Broken Wings

a novel

Carla Stewart

New York Boston Nashville

This book is a work of fiction. Names, characters, places, and incidents are the product of the author's imagination or are used fictitiously. Any resemblance to actual events, locales, or persons, living or dead, is coincidental.

Unless otherwise indicated, Scriptures are taken from the King James Version of the Bible.

FaithWords
Hachette Book Group
237 Park Avenue
New York, NY 10017

www.faithwords.com

Printed in the United States of America

First Edition: June 2011
10 9 8 7 6 5 4 3 2 1

FaithWords is a division of Hachette Book Group, Inc.
The FaithWords name and logo are trademarks of Hachette Book Group, Inc.

Library of Congress Cataloging-in-Publication Data
Stewart, Carla.
Broken wings / by Carla Stewart.—1st ed.
p. cm.
ISBN 978-0-446-55656-9
1. Volunteer workers in hospitals—Fiction. 2. Female friendship—Fiction.
3. Tulsa (Okla.)—Fiction. I. Title.
PS3619.T4937C47 2010
813'.6—dc22

2010031035

Praise for Broken Wings

"Carla Stewart writes with tenderness, insight, and a tremendous amount of heart. Reading her stories emotes the same familiar comfort as curling up in a childhood blanket or laying your head on your mother's lap. This gifted storyteller has a fan in me."

—Gina Holmes, author of *Crossing Oceans*

"A gripping tale of friendship under turbulent circumstances, BROKEN WINGS is told with Carla Stewart's poignancy and skill of storytelling."

—Alice Wisler, author of *Rain Song* (Christy Finalist 2009), *How Sweet It Is* (Christy Finalist 2010), and *Hatteras Girl*

"I smiled through my tears as I read BROKEN WINGS. Those of us who have been abused can cheer for Brooke, who stands up and fights with what she has: friendship and the love of God. Keep writing Carla. We need the voice of hope."

—Shelley Adina, author of the All About Us series

"A relevant story that explores the beauty of friendship as well as the heartache of abuse. Carla Stewart is an engaging storyteller."

—Susan Meissner, author of *The Shape of Mercy*

"With apt descriptions and artful prose, Stewart delves into the vibrant, jazzy 1940s, at the same time creating a true-to-life present. Moving between the two time periods, readers discover what everlasting love is, and how strong a woman must be to recognize it."

—Christina Berry, award-winning author of *The Familiar Stranger*

"Journey along as an unlikely meeting begets a sisterhood of the heart that unlocks the secrets of the past and ends in the purchase of one amazing red dress. Carla Stewart's fine tale will make you want to spread your wings and fly!"

—Lisa Wingate, national bestselling author of *Larkspur Cove* and *Dandelion Summer*

PRAISE FOR CHASING LILACS

"This first-person narrative contains resolute characters and vivid descriptions of a small Texas community in the 1950s. If her debut is any indication, Stewart has a promising future."

—*Romantic Times*, 4½ stars

"Stewart writes about powerful and basic emotions with a restraint that suggests depth and authenticity; the relationship between Sammie and her mother, Rita, the engine that drives the plot, is beautifully and delicately rendered. Coming-of-age stories are a fiction staple, but well-done ones much rarer. This emotionally acute novel is one of the rare ones."

—*Publishers Weekly*, starred review

"... A warm, compelling tale with characters who will stay with you for quite a while... Those who lived during the 1950s will have delightful flashbacks, and those who didn't will get a true glimpse into that era. All will identify with Sammie and the friends and family who deeply influence her search for the truth about her family—and herself."

—*BookPage*

"Prepare to laugh, cry, and pray as you inhale each poignant word of this stunning debut novel. Simply unforgettable!"

—Patti Lacy, author of *An Irishwoman's Tale*, 2008 *ForeWord Magazine* Book of the Year finalist, and *What the Bayou Saw*

"*Chasing Lilacs* is the kind of coming-of-age story that sticks to you beyond the last page. Unforgettable characters, surprising plot twists, and a setting so Southern you'll fall in love with Texas. Carla Stewart is a new talent to watch!"

—Mary E. DeMuth, author of *Daisy Chain* and *A Slow Burn*

"Carla Stewart writes a tender story with such emotional impact, you will hope, fear, cry, and rejoice with her characters. Readers will find themselves cheering Sammie on through her ordeals as she seeks love and forgiveness."

—Janelle Mowery, author of *Love Finds You in Silver City, Idaho*

"Gripping! Nostalgic and filled with bittersweet memories, Carla Stewart's *Chasing Lilacs* captured my imagination, and my heart, from the moment I started reading."

—Elizabeth Ludwig, award-winning author and speaker

"Endearing characters, twists that propel the story ever forward, and soul-searching questions combine to create a heart-tugging tale of self-reflection and inward growth. Carla Stewart's *Chasing Lilacs* carried me away to 1950s small-town Texas... and I wanted to stay. I highly recommend this insightful, mesmerizing coming-of-age tale."

—Kim Vogel Sawyer, bestselling author of *My Heart Remembers*

"Carla Stewart's debut novel, *Chasing Lilacs*, is a deeply emotional masterpiece. Witty dialogue and normal teen antics nicely balance the thought-provoking introspection and dramatic storyline. Young Sammie, the heroine, is both a normal kid and wise beyond her years. Reminiscent of slower-paced days gone by, *Chasing Lilacs* takes you back to days forgotten and leaves you inspired."

—Vickie McDonough, award-winning author of 18 books and novellas, including the Texas Boardinghouse Brides series

"Guilt and redemption are at the soul of this heartwarming tale of a little girl searching for her mother's love. Carla takes us back to a simpler time and a simpler place with wit, wisdom, and insight. God bless her."

—Charles W. Sasser, author of *God in the Foxhole* and *Arctic Homestead*

"Carla Stewart has crafted a wonderful story in the style of *To Kill a Mockingbird* with compelling characters you will care about."

—Margaret Daley, award-winning, multi-published author in the Christian romance genre

"Carla Stewart's lovely voice intrigued me from the start. This well-written story swept me right into Sammie's world and left my heart singing. A beautiful coming-of-age tale, *Chasing Lilacs* is a captivating debut."

—Tina Ann Forkner, author of *Ruby Among Us* and *Rose House*

"Breathe in the scent of *Chasing Lilacs*—nostalgic, yet fresh and real. Carla Stewart has a delicious way with words, and her characters and story are gripping and touching. This is a book to share with friends over coffee and dessert. But your friends will have to buy their own copies because you won't want to let go of yours."

—Sarah Sundin, author of *A Distant Melody*

"Carla Stewart's book *Chasing Lilacs* was a delightful read. The perfect book for a snowy afternoon. It'll warm your heart."

—Jodi Thomas

For Max, with love

[ACKNOWLEDGMENTS]

When I began writing *Broken Wings* and chose domestic abuse and Alzheimer's as the events that would connect my characters, I had no personal experience with either of these life-altering subjects. As a nurse, I had seen both, of course, but only through the lens of it happening to someone else. However, within a month of getting the book contract, my sweet mother-in-law—one of the most giving, caring people I've ever known—was diagnosed with mid-stage Alzheimer's. To Leslie, Chet, Avery, Connie, and my husband, Max—you are my heroes. You are the real-life examples of courage, patience, and love in all seasons. For Dorothy, your life of service has not gone unnoticed. You are loved.

On the lighter side, I had the pleasure of learning about Tulsa's rich jazz heritage and hanging out at the Jazz Depot—the magnificently restored Art Deco building, which was at one time the Union Depot and is now the home of the Oklahoma Jazz Hall of Fame. The museum and concert hall preserves the past and celebrates the present under the inspired leadership of Chuck Cissel. My life and story are richer because of the time I spent there. *The Colors of Oklahoma Music*, an illustrated book by John Wooley, was an invaluable aid as well.

For my agent, Sandra Bishop, you've given me incredible insights and support that far surpass your job description. Every day I am grateful for your guidance and influence in my life.

Myra Johnson, Camille Eide, and Carolyn Steele—you are the best critique buddies in the world. Your honesty and ability to spot the weaknesses in my writing have been such a help, and I thank you for your unique perspectives and the time you've spent reading my pages.

I'm fortunate to be part of several writing communities, and if I listed each individual who has touched my life, it would read like the phone book. Please know that I am humbled and blessed by every note, every kind word, every whispered prayer. To my fellow members of the American Christian Fiction Writers, my local WIN group, the Tulsa Night Writers, and the Christian Authors Network, you've all contributed in immeasurable ways. Likewise, to my friends at Community Worship Center—you are my anchor and source of great joy.

To Anne Goldsmith Horch, my deepest gratitude for your early support of this story. To Whitney Luken, my new and fabulous editor, you are a joy to work with. To the entire team at FaithWords, your work on my behalf astounds me: Jana Burson, Jody Waldrup, Holly Halverson, Shanon Stowe, and the ones who make things happen behind the scenes—thank you. A special mention to Harry Helm, whose phone call greatly encouraged me.

To Jeane Wynn: You've become my friend and my advocate, and you taught me to ride the waves of being a debut author with my face into the wind. You are amazing.

We have a lot of fun in my family talking about Mom's new hobby, but after ten years, I think they get it. You all inspire me and are kind enough to ask what's going on. Thank you Andy, Amy, Brett, Cindy, Scott, Denice, James, and Allison—you are the best kids in the world. A special thanks to my dad, Mike Brune, who still spins a good yarn and will always be the champion storyteller in the family. Donna and Marsha, thanks for all the long chats, for knowing my heart. I'm so glad God made us sisters.

Saving the best for last—Max, you're the music in my life, the melody in my heart. Thank you for your love, for being willing to hop on this journey with me, and for always believing in me.

When all is said and done, my prayer is that my words may be acceptable to Jesus—my Redeemer and friend. To Him be all glory and honor and praise.

Broken Wings

[PROLOGUE]

St. Louis, April 1935

When you're six years old and the only ocean you've seen is in a picture book at Public School No. 16, you don't have a big view of the world. And the other kids running up and down your street in ragged knickers and hand-me-down dresses don't know beans either. To all of us, a mountain was the pile of rocks along the banks of the Mississippi, one we clamored around, spouting truths about the universe as we knew it. And about our Huck Finn dreams of building a raft that would take us all the way to the ocean.

Sometimes when Mama sat with her arm around me on the wood steps of our two-room row house, I'd tell her my ocean dream. And how, if I couldn't have that, I wanted to live in one of those houses on the other side of the green park. The ones that could hold a family our size six or seven times over. I'd fill it with children and get a pony for the backyard and two Great Danes for the front, I'd tell her. And it would ring with laughter and singing for everyone who passed by.

"You're a dreamer, Maggie," Mama would say, and twist my chestnut hair into two ropey braids. "But don't you stop spinning those golden tales, 'cuz as sure as my name's Lorna Beth Poole, I'm going to take you to the ocean, dumplin'. We'll cross the mountains, dip our toes in the water, and collect seashells by the dozen. And that's a fact."

Then Papa would be there, his moonshine jug hooked in the thumb of one hand, a black cigar puffing smoke like a locomotive in the other. And he didn't allow such talk of the mountains or the ocean. Or much of anything. We saved that for when he made his customer rounds the first week of every month.

Papa had been gone four days when that Saturday night rolled around, and I'd been ready to pop out of my skin all day, as if I'd known what was coming. Mama too. She was as skittish as a sparrow caught in a whirlwind.

When Mama slipped the red dress over her head, my belly got the familiar, pinched-on-the-inside feeling. I knew better than to ask where she was going. And I knew exactly what the answer would be if I did—"It's a surprise, but for the surprise to work, we have to keep it a secret. Just between you and me, dumplin'."

Except Mama was the only one who knew what the surprise was, leaving me with all the questions. And the stomachaches.

"Maggie, be a doll and zip this for me, okay?"

Mama took a big breath and pushed the fabric together at the waist so I could tug the zipper over the soft curves, the red satin covering her like the skin on a juicy plum. Turning this way and that, Mama admired herself in the cracked mirror hung cockeyed on a rusty nail. She slipped a stray curl into the fancy knot hugging the back of her neck—a chignon, she told me—then dipped her pinky finger in the rouge pot. Her eyebrows, like two curved mouse tails, shot up as she leaned into the mirror, dotting the rouge over the dark place on her cheek. The one left there by Papa.

She pooched out painted lips, then tilted them into a smile. "That'll have to do." She wiped her hand on a washrag and pulled back the window shade to peek outside.

When she turned back, I opened my hand, offering her the gold necklace from Mama's box of shiny jewelry.

"Not tonight, sugar. This isn't the place to wear Granny's locket. Be a love and keep it for me. And don't forget, Mrs. LeGrange is next door if you need anything." She took another glance out the window and quickly gathered her handbag, a shawl with tickly fringe, and a lace hanky.

As I blinked back the tears, my stomach knotted like my fist curled around the locket.

Sometimes Mama opened the locket and looked sad-faced at the pictures. They tweren't a speck bigger than Mr. Lincoln on a copper penny, but they seemed to make Mama feel better, and before long she'd be humming "Bye, Bye Blackbird."

But not that night. Mama patted my cheek, and I followed her into the front room, where she marched by the mattress on the floor. "Keep an eye on Ruthie, and give Chester another bottle if he fusses. Don't forget to say your prayers."

"Yes, Mama."

"Atta girl. Now, who loves you more than sugar dumplin's?"

"You do, Mama."

She slipped past the sagging divan and out the door. Through my tears, I saw only a blur of red as she went into the night. I brushed my wet face with the back of my hand and ran to the window. Spreading the torn place in the shade to the width of a paring knife, I watched as Mama swung her legs into a sleek motorcar. It shot off with a lurch, its wheels spinning like sunbursts in the moonlight.

A haze from the bulb in Mama's room was enough for me to make out Chester sleeping in his crib in the corner of the front room. Ruthie stretched, then rose from her curled, "playing possum" spot on the mattress and joined me at the window.

Giving her my best grown-up look, I said, "You're s'posed to be in bed."

The thumb stuck in Ruthie's mouth came out like a popping cork. "I can't sleep. Come with me."

We curled into spoons under our frayed quilt. I recited in my head the only prayer I knew.

Now I lay me down to sleep.

Ruthie squirmed like a night crawler beside me, and before I got to *my soul to keep*, she piped up, "I ain't goin' to Mrs. LeGrange's. She stinks like Papa and spits in that can."

I knew the can, the juice in it frothy and the color of motor oil. "We won't have to go if nothin' happens. And nothin' ain't gonna happen, so shush and go to sleep."

The sound of Ruthie's mouth sucking her thumb didn't keep me from thinking about all the things that could happen. It could rain and soak through the crack above our heads. Chester could wake up screaming, and I would have to be careful and not step on a cockroach when I got his bottle from the icebox. I hoped the milk hadn't gone sour, since Papa forgot to put in a new block of ice before he left. Spoiled milk wouldn't help Chester's bawling.

Papa. What if he came home?

This was the worst thought. But Mama said he'd be gone a week this time. Seven days. I recited the days, starting with Wednesday, the day Papa left. And today was only Saturday. Three days left to go.

A happier thought came. Sometimes Papa brought licorice strips if he had a good round of business.

Help Papa have a good trip. And don't let it rain. Let Mama come home soon.

Ruthie relaxed against me, no more sucking noises from the thumb jammed in her mouth. The quilt warmed me as I let its weight and my heavy eyelids pull me into sleep.

The door creaked open, and in my foggy dreams, I smiled. God heard my prayer. Now I wouldn't have to worry—

"Lorna Beth, I'm home. Get yourself out here and give me a big old smooch. Wait till you see what I brung. Lorna Beth?"

Papa. No. No. No!

His boot connected with the divan, and he let out a string of curse words. Then, "Doll face, it's me, your good-lookin' man. Lorna Beth? You hear me?" Boots scraped across the floor as he fumbled, reaching for the light string on the overhead bulb.

I squeezed my eyes shut, pretending to be asleep. It didn't sound like Papa would be pulling licorice from his pocket.

"Quit playing games with me now. Are you sick, woman? Or deaf?" He stepped into the room he shared with Mama, spit out more of those awful words, then started ripping covers off their bed, throwing things against the wall. His boots, heavy and angry, stomped back to the front room, to the edge of the mattress where Ruthie and I cowered under the quilt.

"What do you two know 'bout this? Where's your mama?" He yanked the quilt and whipped it like a bullfighter. "Speak up, you little ingrates. Where's that floozy who calls herself your mama?"

He grabbed me, tangling my hair in his grasp. Thumbs and fingers dug into my shoulders, clamped like a dog's jaw on a bloody bone as he shook me. Feeling with my hands, I tried to hide Ruthie under me, to keep her from Papa.

His slap came sharp against my jaw, and I screamed, but couldn't form the words to answer his question.

Another slap. "Where is she? Answer me, you little twit."

"I don't know. Honest."

Chester started bawling. Ruthie writhed beneath me, and I hid my face in my arms as my body braced for another jolt.

Instead, a gunshot exploded into the room, and I thought Papa had shot me or Ruthie or baby Chester. Plaster rained down from the ceiling, hunks of it scattered on the mattress.

I looked up, afraid of what I might find, but when I did, Mrs. LeGrange stood in the doorway, clutching a rifle.

Papa's eyes jerked like a wild animal, his smell rancid, his lips curled back. He stormed to the doorway, shoved Mrs. LeGrange aside as he went past, and shouted promises of what he would do to Mama the next time he laid eyes on her.

The next morning, Mama put all our belongings in two pillowcases, and the four of us—Mama, Ruthie, Chester, and me—left. Not in a motorcar or paddling a Huck Finn raft. We just struck out, in the opposite direction of the sun peeking over the horizon. Mama never looked back, balancing Chester on one hip, the pillowcases on the other.

My job was to hold Ruthie's hand and carry the hatbox Mrs. LeGrange had packed with food for our journey.

When I asked where we were going, all Mama said was, "We're living your dream, Maggie. We're going to the ocean."

Mama never once told me where she'd been that night, but it was a peculiar fact she left that red dress behind.

[CHAPTER 1]

Mitzi

Present day, Tulsa, Oklahoma

She stumbled into my heart the same way she faltered through the doors of the emergency room that November evening. Bloodied. Bruised. And alone.

With only five minutes until my volunteer shift ended, I busied myself by placing dog-eared *Sports Illustrated*, *Good Housekeeping*, and *People* magazines in the wall rack next to the candy machine, then I surveyed the waiting room of Tulsa County Hospital. An older gentleman with sandpaper whiskers and a urine bag strapped to his leg nodded and hacked into a gnarled fist. I returned the nod, then smiled at a mother with an inconsolable infant. A UPS man, his face as haggard as his rumpled uniform, asked if I knew where to get a cup of coffee. Shaking, he told me his wife had miscarried…for the third time. I brought him a Styrofoam cup of steaming Maxwell House and wished I could do more.

Gathering a Snickers wrapper and a stray Pepsi bottle the housekeeping girl had missed, I heard the ER doors clang open and turned to see a young woman burst through. Strands of dark hair swirled about her face, which bore a crazed look in one eye, the other covered with a bloody towel. It was too early for drunks and barroom scuffles, and car wreck victims usually arrived by ambulance.

A quick look over my shoulder told me that Helen, the intake receptionist, had her hands full, so I bustled over to the distraught woman.

"Here, let me help you."

She jerked at my touch and shrank away. Red splotches like paint splatters had ruined her tailored suit. Definitely not off the JCPenney sales rack. A diamond on the hand clutching the towel caught the light. Two carats at least.

My heart twisted. It wasn't the blood that bothered me, but the dazed expression she wore. Peering through the glass doors, I expected a friend or a husband to come through with the explanation, but only the neon emergency sign glowed outside.

An overhead page crackled, and under her breath, the woman muttered, "He didn't mean it. He didn't..."

At least those were the words I thought I heard, and a chill settled on me.

I coaxed her along, and she followed a step behind me until we reached the half-moon desk that kept Helen, the receptionist, at arm's length from the rest of the world.

Helen told the couple in front of us that the wait would be at least two hours. Maybe longer.

I elbowed past them. "Can we get this patient into a room? She's bleeding."

"They're all full, but I can take her information and get her on the list for the admission clerk."

"But...she's injured. We don't know how much blood she's lost." Already, a small circle of crimson had pooled on the floor, dripping steadily from the saturated towel. The young woman chewed her bottom lip, her one visible eye begging.

Helen flipped her pen in the air, and gave me a blistering look. "Will this day never end?" She sighed. "I'll need some basic info so I can alert triage."

Grabbing a form and another pen, she asked the girl's name.

Brooke Woodson.

Insurance card? No.

Address? Phone? Date of birth?

Each question took more effort, with the girl leaning against the desk for support. "I'm sorry. I had an . . . accident . . . grabbed my keys . . . please, I need help." She dropped the towel from her face to reveal a cut above her cheekbone, an angry red stream tracking toward her mouth.

"It's standard procedure, ma'am. You'll have to call someone to bring your insurance card. Your husband? A family member?"

Brooke hunched her shoulders and stepped back, shaking her head. "No. No one to call."

Helen tapped her pen and looked at me. Not in the eye, but at my name tag. "Mitzi, kindly help the patient find a seat, and someone will check on her soon. And by the way, it's not your place to interact with patients. You should get back to your assigned duties."

My assigned duties as a Pink Lady. Only now we're called "service volunteers." We run errands, make fresh coffee. And once a month, on the third Tuesday, they let me operate the cash register in the gift shop. Unlike Helen, I love my job, and let's face it—there aren't many places an eighty-one-year-old woman can work. Being a Pink Lady suited me more than being a Walmart greeter, that's for sure.

I nabbed a green towel from a linen cart and helped Brooke replace the saturated one, trying to be gentle and not gasp at the injury. Then I led her to a plastic chair.

Accident, my left foot. A gash that size didn't come from bumping into a door.

Perched on the seat next to her, I waited and prayed, the woman seemingly oblivious to my presence as she rocked gently forward and back. Twenty minutes later, a nurse in olive scrubs and surgical shoe covers called Brooke's name.

Brooke winced as she struggled to her feet. After two tentative steps, she turned back to me. "It *was* an accident." Then she disappeared into an exam room.

~

Concentrating on the traffic, I drove the twelve blocks from the hospital to the care center. Maple Andrews, my favorite nurse's aide, met me in the hall on the way to Gabe's room. "My lands, you're running late, Miz Steiner. Gabe's had a rough afternoon. Refused his dinner, and his gums are bleeding again. Maybe you can do something with him."

I nodded and slowed my steps. Our time was running out, Gabe's and mine. We'd had a fine run, but I knew before long the show would be over. *Gabe and Mitzi Steiner—now, they were something.* That's what I hoped people said. Those who remembered, that is. Though I knew that number shrank each day the same way Gabe's frame shriveled more each time I stepped into his room at the Guardian Light Alzheimer's Unit.

I stopped outside his door. Smoothed my hair and took a minute to brace myself. Put on a fresh coat of Pink Salsa lipstick and said a quick prayer. Only then did I enter.

A pillow cradled Gabe's head as he lay on the circulating air mattress between the padded rails. Oh, how I wished my arms could comfort and protect his mind as these devices safeguarded his body when he thrashed about. This man whose voice once rang with laughter and whose presence lifted me to the heavens. His eyes fluttered open when I left a crinkled salsa kiss on his forehead. They held no more recognition now than they had for the past two years.

I turned on the CD player atop his bureau. *Gabe and Mitzi's Greatest Hits*. If anything would bring him back for even a moment, I knew our harmony would.

Humming along to the music, I lowered the top rail, pulled up a chair, and took Gabe's bony hand in mine.

"Maple says you flirted with her today. What am I going to do with you? The minute my back is turned, you're cheating on me." My laugh was tinny. Hollow. With our palms pressed together, I traced the indigo lines on his forearm with my free hand, the shallow dip in his wrist, and the network of vessels like a road map to his knuckles. Ignoring the ravages of age, I focused on the supple, tender fingers that had cupped my chin and caressed my face for sixty-one years. "Memorizing your freckles," he would say, then smother me with kisses.

Dried blood at the corner of Gabe's parched lips reminded me of what Maple had said. His gums were bleeding again. I reached for a lemon-glycerin stick in the bedside table, then stood and leaned over him, smoothing away the crust, gently prying his lips apart so I could clean the fragile interior. He twisted his head and clamped his jaw shut. His knees and elbows jerked together, and with one swift motion he curled away from me into a fetal position.

We were singing "Fly Me to the Moon" on the CD, but I no longer felt like humming along.

When his twitching settled, I said to Gabe's back, "I met a young woman this evening, a patient who came through the ER. Poor thing said she'd been in an accident, but it looked like Goliath's fist split her face wide open. My heart darn near stopped when I caught a glimpse of it. Bleeding to beat everything."

Gabe didn't move. Sometimes I thought he could hear me. That he knew who I was. Like when his breath caught and his eyebrows knitted together. But tonight his breaths came soft and even—a gentle sleep. Sleep was a good thing. And sometimes, you take what you can get.

I tucked the Vellux blanket under Gabe's chin. He always hated having his shoulders outside the covers.

Brooke Woodson. The young woman's name had a musical ring to it. I imagined how lovely her face must have been before I met her. The pity of her coming to the ER alone. I couldn't shake the feeling that more hovered beneath the surface. Much more.

I gave a final pat to Gabe's resting body. Then I raised the bedrail and moved to the recliner. I leaned back, and for a moment, Mama's face came into focus.

Broken. Bloodied.

Eyes pleading for Papa to stop.

Some things you never forget. Not even an old woman like me.

[CHAPTER 2]

Brooke

When I stirred in my sleep, Mom's face was the first thing I saw. She wore the celery green sweater I had loaned her—the one Lance said made me look fat.

Nothing in the room looked familiar, but I had a fuzzy picture in my head of stumbling into the emergency room. Someone—an elderly woman maybe—led me to a desk. Then my name was called, and I followed a nurse through a maze of cubbyholes to a stretcher behind a curtain. The spotlight hurt my eyes, made me feel like an amoeba under a microscope. Prodding. Endless questions. Floating in and out.

The memories stung like needles full of anesthetic meant to take away the pain. The pain in my face and the deeper, hidden hurt that tarnished my heart. Lance. Had he done what I thought he did?

I turned away from Mom, a dense bandage over my face pushing back. I didn't have the strength to think about it. Not now. Thankfully, sleep met me in the space between my pillow and the gauze cushion.

Tiny snatches of conversations with white-coated doctors and faceless nurses filtered in and out, along with Mom's voice, tinged with worry. Waves knocked against me, swallowing me and sucking me under; then a calm held me safe until I saw my reflection in my ocean of dreams. Disfigured. Ugly.

My jerking awake must have brought Mom to my bedside.

"Happy birthday, Brooke." She held a large vase like a trophy. "Look what Lance sent. Aren't you the lucky one? Two dozen roses. With the sweetest note."

"Really?" I tried to smile. "What time is it?"

"Two in the afternoon, and I was getting worried. You've never tolerated any pain medication stronger than an aspirin. I explained it to the nurse, but she said we needed to keep you comfortable."

The scent escaped the red roses, coming at me. Sweet. Smothering. The room faded in and out, and if my head hadn't been spinning, I would have grabbed the flowers, vase and all, and hurled them through the hospital window. Pain medication or not, I was far from comfortable.

Mom babbled on. "Lance called on his lunch hour. Said he had court this afternoon, but he'll stop by with another birthday gift this evening. He's very worried about you, I can tell."

I closed my eyes to stop the spinning, but it didn't help. A million thoughts fought for attention, but only one found its way out my mouth.

"Did he tell you what happened?"

"You tripped on the cat's water bowl and hit your face on the counter. Honestly, that kitten has been more trouble than it's worth. Not to mention the pet deposit you had to pay to keep your precious Cosmo."

Is that what happened? I tripped? I thought I'd fallen last Sunday, could even picture the bruise—no bigger than a dime—on my shoulder. I didn't think that's how I'd gotten the gash on my face. *Lance. No. Please, no.*

"It wasn't Cosmo's fault." No, it was my fault. Again. Lance had never exploded like that before. Not so fast, so wild-eyed. He usually controlled himself, even when I disagreed with him. How could I have been so dumb to forget his meeting?

My arms burned with other memories, distant ones, in which his fingers bit into my flesh. Only once or twice . . . when I was being difficult. I probably tripped, like he said. A simple explanation. And although I was desperate to believe it, I knew better.

Closing my uncovered eye, I wished Mom would disappear. Or at least leave me alone. Which she didn't. "You've always been accident-prone, sugar. That's what I told the doctor earlier. All the times you skinned your knees riding your bike as a child. Forever bumping into things. He thinks you could have an underlying seizure disorder, lapses in your brain activity making these things happen."

"There's nothing wrong with my brain." *Except my fiancé tried to put his fist through it.*

Mom couldn't find out. It would crush her and her dream of me marrying Lance. That both her daughters would find worthy husbands—not the kind like my dad, who disappeared before my sixth birthday. And Lance was perfect for me. The dream guy I never thought I'd find. Me with Tulsa's most eligible bachelor? An attorney who was mere inches away from launching his first political campaign? No wonder he'd reacted—he had a lot on his mind. How could I have been so thoughtless?

The answer was simple. Mom wouldn't have to know. I would try harder to make it work. Lance's face came to me, his fingers running through my hair, the back of his finger whisper-soft on my cheek. A hitch came in my chest, and it was Lance I longed for. His arms. His kisses.

Mom hovered nearby, still admiring the roses. "Lance is so perplexed. Said he saw your face bleeding and ran to the bathroom to get a towel, but when he came back, you'd disappeared. He thought you came to my house and called to see if you had. Lucky for you, the hospital checked with me."

She caressed a red petal, not looking at me, and another piece of the puzzle fell into place. My old records. Even a paralegal like me knows you leave traces of where you've been. And with my accident-prone childhood, I'd left a record a mile wide. I couldn't explain why I'd fled the apartment. To get away... or was I afraid I'd do something stupid? I didn't know.

Mom peered at me through the flowers. "Lance would've been happy to drive you and explain everything. Instead, you gave such vague answers to the doctors that they are somewhat suspicious. Lance doesn't deserve that."

"Ummm. Excuse me."

A Pink Lady stood in the doorway holding another flower arrangement. Good grief, did the whole world know I was in the hospital?

Mom grabbed it from her and plucked the card out. "You want me to see who it's from?"

The woman stepped toward her. "Actually, I can tell you. It's from me."

I did a double take. "I think I had a dream about you. After the doctor came in this morning."

"Must've been some crazy dream." When she smiled, laugh lines crinkled her face. "You may not recall, but I was in the ER last night when you came in. My name is Mitzi Steiner, and I've been worried sick. You were all alone, and I came to check on you... to see if you needed anything."

"I do remember. Vaguely. You sat with me. I'm sorry I didn't feel much like talking last night."

Her dark eyes, behind frames with rhinestones dotting the outer corners, darted from Mom to me. "It's understandable. And I didn't mean to interrupt. I didn't think... well, I wasn't sure if you had family or friends to pop in."

Mom grabbed her purse—a new Dooney & Bourke she'd gotten

off the Accessories Galore Network. "No problem. I'm just leaving. I have to take my car in and see if they can figure out where the clunk under the hood's coming from." She changed gears, setting her mouth in a way that let me know she'd be tacking on a message: "You oughta thank your lucky stars you won't have to worry about driving junk cars the rest of your life."

She jingled her keys and gave me the look. The one that said I'd better not screw up my relationship with Lance Evans, the prince of every girl's dream.

"You get some rest, and I'll check on you later. And by the way, I called CiCi to let her know we'd celebrate your birthday when you get home." She blew me a kiss, then sashayed out the door.

"Your birthday?" The Pink Lady set the bowl of sunshine daisies on the bedside table. Hesitation dangled in her voice, the slight lift in her eyebrows inviting me to explain.

"Unfortunately. Not the party I had planned."

"I'm sorry. You want to talk about it?"

"Not really." The fuzziness had left, leaving me with a washed-up-on-the-shore heaviness. I needed time to think. Sort out the mess I'd made, and I didn't think this woman would have a clue how to help someone who was a pro at sabotaging her love life.

"You probably need some time to yourself. Out of curiosity, though, would the roses have anything to do with your accident?"

"Of course not. They're from my fiancé . . . for my birthday. The big three-O, in case you're wondering. And honestly, I can't see why you would. Don't you need to get back to work at whatever it is you do?"

She shrugged. "You're probably right. It's none of my affair, but I'm not due in the gift shop for another thirty minutes. I came in early today to see you."

"Why? Why would you care?"

"I saw the look on your face last night. Being wounded like that is difficult to hide. Today, you've had time to think it through, come to some conclusions—"

"I don't need time to analyze it. I'm a klutz. I had an accident and it happened to be on the eve of my birthday. I'll get over it. I'm a fast healer."

The volunteer shook her head. Not in disagreement, but as if she were sorrowful. Her hands, spotted but delicate, rested on the rail of the hospital bed. Rails on either side would keep me safe for a day. Or two. Then what? Try and be a better person. One who didn't stumble into situations that irritated Lance. He had a stressful job. An important one. And any single woman would trade places with me in a flash.

My face throbbed beneath the bandage, an uneasiness twisting in my gut like a corkscrew. Seeing Mitzi Steiner's hands poised to bridge the gap between us, I felt an offering. Of what, I wasn't sure, but at the moment, I knew I needed a friend.

[CHAPTER 3]

Mitzi

An awkward pause hovered between Brooke and me. Rendering my opinion of abusive men tempted me, but no one appreciates reminders of making bad judgments. Especially about men.

I cleared my throat and patted Brooke's arm, then reached in my pocket for one of the cards I always carried. With my supervisor's blessing, I passed them out as encouragement—sometimes to a patient, other times a distraught family member in one of the waiting rooms where I served coffee and offered magazines.

The cheerful lemon-colored cards showed a tiny sparrow hovering at the edge of a nest—a creature on the precipice of life.

Brooke took the card, turned it over, and as she read the words printed on the back, I whispered them silently to myself.

I sing because I'm happy,
I sing because I'm free,
For his eye is on the sparrow,
And I know he watches me.

Brooke mumbled her thanks, then cocked her head with a curious expression. "I'm not sure what this means. Everyone flies from the nest eventually. I've been on my own for ages."

"True, but sometimes the flights aren't what you expected. That's the chorus to a favorite song of mine. Maybe I'll sing it for you one day..."

A nursing assistant came in pushing her blood pressure machine. "Time to check your vitals, hon."

Stepping aside to give her room, I smiled at Brooke. "I'll check on you tomorrow."

"Good to see you, Miz Steiner," the nurse said. With smooth efficiency, she pulled the cuff from the basket on the machine's post and Velcroed it around Brooke's arm.

As I slipped through the door, Brooke asked the assistant, "You know her?"

"Oh my, yes. Don't you?"

Curious, I hesitated and eavesdropped like a child at a keyhole, but I didn't hear what Brooke said, if anything.

Then the nurse. "Where you been, girl? That was Mitzi Steiner, one of the jewels of Tulsa. Don't tell me you ain't never heard of Gabe and Mitzi Steiner?"

A jewel? I chuckled, embarrassed at my own curiosity. What if she had said I was an aging matron with vocal chords as rusty as nails? Now that would have been closer to the truth.

Scooting down the hall, I nodded to a couple as the man pushed the IV pole for his wife. The woman, whose head was bald and smooth as a baby's bottom, returned a valiant smile.

Cancer—but she looked so young.

Life was full of cruel twists.

And I know he watches me.

[CHAPTER 4]

Brooke

The nursing assistant, Lucretia, according to her name tag, fussed over me, babbling about Mitzi, who I confessed I'd never heard of. I asked if she and her husband were benefactors of the hospital.

"Wouldn't surprise me, but no, they're a singing sensation from back in the fifties and sixties. Maybe even the seventies. Mr. Gabe was a patient here a few years back. Sharp as the crease in a new pair of pants. I heard he got the Alzheimer's and lives over at the Guardian Light now." She jammed the electronic thermometer in a receptacle and pulled it out with a plastic sleeve. She opened her mouth for me to follow suit.

I studied the card until the temp indicator in my mouth beeped.

I sing because I'm happy. I sing because I'm free.

Mitzi certainly seemed happy. A little daft, perhaps. Or lonely, if her husband was in the nursing home. I did know the Guardian Light. One of our clients had had her mother committed there after a big family tussle.

"Your vitals are right as rain. Anything I can get for you?"

"Yes. The phone, if you don't mind."

"Sure thing, hon. You take care now." Humming in a deep, rich voice, she wheeled the machine out.

I punched in the number of Jenna's private line at the law offices of Cooke, Harrington, and Baumgartner. She picked up on the second ring.

"Hey, Jenna, it's me."

"Brooke! Hey, girlfriend, I heard you had an accident. What happened?"

"It's a long story. Was Mr. Harrington upset when I didn't show up today?" I seemed to have that effect on people of late.

"What do you think? Good thing for you Lance popped in around break time and told us you'd taken a nasty fall. Stitches and everything, huh? Are you home from the hospital?"

"No. Probably tomorrow. The doctor should be in later to let me know. I forgot I had a brief to get ready—"

"No prob. After Lance showed up, Mr. Harrington had one of his other peeps do the brief. You are one lucky chicky, you know. Man, Lance looked pitiful. Said he felt bad that you had to spend your birthday in the hospital. So what did he get you? A diamond necklace? A jeweled tiara? Sheesh! The guy worships the ground you walk on. Why can't I find someone like Lance?"

The hospital room was spinning again. Jenna meant well, I knew. I muttered something about her finding the right person someday, then thanked her and said I'd be in touch.

Lance had made my excuses for me. I should be grateful. I *was* grateful. I had a dream job at Tulsa's premier domestic law firm. A far cry from the Legal Aid work I was doing when I met Lance at the Ethics and Practices Symposium he co-chaired. When he asked for my phone number, his intense blue eyes laughing, flirting, I gave it to him, reeling that he'd noticed me at all. He brought me flowers on our first date, took me dancing on the second. A few weeks later, he gave me a recommendation at Cooke, Harrington, and Baumgartner, a group that handled civil cases—enormous divorce settlements, lawsuits, child custody work. The new job doubled my salary and allowed me to work in the same office tower as Lance—convenient for quick kisses in the break room and lunch hour strolls through downtown.

It was foolish of me to complain. It was more than I'd ever dreamed possible. A secure job. A criminal defense attorney who wanted to spend the rest of his life with me. If I screwed up now, my job, my future would be in jeopardy. I shuddered and vowed to never let that happen.

When a nutrition assistant lifted the Styrofoam lid covering a piece of pale, limp chicken and a noxious-smelling broccoli-carrot medley, I nearly gagged. Waving away the worst of the smell, I settled on a dinner roll and searched the tray for a pat of butter, but only came up with salt, pepper, and an Equal packet. I nibbled the roll, surprised at how good it tasted. I'd eaten almost half of it when a young physician came in, chart in hand. She introduced herself as Dr. Craft.

"Your X-rays came back clear. No neurological symptoms, but we are going to follow up with an outpatient EEG to check if you might have an underlying seizure disorder. The doctor in the ER asked me to see you since my specialty is cosmetic surgery."

The damage. Just tell me about the damage to my face.

As if she was on the same wavelength, Dr. Craft went on, "I'm afraid that even if the neuro is negative, your face will be scarred."

I swallowed and knitted my eyebrows together, the tape pulling the skin on my forehead taut. "What do you mean? The doctor who stitched me up said my scar would be barely visible."

"It all depends. I'll do a complete evaluation when I remove your bandage tomorrow before we release you. First, though, I need some history. Tell me again, what happened?"

My mind went blank. I had a vague recollection of telling someone in the emergency room I'd run into my pantry door, but then Mom had told me Lance's story about the cat bowl and falling to the counter so I wondered if she'd told them that while I was being stitched.

I gave a lopsided grin. "I fell . . . tripped, actually, and hit my face. I blacked out for a second, but when I realized I was bleeding, I grabbed a towel and came to the hospital."

"You were home alone?"

"No. My fiancé was there, but he had just left."

"Before you fell?" Her manner was professional, yet casual, and it caught me off guard. Confide in her or just let her do the job she came to do? Which would be to fix my face, not my heart.

Taking a big breath, I made a decision. "Yes. Before the accident."

"Can you tell me anything else that might be relevant? Were you upset about something? Feeling ill?"

"No. None of those things. Just clumsy, I guess."

A look passed between her and the nurse, and I thought the nurse raised her eyebrows a fraction.

I averted my eyes and took a drink of the watery tea from my tray.

"All right then. The nurse will notify me if you have any problems tonight."

Dr. Craft clicked my chart shut and was out the door in an instant.

My appetite, what little there was, had gone, so I called Mom and gave her an update.

She seemed relieved. "I'll stay home tonight then, and pick you up in the morning. I'm getting your old room ready—you can stay with me for a few days."

"I'll be fine at my place, Mom. Besides, you're not used to having a cat, and I miss Cosmo."

Cosmo. I'd forgotten about him. "I do need someone to go check on him. I have my apartment keys here if you don't mind coming by."

"I'm tired, Brooke. Being up half the night with you and missing work today. Besides, I don't have a car anyway. I had to leave my car at the shop and call CiCi to bring me home. Six hundred dollars for a new part that wiggled loose. I don't know where I'm going to come up with the money. Why don't you have Lance run by and check on Cosmo? I'm sure he'd be happy to."

"I'll see." Lance and Cosmo weren't on the best of terms. For some reason, Lance bristled at the idea of me having a cat, and Cosmo, sensing Lance's disdain, always conveniently disappeared when he came over. Cosmo would have to be on his own until morning. Besides, Lance had a dinner meeting with the couple endorsing him for district attorney. It was my forgetting about the meeting that had started our argument in the first place. My sister, CiCi, and her husband, Todd, had wanted to celebrate my birthday at Los Cabos on the Riverwalk and then have us stop by their new house in Jenks. CiCi was so excited for Lance to see their sprawling Tudor that I'd immediately agreed.

Lance's big dinner totally slipped my mind. The Parsleys were the richer-than-King Tut benefactors who wanted to finance Lance's campaign, and I had put my own trivial birthday ahead of his future. He'd gone with the Parsleys, I was sure.

CiCi called while I was mulling over the Cosmo situation. A quick how are you, do you need anything, happy birthday, we'll celebrate later.

My younger sister. Perky. Six months pregnant with her first baby. Perfect marriage to Todd, an orthodontist. They were on track with their fairy-tale life.

"We'll have our small group pray for you, Sis."

"Thanks. I could use it. Give Todd my love."

Some people are too perfect, you know. I'm not one of them. Still, a prayer might help, and going to church on a regular basis had certainly put a sparkle in CiCi's eyes.

I gave up on my pity party when a nurse brought my pain pill at bedtime. A good night's sleep was all I needed.

Lance's kiss woke me. At first I thought it was a dream, but when I inhaled his lime aftershave, I knew he'd come.

"Hello, sweetheart. How are you, baby?"

Feigning sleep was an option, but his warmth and strong hand clutching mine flooded my senses. I opened my right eye, the one not under the bandage. He stood above me, his profile barely visible in the glow of the streetlight slanting through the window's vertical blinds. Lance was handsome in a rugged way, with a bump on the bridge of his nose and sandy hair, stylishly mussed.

"I'm doing okay. Home tomorrow, the doc said. How was your meeting?" Keep it light, my gut told me.

"Unbelievable. The Parsleys are ready to move on getting me into the DA's office. They're fed up with the current system and the petty lawsuits the city's involved in. They're excited about fresh ideas for Tulsa's future. Remember my last case, where I got a reversal on the manslaughter charges for the poor guy who shot an intruder? They were impressed with my stance on citizens' rights."

His passion stirred in me. We needed more people like Lance, who would fight for justice. I wanted to apologize for upsetting him, but now that he'd come, a part of me wanted to hear him say he was sorry too. That he hadn't meant to hurt me.

Lance took off his overcoat and folded it on a chair before he continued.

"Hey, sweetheart. This isn't only about me. This is our future. We'll be in this together. I told the Parsleys how beautiful and smart you are. How much you wanted this, too."

Beautiful? Not now. What about my scarred face when I stood beside him on the campaign platform? And smart? I'd already messed up his first influential meeting. Did that make me a liability or an asset? And why was he ignoring my accident as if it never happened?

He must have read the doubts tumbling in my head, for he sidled beside me, sitting on the edge of the bed. "You are with me on this, aren't you?"

A slight edge in his tone sent ripples in motion in my stomach. Either that or the latest pain pill was burning a hole from the inside out. "If it makes you happy, sure. But I think we need to talk about what happened—"

He stiffened slightly. "I'm sorry. I wasn't thinking. You're lying here in the hospital thinking about last night... I admit my feelings were hurt you'd forgotten our meeting with the Parsleys. We both overreacted, I'm afraid. I didn't mean it... You know that, don't you?"

"I'm not sure, Lance. I want to believe you, but—"

"Look, I'm sorry. I've been under this pressure... It won't happen again. I promise." He kissed the tip of my nose. "As a matter of fact, I have something to prove how much I love you."

He jumped from his sitting position and in two quick strides retrieved his overcoat and fumbled with it in the haze filtering in from the streetlight outside the window. Then he was back beside me, holding out a small wrapped package. "Your real birthday present."

Using the control on the rail, I turned on the softer of the two lights above my bed. The thin, square box was cold in my hands. Silver paper. A Simmons Fine Jewelry sticker on the outside. My heart thumped with excitement, matched beat for beat beneath the bandage covering my eye. Swallowing the lump in my throat, I relaxed against the pillow. "I'm sorry. I'm having a hard time focusing."

His hands enveloped mine and the box. "It's all right. I'll help you with it." Then, like a parent helping a child with a Christmas gift, he worked my fingers over the tape, deftly pulling the paper off and lifting the lid for me to see what was inside.

Four rows of baguette diamonds on a silver cuff bracelet winked at me. Simple. Elegant. Breathtaking.

His eyes studied my face, expectant, hoping I approved. Then it hit me—it wasn't the gift that needed approval, but Lance himself. An only child, he'd once told me how difficult it was for him to meet his parents' expectations. The pressure his senator father put on him to follow in his footsteps. The distance he felt with his mother. Then, before he'd finished law school, they'd been killed in a plane crash. My mom was annoying at times, but at least I still had one.

With childlike exuberance, Lance lifted the bracelet from the velvet lining and slipped it on my wrist. "It's one of a kind. Special order. I've been anxious for your birthday to get here so I could surprise you."

My doubts began to crumble when I saw in his face, in his tender eyes, the approval he hoped I'd give. The approval he needed. "It's gorgeous. Thank you."

His lips were warm and soft against mine. "I love you." His

breath, inches from my face, promised everything I'd always wanted. Love. Security. Marriage.

I inhaled his scent, intoxicating, like a fine Cabernet that tingled as it slid smoothly down the back of the throat. My remaining doubts, my fears, melted as I closed my eyes and answered him back with a kiss. *I love you, too, Lance Evans.*

[CHAPTER 5]

Mitzi

The mornings were the kindest to Gabe, so over time I learned to adjust my schedule to meet his. I arrived before six thirty, anxious to share my concerns about Brooke. Not because Gabe could give me a rational answer or shed light on why Brooke weighed so heavily on my spirit, but Alzheimer's or not, after sixty-one years, I still discussed everything with him. Always. This was no different.

I raised the head of his bed, washed his face, and kissed him good morning. Then I took the Bible from his nightstand and read from the Psalms.

"O sing unto the LORD *a new song; for he hath done marvelous things . . ."*

Gabe's lips moved as I read through the passage.

"Sing unto the LORD *with the harp: with the harp, and the voice of a psalm."*

I paused, wondering if, sandwiched in the plaque clogging his brain, the words still held meaning. My lapse in reading brought a look of alarm to his eyes. He knew I'd stopped mid-verse. I waited, hoping he would say something.

He did. His deep voice croaked out, "Harpo. Groucho. Now

they knew a good cigar." He wiggled his eyebrows and pursed his lips as if blowing smoke.

I finished the Psalm, then took his hands in mine and prayed a blessing over his day. The Marx brothers. Ahhh, yes. And for a minute, I wanted to crawl into Gabe's brain and relive the old days of television when we'd laughed at Groucho on *You Bet Your Life.* Instead, I fed Gabe his brown-sugared oatmeal and scrambled eggs, but when I offered the Ensure, he clamped his mouth shut and turned away.

Forcing him to eat would only end in a battle, one that I wasn't up for. In the earlier stages of Gabe's disease, my fussing over Gabe and his hygiene—or lack of it when his mind began unraveling—was met with thrashing, shouting, and more than a few wars of the world. His resistance stung with rejection, but as the staff at the Guardian Light counseled and educated me, I quit giving Gabe his bath and stuck with routines that didn't bring out the grizzly in him. Oddly enough, one of those was doing his range-of-motion exercises, or as I preferred to think of them: the geriatric tango.

Lotion first on his feet and legs. Then gentle massage to relax his muscles. When I hit his ticklish spot, Gabe jerked reflexively.

"You're the cat's pajamas, Gabe Steiner." I exercised his toes, rotating them each in turn, then flexed his ankles one at a time toward his shin and back toward the foot of the bed.

"Remember when we added a few dance steps to our singing routine, and it made all the girls in the audience swoon? They couldn't get enough of you."

I chuckled and moved his feet from side to side, the long bones of his feet almost visible beneath transparent flesh. "You made me jealous, you old scamp. Having the admiration of all those women."

Pulling clean socks over his feet, I let my memories of our lives then and now mingle together.

"Those were the days, Gabe."

Still wide-eyed, he looked toward the window where a cold drizzle streaked the glass.

"Forty-two degrees out there. Perfect for a cozy fire and a cup of cocoa." I tried the Ensure again. Offered him the straw.

He tightened his lips.

"All righty. I know it's not cocoa, but it is filled with all those yummy calories. A few more sips, then I'll tell you what's on my mind."

His lips parted for the straw, his cheeks sinking in at the effort of drinking. One swallow, then another. A slurping sound as the can of Dutch chocolate was emptied. Dotting the corner of his mouth with a napkin, I smiled, and although he didn't return the smile, I knew he was listening.

"I told you about the girl I met night before last. I saw her again yesterday. Her name is Brooke. Isn't that lovely?"

Gabe stared at a spot somewhere behind me, but I plunged on with the idea that had flirted with the edges of my mind all night. "Someone...her fiancé, if I were guessing...hit her. She's wounded and in denial I think, but all night I wrestled with what I could do to help her. She reminds me of Mama. Proud. Beautiful. Trapped. If someone had given Mama an alternative, things might've turned out different. I want to give this girl a chance to get some perspective about her life. I'm going to see her again this morning and offer her a room in our home."

Gabe's eyebrows, speckled still with black bristles among the white, arched up, and whether it was my imagination or only my eternal optimism, I believed he was listening.

"I know it's risky, but at our age, everything we do is a risk, so why not? She seems like a nice girl, but I was hoping you might give me your opinion."

Even a garbled word salad offering from him would be enough. Without thinking, I had slipped my hand into Gabe's, and when I paused, his fingers curled around mine. Weak. Warm. The slightest grasp that whispered affirmation.

I returned the squeeze and leaned over to kiss Gabe's cheek. His eyes closed, a calm resting on his face, and I let the wonder between us linger.

Love is many splendored.

~

When I knocked on Brooke's door, I didn't get an answer, so I peeked around the corner. My heart sank. The bed was empty. But before I'd had time to think of what to do next, she stepped from the bathroom, a surprised look on her face.

"Mitzi?"

"Good morning. Told you I'd be back. You must be feeling better to be up and around. And dressed."

"Much better. Going home, as a matter of fact. Mom's gone to get the car."

"Then I won't have time to hem-haw around, will I?"

"As in?"

"I know I have no business prying. Not like me at all, and of course you don't know me, so you will have to take my word for it. When I saw you the other night, it was like seeing my mother all over again. There's no mistaking the raw, exposed look of being abused." My insides quivered from having spewed out everything so quickly, but seeing Brooke had also opened up a wound that felt as fresh as it did seventy-some years ago.

I gulped in a bucket of air and went on. "No one deserves being the object of another person's wrath or insecurity or plain old meanness."

Brooke's mouth tightened into a terse line. "Lance is not mean. Or insecure. He's a successful attorney, an advocate for citizens' rights. You may have heard of him. Lance Evans. One of the brightest new legal minds according to *Tulsa About Town* magazine."

"I didn't say he wasn't smart or prominent. Abuse knows no social boundaries. The point is—"

"The point is, he lost his temper once. This one time. Unfortunately, it was my fault, and we've worked things out. He says it won't happen again, and I believe him. He needs me..."

She shrank away as she had the night in the emergency room. Arguing would be futile at this point. I could see that. He gave his word—a cotton candy promise—sweet, but full of air. And Brooke had bought it. Oh, how I hoped she was right. I walked toward the window, giving her space, before I turned back around.

"You have my blessing and best wishes. I'm not sure why our paths have crossed or what I could possibly offer you except friendship. Maybe a place to stay if you need to get away and think things through. I come and go at odd hours, but I live in a quiet neighborhood and would love to have you."

She jutted her chin up. Tears brightened one eye, the other swollen and discolored. "It's sweet of you, and I do appreciate your offer, but I prefer to be in my own apartment. I'll be off work until after Thanksgiving, which should give me plenty of time to think."

"Think about what?" Brooke's mother bustled into the room, shivering under her raincoat.

"Nothing, Mom." Brooke blinked and swallowed hard, as if she didn't want her mother to see her crying. "You remember Mitzi? I'm sorry, I've forgotten your last name."

I extended my hand. "Mitzi Steiner. And I didn't catch your name yesterday."

"Beverly Woodson." She ignored my hand and turned to Brooke. "I thought you were going to have someone load these flowers on a cart. They are too bulky for us to carry, and I've already pulled the car into the patient loading area."

"Sorry. I'll call someone."

I stepped in. "I'll be glad to help you. It's one of the things I do know how to do as a volunteer. I'll be right back with a cart."

We wheeled the things to the automatic doors, and before Brooke got into her mother's car, she stopped. "I forgot. I have my car in the parking lot. Mom, can you take me around to it and follow me home?" She gave me a bright smile. "Thanks for helping with my things."

"Take care, Brooke. And remember..."

She closed the car door before I finished, so I stood at the curb and watched them pull away. A brisk breeze whipped a candy wrapper through the air, spiraling, twirling around and around, aloft in the November cold.

And for some reason, thoughts of Mama and that time so long ago swept through me like the wind.

[CHAPTER 6]

Mama never did get to dip her toes in the ocean. Or see a mountain. We'd only gone a mile or two down the road outside of St. Louis when a man with a streaked beard and his lumpy wife picked us up. They were headed west to get away from "the insufferable Depression" and squeezed us into the backseat of their Model T. Bouncing along mile after mile, day after day, Ruthie and I kept our eyes peeled, looking for the mountains, but after the hills in Missouri, all we saw was dried-up earth from one side of the horizon to the other.

Mama sang "His Eye Is on the Sparrow" to soothe baby Chester between bottles of thin milk made with grainy powder and water from one of Papa's jugs. When we stopped near sunset, Mr. Meade would get out his shotgun and shoot whatever birds he could scare up. I trembled to think they might be the poor creatures God had his eye on. He plucked feathers while Mrs. Meade, her hair coiled into earmuffs, made a campfire.

"Maggie, you should try and eat a bite," Mama would say, and offer me one of the cooked birds.

But I couldn't. If God had his eye on the sparrow and Mr. Meade shot it, then what about me? Mama sang he was watching us, too.

We'd been in Kansas two days when Mr. Meade had his vision. He woke up wild-eyed and yanking his beard, which came to a point at the top button of his shirt.

"The Lord done told me we're headed in the wrong direction. Only the fools are going to Californy. We ain't nothing but a bunch of nomads like Moses in the wilderness." He dove into the Model T and came out clutching a Bible in one hand and waving his shotgun in the air with the other, looking up at the sky. A couple of puny white clouds drifted by.

"There now, you see it? God's pointing the way. A fire by night and a cloud by day. We're going in the direction of the clouds. Everybody, get loaded up. We'll burn in hell if we rebuke the visitation of the Lord."

Mrs. Meade ducked her head and obeyed, but while Mr. Meade had his head under the hood of the car, she whispered something to Mama.

Mama quickly removed our things from the car, thanked Mr. Meade for the ride, and said she changed her mind about going west.

Mr. Meade stroked the beard, fire nearly spitting from his eyes. "Vengeance is mine, saith the Lord. I'll call down fire and brimstone from heaven to smite you for your disobedience. Perish! Perish!" Saliva foamed from his mouth, oozing into the peppered beard.

"I'll keep that in mind," Mama said, and headed us back the way we'd come.

"Are we disobeying?" Ruthie wanted to know.

"No. Mr. Meade has spells from time to time, and Mrs. Meade said we ought to go back to the fork in the road we passed last night. The road to Oklahoma. Lots of Okies are moving in the direction we want to go. Besides, we could use the exercise. My goodness, my hip bones are pert near rubbed raw from bouncing on that loose spring."

At the place where the road split, a board on a fence post said it was twenty miles to Paris, Oklahoma. Mama loved the sound of that.

"Who knows? We might stay in Paris awhile. Maybe I could get a job and settle us into a nice cottage." Her eyes shone with possibilities.

We walked all day, Mama humming and Ruthie skipping off the road to chase butterflies. Nothing but the sun on our backs and air buzzing with anticipation. The road was straight, but with soft, rolling hills, so at every rise, we held our breath thinking we'd see Paris. Time after time, our hopes were dashed. Blisters covered the soles of my feet from miles of walking on the hot dirt, but we kept on until we came to a snowy thicket. Only it wasn't snow, but clouds of tiny white blooms that covered the bushes jutting from the ground.

"Oh, I haven't seen wild sand plums since my brother and I were kids back in Missouri." Mama danced around touching the branches, breathing in the scent. "Come June, these will be loaded with the tastiest little fruits you ever laid eyes on. So juicy and tart they'll bring tears to your eyes. And they make the best plum butter in all the world. Oh my, a taste of heaven."

She had a dreamy expression on her face like she'd already found heaven. A rumble in my tummy reminded me we hadn't eaten anything but crackers all day.

Mama hollered from the other side of the plum thicket. "Over here, kids. There's a creek."

A trickle of water cut through sandy banks, where scraggly trees with stickery offshoots nipped at us if we got too close. Mama kicked off her shoes and dipped her toes in the water. Then she kicked up a spray and started giggling. She bent over and scooped up handfuls of water, patting her face, inviting us to join her. We traipsed up and down, splashing, laughing. Even baby Chester got in on the fun, sitting in the shallow edges, waving his arms.

Ruthie was the first to stop us. "I think we should get going. The sun's about gone, and I'm scared of the dark."

"Looks like we won't make Paris tonight, dumplin's, but maybe we can find a soft spot to lay our heads. We can look at the stars and count our blessings."

Winding along the creek banks searching for the perfect spot, we found an old hut, pitiful looking, with the door hanging on one hinge. "Mercy sakes." Mama raced over and looked inside.

"It's a mite dusty, but there's an iron bedstead. We'll cover it with our quilt, and tomorrow we'll find Paris."

Mama made Chester's bottle with fresh water from the creek and sang "Amazing Grace" while she brushed and braided Ruthie's hair, then mine. "Let's say our prayers, dumplin's, and call it a day."

When we woke, the sun was already halfway up the sky, and the blue overhead so bright it hurt my eyes.

"Is this heaven?" Ruthie asked, and popped her thumb back in her mouth.

"I do declare, it might be." Mama leaned on the door and craned her neck. "Tell you what, kiddos. I'm going to get some fresh water for Chester's bottle and see if I can find a farmhouse nearby. I'll be back before you know it."

She grabbed one of Papa's jugs and a cup for dipping water from the creek. "Stay close to the hut and look after Chester, okay?"

Ruthie and I played patty-cake with Chester, then we went outside and found a stick so I could show Ruthie how to write the letters of her name in the dirt. I kept an eye out for Mama and was bouncing Chester on my hip when Ruthie pulled on my dress.

"Look over there." She pointed over her shoulder.

A thick black line came up over the plum thicket where Mama had disappeared. It grew wider with each blink of my eyes.

"What does it mean, Maggie? Is it the devil? Is he coming to take us to hell like Mr. Meade said?"

"Don't be silly, Ruthie. It's a rain cloud. Come on. We'll wait for Mama inside the hut."

The wind picked up, lifting my dress like a blast of winter and almost knocking me down. I hurried into the hut, shooing Ruthie in. The wind slammed the door behind us. Ruthie whimpered. "Mr. Meade was right. We shoulda gone with him."

"In case you didn't notice, Mr. Meade was crazy. Mama's the one we got to trust. And God. His eye is on the sparrow and he's watching over you. And me. And Mama." I tried to sound brave while dust as fine as Mama's face powder blew between the boards. Outside, the wind moaned

and howled. We huddled in the shack, the thin walls creaking with each gust.

I rooted around in the pillowcase for the box where Mama kept her locket. In the shadowy light seeping through the cracks of our refuge, I fastened it around my throat and prayed it would make me feel better like it sometimes did Mama.

Chester howled along with the wind, while Ruthie leaned into me, sucking her thumb. I sang Mama's songs twenty times. Maybe thirty. And still the wind howled.

When I started singing again, Ruthie covered her ears and cried, "Stop it! Singing ain't going to help. And I have to potty. Do something, Maggie!"

Dust blew in every crack, the fine silt slanting like a dune against the wall. We covered our faces with our scrappy clothes from the pillowcase to keep from choking on the particle-filled air.

I tried to think of something. Anything. But there was nothing to do but wait.

Ruthie tugged on my arm. "I wet myself." She started coughing and crying. "Mama ain't coming back and we're gonna die. Die, Maggie. You hear me?"

Closing my eyes, I tried to block out her wailing . . . her endless prophesying like the bearded Mr. Meade.

It turned out Ruthie was right about one of those things.

[CHAPTER 7]

Brooke

Leaning into the bathroom mirror, I examined my wound. Pale yellow with a hint of green. The suture line, while still red, had lost most of the swelling, leaving an inch-long ridge along my cheekbone. Miraculous what two weeks would do. I hoped Dr. Craft was right and the cream she'd given me plus a few microabrasion treatments would be all I needed.

The doorbell rang as I patted the concealer I'd picked up at the mall on the scar. Lance. Right on time to go to CiCi's for Thanksgiving dinner. Lance's idea, which had sent Mom into orbit, gushing about how perfect Lance and I were together.

And the truth was, since my accident, Lance had treated me like a princess, checking on me every day and spending hours watching the boxed set of old *Frasier* episodes he'd bought me. I helped him make a list of potential supporters, and together, we designed a flyer for his team of volunteers to deliver to every home in the county. Lance carted my files back and forth to Mr. Harrington, who'd agreed to let me work at home, much to Jenna's chagrin. She called with the latest office gossip and told me she'd love to work in her pajamas. Poor Jenna. I sometimes cringed at her wardrobe choices—more punk rock than professional—but Ben Harrington was not only her boss, he was also her uncle, so I kept my opinions to myself.

Lance greeted me with a kiss and a bouquet of roses. The third vase since I'd returned from the hospital.

"You're spoiling me, Lance Evans."

"That's the idea. You're worth it. And more." He put his arms around me and nuzzled my neck.

I relaxed against him. "Are you sure you want to be with my family today? We could—"

"—Cuddle on the sofa? Is that what you had in mind? I'd love to, but your family and holiday dinners are important to me. That's something I wish I'd had more of, but my mom..."

He didn't finish, but left it hanging the same way he did every time he mentioned his mother. Once I'd asked him to explain, and the most he would say was that she was complicated. Fragile. Thanksgiving was no doubt a tough time for him.

I grabbed my coat and purse. "All right then, let's go."

The air swirled with sunshine as we zipped south on Riverside in Lance's Lexus. Joggers dotted the trail winding along the river's park front, and I was watching a boy throw a Frisbee for his golden retriever when Lance slammed on the brakes.

"What an idiot! Did you see what that creep did? Cut in front of me, no turn signal or anything." He smacked his palm on the horn, blasting it long and hard. Jerking the steering wheel to the right, Lance came alongside the elderly man who'd cut him off, screaming through the glass at the poor man, who seemed oblivious.

The space inside Lance's sports car suddenly felt too thin, my jacket too warm. "Good thing you were watching the road," was all I could squeak out.

"Darn straight, I was. You have to keep your eye out all the time for these morons. Whoever gave that old man a license should be shot."

Closing my eyes, I chewed on my bottom lip, praying he would calm down. Things had been going so well; we didn't need an inattentive driver mucking it up.

The vein in Lance's neck bulged above his cream turtleneck, his jaw set. His right hand curved tight around the steering wheel, sunlight bouncing from the center of the tigereye ring I'd given him for his birthday in September.

A shudder ricocheted through me. The ring that had cost me half a paycheck was the very thing that had split my face with Lance's fury behind it. I was pretty sure he hadn't been wearing it during the past two weeks. The old apprehensions stirred.

Then, just as quickly, Lance gunned the engine, zoomed ahead of the offensive driver, and whipped back into the center lane. Smiling, he turned to me, the explosive moment erased. "You suppose your mom's bringing pecan pie?"

"I'm sure she is. She knows it's your favorite." My voice was cheerful, but inside, I quivered, hoping the wobbly start to our morning had passed.

Thanksgiving smells and wood smoke tinged the air as we ambled up the short walk to CiCi's house. The upscale community where my sister lived her charmed life was so unlike the cookie-cutter neighborhood we grew up in, with haphazard yards and basketball hoops tethered above garage doors. I was truly happy for her.

Todd ushered us into the great room, with its marble fireplace and oak-planked floor. When he hugged me and offered to take my coat, his breath was minty fresh. CiCi appeared, her face glowing as she patted her melon-sized tummy beneath her sleek maternity top. Chattering how happy she was to see us, she whisked the relish tray I'd brought to the kitchen. I gave Lance a quick kiss and told him I'd better help with dinner.

Mom's head popped up when I entered the kitchen. "Just a minute and I'll give you a hug. Got to get these rolls into the oven.

We can't have CiCi overdoing in her delicate condition." She wiped dots of perspiration from her forehead with the back of her hand.

"It smells divine." I pecked her on the cheek. "Great outfit. Have you been shopping?"

"Matter of fact. Got this for 40 percent off retail on the Bling Shopping Network."

Too shiny for my taste, but it suited Mom. Her bracelets jangled when she handed me a jar of pickled okra. "Could you add those to your relish tray?"

I went to work lining them up, rearranging the sweet gherkins and black and green olives scrambled together from Lance's swerving in and out of traffic.

When CiCi left to light the candles on the dining table, Mom pulled me aside. "Don't say anything more about my outfit. CiCi's having a fit—my *habit*, she calls it. And her with her hormones all over the map like the stock market—"

"I heard that." CiCi stood in the doorway waving the butane candle lighter. She pointed it at me. "Just wait till Mom hits you up for some cash to pay her maxed-out charge card. She couldn't even pay for her car repairs. Todd had to write her a check."

Mom glowered at CiCi. "You don't have a clue, do you? All my life I've sacrificed for you two. I deserve nice things. You don't know how lucky you girls are to have men who can pamper you. Look at Brooke. I'd bet my last Dooney & Bourke those diamond earrings she's wearing cost more than I make in a month."

CiCi waved the candle wand in Mom's face. "Talk about hormonal." She turned to me. "You think you could put the ice in the glasses? And be careful; I don't want any broken crystal."

Wincing, I had second thoughts about our sweet family Thanksgiving and busied myself, trying not to chip a glass or stumble carrying them to the table.

Mom checked the rolls in the oven. "Two more minutes and we

can eat." She winked at me. "So, tell me. Have you and Lance set a date?"

"For what?"

"Don't be so dense. Your wedding, of course. I don't know why you're dragging your feet. Your biological clock is tick, tick, ticking away, you know."

"Don't start, Mom, okay?" I tried to sound casual. Going from weddings to biological clocks in one breath? Come on.

My hint that I didn't want to discuss it went unheard, or unheeded, as Mom went on, "I read another article last week that a woman's fertility rapidly declines after age thirty-five. That's why there's so many test-tube babies nowadays."

I popped a green olive in my mouth, glad for the vinegary tartness that puckered my mouth and matched my mood. "I'm barely thirty, in case you forgot. There's plenty of time for kids. And weddings." I brushed past her with a bowl in each hand.

The dining room sparkled, with flickering candles and an artsy centerpiece in vibrant fall colors. Not the papier-mâché cornucopia I'd made in grade school that paired up nicely with the construction paper pilgrims CiCi made the same year. Thinking of those homemade decorations, though, brought an unexpected lump to my throat.

As infuriating as Mom was occasionally, we did have good times, and for an instant, I wanted to go back to my childhood. Fix the regrets. Hang onto the magic moments that had occurred here and there. Perhaps I would be graceful and elegant, accepting the praise people heaped on me for the ribbons I won at the art fair. And I would stand up for myself and insist on taking the art scholarship instead of the academic one for pre-law.

Having a milestone birthday hadn't given me these insights; I'd always done what other people thought best for me. Pursued the safe course in college that promised a steady paycheck. Being the paralegal assistant to a partner in a reputable firm was as steady as it gets. But making spreadsheets to track facts, dates, and addresses of our clientele didn't exactly lend itself to artistic expression. Even the simple act of lining up pickles and olives in a crystal dish was infinitely more creative.

Mom shook my arm. "Brooke, are you all right? You're staring into space. Oh goodness, I hope you're not having one of those mental spasms again."

If Mom hadn't looked so worried, I would have laughed. Instead, I reassured her. "My EEG came back normal, remember? Nothing wrong with my brain. No seizures." I gave her a hug. "I was thinking of all the things you did for CiCi and me growing up, and I don't think I ever thanked you."

Her jaw dropped open. "What a sweet thing to say." She blinked to gain control of her teary eyes. "Now, let's all sit down and eat before the dinner gets cold."

Todd held my chair for me before taking his seat at the head of the table. CiCi and Mom sat across from Lance and me, and after Todd asked the blessing holding mine and CiCi's hands, Lance rose from his seat.

"Thank you, Beverly and CiCi, for preparing such a feast. And Todd, I gotta hand it to you. You guys have a great house." He picked up his water glass. "A toast? To many future family gatherings."

When I lifted my glass along with the others, it bobbled and water dribbled onto my plate and down the front of my silk blouse. Todd and Lance reached over with their napkins at the same time to dry my plate. Lance's eyes narrowed ever so slightly in Todd's direction, then with a flourish, Lance blotted my water-stained blouse. "Allow me."

Embarrassed at my clumsiness, I shooed them both away and reached for the bowl of cornbread dressing. We ate, the conversation polite until Todd mentioned he had tickets to the OU–O State game on Saturday. Bedlam to those who lived for the annual rivalry.

Todd gave an exaggerated wink. "'Fraid your Sooners are due a whupping from my Cowboys."

"In your dreams, bud." Lance, whose blood ran crimson and cream, snickered.

Barbs flew back and forth until Mom piped up, "You two are wearing me out. Maybe you can duke it out while the girls and I do the dishes."

"Maybe if Todd put his money where his pearly whites are—"

"You're on. Five bucks says the Cowboys win." Todd did a thumbs-up.

"Shows how much faith you got in your rookie quarterback." Lance flicked a bread crumb to the center of the table, then encircled my shoulders with his left arm, his grip firm. He glared a final time at Todd before tapping his water glass with the tigereye ring on his right hand. "I have some good news, and if Todd can put aside his misguided loyalties for a minute, I want y'all to hear it first."

Todd leaned back and nodded. "Sure thing."

Beside me, Lance shifted, sitting taller in his seat. "Certain people behind the scenes have decided to back me for the next Tulsa County DA. Since you're practically family, I wanted you to know that come Monday, the news will be official."

My fork clattered to my plate. "Lance, you hadn't told me Monday was the day."

"Sure I did, sweetheart. You must've forgotten."

While I racked my brain trying to think of when he'd told me, Mom's face beamed like she'd won the lottery. "Oh my gracious—my future son-in-law—the next district attorney. Tell us, what happens now?"

"First, the press conference. Then fund-raisers. And, of course, it will be good publicity for Brooke and I to get married during the campaign. Everyone loves a romantic twist."

CiCi puckered her lips. "Please don't get married before I have the baby."

Todd patted her hand. "What's wrong with a pregnant matron of honor?"

"Brooke won't want me standing beside her all ugly and fat." CiCi looked incredulous that Todd would consider such a thing. I was incredulous a wedding was even being discussed, fearing we'd gotten offtrack from the real purpose of Lance's announcement—his budding career.

Mom said, "Don't worry, CiCi. It will take a while to make the plans." She added on her fingers, counting off the months. "But we could surely pull it all together for late spring or early summer."

"What do you say, sweetheart?" Lance's solid hand squeezed my upper arm, a little too enthusiastic.

The candle before me flickered, wax oozing slowly down the side until it congealed, and I couldn't take my eyes from it. Mom and Lance were trying to light a flame under me, rush me into a wedding I wasn't ready for. Like the melted wax left a scar on the taper, my own face carried a reminder of why I was so reluctant to commit. Time. I needed more time.

The air thickened, four chilly pairs of eyes trained on me. Lance's grip on me hadn't loosened. If anything, the pressure of his hand dug deeper into my arm.

I lifted my chin. "When's your due date, CiCi?"

"March tenth, but you knew that." Her pouty look told me I'd hurt her feelings.

"Well, then, sometime after the baby comes." It was the best I could do, and conceding that left me weak, bereft. Telling myself to get a grip didn't help. How can a person grip something so slippery as happily ever after?

Mom jumped in with, "Thank goodness. I was afraid you two would never set a date. I have a surprise of my own. I've registered Brooke with the Designer Showcase Bridal Fair at Utica Square next month—"

"What? You did this without telling me?"

"Your lack of direction has always been a problem, Brooke. I thought seeing all the lovely gowns, wedding themes, and cake choices might inspire you and help you decide. Now that you have, we can focus on your dream day." Her eyes glistened, the flickering candle making twin flames in her eyes. "We can schedule time with one of the wedding planners, and they'll guide us in putting together an event suited for the next district attorney."

"Hear, hear." Lance clicked his crystal stem with mine, but his eyes shone toward Mom. "Thanks, Beverly."

"Please, call me Mom."

"You got it... Mom." His position shifted, his arm now draped across the back of my chair, his fingers toying with the back of my neck.

Everything seemed off. While I'd failed once again to express my truest feelings, I'd also caught a bit of Lance's enthusiasm. Beneath his feathery touch, my skin tingled with a grain of excitement. Maybe all I'd needed was a prompt in the right direction.

When we started home, Lance turned to me. "What's going on with you and Todd?"

"Excuse me?"

"I saw the way he looked at you. All those hugs and standing close to you." His voice was even. Controlled. But I wasn't sure if he was being critical or merely making an observation.

"I guess I didn't notice."

"How could you not? He practically drooled at your cleavage when you spilled water on your blouse. Honestly, I don't trust the guy."

He revved the engine waiting for a stoplight to turn green, and I tried to picture what had now turned into an accusation. *Stay cool. Keep it light.*

"He's my brother-in-law, my sister's husband. I'm sure he didn't mean anything by it."

"So you did notice? That's what I'm asking."

"Not really. Todd's a nice guy, that's all."

"Too nice, if you ask me. Let me tell you something. Guys with pregnant wives let their eyes wander. If I were guessing, I'd say he's turned off by CiCi's excessive weight gain. What do you think? Thirty pounds? Jeez, by the time the baby comes, she'll look like a sumo wrestler."

Blood rushed to my face. How rude. And unfair. Not only to CiCi, but to women everywhere. Those were the kinds of things Lance obsessed over and pushed to the limit. *Had* Todd come on to me? Or was there some sort of testosterone surge men got in the presence of women that made them want to challenge each other to a duel? Should I be flattered or mad at Todd? He and CiCi were happy—dripping-with-syrup happy—so why would Lance bash Todd?

Staring out the window on my right, I focused on the Christmas lights that had popped up overnight. Shining, twinkling. Feathery dusk had settled on Tulsa, the downtown skyline rising ahead of us. My apartment nestled in the shadow of those tall buildings. My pricey, chic apartment that was nothing like the cozy suburban home of my sister.

A part of me wanted to defend CiCi and Todd, but the sensible side told me to let it go. I changed the subject. "So, when will the campaign start?"

"It won't get rolling until after the holidays, but Monday the Parsleys will make the announcement to the media and outline my qualifications. A character reference so to speak. Which is why I need to know I can trust you. My opponent will be looking for any detail, any trivia to cast a shadow on my reputation. I think for now, it might be best if you don't visit your sister. You never know when Todd might be around, and trust me, his eye is wandering."

Say what? My jaw twitched, aching to disagree, but I kept quiet. His point about the media was valid—they were vicious. But to suggest I not see my own sister cut through me.

Lance must have sensed my hesitancy to agree. "It's only for a while. I know you'll want to be with your family at Christmas. I'll take some time off and join you." He gave me a reassuring pat on the knee. "Besides, we're going to be busy with all the charity balls coming up. I can't wait to show you off, start placing in people's minds the next couple who will be district attorney. It is the two of us, you know." Excitement and passion now laced his voice. His childlike exuberance was one of the things I loved most about Lance. The jealous streak aside.

Lance pulled up to the entrance to my apartment, letting the car idle, his fingers drumming on the steering wheel.

"Aren't you coming in?"

"Not tonight. I need to start writing my speech for the press." He leaned in offering a kiss.

Quick. Dismissive. Then he was gone.

After changing into sweats, I curled up on the sofa with a fleece throw. As Norah Jones crooned softly through my stereo speakers, Cosmo came out of hiding and jumped on my lap. Stroking his dense silver fur, I tried to psych myself up for looking at wedding gowns and choosing cake flavors. Maybe setting a date would give me the incentive to get jazzed about saying I do.

Reaching for the mini-calendar on the coffee table, I knocked something off—a receipt or piece of paper. I stretched to get it before Cosmo batted it under the sofa, and came up with the card Mitzi Steiner had given me. The one with the picture of a sparrow clinging to the nest with its tiny, needlelike toes. I held my breath as if doing so would keep the fledgling bird from plummeting to the ground. The card quivered between my trembling fingers as an idea flittered through my head.

Don't be absurd.

The image wouldn't leave, so I rose from the sofa and went to the desk in the corner. Scrambling through the contents of the center drawer, I found what I was looking for. A pad of white paper. A lead pencil. An eraser.

Then I propped myself back on the sofa, and after a brief look at Mitzi's card, I sketched a bold outline. Holding the paper up, I tilted it this way and that to check the proportions. An energy buzzed through me, quickening a place deep inside. The pencil felt solid in my hand, my fingers gliding across the paper, my heart instructing them where to make the next line. Short strokes, subtle shading, a beak with two tiny air holes. Eyes that took in the world.

My breath came in short bursts, my lungs hungry for air as the body and wings took form, the legs as fragile as toothpicks. Time was of no consequence, and yet I knew the exact moment it was finished. Another mark would be one too many. I leaned my head back and closed my eyes, a warmth coursing through me. Weakness, too—as if a plug had been pulled, and all my energy had drained from me. But it was a cleansing, freeing sensation.

Why had I given up drawing and painting? Just because I didn't pursue art as a career was no reason I couldn't enjoy it now. I no longer owned a set of pastels or charcoal pencils. Not even a sketchbook.

Tomorrow. Why not buy a few art supplies?

Cosmo purred beside me, his whiskers twitching in his feline dreams. I stroked his fur, lost in thoughts that had nothing to do with bridal fairs or wedding cakes. When Cosmo stretched and began kneading his paws against me, I shifted my position and looked again at my penciled effort.

Nice contrast. Silky feathers I could almost feel. I'd sketched a sparrow without doubt.

A tiny song sparrow with a broken wing.

[CHAPTER 8]

Mitzi

The day after Thanksgiving, I loaded my worn-out Mercedes with boxes. Tinsel. Christmas ornaments. A tabletop artificial tree to bring a spot of Christmas to Gabe's room. When I ran back in for my purse, the phone was ringing.

"Mitzi. It's Drew."

Drew Caprice. Hearing his voice brought tears to my eyes.

"Drew. Oh my, I haven't heard from you in way too long. Is everything all right? You doing well?"

"Doing fine. And how's my favorite girl?"

"Perfect now that you've called. Gabe, not so well. The nature of the beast with Alzheimer's, I'm afraid. So what do I owe for this unexpected pleasure?"

"A favor. I'm applying for a pediatric residency in Tulsa. Boston is crawling with candidates, and I'm ready for a smaller town. Only problem is, they can't see me until a couple of days before Christmas. How about I spend Christmas with you?"

My heart raced. Yes! Just like old times, when Gabe and I spent our holidays with our dearest friends, Lou and Mary Ruth Caprice. The years tumbled one after another in my head. Life on the road with Lou, our lifelong career manager. Mary Ruth going into labor with Henry the night we opened at the Sands in Las Vegas. Being godparents to Henry and then holding the honorary distinction again when Henry and Jill brought Drew into the world. Precious Drew, who now wanted to come for Christmas.

I was still babbling an hour later as I decorated the tree in Gabe's room. "Can you believe it? Drew spending the holidays with us. And if he gets a residency in Tulsa, he'll be nearby all the time. Not sure he'll have much time for us, but still."

Gabe blinked at the tree's twinkling lights, and I wondered if he remembered Drew. Or Henry. Or even Lou and Mary Ruth, who'd both passed from cancer six months apart. An awful time for all of us. Attending Mary Ruth's service in California was the last trip Gabe and I made. Even then, the Alzheimer's had begun, and if not for Drew's steady hand to help while we were there, I couldn't have managed Gabe. A swell of memories lapped at my heart.

Going to Gabe's bedside, I kept up the patter. "Drew wants to go to the Jazz Depot when he comes and see our plaque. Remember when they inducted us into the Oklahoma Jazz Hall of Fame? I told Drew they'd put our gold record in a glass showcase. Who knew your song 'I See Heaven in Your Face' would be our ticket to fame?"

A tear formed in the corner of Gabe's eye, and rather than whisk it away, I leaned over and kissed his forehead, a tear of my own mingling with Gabe's.

With my thumb, I brushed the wetness from his face, but his eyes had drifted away, his body easing into sleep.

Sighing, I sat in the recliner, content with my memories and the sounds of Gabe's soft breathing.

[CHAPTER 9]

Brooke

Sparrows populated my apartment. Dozens of them etched with my new charcoal pencils. On some I'd added a touch of color—a yellow beak here, a crimson leaf there. A pair of pink-tinged hatchlings, crouched in the safety of a nest.

My favorite, though, was still the one I'd drawn on Thanksgiving—the sparrow with the broken wing. Matted and framed, it hung in the corner next to my bed and was the first thing I saw when I woke up. The last image in my head when I went to sleep.

My first morning back at work, Ben Harrington dumped an armload of files on my desk. "Busy time of year. Why do people wait until the holidays to get their hackles up over their visitation rights? Check through these, then flag the ones with a legitimate request, and I'll take it from there."

The requests varied from the annual tug-of-war over who would spend Christmas with mommy to those where an elderly family member was on his deathbed and the noncustody parent wanted the child present for one last Christmas. My job was to verify if the dying person existed or if it was a manufactured excuse to keep the waters churning in a battle of wills. It baffled me how two people who fell in love and brought children into the world could become so vindictive when they divorced.

Like Mom and Dad. They divorced when I was five, and Mom never shielded CiCi and me from her bitterness about Dad running off to Texas with another woman. When the child support came each month, she'd sniff and say, "Even a rat takes care of its young."

As far as I knew, Dad had never asked for visitation rights with CiCi and me. Maybe an angry tussle or two between my parents would have given me a sense I was worth fighting over. Or maybe Dad was a gutless wonder like me who fled my mother's rants when he got the chance.

Whatever.

Lance didn't invite me to the press luncheon at Southern Hills Country Club to launch his campaign, but that evening he took me to dinner and gave me a list of the charity balls and social events we would be expected to attend.

First up, attending the season premiere of *The Nutcracker* with Jim and Roberta Parsley on Friday night. Knowing it was my first test with Lance's mentors, I'd changed clothes five times and ended up wearing a black silk dress I'd bought at the Gently Worn Consignment Store. I swooped my dark hair up, leaving my bangs ruffled, hoping the makeup-covered scar wasn't too noticeable. The diamond birthday bracelet complemented my outfit perfectly, its sparkle giving me a false sense of bravado.

Roberta effused money, charm, and good manners while maintaining the aura of a patronizing aunt. "Lance has told us so many nice things about you. So clever of you to choose St. Luke's for your wedding. It's perfect for publicity, with their wonderful organ and miles of stained glass."

I thought I'd heard wrong. St. Luke's? My chest felt as if I'd fallen from the balcony two levels up. I blinked, aware of my mouth gaping open. "Actually, we're still considering our options."

"Oh, but St. Luke's is perfect." She gave me a quick hug, her ample bust draped in gold lamé. With a throaty laugh, she asked, "What's the date?"

Lance's eyes met mine with an I-can-take-it-from-here look. "June third. Lucky for us the church was still available. The reception will be at Southern Hills, of course."

I struggled for air, contorting my face into a smile. When had he done this? Set the date? Booked the church? And why hadn't he told me?

"Excellent choice." Jim and Roberta's twin smiles told me Lance was a quick learner in the political arena.

The lights above me twinkled, while the murmurs of the theater patrons buzzed in my ears. Jim Parsley handed me a glass of champagne and hoisted his in a four-way toast. It was acid on my tongue, effervescing into a million pricks in my mouth, down my throat.

Just then, a man to my left held up a camera, a heavy, professional-looking model, and asked for a smile. The four of us scrunched together as the man—a reporter, I assumed—clicked away. Lance draped his arm around me and whispered, "Can't wait to see that in the papers. You look beautiful, hon."

Taking advantage of the close encounter, I hissed in his ear, "Never mind that. How could you have made all those arrangements without consulting me? You know I can't afford a reception at Southern Hills."

He tilted my chin up with his hand, his blue eyes searing into mine. "No worries. I'll be paying for that. Only the best for you, my love. I thought you'd be pleased." Another camera flashed capturing our tender moment. I was anything but pleased with the way the evening was going.

When the lights flickered, signaling that the show would soon begin, we found our way to the orchestra section. Fifth row. Center seats. And as the curtain lifted, I saw not sugarplum fairies and dancing flowers on the stage, but my life being scripted for me. Each step carefully measured. One misstep, and I would ruin the show.

Long after our late-night coffee with the Parsleys and Lance seeing me home, I had still not recovered from the feeling of being backed into a corner. That somehow what I wanted didn't matter. Was that it? Lance said he loved me, but as his campaign took shape, I felt like window dressing, a marionette at the end of a string. He hadn't bothered to ask what I wanted or needed. And sadly, I wasn't certain myself.

My eyes rested on the framed sparrow beside my bed. I should have pressed the point on the wedding plans with Lance, but it hardly seemed worth the effort, and I didn't want to jeopardize anything with his campaign.

Broken wings can heal. Tiny birds can learn to fly again.

And for a moment, I dreamed of soaring high and far away.

On Sunday afternoon, I drove across downtown to Swan Lake with my sketch pad and charcoal pencils in tow. The sun warmed my back as I perched on a bench and looked beyond the black wrought iron fence circling the small body of water. There, some of Tulsa's finest vintage homes stood welcoming me.

As my hand found the freedom to experiment with shading and drawing the elegant curved necks of the resident swans, I shoved thoughts of my upcoming wedding aside. Like the water lapping the fringes of the feather grass around the lake, though, they wouldn't lie dormant. June was only six months away. How could I be of any help to Lance's campaign while worrying about the details of the ceremony and reception at the same time? My life would be consumed with planning, fittings, photographers, florists. Surely Lance's budding political career was more important at the moment. We hadn't even seen each other on Saturday; he had golf plans with Jim Parsley, then dinner at the Petroleum Club with more potential financial supporters.

The mossy wet smell and the distant chatter of children playing gave me a heady feeling. I wanted to run barefoot through the grass, let the wind fly through my hair, not be locked into wedding plans. I would have to convince Lance—and Mom—and now apparently Roberta Parsley—to put the wedding on hold. Maybe a year from now—after the election. A backlash was inevitable. Lance would insist on going through with it. Mom would lecture. I didn't even want to ponder what the Parsleys might think.

The swans, two regal snowy white creatures, skimmed by, glibly unaware of me and my inner turmoil. My fingers curled around the charcoal pencil in my hand to capture their elegance, the lazy circles rippling out behind them. An errant leaf, brown as the crust on a piece of toast, landed in the water. Caught up in the wake of the swans, the leaf drifted, tipped, and turned, then disappeared into the murky undertow.

A chill came in the air as the soft blur of dusk approached. Gathering my pencils and paper, I took a last backward look at the swans. One of them—which I liked to think was the female, although I didn't know how to tell the difference—curtsied on the water. Her mate responded with a tiny nuzzle on her neck. Then, side by side, they swept through the water in a dance no choreographer could orchestrate.

When I pulled into my apartment's parking garage, Lance pulled in right behind me, his eyes bright, his mouth in a tight pose. With a long box tucked under his arm, he hurried to my car and opened the door for me. "Where have you been? I called your apartment. And your cell. And why are you wearing that old jacket?"

Doing mental calisthenics, I tried to remember if we'd made

plans I'd forgotten about. Gaining time to think, I pulled my sketch pad and art case from the passenger seat before I answered. "Just out for a drive, and I took my sketch pad to Swan Lake. Must've forgotten to take my cell."

He gave me a half frown, but followed me up to the apartment, talking about his afternoon. Every Sunday, no matter what else was going on, Lance visited Judith Zabel, a widowed friend of the family. Sweet, really. They played Scrabble, and she served him gingerbread.

"She beat me two for three this afternoon." Scrabble. "And instead of gingerbread, we had pumpkin cheesecake a neighbor brought over for Thanksgiving."

"Sounds good. I'm sure Mrs. Zabel enjoyed your visit."

"It's the least I can do. She's lonely, and I cheer her up."

Our footsteps gave a muffled echo in the stairwell as we went up to my second-floor apartment. "So what's in the box?"

Mischievous grin. "A surprise. You'll have to wait. But I can be bribed with a kiss."

He leaned over and offered his lips.

Cheesecake-flavored kiss. With a bourbon chaser.

My antennae went up, and when I slid the key into the lock of my apartment, I prayed Lance didn't notice the tremble in my fingers.

Cosmo flew like an airborne skid mark and disappeared under the sofa. I tossed the art supplies on my desk, then slipped out of my jacket.

"Still curious?" He held out the box, which had a lavender ribbon and gold sticker from La Belle Formal Wear. After removing the ribbon and paper, I lifted an exquisite deep teal creation from the tissue folds. The sequined bodice felt weighty in my hands, and as I held it up I could tell the neckline plunged dangerously low. As always, an expectant gleam danced in Lance's eyes.

"Oh, it's gorgeous. Fabulous." And it was. So not like the tailored me, but breathtaking and sparkly and provocative. The kind of dress Mom would drool over. I held it next to me and twirled around the living room imagining the music as we danced at the Christmas ball. "So which event is this for?"

"Next Friday. I gave you the list and hoped you would remember. It's either the Cure for Diabetes or the Tulsa Zoo Gala, but we'll be the stars. Go. Try it on. Let me see you."

"Wait. I'll check the list and see which party it is." I handed him the dress, then scrabbled through my desk, pulled out envelopes, stamps, a receipt for my art supplies, a get-well card from Jenna at the office, and a handful of pens, nail files, and junk. No list. "I must have put it in my Day-Timer."

"Do you think you could get any more disorganized? Honestly, how can you expect to be of any help as my wife if you run off and spend your afternoons drawing silly pictures and can't keep track of a simple list?"

"It was a beautiful day. And they're not silly pictures. Here, I'll show you."

"Some other time, okay? Just try on the dress." He shoved it at me.

In my bedroom, I peeled off my sweatshirt and jeans, stepped into the gown, and shimmied it up over my hips. Uh-oh! No way was this going to fit. The label verified my brilliant conclusion. Size 4. And I wore an 8 on a skinny day. Dropping to the edge of my bed, I dreaded telling Lance. Even if I wanted to be petite, it wasn't as if I could change my bone structure. On the other hand, maybe I should be flattered that Lance envisioned me as thin as a runway model.

Bending over, I scooped my jeans off the floor to put them back on, then thought better of it. Why not something softer, more appealing? In my walk-in closet, I found a pair of wool pants and a soft, clingy red sweater. When I stepped back into my bedroom, Lance stood with the glittery gown in his hands.

"I thought you might need some help."

My throat clogged as I held the sweater and slacks awkwardly in front of me, trying to hide my near nakedness. "You scared me. The dress . . . uh . . . it's too small. I was getting dressed. Can you wait outside?"

A corner of his lip went up. "Jeez, we're engaged. You think I won't see you getting dressed every day for the rest of our lives? Come on, give me a hug. I've missed seeing you this week." His eyes, looking more gray than blue, softened, as did the curl of his lips. Momentarily, my embarrassment fled, but I couldn't bring myself to step toward his outstretched arms.

With a catch in my throat, I willed myself to shrink behind my clothes. I wasn't a prude. Most people would say I was an idiot because I didn't let Lance sleep over, try out sex before marriage. I couldn't do it. Images of Chad Lamb flashed through my head. My boyfriend when I was a freshman in college. He duped me into believing we had the real thing and an engagement ring was right around the corner. How naive. And stupid. After the third time we slept together, he dumped me like an empty McDonald's bag. It would not happen again. Not without a marriage certificate.

My face felt hot and had probably turned the color of the sweater I artfully held in front of me. "Lance, please. You know how I feel. Call me old-fashioned, but I'm so not comfortable with this situation. Can you wait in the living room until I get dressed? Then we'll talk."

He was at my side, his fingers on my skin sending electric impulses fluttering through me. When I relaxed, giving into the sensation, Lance gently took my clothes and tossed them on my bed, then pulled me into an embrace.

My skin prickled, but not in arousal. More like panic. Clogged throat. My body rigid. The cashmere of Lance's sweater was soft, wooly against my bare midriff, my shoulders. Shrinking back, I crossed my arms across my chest, giving him what I hoped was a playful shove, but it came out with more force than I intended.

"What is with you?" His eyes flashed. "One minute you're dancing like a ballerina around the coffee table, the next you're the ice queen."

"I'm sorry, Lance. Please, can you let me get dressed?"

"Sorry is right. You're my fiancée—or did you forget that minor detail? Even old-fashioned girls—as you put it—get caught up in the heat of the moment. There's nothing wrong with that."

He grabbed my elbows, pulling me into him again, but I ducked my head, turning away from his breath, which now reeked more strongly of bourbon. Had he brought it with him? I didn't keep bourbon, much to his chagrin, and he had, on occasion, brought his own.

"Look at me!"

I lifted my chin and met his gaze, shivering in my underwear. "Lance, please."

"I'll take that as a yes."

Before I could protest, he put a vise grip on my elbows and led me to the bed.

"Stop! You're hurting me."

In the next instant, he hurled me onto the mattress. My head swam as the feeling of sinking overtook me. I fought for breath, my arms and legs thrashing to get my head above water. Instead, pinned under his weight, I plummeted deeper, my insides screaming, *Please, we need to talk about this.* But the words clogged in my throat, my plea only a guttural moan.

Lance's face touched mine, but it was Chad Lamb's eyes I saw, eager, laughing, taunting. I gulped for air, this time my words breaking free and begging, "No! Stop! Please."

Writhing, I tried to surface, to gain traction and push myself away. That was when the first blow pushed the air from my lungs. Then another. And another. A garbled voice filled my ears, but I couldn't tell if it was me moaning or Lance grunting.

Breathing took all my effort as I was sucked into the swirl. Drifting. Rolling. Desperate for air. Tentacles grasped my hair, my head yanked askew on my shoulders. When the pain of it subsided my arm was wrenched from another direction. A crack, like a tree limb snapping, filled the space, a searing white pain taking the last bit of air from my lungs.

As I tumbled deeper, a voice above me screamed, "Look what you've made me do. You're no different than her. Weak. Ungrateful." Swirling lights, psychedelic pulses in my brain took away all sense of time as the angry strains continued. "After all I've done for you. After buying you nice things you don't deserve. Jewelry. Dresses. This is the thanks I get."

I reached up to touch the spewing lips, to protest, but another blow into my ribs sent me tumbling into darkness. Into the deep.

[CHAPTER 10]

Mitzi

Christmas lights framed the roof and front door of the Guardian Light care center. Another half hour before daylight would come. A cold front had blown in during the night, bringing a bone-chilling rain and predictions of an ice storm. How it could be seventy-five degrees one day and bitter cold the next was a conundrum I'd never figured out, even though I'd lived a good part of my life in Oklahoma.

"Good morning, Miz Steiner." Hadley Davis held the door for me. He spent more time than I did at the Guardian Light, caring for his wife, Lily, who had a room two doors down from Gabe. A kind soul and wicked gin rummy opponent, Hadley and I spent many an hour playing cards and arguing over whether Miles Davis or Duke Ellington was the greatest jazz performer of the last century. Hadley delighted in yanking my chain, telling me Miles was his cousin on his daddy's side. The truth of it didn't matter. What did matter was that we teased and laughed through hours we might've spent dwelling on the future of our spouses.

Hadley waited while I stomped the wet from my shoes. "Got a mite chilly, didn't it? Any ice on the roads when you came in?"

"Not yet, but if this weather keeps up, I'll probably make it a short day here. How about you?"

"Not rightly sure. I spent the night holding Lily's hand. She's a fright when the weather changes. Got her settled now, so I'm stepping out for some breakfast. Can I bring you something?"

"I'm fine, but thanks for asking. Be careful."

Gabe, blessedly, was not bothered by the change in weather and had to be shaken awake for his breakfast. While I fed him, I kept an eye on the window, watching for signs of ice. A storm could keep me housebound for days—days away from Gabe—but I didn't relish spending the night in the recliner beside his bed either. Perhaps the front would zip through and spare me from making a decision.

It turned out, I had another mission. While I went through the paces of Gabe's range-of-motion exercises, the phone rang.

"Mitzi, I hope it's all right to call you at this number." It was Betty Wardell, the volunteer administrator from the hospital. "I'm in a bind over here. Three people on the schedule have called in sick, and I don't know whether you've seen the news or not, but there's been a huge pileup on the Broken Arrow Expressway. The ER is crammed with people, and I've got requests for coffee and what all and could use some help. Any chance—"

"I'm on my way."

When I turned around, Gabe had fallen back asleep. I pulled on his socks and tucked the blanket under his stubbled chin. When I kissed his cheek, he didn't even stir.

A steady drizzle fell as I left the care center, but as the windshield wipers swished, I was grateful to see that no ice crystals had formed. At the hospital, I pulled into a spot reserved for volunteers on the lower floor of the parking garage and ducked in the back entrance. Betty gave me the assignments for two of the missing-in-action Pink Ladies. Coffee patrol and delivery girl for the gift shop. She tucked a pager in my hand and sent me on my way.

After making sure all the visitor waiting areas had fresh coffee, I went to the ER. The air buzzed with talk of an overturned eighteen-wheeler and black ice, and rants about why the city hadn't been quicker with the sanding trucks. Since I'd been chastised by Helen for interacting with patients, I steered clear and stuck with making coffee. I'd just started the Bunn coffeemaker when a line formed to get a fresh cup, and my pager buzzed with the code for the gift shop. I hurriedly set out clean cups and supplies and started in that direction.

Pages crackled overhead.

"Doctor forty-nine to OB."

Ahead of me, a male nurse pushed a wheelchair, when another page announced, "Code Blue in ER six."

The nurse stopped and whirled around, eyeing me in my pink smock. "Can you take this patient to X-ray? We've got a code." He shoved the chart into my hands without waiting for an answer.

A woman with tangled hair, undoubtedly a crash victim, slouched in the wheelchair as I pushed her toward the radiology department. I said, "So sorry about the pileup on the BA. That must've been something."

No answer.

"Were you driving or a passenger?"

Nothing.

"Here we are."

I turned the wheelchair around to back through the swinging doors to the X-ray department. When I did, I saw the woman's face.

"Brooke? Brooke Woodson. Oh my, I had no idea you were one of the accident victims."

Her eyes filled with tears, whether from seeing me or because of pain, I didn't know. A closer look and I saw she wore a hospital gown and fuzzy red scuffs. Mascara-smudged eyes peered through coils of uncombed hair.

"Mitzi." The effort at saying my name seemed more than she could bear. Wincing, she lifted her right hand and squeezed mine until I thought my fingers would break.

In my pocket, the pager hummed again. As I wheeled Brooke into radiology, an X-ray tech pointed to a waiting area crowded with patients in wheelchairs and on gurneys. "Find a spot there. Do you have the chart?"

I handed it over, then positioned Brooke in an empty space. "Can I call someone for you? Your mother? Anyone?"

"No. Not my mother." Her eyes darted around the room. "Please, no. I just hurt my shoulder... in an accident."

My pager hummed again. "Hang on. I'll answer this and tell them I'm tied up in the ER."

"I'm fine."

"Hmmph. And I'm the Queen of England. Look, you may not realize it, but with all the activity around here, you could be stuck for hours and get lost in the shuffle."

"I'm not going anywhere today anyway." She stared at her feet, then lifted a quivering chin. "I can't go home. Not yet."

"We'll talk later." It was not the time to ask what happened, but the dullness in her eyes, her weary words gave me a sick feeling. The freeway pileup was not the cause of her accident. No matter what she said, I didn't think she'd been going to work when trouble had come her way. No one wears fuzzy slippers to work.

~

It was one o'clock before I got a lunch break. With a vending machine sandwich, I went to the ER and slipped past the reception area to the workstation and maze of cubicles. A clerk behind a computer monitor directed me to Brooke's cubicle.

When I peeked around the curtain, alarm flashed in Brooke's eyes until she saw it was me. "Mitzi. Come in."

"Want to share lunch?"

"No thanks. I'm not allowed to eat or drink anything until I get my test results. They've mentioned surgery if my shoulder is broken." She cradled her left elbow in her other hand and winced when shifting positions. "It feels like it might be."

"Want to talk?"

"No... but... well, I'm not sure. I've gone over it a million times in my head, and..."

"I'm a good listener."

"I don't know. Things were going so well... Something just came over him... I'm trying on the dress one minute, then the next, he's wanting me to..." She stared at the ceiling like the answer might fall from the tile.

"I'm guessing you're referring to your fiancé."

She nodded, the wary look back in her eyes. "Lance. He's pressing me to get married. He's picked out the church, the country club, the date, but it's all very complicated. He's running for a political office, and he's under all this stress. A wedding would be too much."

"Have you told him your concerns?"

"I never get the chance. Between him and my mother, I feel like I'm being forced into making snap decisions. And telling you all of this makes no sense at all."

She had a point. I was a doddering meddler who had no business interjecting myself into someone else's life. But I couldn't shake the coincidence of our paths crossing not just once, but twice. I'd learned long ago that coincidence had nothing to do with chance and everything to do with a master plan. Divine providence.

"Sometimes it's easier to tell a stranger your troubles."

The ER doctor stepped inside the cubicle, chart in hand. "Brooke Woodson?"

Brooke looked up and nodded.

"Your shoulder? You have much pain?" The doctor ran his fingers along the joint and asked her to raise her arm. Tears streamed down her cheeks as she tried to comply, then apologized when she could only lift it a few inches.

The doctor's brusque manner, coupled with his foreign accent, made it difficult for me to follow, and poor Brooke looked miserable and confused. The doctor frowned and said, "No fracture was found on your X-ray, but the MRI shows a torn ligament and deep muscle damage. We will fit you with a shoulder brace and a rib belt. Lucky for you, the ribs didn't fracture in the accident. You might have received a lung puncture." He shook his head and scribbled in the chart.

So Brooke had told the medical personnel it was an accident. Mercy. What a mess. And why would she do such a thing?

"How long until I can go back to work?" Brooke asked.

He shrugged. "You must see an orthopedic doctor. I would estimate at least one week. For now, no driving. No lifting more than five pounds." A nod in my direction. "Your volunteer here can call someone to drive you. A nurse will give you prescriptions and the calling number of a specialist for an appointment. Any questions?"

No. Just a look of confusion when the doctor left the cubicle.

Then to me. "I guess I'm going home, but how am I supposed to get there if I don't drive?"

"You sure you want to go to your own place?"

"I have no choice. Someone has to be there to take care of Cosmo."

"Cosmo?"

"My cat." Her eyes lit up. "He was a rescue kitten, a Russian blue according to the vet. He's different from any cat I've ever seen. Short, thick fur in a dreamy silver color."

"Sounds like Gabe."

"Huh?"

"Gabe, my husband. There's no one like him on earth. And he's definitely got the silver hair." Checking my watch, I saw my lunch break was over. "Guess we've both got a dilemma. I have to get back to work, but only until the two o'clock shift arrives, providing they do. About your driving—don't worry. I'll take you home. Better yet, my offer still stands... You're welcome to stay with me. You and Cosmo."

"You'd let me bring my cat?"

"Honey, I was raised on a farm. It's been years since I've had a cat around. So, what do you say?"

"Yes. Thank you. No, wait. How will I get my car home?"

"Don't worry. I'll think of something."

[CHAPTER 11]

Brooke

When my discharge was complete, Mitzi loaded me in her vintage Mercedes and we roared off toward the care center to check on Gabe. I waited in the car, woozy from the Percocet the ER nurse had given me and cross-eyed from watching the raindrops splat on the windshield. Then, as my eyelids grew heavy, Mitzi dashed out with an elderly black gentleman so thin I thought the wind might whisk him away. Gabe? I didn't think so. The man climbed into the backseat.

"Brooke, this is Hadley Davis," Mitzi said as she took her place in the driver's seat. "He's going to drive your car and help us gather up the things you'll need from your apartment. Don't let his looks fool you. He's strong as an ox and needs something to keep him out of trouble."

"That I do. Pleased to meet you, Brooke. And don't you worry none about Miz Steiner. Underneath her bossy exterior beats a heart of pure mischief."

So I had entrusted my life to two strangers. Geriatric comedians at that.

In the end, Hadley drove my Mustang and followed us to my

apartment. They packed while I tried to think of everything I needed. Clothes. Shoes. Toiletries. Laptop. All of Cosmo's essentials. Doubt danced in my head. Was running away from my problems the right solution? I knew nothing about Mitzi—only what I'd seen of her in the hospital. And this Hadley guy. He seemed too eager, you know. *What if I've done the wrong thing again?*

Fresh pain barreled its way from my ribs to my shoulder, taking my breath away. I'd be certified if I didn't get away. And maybe there were a few decent people left in this world. All I could do was hope.

Cosmo got in the way of the packing, rubbing against Hadley's leg, begging for attention. Hadley stooped and scratched behind Cosmo's ears with his bony, black fingers. Cosmo flipped onto his back, inviting a tummy rub. At least one of us trusted Hadley.

After several trips to the cars, Mitzi asked what else I needed. I walked in a daze through my bedroom. The box with the teal dress protruded from under the bed. Had it been there all along? In my stupor I hadn't seen it, but now it lay like a snake ready to bite my ankle. Should I take the dress and return it to Lance? The memory of the previous night jolted me. Lance had left me in a heap. I'd pretended to be passed out, but heard him snorting, slamming things around, and finally... blessedly, he'd left. I'd lain there all night too sore to move, too tired to care. The tape replayed in my head, and I wondered briefly if Lance had raped me. I remembered the swirling, sinking feeling while he... I cringed at the thought. No. I was certain the assault wasn't sexual. When I finally rose from the bed, I still had on my underwear, and I would have known, wouldn't I, if something more had happened? By dawn I knew I had to get medical help and somehow mustered the energy to drive myself to the emergency room.

I inched the dress box out with the toe of my shoe, then reared back and kicked it into the corner. The dress could wait the way I had. Gritting my teeth, I yanked the cord for my alarm clock from the socket and saw the picture of the sparrow on the wall beside my nightstand. I tucked it under my incapacitated arm.

Bills. I had a couple due soon and retrieved them from under the sketch pad on my desk. Mitzi stood beside me, taking the things I handed her.

"I didn't know you were an artist." She nodded at my recently acquired art box.

"It's only a hobby. Do you think we'd have room for this?" When I picked up the sketch pad, the swan pictures fluttered out. Someone had ripped them all in half.

I grabbed the back of my desk chair with my good hand to steady myself. How could he? Just because Lance thought they were silly, he didn't have to ruin them. Bile fought its way into my throat.

Mitzi patted me on the shoulder. "Hadley says we need to get on the road before dark."

Hadley nodded. "We shore 'nuf do. Temperature's dropping. The rain'll be turning to ice." He stooped to pick up the torn sketches. "Here, I'll get these."

I stuffed my cell phone and charger in my purse and gave a last look at the apartment. Heaviness bore down on my bones, but when I closed the door behind me, the cool air kissed my face, and a flapping sensation, like a tiny wing, fluttered in my chest.

~

The next morning, I woke to stillness, trying to get my bearings. How had I gotten to this room? This bed? I vaguely recalled a hot shower and Mitzi fumbling with my shoulder brace and the wide elastic thing around my ribs. The smell of coffee and cinnamon brought me wider awake, and I made my first attempt at movement. Every muscle in my body groaned as I struggled to a sitting position and discovered I had on my own flannel pajamas, the left sleeve flapping free with my arm secured underneath.

The only thing that seemed normal was my bladder, which felt like it would burst if I didn't go soon. A bathroom had to be nearby. Two doors were opposite the four-poster bed where I'd slept amid clouds of down. I threw off the duvet, covered in an old-fashioned cabbage rose print, and slipped into my scuffs and tried the door on the left.

A closet. The smell of cedar greeted me from the deep walk-in space. Fur coats. Long dresses that swooshed when I fumbled for a light switch. If not for my urgent need to find a toilet, I would have explored, run my hands along the mink and fox, crinkled the satin and chiffon in my fingers.

I found the bathroom behind the other door. When I'd finished and splashed water on my face with my one available hand, I did a quick survey. I didn't think this was where I'd showered as I didn't see a showerhead or curtain around the claw-footed tub. Mosaic tiled walls spoke of a different era; the plush towels like those of a luxury hotel.

This was not the home of an ordinary Pink Lady.

Still a bit uneasy, I draped my terry spa robe around my shoulders and followed the smell of coffee downstairs. There I found Mitzi in an overstuffed chair in a large room that was both kitchen and a cozy sitting area. Head against the chintz cushions, feet propped on an ottoman, she rested with her eyes closed. Curled into a ball on her lap was Cosmo.

I crept softly to the cabinet and gazed out the window above the sink. Snow blurred the sky, patches of it sticking to the window screen. I filled the cup waiting beside the coffeepot and took it to the matching chair beside Mitzi. She awoke with a start when Cosmo sprang from her lap onto mine.

"Good morning, dear. Sleep well?" She reached for her rhinestone-trimmed glasses from atop an opened Bible.

I nodded. "You didn't tell me you lived in a mansion."

"Not a mansion, my dear. Just a lovable old wreck of a house. Wait till you hear the plumbing groan. Makes a nice duet with the wind whistling through the chimney." She rose and patted my leg. "Hungry? I've made a streusel coffee cake. A box mix, I'm afraid. I seem to have misplaced whatever cooking talents I once had."

We ate in a tiny alcove with a view of the front yard. Across the street a two-story house that could have been the inspiration for a Victorian Christmas card was decorated with evergreen boughs, white with the snow. Icicles hung from the eaves in a wintery fringe. I sipped my coffee, its warmth and caffeine welcoming. Like Mitzi.

Clearing my throat, I tried to find the words. "Hmmm. Mitzi? Is it okay if I call you that?"

A wide smile. "Absolutely."

"Thanks. I hardly know how to thank you. Rescuing me, taking care of me last night. And this coffee cake is delicious."

"No thanks needed, my dear. Here, have another piece. I'm delighted you're here. It'll be nice to have someone to chat with. Gabe's been at the care center two years, and trust me, living alone is not the peaceful, serene life it's cracked up to be."

"You do understand it's only until I sort things out. A couple of days at most."

"One day at a time, sweetie. God only promises today, nothing more."

My cell phone's familiar ringtone sounded from another room.

"That's the third or fourth time this morning your purse has gone off." Mitzi's eyes sparkled over her rhinestone-tipped glasses. "As nosy as I am, I couldn't bring myself to dig in your purse and find it. Besides, I wouldn't have a clue how to answer it if I did."

"It's all right. Not sure I want to answer it either." Revulsion heaved in my stomach. No, I was definitely not ready to talk. "I should probably check the messages, though. And I have to call the office sometime. To let them know I'll be out for a few days."

I had missed calls from Mom, CiCi, and Lance. They'd all left almost identical voice messages.

Where are you? Are you all right? We need to talk.

Lance had added, "Sweetheart, I'm sorry about the dress. Could we have lunch on Wednesday? I can squeeze my afternoon clients to Thursday and take you shopping. We'll make a day of it. Oh. I found out the Friday night party is semiformal, not black tie, and it's the zoo fund-raiser. Love you."

The swirl of black ocean engulfed me. His voice—so cavalier—sent waves rippling through me. My hands shook as I pressed save and steadied myself. Tucking Lance's call into the "later" file of my brain, I punched in the number of my office. No clue how I would explain being AWOL the day before and that I would, in fact, be out all week. Weather? Car trouble? My fiancé beat me up? Yeah, like that would fly.

Maybe it would come to me as I talked to Jenna.

Ben Harrington, however, was the one who answered. "Brooke. I didn't expect to hear from you."

"You insist on running a close tab—" A pain shot through my shoulder. Raw. Intense.

"Right, I do. Not that you've adhered to that recently though."

"Well, it's Lance—"

"Yeah, he called me."

"What?"

"Gone to Texas, huh?"

"Texas. Well..." It was my shoulder that was injured, not my brain, but none of what Ben said made sense.

"Too bad about your dad."

"Uh..."

"Open-heart surgery, is that right?"

"Well..." It came into focus. Lance called and lied to Mr. Harrington. How convenient. Still, an opportunity presented itself, and I made an instant decision.

"I won't be in for a while longer. A week or so. I'll be in touch." I disconnected before I blubbered out something foolish. *Lance. Always the hero.*

The irony swelled in my throat, bitter tasting, but when Mitzi appeared, carrying a split log for the fireplace, I swallowed hard and smiled.

She said, "Everything okay?"

"Peachy." I hoped she didn't detect the venom in my voice.

"As long as we're here for the duration, I thought we'd have a fire."

"Sounds wonderful. I'll join you as soon as I get dressed."

I found my suitcase where Hadley Davis must have put it in my room upstairs. A perfect day for sweatpants and a ratty sweatshirt. A splash of cold water on my face calmed me a bit, and, mechanically, I descended the stairs and found the den.

The room had tall ceilings, its worn but well-built furniture piled with a myriad of floral cushions—mismatched, but cheerful. Pictures on every surface of a smiling couple, Gabe and Mitzi, I presumed. The hairstyles and fashions were clearly from another era. Oversized pictures of jazz scenes dotted the walls. A wing chair by the fireplace had a smoking stand nearby topped with a pipe collection. Gabe's, no doubt. Eerie. I could almost feel his presence in the room.

Mitzi brought hot cocoa for the two of us and curled up on the opposite end of the overstuffed sofa. "It's been ages since I've sat in this room. Too long." She blew on the cocoa's surface. "Are you comfortable? Need something for pain?"

"I'm good. I took a pill when I went upstairs. If I nod off, it's because they make me loopy. Poor tolerance, my mom says."

"Did you talk to your mom?"

"No. Since no one knows I'm here, I'm going to leave it for now. How about you? Did you check on Gabe this morning?"

She nodded. "Nothing new. He's in good hands." Her eyes drifted off to one of the shadow boxes hanging on the wall. It contained an old record cover and a vinyl disc. A much younger Mitzi with honey brown hair, her head tilted, looking into the eyes of her partner, a handsome dark-haired man with strong features and a dazzling smile.

"Will you play some of your records for me?"

"Mercy. Why would you want to hear those old songs? I have more modern tastes now myself. Michael Bublé. Norah Something-or-other."

"Jones. Norah Jones. She's one of my favorites. Is that what you sing? Jazz? I'd love to hear you." Focus on Mitzi. Let her do the talking.

"You get me started, and I might not know when to stop. Better yet, why don't you tell me about yourself first?"

My mind fuzzed over. Sipping my cocoa, I shrugged. "Not much to tell. There's Mom, who you met. One sister named CiCi who's married to Todd. My fiancé, Lance, who . . . well . . . you know. And I work as a paralegal. Nice job, but . . ."

Hearing myself talk made me realize how much I didn't want to go into the details. And without so much as a flick, I let an invisible shield slide up and stared into the flames dancing in the firebox.

Mitzi didn't prod. Rather, she settled into the sofa cushions and waited.

The fire hissed and crackled, and when I glanced at Mitzi, her sharp eyes bore into me.

Forcing a weak smile, I said, "Your turn. You said you grew up on a farm. How did you get in the music business?"

"We need a cocoa refill before I launch into that." She took my cup and with a sparkle in her eyes said, "Matter of fact, back then I wasn't Mitzi at all, but a little girl with pigtails named Maggie."

[CHAPTER 12]

As we huddled in the shack, our eyes and throats scratchy from the dust, baby Chester wailed until he wore himself out and fell asleep. When the wind stopped howling, everything got spooky quiet. We stared at the dark coming through the cracks, hoping any minute Mama would pop through the door. Instead, it was the following morning when we heard shouting outside.

A man in overalls yanked the door open, blinding us temporarily with the light. Behind him, a stout woman craned her neck, her eyes growing wide, then filling with tears as she rushed in and gathered us to her yeast-smelling bosom. Our rescuers were Hattie and Jess Barlow, homesteaders outside of Paris, Oklahoma. We later found out that we'd lived through the worst dust storm in history, the one that became known as Black Sunday. Hattie pulled Chester out of my arms and declared that we were orphans in need of a home despite my cries that Mama had to be alive somewhere. From that minute on, her twelve-year-old daughter, Liberty, took over my baby brother and nicknamed him Chet, calling him the answer to their prayers.

I had my own prayers. Every night I knelt beside the bed and prayed that Mama would appear on the horizon and say she'd come to take us to the ocean. Instead, after we'd been living with the Barlows for two years, Sheriff Smith came calling. He pulled a crusty, tattered piece of cloth from a paper bag.

My throat closed up. Mama's dress. I knew what he was fixing to tell me was the end of my dreams. And Mama's.

He called me a lucky girl to have the Barlows for a family, and I agreed. It sure beat the pants off being raised by my papa, Finster Poole, but from that day forward, no talk of Mama was allowed. She was dead to the world. And us.

I hid Mama's gold locket in the chest of drawers, along with a letter I found in one of the pillowcases from St. Louis. The envelope carried a postmark from Quincy, Missouri. No return address. The note inside read:

> Our dearest Lorna Beth,
>
> Your Daddy and me are plumb tore up from your last letter. We had no idea Finster was treating you so badly. Before he lays another hand on you, please, pack up your things and get out. Come to us. We can't wait to see the children.
>
> Love, Mother

The two tiny pictures in the locket had to be my grandparents. People who loved me and would welcome me. While I rubbed the locket shiny as a new penny in my fingers, my insides burned with desire to find them—my own family. I would take Ruthie and baby Chester along with me. Then the winter Ruthie was eight, she came down with erysipelas and broke out in blisters over her whole body. Racked with fever and delirium for six days, she grew weaker and weaker and died in Maw Barlow's arms.

Loneliness descended on me like a turkey vulture on a dead rabbit. First Mama. Now Ruthie. And no matter which way I turned it over in my head, I was stuck on the Barlow farm. Tending the chickens, milking the cow, hoeing the garden. Hattie, bless her, tried to be the mama I'd lost, but not a day went by that Jess Barlow didn't remind me of the favor he'd bestowed by taking us in. My rescuer, yes, but also the one who never let me forget I was beholden to him and his generosity.

Two years out of high school and keeping books at the Boyd Brothers' feed store, the hopes of me ever finding out who I was seemed as remote as my dreams of the ocean. I was nineteen years old and still living at home. One Sunday in late May, Hattie rose early and gathered the eggs while I rolled out the biscuits. With a snuff glass, I cut them in perfect circles, then I placed them in the bacon grease I'd melted in the skillet. After I slid them into the cast-iron stove, I hollered up the stairs for Chet to hurry up or we'd be late for church.

Hattie appeared at the back door. "Can you take the eggs, Maggie?" She held out the wire basket and steadied herself on the screen door, her round face drained of color. A flash of something in her eyes alerted me.

"Hattie, you okay? You see a snake?" The fear of anything that slithered was, honest to goodness, the only weakness Hattie possessed.

She shook her head. "I got light-headed coming up the porch steps. 'Taint nothin' to fret over. I'll sit a spell in the rocker while you finish up what you're doing."

She leaned back and closed her eyes, and I figured she was saying her morning prayers. A tiny string of spit oozed out the corner of her mouth, like she must be deep in the spirit talking to God.

I set the pitcher of milk on the table and got a new jar of plum butter from the cupboard. When I turned around to ask Hattie how she was doing, her head lolled back at an awkward angle, her arms sprawled open. The plum butter crashed to the floor as I flew across the room.

"Hattie! Can you hear me?" But even as I shouted I knew it was no use. Hattie was gone.

The next day, I took the money I'd saved to go to secretarial school and bought a cardboard suitcase and three new dresses at McAfee's Dry Goods. Chet, though grieving something fierce over Hattie, was busting his buttons about driving tractor for Sheriff Smith. He had his summer planned out, and I knew Doralee Smith would fill Chet's stomach and look after him.

As would my stepsister, Liberty. Later, if everything worked out, I vowed to send for Chet—bring him to his real family.

The day after we buried Hattie Barlow, I left Paris, Oklahoma, with Mama's locket and the yellowed letter from Quincy, Missouri. Liberty took me to the bus station forty miles away. The last thing I saw was her clinging to a child on each side, her belly swollen with the one in the breadbasket. As the Trailways bus lumbered east on Highway 412, Jess's words burned in my ears. "You're a foolish twit, you know that, Maggie? How can you turn your back on us when we need you the most? After all we done for you?"

Foolish or not, I chose to look straight ahead, not back. My ticket was for Tulsa, where I would have to change buses and get my ticket to St. Louis. When the bus stopped in Enid, I stretched my legs and bought a pimiento cheese sandwich in the café attached to the bus depot. At the cash register, I saw a map with Arkansas on one side and Missouri on the other and tossed an extra dime on the counter. For the rest of the day I studied the map and memorized the towns we'd pass through once we got to Missouri. Joplin. Springfield. Lebanon. Sullivan. Then sprawling like a spider on the map . . . St. Louis.

Mama always called me the dreamer, and now the floodgates of my memory ran wild. Jenkins. The name came to me, singing like the tires on the bus. My mother's people. She'd talked about Aunt Opal on the Jenkins side. My brother, Chet, had been named Chester after my grandpa. I hoped it was the one on Mama's side.

What if I arrived and found Papa's kin instead? My insides tumbled.

Perhaps if I arrived with a name no one knew, it would be safer. Then, if my memory had failed me, I could move on. No one would be the wiser. Of course, no one knew me by Barlow, so I could go with that, but I needed a new first name. Something modern. Sophisticated. And whimsical. Definitely whimsical. When the name Mitzi popped in my head, it was like God handed it to me on a stone tablet.

Mitzi Barlow.

And that's who got off the bus in Tulsa, Oklahoma.

I stretched and craned my neck at the tall buildings, my courage dashed. I was nothing more than a stray minnow in the Pacific Ocean.

"This way, ma'am." The bus driver pointed to a neon light above the entrance of the bus station.

"Wait. I'm changing routes here. I'll need my suitcase."

A black man stood beside a pile of cardboard boxes and assorted luggage. "Which one your'n, ma'am?"

After I pointed it out to him, he hefted it to the curb and waited, eyeing me. Shivers ran up my legs landing in the pit of my stomach.

"Thank you, sir."

He opened his mouth as if to speak, but when an older gentleman in a dusty suit asked for his luggage, the porter turned his attention away from me. After scurrying toward the entrance, I glanced over my shoulder and saw the porter receive a coin from the traveler. A tip. He was waiting for me to give him a nickel for his trouble.

I fumbled in my purse, came up with an Indian-head nickel, then went back to the curb and held out my hand. He palmed the coin. "Thank ye, ma'am."

"Please. You can call me Mitzi."

With a swagger in my step, I waltzed into the bus depot. The bank of ticket windows glared yellow in the dimly lit lobby, where hordes of people waited on benches and stood in line. Taking my place, I waited my turn.

"One ticket to St. Louis, please."

"Last bus left an hour ago. Next one at 6:18 in the morning."

Not expecting that, and planning to sleep overnight on the bus, I stammered, "Are you sure?"

"Take it or leave it. Two other departures tomorrow. You want the times?"

"N... no. I'll take the 6:18." I paid for the ticket and spun around. Then pivoted back. "Wait. Where will I spend the night?"

"We sell bus tickets, lady. We're not a travel agency. Next?"

A hefty woman with long, greasy hair and two top teeth missing shoved her way past me. "Tahlequah, please."

My insides rumbled, reminding me how long it had been since I'd eaten the pimiento cheese. I scanned the crowd for a friendly face to ask where I might get a bite to eat. Seeing none, I sat on the nearest bench to put my ticket safely in my handbag and consider my options.

My money had to last for an indefinite time. A few dollars for a hotel room was foolish. Like me, according to Jess Barlow.

If I spent the night in the bus station, at least I wouldn't take the chance on getting lost amid those skyscrapers. Nearby, an Indian woman with two small children rested her head against the wall. A man with a whisker-stubbled face stretched out on one of the benches.

Pretending to know what I was doing, I got a Milky Way from the machine next to a bank of lockers. A seat on the opposite wall looked promising, with a place to lean my head into the corner and still have a good view of the waiting area.

I sat down, my suitcase snug against my ankle, and clutched my purse with one hand, the fingers on the other automatically rubbing the locket around my neck. Soon. Very soon I'd find my kinfolk and learn who I was. Pictures danced in my head of embracing my grandmother, who, in my mind's eye, looked identical to Mama but with white hair. She would call me dumplin' and show me pictures of Mama as a girl, and I would tell her my story. We would cry together, entwined in one another's arms.

As I nibbled the candy bar, the racket around me settled, punctuated with soft snores from other weary travelers and the tick of the clock on the back wall. When my eyelids grew heavy, I pinched myself to stay awake. Afraid to rustle the map and disturb those sleeping, I counted the wall lockers. Then the seats in the waiting room. Seven long benches. Three shorter ones. Twenty-six chairs.

A few minutes rest, then I would stretch my legs. Instead, sleep stole me away.

I dreamed of finding the Jenkins house where roses climbed a porch trellis.

Slowly walking up the curved sidewalk, I planned what I would say when my grandmother opened the door. The screen door burst open in my dream, and Papa stood on the porch. "That you, Lorna Beth?"

My heart, so ripe with anticipation, tumbled, rooting my feet to the ground. Papa stepped closer to me. "Fool girl. I knowed you'd come crawlin' back someday."

"No! I'm not Lorna Beth. You're wrong. My name is . . ." My tongue searched for my name, finding nothing. But my head told me to run, and whirling around, sweeping my suitcase through the air, I retreated the way I'd come.

His taunts echoed in the air. "Who says I'll take you back? Stealing my little 'uns the way you did."

My eyes popped open, my scalp damp with perspiration. How long had I been asleep? The clock on the wall showed 10:30. Twenty minutes? How could I have slept so long? Something wasn't right. People stirred around the waiting area, stretching, shifting positions. Outside the glass windows, a bus pulled away from the curb, a puff of exhaust trailing behind.

I curled my fist around what should have been the strap of my handbag, but a crumpled candy wrapper was all I held in my hand. My purse had vanished.

Panic ricocheted through my gut as I searched the area around me. I marched to the ticket window and rapped on the glass.

"No, didn't see nothing unusual, ma'am." The clerk pointed to a sign.

WE ARE NOT RESPONSIBLE FOR MISPLACED OR STOLEN ITEMS.

Misplaced? No. Stolen? Yes.

My handbag. My ticket to St. Louis. Every penny I owned.

And the letter from my grandmother.

[CHAPTER 13]

Brooke

My cell phone's ringing interrupted Mitzi's story of her stolen handbag. Fumbling in my own purse, I pulled out my BlackBerry to see who was calling.

Lance. Again.

I switched my phone to silent mode and tossed it on the table. "Too bad you didn't have cell phones then. You could have called your number and found out who took your purse."

She laughed. "We didn't even have a phone in the farmhouse where I grew up, and only a handful of people in Paris had them. You can imagine what a country bumpkin I was, stranded in a city the size of Tulsa. Jess Barlow was right on one thing. It was pure foolishness for me to take off the way I did."

"So how did you make it home?"

Mitzi's eyes shone with remembrance. "I didn't. I couldn't. Jess Barlow made it clear I couldn't come crying to him if things didn't work out. The old 'You made your bed, now you have to lie in it.' One of life's bittersweet lessons, I'm afraid."

"Did you ever go back?"

"No. I kept up a correspondence with Chet over the years and met him once in Guymon when we played the fairgrounds there.

Quite a pleasant man. Good-looking, too, but it was apparent with him in his farmer's overalls and me with a microphone in my hand, we had nothing in common."

"I'm sorry. Did you get to St. Louis?"

"That's a story for another time. You looked on the verge of nodding off while I was talking. Why don't you take a nap while I make us some lunch? I wonder if I can still make biscuits?" And off she went.

I checked my messages on the BlackBerry. Another voice mail from Lance. "Brooke, are you stranded in the snow? Why aren't you returning my calls? Where are you? Can we talk about this? About us? Please."

Pleading. Begging.

And for the first time, when I pictured his tousled hair, his stormy blue eyes changing like the temperamental Oklahoma weather, I wasn't moved to make excuses for him or overlook his violent nature. A numbness wrapped around me, deflecting his charm as I saw our future clearly for the first time.

He was right about one thing: we did need to talk.

Lance Evans, though, would not be happy with what I intended to tell him.

Snuggling into Mitzi's sofa cushions, I pulled up a wooly throw with my good hand and watched the embers in the hearth fade from their crimson glow to white-hot ashes.

Three days later, the sun came out, and with the brighter weather, Mitzi sprang into action, too. She sorted through stacks of magazines, made countless trips up the stairs, taking things up, bringing linens down for the laundry.

"You're wearing me out," I said, knowing her burst of energy was in anticipation of the upcoming visit of the grandson of an old friend from her singing days.

"Drew's a bit shy, devoted to his career. His specialty is pediatrics, and I have a feeling you'll like him."

I had no intention of staying at Mitzi's until Drew arrived, but I didn't tell her that. Instead, I said, "You'll have fun pampering him the way you have me. Just don't make him eat any of your biscuits."

She held up her hands in mock horror. "That's the thanks I get. Mercy, even the birds wouldn't eat the charred leftovers we threw in the snow."

We laughed and sat by the fire for a while. Then Mitzi popped up and went to the front window. "Look at that. Traffic is moving along out there. Guess we won't be housebound much longer."

"You'll be able to go see Gabe in the morning."

"I'm going if I have to crawl. When you don't know how much time is left, you tend to view every day as a gift from God. And tomorrow's a Pink Lady day, too, so I'll be out of your hair. You can lounge all day in your jammies if you'd like."

"Probably not. I'm itching to get out my sketch pad. And I should probably report in to Mr. Harrington. Let him know I'll be back at work on Monday."

"You sure?"

"Positive. Time to face the giants and take my life back."

She looked over the top of her glasses, an invitation for me to explain.

"And yes, figure out what I'm going to do about Lance... about delaying our wedding."

Her eyes widened. "Delay? Mercy, child. I'd think you'd be wanting to be rid of him for good."

"He says he wants to talk, and no matter what you think, Lance is a nice guy."

"Nice like a root canal." She sucked in a breath as if she'd said too much and looked sheepishly over her glasses.

"I don't expect you to understand. I hardly do myself, but I can't help thinking of all the good times, the way Lance made me feel special, loved in a way I'd never had before. It's only when I said stupid things he did the things to hurt me."

"I don't doubt you loved him, but knowing what you do now, would you have been so quick to fall in love?"

"I honestly don't know. I realize we're in one of those I'm-so-sorry cycles where he promises not to hurt me..." Hearing myself utter those words sent a wave of realization through me. I knew giving Lance back the diamond would shatter the cycle.

"...Until next time." Mitzi finished my sentence.

"What should I do? Keep the ring and ignore him? I work in the same building. I can't hide out here forever."

"Being honest and upfront is always best. Not that I'm one to talk with all the trouble I got myself into changing my name to Mitzi. Still, promise me you'll take a friend with you or meet in a public place. Don't allow yourself to be alone with him."

"Good point. I'll try to remember."

"Sweetie, you're going to need a covering of prayer when you see Lance. Not only knowing what to say and do, but also for your protection and boldness in doing the right thing."

"I'm not all that religious. Prayer...maybe, but I'm not even sure God remembers me. It's been a while since I went to church...not since my youth group years ago."

"I'm sure he remembers. Why don't you ask him yourself and see?" Mitzi tilted her head, the laugh lines in her face as soft as crushed velvet. Her dark eyes, bright and twinkling, shone with wisdom.

"I don't know." I rose from the sofa, uncomfortable with what God might say about the mess I'd made of my life. Knowing, too, that it might take God and an army of angels to keep Lance from killing me if I said the wrong thing. I joined Mitzi, who was staring out the window again.

"Thanks for being here for me. I owe you big time."

"Don't be silly. I'm only passing along some of the kindness that's come my way over the years."

"You promised you'd tell me what happened after the bus station."

"So I did."

We linked arms and went to the sofa, content to step back to another time.

[CHAPTER 14]

Someone had stolen my purse.

Panic rose in my throat, the pit of my belly as hollow as the fifty-five gallon rain barrel back on the Barlow farm. The Indian woman in the bus station clutched her small children to her breast as I stomped around, asking if anyone had seen what happened. Deranged. That's what people thought about me. Hot tears ran down my face as I searched in vain, then took my suitcase into the bathroom, digging through its contents in hopes a twenty dollar bill would magically appear.

Returning to my corner of the bus station, I perched myself atop my suitcase, determined to go to the police station and report the crime at first light.

The officer who took my statement shook his head. "Young girls shouldn't be traveling alone. Settin' yourself up for trouble, you are. Here, use our phone. Call your folks and reverse the charges. Maybe they can wire you the money to get yourself back home."

I glared at him and marched out of the station. Even if the Barlows had a phone, that wasn't the point. I wouldn't go home begging. Not yet.

You got yourself into this mess, Maggie Barlow. You can get yourself out.

Back out on the street, tall buildings peered down at me, mocking me. I set my suitcase down and looked at a sliver of blue heaven above the sky-

scrapers. Raising my arms, I shouted, "I may not have any money or brains, but God, if you're up there, I'd like to find my way out of this maze and on to St. Louis. And if it's not too much trouble . . . some food to give me strength would be appreciated."

Men in business suits and women with shopping bags streamed by, none of them paying a bit of never mind to me. I clutched the handle of my suitcase and struck out, sure the Lord Almighty was directing my steps.

My shoulders ached from carrying the suitcase, and when I thought I couldn't take another step, I came to a row of three-story brick houses. Cardboard FOR RENT *signs hung in several of the front windows. An idea germinated: I'd offer my services as kitchen help in exchange for a room. One landlady slammed the door in my face; the next said she was full up and forgot to remove the sign. At the third house, a scrawny woman with a pocked complexion listened to my story, then jerked her head, pointing to the upstairs.*

"You's lucky, a vacancy opened up yesterday. I don't hire no help, though. You'll have to find yer own job, but bein's you look nice enough, I'll give you a week to come up with the rent. If you can't, you'll have to find someplace else." She blew smoke from her cigarette and told me supper was at six o'clock. I didn't even think to ask her name.

It was more than I'd hoped. A room. And a promised meal. After thanking her profusely, I sat on the saggy single bed in the second-floor room she pointed out. I'd only been gone a single day, and already, my life had taken a desperate turn. Rubbing Mama's locket, I curled up on the chenille spread and wondered what would happen to me.

First off, I needed a job. From my bookkeeping job at the feed store, I had skills and experience, but I couldn't give the Boyd brothers as a reference. Not without Jess Barlow finding out, giving him the I-told-you-so satisfaction. No, something else. The bed felt wonderful after the sleepless night in the bus station, and while I turned over the job possibilities in my head, my eyelids fluttered shut.

The smell of sauerkraut woke me. Hunger pains rumbled as I opened my suitcase and retrieved my hairbrush and toiletry items. I found the bathroom at the end of the hall, splashed water on my face, and kicked myself because my only tube of lipstick had disappeared with my purse. I dusted my pale cheeks with powder and went down to meet my housemates.

Three girls sat around the oak table in the front room of the boarding house. Lingering in the doorway, uncertain of the protocol, I waited for one of them to greet me or ask me to sit down. Nothing. A moment later, the landlady appeared. "Coming through." I stepped aside as she plunked a steaming pot on the table. "Ladies, we have a new boarder. Meet Miss Harlow, who's only here if she can come up with some rent money by next week."

"Barlow. M— Mitzi Barlow." I nearly said Maggie, but then I made a snap decision to continue on with my new identity. "This seat taken?" I pointed to one of the empty chairs and slid into it when no one objected.

"Smells good, Idella." This from a plump-cheeked girl who sat next to her identical twin. "Mitzi, glad to meet you. I'm Ann. And this is Nan. We work at JCPenney. Are you new to Tulsa?"

"Just arrived. I'm hoping to find a job. Do you like working at a department store?" Already the prospect of working in a respectable business had occurred to me, and I could hardly believe my good fortune to meet someone who did and could introduce me.

"Oh my, yes." The twin named Ann dipped out a heaping spoon of sauerkraut and weenies for herself. Another for Nan. "And we get a 15 percent discount on personal purchases." She giggled and reached for the bag of Rainbow bread. "Sorry to say, they're not hiring now."

So much for that. But there were other shops and stores. With my three new dresses, I'd be sure to find something suitable.

Ann handed me the serving spoon to take my portion of the main dish, which smelled sweeter than manna from heaven. A slice of white bread and a dish of applesauce rounded out the meal. Silently, I said a quick blessing, ready to dig in.

The girl next to me hadn't uttered a word, but she gave me a sidelong look, her long eyelashes the most gorgeous I'd ever seen. She had a pixie face, with a turned-up nose and a creamy complexion. "I'm Penny Vaughn. You ever done any waitressin'? My boss is looking for someone." The twang in her voice didn't match the cherub face, but she seemed sweet. Sincere.

"Sure, I've waited a few tables." The annual Groundhog Day Pancake Supper ought to count for something. I'd done it for at least eight years.

Idella had disappeared, leaving us to our meal and conversation.

Penny picked at her food. "I'm fixin' to go to work if you wanna come along. We make real good tips, and Red's swell to work for. Just don't pester him too much on the weekends. That's when we get lots of out of towners."

Ann and Nan passed each other hooded looks, but I ignored them. My luck had turned. A roof over my head and the prospect of a job. I inhaled my food, then went upstairs to change into my best gingham blouse and black skirt—which wasn't new but looked waitresslike. Penny told me Red would give me a pinafore when I got there.

I didn't even think to ask the name of the restaurant.

"You do smoke, don't you?" Penny asked when we stepped into the alley behind the Carlisle Club. Not a restaurant, as I'd thought, but a nightclub. And my pinafore turned out to be a tight-fitting blue satin blouse with a plunging neckline that, had he laid eyes on me, would have made Brother Angus back home preach a Freewill sermon on the world's oldest profession.

I waved away the curling blue smoke from Penny's cigarette and shook my head. "Penny, about this job. It's not exactly what I'm looking for." As I jingled the tip change in my skirt pocket, a vanload of musicians started carrying instruments into the entry marked STAGE DOOR.

"You've only given it two hours. Red's a good boss, and he pays more'n most of the club owners here in town. Besides, you haven't heard the band yet." She blew a smoke ring, then ground out the cigarette with her open-toed pump.

"You don't understand. This isn't the way I was raised. The only restaurant I ever went to was the Club Café on Main Street in . . . where I grew up. I'm a churchgoing girl."

She waved her hand at me. "Time for you to expand your horizons, chicky. Red says you got the girl-next-door look, the kind customers like." She cocked her head. "Your makeup could use a few tricks, though. I'll help you with it tomorrow."

Red must've hired her for her innocent look, too, but she had an edge about her I couldn't quite put my finger on. Is that what came from working in a nightclub? Something in her voice, though, said she was looking for a friend. That would make two of us.

Pursing my lips, I followed her back in and served up burgers and deep-fried onion rings to a rowdy table of eight who had ordered before our break. Now they wanted a round of beer. Oh my. Jess Barlow would have a righteous conniption if he saw me.

Balancing the tray in my hand, I kept one eye on the stage, where the musicians warmed up their instruments—sax, trumpet, drums, and a string bass two feet taller than the mahogany-faced man who strummed it. They had a catchy beat when they got rolling, sorta blues or jazz—I didn't know which. With a flourish at the end, the trumpet player's cheeks puffed in and out, the horn catching the green and red lights aimed at him, ending on a high note. The audience broke out in applause. He did a bow and came up smiling, his teeth gleaming like pearls on his licorice face. He held up one arm and counted out the beat to start the next number, a tune I recognized at once as "Sentimental Journey."

The room swayed with the music, teasing the edges of my memory, like I should recognize something. The words? Or the sound? I didn't know, but a familiar clench seized my insides, and when a paunchy man with a ruddy face motioned me over, I jumped like a spooked toad.

"My missus here wants a 7-Up. And make mine a Coca-Cola." He gave me a wink.

When I returned with the sodas, he held the glasses below the edge of the *table and poured a splash of something from a small flask. Then he did the winking thing again.*

The only person I knew back home who drank liquor was Widow Carr, and it was medicinal. At least, that's what she told folks. I had more to get used to in Tulsa than I had figured on. Lots more.

With a tray of empty glasses, I headed toward the kitchen in time to see three girl singers take the stage. Through the smoky haze hanging in layers inside the club, I made out their ebony faces and their lithe bodies in matching satin dresses. The one in the middle stepped to the microphone, and in a deep, buttery voice began:

Pack up all my care and woe,
Here I go, singing low.

The haze swirled around me, my legs buckling as I juggled the tray. Gulping in stale tobacco air, trying to clear my head, I slammed the tray down. The glasses tumbled over, clinking. Backing up, I tried for another breath, my ears burning at the line I knew was coming.

Bye, bye blackbird.

One of Mama's songs.

I fell backward, landed on the lap of a customer, and slid down to the floor that vibrated with the beat of Mama's music.

My insides moaned. Screamed. A heaviness pressed in on me, like something had scraped a seed hull inside me and released a fertile sprig.

And in that moment, I knew it wasn't Mama's family I'd set out to find, but Mama herself. Instead, her music found me.

[CHAPTER 15]

Brooke

Goose bumps covered my arms. "What a way to find out you were meant to be a singer. Didn't you ever have the feeling you were supposed to sing one day?"

Mitzi stared into the fire, her voice husky from talking so long. "Far from it. I hummed and sang the way kids do. Even sang a solo at church one Sunday. Afterward, Brother Angus drew me aside and told me he was disappointed I hadn't shown the proper reverence for 'Bringing in the Sheaves.' I don't know if it was the way I snapped my fingers or drew out the phrasing on *We shall come re-joicing, bringing in the sheaves.*"

She gave a demonstration, her voice strong, rich. "Anyhow, Brother Angus never asked me to sing another solo."

"What happened at the club? Did you get to keep your job?"

"Yes. Red Carlisle thought I swooned since I was so skinny, so he took me to the kitchen and had the fry cook fix me a T-bone steak from the stock he kept for special customers. I've a lot to thank Red for. A job. Food. And my first opportunity to stand on the stage."

"I can't wait to hear—"

"Not now, sweetie. I'm tuckered out. I'm turning in, so I can get an early start in the morning."

After Mitzi went to bed, I turned out the lights, scooped Cosmo up, and went upstairs. Without turning on the lamp, I went to the window. The moon shone on the last of the snow, making a black and white kaleidoscope below me. My gaze skimmed the rooftops, the naked branches of the winter trees, and a clearing beyond that. As I leaned into the glass, my breath caught. Bits of moonlight danced like gold glitter on a small pond. A wrought iron fence curved around one end, the gnarled trunk of a tree leaning across the water.

Swan Lake.

My chest tightened around my hammering heart. Swan Lake? Right here at Mitzi's doorstep? Exhilaration bubbled inside. I twirled around the room, scaring Cosmo into a dive under the bed. Switching on the lamp, I quickly changed into my pajamas, noticing my shoulder now moved without searing pain.

Tomorrow, I'd get out my sketch pad. Could painting be the part of me I'd never allowed to flourish? Oh, if only I were as brave as Mitzi.

Later, in the floating twilight before sleep, a cloud passed over the Swan Lake of my dreams. My body jerked, bringing me wide awake. Perspiration covered my forehead, a sense of foreboding skating along my bones.

Mitzi drove me to work on Monday and offered to pick me up at five o'clock. We'd both had a good weekend—her with Gabe, and me filling a sketch pad with drawings—the white swans, the fountain that sprang to life on Sunday afternoon, the lovely homes with their stone steps and lawns dressed in the drab of winter.

Even so, the feeling that my life was crumbling kept me on edge. Being cocooned at Mitzi's home was only a temporary respite, one to which I clung as I pushed thoughts of Lance and my mother to the deep furrows of my brain. Finding the right time to tell Mitzi I should move back to my apartment eluded me. A few more days. That's all. Wait and see how things go with Lance.

As Mitzi pulled away from the curb of the office tower where I worked, I sucked in as much air as my cracked ribcage would allow, stepped into the lobby, and punched the elevator button to take me up to the office.

Jenna's reception desk was empty, her usual Starbucks cup beside her monitor. Out for a last-minute smoke, I guessed. I went toward the break room for a cup of coffee and nearly bumped into Ben Harrington, headed in the same direction. I jumped like I'd encountered a ghost.

He didn't seem to notice and held the door for me. "So you made it today? I was beginning to think we'd never see you again."

"I left a message on your voice mail last week. Didn't you get it?"

He shrugged. "Do you know how many messages I get a day? Guess yours slipped through. So how's your dad doing?" He went to the espresso machine, tamped the coffee into the stainless steel cup, and switched it on, keeping his back to me.

Ben Harrington was the consummate attorney for his rich clientele. Designer suits. Italian leather shoes. Diamond cuff links. Having been with the firm just over a year, I knew the line between being the hired girl and part of the inner circle was clear. I knew my place. For Ben to ask about my dad was a smidgeon out of step with his usual brusque manner.

"My dad? I need to talk to you about that."

He swiveled around, his mouth a tight line. "Please don't tell me you're taking off again. Do you have any idea how many files I've got piled on my desk?"

"I know there's a lot of work, and I'll make it up. I'll take work home. Whatever needs to be done, I'll do it. That's not what I meant. I... I didn't go to Texas. My dad was never sick... and—"

"Are you saying you made up the story? What possessed you to do that? Does Lance know you were lying?" His normally bland complexion flared with color.

"Lance acted on his own telling you I went to Texas. I played along when I talked to you, since I couldn't come to work anyway."

"You seem to be absent more than in the office of late."

"I'm sorry about the absences. If I could explain..."

"Please do." He crossed his arms and waited.

"Lance and I have had some issues... a lot, actually. I'm not sure I'm ready to go through with marrying him."

"This took a week? A week when you could have been here working? Lance said you'd been acting strange lately. If I were betting, I'd say you're afraid Lance is going to dump you, so you're playing some game." His eyes bored into mine. "I. Don't. Do. Games. Not when there's work to be done."

A slap couldn't have hurt more. And before I had time to set things straight, the break room door swung open. Jenna.

"Hey, Brooke! You're back. Morning, Unc. Sorry I haven't made the coffee. I'll hop right to."

Ben lifted his ceramic cup. "I've already got my espresso. You can bring me a cup of the other when you get it done." To me, he said, "I'll see you in my office in three minutes."

He turned before seeing me nod in agreement.

"Whew! Someone's grouchy for a Monday morning." Jenna made a face at the closed door Ben had just exited through. "So, Brooke, where've you been? Your mother's called here every day looking for you, talking ninety to nothing about plans for the bridal fair. She says it's coming up this Saturday."

"What did you tell her?"

"What Mr. Harrington told us—you were out of the office. I

didn't mention your dad since I wasn't too sure of the connection there... Man, everyone's got their panties in a wad about you missing another week of work. Some of the other paralegals are betting you went to get the plastic surgery on your face done and decided to have some extra enhancement at the same time."

She stood back and gave my chest a once-over. "Hmmm. I guess not."

Excuse me? I wanted to spit. "Sorry to disappoint you and the gals, Jenna. And I'd love to stay and chat, but Ben's expecting me in less than a minute." Sheesh! Already I was sorry I'd not worn my shoulder brace. A nagging ache had run up my neck, settling into the base of my skull. And I hadn't had a cup of coffee yet. I wondered if Mom had talked to Lance and what story he'd given her. I would call her on my lunch break. Get her out of the way while I worked up the courage to face Lance.

Mr. Harrington cradled the phone to his ear when I stepped into his office. He glared at me and pointed to a pile of folders on the corner of his desk. Thankful not to hear another lecture, I went right to work. By noon, a pain like a hot coal had embedded in my shoulder joint, but the headache had gone. Surprisingly, I'd whittled Mr. Harrington's pile of urgent folders down by half, but there were a lot left to go. If I grabbed a sandwich from the deli and ate at my desk, I'd have time to call Mom and get back to the folders before Mr. Harrington got on my case again.

When I left the office, Jenna had already gone, off to eat with the girls, I assumed. My ears burned with what I imagined they were saying. Ginger, one of Mr. Cooke's paralegals, and Lisa from accounting had both poked their heads in and asked how my dad was, and then eyed my chest when they didn't think I was looking. Oddly enough, I wished they'd ask me to go to lunch with them. Maybe I'd tell them the real reason for my absence.

Lance detested me going out with the girls—"flaunting themselves, flirting with any guy who'll look at them," he said. His jealousy was sweet at first, but now I saw it for what it was—his desire to control my friends. And my life. If we didn't have lunch plans, I brown-bagged it and ate at my desk alone.

Stepping out into the sun, I paused for a moment to look for my sunglasses, but then I remembered they were in my Mustang in Mitzi's garage. Pigeons fluttered and hopped at the curbs and scattered aimlessly before me as my heels clicked on the sidewalk. I could see my breath in the crisp air as I hurried to the corner crosswalk, the fresh bread smell from Pete's Deli drawing me.

A group of the lunchtime crowd streamed toward me when I started across the street, and halfway across, an arm yanked mine, sending a fresh jolt through my shoulder.

"Brooke!"

I closed my eyes, reflexively pulling my left arm into my chest.

Lance.

I didn't say his name. I couldn't. My throat felt dry and scratchy, my tongue frozen and unable to form words.

Talk to him in public.

Not alone.

Mitzi's words.

Lance had a viselike grip on my left arm and spun me around, half pushing me in the direction he was going.

No! I stopped at the sidewalk, my shoulder blazing with pain, my knees as crumbly as the pothole at the curb.

I glared into Lance's clear blue eyes. "What do you think you're doing?"

He leaned in close. "I've been in a meeting and just found out you were back in the office. Want to go to lunch?"

"No. I'm grabbing a sandwich to take back to the office. My desk is swamped."

"Ben will understand. A girl's gotta eat. We've got a lot of catching up to do. Man, I've missed you. You look great. New perfume?"

His tone, so cocky yet intimate, sent chills to my toes. Words as smooth as honey.

My gut twisted. "No, same perfume, but yes, it's time we talked. About us."

Wrenching from his grasp and not waiting for him to respond, I pointed to the deli. "Over there. Now would be a perfect time."

Lance carried the tray with our sandwiches through the crowded deli and slapped it on the table. "We could be having a quiet lunch at Lagucci's instead of this dive."

"This is fine. I need to get back as soon as I can." My hand cupped the engagement ring I'd removed from my finger, its diamond biting into my flesh. When Lance settled into his seat, I opened my fist, palm up.

"Here. This is for you." My voice shook, thin and squeaky. "I'm sorry. I don't think things are working out too well right now."

His confused look turned at once to stone, the only movement a twitch in his clamped jaw. Then, in a flash, his shoulders relaxed and a smile formed at the corners of his mouth. "For a minute there, I thought you meant you didn't want to marry me ever. The last few days, I've had some time to think. Honestly, you wouldn't believe the agony I've been through. At times I wanted to strangle you for what I now realize was only you acting on your convictions. So, I take the blame for . . . er . . . our misunderstanding. And I agree, perhaps we rushed the wedding plans. Your mother had us both going with her enthusiasm, and—" He looked over his shoulder and cast a furtive glance at the other diners. "This probably isn't the time or place to discuss this."

I leaned against the chair back, the ache in my shoulder a ready reminder of what I had to do. In a calm voice, nothing like the earthquake I felt inside, I said, "Yes. This is the time and the place. I can't go on... with your abuse."

He flinched at my words, his eyes stormy. Through clenched teeth, he whispered, "Abuse is a very hateful word." He leaned in closer. "Do you know what it would mean to my career if you started throwing out such rubbish?"

"We both know it's not rubbish. Whatever I did to set you off, I'm sorry, but I can't live like this." I wrapped my sandwich in the paper wrapper, whatever appetite I had gone. "I need some time... maybe a lot of time, who knows? I'm sorry." I wanted to kick myself for saying sorry so many times.

"Not nearly as sorry as I am. Look, I'll come over to your place tonight, and we'll talk some more. You know I've never loved anyone the way I love you. Maybe we've both learned our lesson in this. I'll make it up to you. I promise."

I shook my head, disgusted that he'd included me in the blame—that I needed to learn a lesson. "No. You've cost me too much already. Not only in missing work, but also my medical bills. It's a miracle my shoulder wasn't broken."

"If it's the money, don't worry. I'll take care of it. And Ben Harrington, too. What do you think I was doing by telling him you'd gone out of town? I was covering for you, sweetheart. Protecting you."

"I can take care of myself." I scooped up my purse and stood, then leaned in, looking into his vaporous blue eyes. "And by the way, I told Ben the truth about not going to Texas."

His nostrils flared. "Why? Can't you see I'm trying to help you? Some thanks I get." His jaw muscles twitched as he tried to control his tone. "You'll regret throwing this in my face. Then we'll see who's sorry. You hear me?"

His hand clamped onto my wrist. "You will regret this."

"Good-bye, Lance." I jerked from his grasp and bolted from the deli, hoping, praying he wouldn't follow me, his words searing my brain.

Blindly, I ran into the street, weaving in and out of pedestrian traffic to the safety of my office tower. By the time I got there—alone, thankfully—Jenna hadn't returned from lunch. Out of breath, I locked my office door behind me and slumped into the chair. Waves of emotion licked at my insides—disbelief that I'd broken my engagement. Shame that I'd allowed myself to be in this position to begin with. A broken shoulder was nothing compared to my shattered morale. Embarrassment crept up my neck like a fever. I dreaded telling Mom. And CiCi.

Despite the heat in my face, my hands had turned to ice, numb like my feelings for Lance. Another thought corkscrewed through me. I had to call Mom before Lance did. She would see it his way. She always did.

Shivering, I pulled my BlackBerry from my purse.

Mom answered on the second ring. "Brooke, oh my gosh, where have you been? Never mind, we have an emergency. It's CiCi. She's in labor, trying to have the baby, but it's too soon—only twenty-eight weeks—the baby—my first grandbaby. Can you come? Where are you?"

It came so fast, I couldn't absorb it all. CiCi? Premature labor?

"I'm at the office. Things are awfully busy here today. Where's CiCi?"

"St. Francis, but I thought you would know that. I'm sure she told you."

"I forgot. Are you there now?"

"Yes. Another day off work."

So Mom and I'd both become slackers in the job department. But poor CiCi. And Todd. The piles of unfinished work listed sideways before me. Another stack of less-urgent files sat on the corner of my desk.

"Mom, I'll be there as soon as I get off work. What room?"

"Gracious, I hoped you'd be more concerned and come right over. But then, after you disappear for a week and don't answer your phone, I guess I should be thrilled you're coming at all. Whenever it suits you will be fine. And I don't know what room. Just ask at the information desk." She hung up.

[CHAPTER 16]

Mitzi

My hands gripped the steering wheel of the Mercedes as I circled block after block downtown trying to find Brooke's building. The towering skyscrapers all looked the same from ground level, leaning into me until my sense of direction was out of whack. I tried to concentrate, but Gabe flitted in and out of my thoughts.

He'd been twitchy all day, his mutterings garbled as he slid from one timeline to another. First he'd cried over breakfast, telling me over and over he hated meatloaf. It was oatmeal I was trying to feed him.

Then a convoluted tale about going to Coney Island as a boy. Yelling like a carnival barker as he ranted for thirty minutes about the Ferris wheel where his rabbi uncle lost his *kipa*—his lucky skullcap. I'd heard the family legend a dozen times, but today Gabe bellowed and cried. Uncle Rez had been hit by a bus the day after the *kipa* rolled into the sea, and Gabe relived it as the young child he was at the time.

When I did his exercises he banged his legs against the bedrails. More shouting—this time about minefields and the Battle of the Bulge, where he'd fought during World War II.

I felt I'd been through a war myself.

A familiar building loomed ahead. I pulled to the curb hoping it was the one where Brooke worked. I breathed a sigh of relief when she emerged, clipping along pert and businesslike.

"How was your day?" I patted her knee when she slid into the passenger seat, stowing her briefcase at her feet.

"Long. Thanks for picking me up." She went into a spiel about CiCi and premature labor and for a minute, I couldn't remember who CiCi was. Her sister. Of course.

"Would you mind taking me to St. Francis? I know it's clear across town, but I need to be there for her and Mom."

"Yes, you do. Your family must be worried out of their minds. How far along is your sister?"

"Seven months. No, six. Whatever twenty-eight weeks is."

My fingers tightened around the steering wheel; I knew from past experience twenty-eight weeks wasn't good. Not good at all. I flicked the turn signal for a left.

Brooke grabbed my arm. "Wait. That's a one-way street. Go to the next light."

"Right. I never can keep straight which ones are one-way down here." I squinted through my glasses at the slashes of sky breaking up the shadowy buildings with a funny blue twilight. Concentrating on the street signs, I turned on Cincinnati and did the stop-and-go at every intersection until we got to the Broken Arrow Expressway, where the cars whizzed past at breakneck speed. A short five or six miles until we exited on Yale and began the slow traffic crawl toward St. Francis.

I missed the hospital turn-in and had to go to the U-turn lane farther down. The Mercedes groaned as I cut the wheels sharply to the left to avoid the curb. Then out of nowhere a black SUV as big as a tank zipped by inches from my face, the horn blaring.

My muscles bunched up in my shoulders and my neck, relaxing only a fraction when I pulled into the drop-off at the entrance of St. Francis. "What time do you want me to pick you up?"

"Don't worry. I'll figure out a way to get back. Mom or Todd can drive me. It may be late, anyway."

"You sure you want to give away your location?"

"It's all right. I'm going to tell them everything." She dangled her left hand in front of my face and said, "Like I did Lance."

It took a minute for me to process what she meant, then my skin went clammy. "You gave his ring back? Oh gracious, how did he take it? He didn't do anything harmful, I hope."

"Nope. Everything's fine. I'm relieved, in a way. I don't know if I would have had the nerve if I hadn't bumped into him in the middle of the street. Talk about coincidence."

"Coincidence, my hind leg. I'd say your meeting was orchestrated by someone watching out for your best interest."

"Maybe. Maybe not. I did take your advice. Gave him back the ring in the middle of Pete's Deli. He was ticked, but there wasn't much he could say. I feel I'm ready to get on with my life. Hiding out at your place can't last forever."

A stooped gentleman in a St. Francis smock rapped at her window.

"Do you need help, miss? A wheelchair or directions?"

Brooke shook her head. "No thanks."

I cleared my throat. "Honey, I'm glad you took the first step. But he won't give up easily. His type never does. Please promise me you'll stay at my house a while longer."

"I think I can do that. Besides, you haven't told me the rest of your story." Brooke gave me a quick smile, gathered her briefcase and purse, and got out. Then she poked her head back in the car. "Be careful going home. And thanks . . . for everything."

Blinking, I put the car in gear and inched forward, noting the lights of downtown far away on the left side of the windshield. As I pulled out onto Yale, the headlights of oncoming traffic glared, their beams splitting into a million piercing fragments. My fingers curled tighter around the steering wheel as I held my breath and concentrated on the road.

[CHAPTER 17]

Brooke

The stooped gentleman gave me directions to obstetrics. The waiting room—the second door on the left out of the elevator—teemed with people, none of whom I recognized. Then, from the crush of people, Todd appeared, concern etched at the corners of his eyes.

"How's CiCi? What about the baby? Can I see her?"

"I'll show you the way." With a nod, he led me down the hall and into CiCi's room, where Mom hovered over my sister as she'd done with me when I'd been in the hospital.

Mom's head jerked up on seeing me. "You did come."

I ignored the insinuation and went to CiCi. "How are you?"

"Still having a few contractions." She reached for me, her hand cool and limp in mine.

Mom added the details. Brethine drip. No distress of the baby according to a strip of paper that slowly unrolled from the fetal heart monitor. A hum came from the box she pointed out, interspersed with the scritch of a needle apparently recording the baby's activity. It was all foreign and intimidating, so I chose to focus on CiCi.

Todd offered to step out and let us visit, murmuring about wanting to talk with the people from their small group. Were all those people in the waiting room their friends? People who stopped their lives to keep vigil with Todd and CiCi? My throat filled with a fist-sized lump.

CiCi smiled at me... "Mom says you've been gone. Did Lance take you somewhere?"

I could only imagine what Lance had told Mom. Not wanting to upset CiCi and make her worry, I wrinkled my nose. "Yeah, I've been gone a few days. Not with Lance. Just doing some thinking."

Mom stood on the opposite side of the bed, frowning, trying to read my mind, it seemed. Let her wonder. Mom's welfare was of much less concern to me than CiCi's, and yet my stomach gnawed with the truth I had to tell her about Lance.

I sat in the chair closest to CiCi as her eyes drifted closed. A moment later they flew open, her face twisted in pain.

"Darn. I thought I wasn't having as many contractions." She breathed through pursed lips, shutting us out. Then almost as quick as the pain started, she relaxed. "Only ten seconds that time."

"What do the doctors say? How long before they know anything?"

"They're confident we can stop the labor, but I'll have to stay on bed rest until the baby comes. I know people are praying."

Nodding, I couldn't think of anything to say. Friends. Prayers. A great husband. A corner of my heart envied CiCi. She looked so helpless lying there, machines and IVs everywhere. But she had a peace I couldn't describe. And maybe that's what made me jealous.

When Todd came back, a drip of mustard on his chin, CiCi brightened. "You rat. Going off to eat, while I lie here starving." She laughed and puckered her lips for his kiss.

Mom and I told them we'd wait outside and would check back in an hour or so. When we got to the waiting room door, Mom turned to me. "Not there. Let's find something to eat in the cafeteria."

With my second deli meal of the day, I sat across from Mom at a small table away from a boisterous group of hospital employees in scrubs and lab coats. She lowered her head and looked up at me with her let's-get-this-over-with glare. "Well?"

I bit into my turkey sandwich. "Well, what?"

"Don't mess with me, Brooke. What's going on? And don't think for a minute I didn't notice you're not wearing Lance's ring."

"I'm glad you noticed. I called off the engagement."

"Why? How could you?"

"Mom, it's complicated, and I want you to listen. Really listen to me."

She let out a noisy breath through her nose. "It's not enough your sister's in early labor, but you have to have a crisis, too."

"This has nothing to do with CiCi. I'm worried the same as you are." I sipped my Diet Coke. "Here's the thing. Lance is not what he appears to be. He gets upset over... well... over a lot of things." A tiny pulse throbbed in my jaw.

"No relationship is without a few bumps. It's part of the package. Working them out is the hard part."

A sarcastic remark about how well she and Dad worked things out crossed my mind. Swallowing the words before I said them, I smiled at Mom. "Under normal circumstances, yes. This is not a normal circumstance."

A look of realization marched across her face. "Lance hasn't found someone else, has he? I've been horrified that would happen. Him in such a visible position, and let's face it, Brooke—his social standing is a couple of rungs up the ladder from ours."

"Relax. If Lance has found someone else, it's news to me. It's his temper, his outbursts. I can't take any more." I jutted my chin out, running my finger over the scar on my cheek, not ready to say aloud what I wanted Mom to know. I didn't have to.

"You argued and had a scuffle? 'The accident,' you called it. Oh my word, it was Lance who tripped you then."

"I didn't trip."

Her lips drew into a flat line, the muscles in her throat clenching and relaxing as she swallowed. "What did you do to antagonize him, Brooke?"

"I forgot a meeting we were going to. If he'd yelled or screamed or stomped out, I would have understood. Then later... a week ago..." My throat clogged with what I ought to tell her. Why couldn't I simply blurt out that Lance half raped me and beat the crap out of me? I hated not being able to say the words and admit what happened.

She toyed with her salt and vinegar chip, her eyes on the Styrofoam plate before her. "So, was this your idea or his?"

"Mine. All mine."

"Fine. Looks like you've made me the fool, too. Did you forget the bridal fair on Saturday?"

"Not happening. Sorry." That word again. Sorry.

She made a soft snort and crinkled the remains of her sandwich in its wrapper. "I've never understood you, Brooke. What you don't seem to realize is all men are flawed. The sooner you grasp the concept, the better off you'll be."

Flawed. Like Dad. Was her own failed marriage what made Mom so bitter?

"You may be right, but you and Dad didn't work it out, as you say."

"That was different."

"How so?"

"You know he left me. I couldn't compete with the other woman."

The one who took my dad and left me stranded in the clutches of a mom who was a control freak.

Hot tears stung my eyes; words lay unspoken on my tongue. *Don't go there, Brooke. You'll only make things worse.*

The table of hospital employees exploded in laughter, but in the midst of their joke, Mom's words rang out. "Don't be a fool, Brooke. Lance was probably the last chance you'll ever have at finding a husband."

The way she said it made me think I had grown horns and buck teeth and would never be attractive to another man. And at the moment, that was the last thing I wanted.

With a smirk of dismissal, she stood and marched toward the trash receptacle and didn't look back to see if I would follow.

I left the obstetrical floor at midnight, without mentioning to Mom or Todd my need for a ride. Mom spoke only in clipped tones the rest of the evening, avoiding me whenever possible. When CiCi went two hours without having a contraction, I said good-bye and promised to come back the next day. My shoulder ached as I walked across the lobby to the information desk, hoping they had the number of a cab company. When I approached the lobby's seating area, a thin, black man rose and stepped toward me.

Hadley Davis. A flicker of panic went through me. His wife. She lived at the Guardian Light. I hoped something hadn't happened.

"Hadley. What are you doing here? Is everything all right?"

He nodded. "I heard you was in need of a ride, so I've come to fetch you... At your service, ma'am." He did a swooping bow.

"Oh my. You shouldn't be out so late. I was going to call a cab. And how did you know I needed a ride?" Of course I knew, but why would Mitzi go to all the trouble?

"It's not important—"

The flicker went through me again. "Oh my. It's not Gabe, is it?"

He squared his thin shoulders, straightening even more erect than normal. "No, child. It's Mitzi. There's been an accident."

[CHAPTER 18]

Mitzi

I'd nearly paced a rut in the carpet waiting for Hadley to deliver Brooke back home. At every sweep of headlights in the front window, I went to see if it was them. Then back to staring into the cup of tea I'd made to calm my nerves. My worries seesawed between Brooke's sister, who I'd never met, and explaining to Brooke what caused the collision at the end of the expressway's exit ramp.

Foolish. Why didn't I see the car beside me when I merged into the oncoming traffic? Had I put on my turn signal? I couldn't remember. I had only fuzzy memories of squinting at the taillights ahead of me. And now, the recurring tape in my head of tires screeching, glass splintering, and metal shrieking. The wail of the ambulance came at the same time as the blaring fire truck. If only my eyesight had been as good as my hearing.

The teen driver, whose car I'd plowed into, cursed, calling me names I deserved, promising me a day in court. Thank goodness I had full-coverage insurance.

The throbbing in my arm reminded me how lucky I was. The splint running from my fingertips to my elbow held my fractured ulna in place.

"A simple fracture," the ER doc had declared.

Simple? Nothing could be simple about having my arm hobbled.

"We'll give it a few days for the swelling to subside, then fix you up with a cast." The physician must have seen my grimace, for he added, "You look like a bubble gum pink gal, but of course, they'll let you choose whatever color you want." He clucked his tongue and disappeared, leaving me to await the nurse's instructions.

The clock in my antiseptic-scented cubicle read nine thirty. Three and a half hours of giving statements to the responding officer, being wheeled to X-ray, then off to get an EKG because the fright of my mishap might have given me a heart attack. Nursing assessments. Physicians prodding my internal organs. Somehow, I'd survived the ordeal, with a Velcro splint and a hefty traffic ticket to show for it.

The only person I could think of to call and retrieve me was Hadley Davis. Why I couldn't think of anyone else baffled me, and if I'd let on my brain was a jumble, the doctor might've called for having my head examined.

Hadley, bless his heart, came immediately, and when he deposited me at my house, he picked up on my alarm that Brooke hadn't returned. Being the dear man he was, he offered to check on her at St. Francis.

Another car crept along the street, slowing at the intersection two houses down before turning onto Utica. What was keeping Hadley? He'd promised to let me know if Brooke decided to spend the night or made other plans. What about her sister? CiCi, wasn't it? Was twenty-eight weeks far enough along for an infant to survive? Probably, but not without being in neonatal for eons. Prayers skated through the muddle of my thoughts.

Prayers I'd cast heavenward so many times myself. None of my pregnancies had ever advanced past twelve weeks. Not even long enough to feel the flutter of life of my three babies.

Then, there they were. Hadley and Brooke, rushing in the side door. Brooke running to me and pulling me into an embrace.

"Mitzi. Are you sure you're all right?" Eyeing me up and down, she whooshed out a breath. "Your arm. Hadley said it's broken."

"Just a simple fracture. I'll be new in no time. What else did Hadley tell you?"

"That the invincible Mercedes saved you."

"Sacrificed its life for my pitiful soul, I'm afraid. And I'm sure he enlightened you regarding what a fool I am." Brooke's icy hands clutched my free one. "Which I don't want to hear, anyway. How's your sister?"

"So far, so good. The contractions have stopped. The baby's fine. It'll be another day or two until they know for sure if they can keep her from an early delivery."

Hadley hadn't moved from his spot beside the door.

I waved him over. "Hadley, come on in. I'll make you a cup of tea."

"Thanks, Miz Steiner, but I need to get on home. Us old folks need our beauty sleep."

"Who're you calling old?"

"Figure of speech, that's all. Anything I can do for you ladies, you know where I'll be."

"It's a sorry day when I can't get a fuss out of you, Hadley Davis. Go on home, if you need to. Brooke and I will be fine. And thanks. You're a treasure."

"Thanks, Mr. Davis." Brooke dumped her things on the sofa and went to lock the door behind him. She turned to me. "I'm sorry I asked you to drive me to St. Francis. This would've never happened—"

I held up my right hand. "Stop. We won't worry about who's to blame. What I can't figure out is why I didn't see the other car. Now I've put us both in a jam. No help to you in getting to work.

Me having to figure out how to get back and forth to see Gabe. It's a fine tattered mess."

"Don't be silly. You're not responsible for me. I'm the queen of getting into trouble, in case you've forgotten. And as for you, maybe it's time you let someone help you for a change. You obviously can't drive, but I think my shoulder's strong enough to get us where we need to go." Brooke rolled her shoulder to demonstrate.

"I'm accustomed to taking care of myself, Brooke. If you haven't figured that out by now, you're not the smart cookie I made you out to be."

"I have noticed your independent streak, but tonight we're both tired. How about we decide in the morning?"

Brooke headed up the stairs while I rechecked the doors and turned off the lights. In spite of my weariness, a warmth caressed me. I carried on about being self-sufficient, but Brooke didn't know how welcome her presence was. How cold and frightened I'd become at the thought of being alone.

[CHAPTER 19]

Brooke

After dropping Mitzi off at the Guardian Light, I arrived at CH&B to find Jenna decked out in an emerald spandex top with a streak of green hair hanging casually over her left eye.

"Hey, Brooke, Lance called. Wants you to call him." She raised her pierced eyebrow, her expression curious. "When you do, why don't you hint around I'm looking for an escort to the Christmas Bash next week? It's so lame to show up like I'm on the prowl, you know."

Grrrr. The annual Attorneys Association Christmas party. How could I have forgotten? The biggest booze-guzzling, back-slapping event of the season. Last year I'd floated through the whole afternoon, beaming with Lance at my side, dreaming of spending my life with him.

Not this year. But instead of being gracious and suggesting that Jenna and I go together, I muttered, "The entire affair is overrated, in my opinion. I may not go myself this year."

Her jaw dropped. "What's the matter? Did you and Lancey-poo have a tiff? He did sound a little irritated on the phone, if I recall."

Whatever. Let her think what she wanted, and under no circumstances would I be calling him. He was simply going to have to adjust to our nonengagement.

Mr. Harrington buzzed the minute I got to my office and gave me another stack of files to work on. Crisp. Business as usual.

During break, I made a quick call to CiCi in the hospital and was relieved she'd made it through the night without a contraction. "I'll stop by later in the week when you get home then."

As I went through the mechanical rhythm of fact-checking and updating computer files, an interoffice memo popped up on my monitor. The official announcement of the Christmas party. Maybe I'd come down with strep throat or get hit by a bus. Plotting ways to get out of what would be an awkward, agonizing event, I entered the wrong information on a client and spent thirty minutes checking to see what other dumb mistakes I'd made.

Concentrate on your job, girl. Why should you let Lance taint every part of your life?

Indeed. I'd done nothing wrong, except fall for the wrong guy. I rubbed an ache that had crept into my shoulder. Maybe it was time to face my fears. And for one gleeful, mad moment I saw myself facing Lance down at the Christmas party. Yes. It was definitely time to get my life back on track.

At five thirty, I turned off the computer monitor and left the office, glad Jenna wasn't at her station. Give Jenna a sniff of gossip, and she was like a bloodhound. I didn't relish deflecting whatever rumors tangled the grapevine about my "tiff" with Lance.

A wintry chill and the smell of exhaust from the five o'clock exodus met me when I stepped off the elevator to the parking garage. I shrugged deeper into my wool jacket and shuffled across the fluorescent haze toward my car. Hit the keyless remote and ducked inside, tossing my briefcase in the passenger seat. When I jammed the key into the ignition, I saw a flyer stuck under the wiper. What now? An ad for a bargain oil change or notice of a new tattoo parlor? Maybe a fortune-teller in the Blue Dome district who offered deep discounts on your first visit?

I stepped out and bent between the door and car frame to snag it from the windshield. On ecru letterhead paper, I read the words scrawled boldly across it.

Table for two at O'Malley's tonight at 7. All is forgiven.

No signature. Not that it mattered—I recognized Lance's handwriting. I crumpled it into a ball, jumped back in the Mustang, and threw the note on the floor. The tremors started inside, jerky quivers at first, then full body shaking. I clenched the steering wheel in both hands for control, telling myself it was nothing.

All is forgiven? What gall.

I started the car, gunned the engine, and backed up fast. Hit the brakes, then roared out of the parking garage. Taking a circuitous route through downtown, I wound up on I-244 and had to go miles out of the way before I pulled into the Guardian Light at six fifteen. Mitzi was nowhere in sight, so I parked the Mustang and went inside looking for her.

Expecting the smell of old people and bedpans mixed with disinfectant, I was surprised at the inviting cinnamon scent in the lobby. The soft strains of "Angels We Have Heard on High" filtered through the air. Before a gas-log fireplace, a semicircle of wheelchairs were parked with bent-over passengers muttering to each other, one a tiny lady with hair so thin it looked clear.

Her face lit up when she saw me. "Oh, honey. You came. I told the fellas here you'd be by any minute." She turned to a toothless man wearing Reeboks and a bright red wind suit. "See, Herman, I told you my Missy would come. It's Christmas."

Words fumbled in my mouth as I shook my head. "I'm sorry . . . I . . ."

The lights from the decorated tree in the corner couldn't have blinked brighter than the poor woman's crystal blue eyes. Touching her lightly on the shoulder, I wished her a merry Christmas, then backed away in search of a reception desk.

A hefty woman in a violet floral scrub top gave me directions for finding Mitzi. Second door on the right. As I stood outside Gabe's room gathering my courage, a shrill voice rang out down the hall, "Help me! Someone, please help me!"

The plea echoed in my head as I rapped lightly on Gabe's half-opened door. No answer. I peeked into the room. Mitzi's back was to me, her form hovering over the bed where Gabe lay. My heart rate ratcheted up a notch, and I almost turned to run out. I could just as easily tell the nurse to give Mitzi the message I was waiting.

Mitzi's sparkling voice, though, kept my feet planted to the floor. "Here you go, Gabe. A few more sips and I'll quit pestering you."

I cleared my throat. "Hey, Mitzi. Sorry I'm late."

She lifted her chin, her lips curved into their perpetual smile. "Hey yourself. Come in; it's about time you two met."

While I stood at the foot of the bed, Mitzi made the introductions. Politely, with more confidence than I felt, I said, "Good to meet you, Gabe. I've heard great things about you."

His gaze brushed past me, lingering on the world outside the window. His gnarled body, long arms lying loosely at his side, and cheeks like moon craters gave my insides a twist. This was not the picture I had in my head of the robust man laughing in the framed pictures scattered all over Mitzi's home. The figure in the bed sported a shock of silver-white hair, as fine as silk, with a boyish cowlick on the left, but his eyes, as dull as dark clay, haunted his face. My heart swelled with sadness for Mitzi and compassion for this dear man who was the reason Mitzi lived and breathed.

Mitzi clucked over Gabe, pulling the covers up under his neck. She winced as she guarded her arm, held snugly against her with a sling, and bent over the shriveled figure, skimming his cheek with a kiss. "Gabe, you behave yourself tonight. Sweet dreams."

Tears glistened in her eyes as she gathered her coat and purse and lifted her chin toward me. "I'm ready if you are."

I could barely breathe as we ambled through the lobby, Mitzi's head held high as she said a cheery good-bye to the nurse I'd seen earlier. When we passed the huddle of wheelchairs, she crooned, "See you all tomorrow."

The cinnamon smell now burned my throat, my eyes. Our worlds—mine and Mitzi's—were so different, and yet what I felt inside was yearning—a mournful, silent thirst for a sip of whatever it was that gave Mitzi her strength and zest for life.

Granted, her energy had taken a dive by the time we'd finished our Lean Cuisine dinners an hour later, and without much urging on my part, she went to bed early. I stretched out in the chintz chair in the corner of the keeping room, my feet on the ottoman. I'd brought home a thick stack of files to read so I'd have a head start the next day. The words blurred before me, and while I was considering dragging out my laptop, my cell phone rang.

Lance.

Ticked I hadn't come to O'Malley's, I was sure. I half suspected he was trying to re-create the night he'd proposed to me in the upscale steakhouse whose only resemblance to its Irish name was the hearty lamb stew they served.

Ignoring the call, I got up and put a cup of water in the microwave for some tea, then tiptoed upstairs and put on my flannel pajamas. Not until I sat sipping the lemongrass and peppermint tea did I check my messages.

Two. One from Mom, telling me CiCi wouldn't go home until Thursday. The other from Lance.

You must not've got my message. I waited over an hour for you at O'Malley's.

Long pause where I thought I detected a hiccup. Drowning his rejection in bourbon? His voice started again.

I'm sitting outside your apartment waiting for you to come home. Kinda late to be out alone, isn't it? At least I hope you're alone. See you soon.

I exited the message program and leaned my head against the sofa cushion.

Waiting for you.

It irked me that he wasn't giving up. He'd assumed that I was with someone else, cheating on him, making it sound like *he* was the victim. What if I *had* shown up at my apartment, what then? More bodily harm? I was the poster child for that already.

A more disturbing thought—if he was watching me, it wouldn't take long until he figured out my refuge. Mitzi. Would he approach her? Lance wasn't one to accept rejection gracefully. What if my staying with Mitzi put her in danger? But I couldn't leave her with a broken arm and no one to drive her to see Gabe. Some things are more important, you know?

I would simply have to be careful. Inside, though, I trembled. Lance Evans just might be a hissing volcano.

[CHAPTER 20]

Mitzi

Crashing my car was an idiotic thing. Horrible timing. Brooke was already weary from her own recovery, and now she was saddled with me. Clearly Lance's message had upset her, or she wouldn't have mentioned it at breakfast the next morning. There's a time for silence, but this wasn't it.

"Brooke, I know Lance's type. He's frustrated you've rebuked him, that he no longer has the upper hand. Now he's trying to woo you back into his trust. It's another form of control. He's trying to soften you up so you'll feel sorry for him or, God forbid, think it's all your fault. Once Papa gave Mama a black eye and a busted lip for not kissing him the minute he stepped over the threshold. She was nursing my baby brother at the time."

Brooke crossed her arms. "Our situations may be similar, but Lance will get tired of wooing me, as you say, and move on. I'm sure of it."

"You don't sound convinced."

"It's partly my fault—for letting our relationship get serious when I had doubts. I keep thinking I should've seen the signs, but let's face it, Lance had an amazing flair that drew me in, charmed me."

"Abuse is not charming, and Lance will not give up without a fight. Losing is not in the genes of people like him, and if you think about it, you know I'm right. You need to get a restraining order. Now. Later might be too late."

Brooke broke off bits of the burned crust on the toast I'd made with my terrific culinary skills. Even then, she only nibbled at the remains. "I know how much good protective orders do. I'm a paralegal, remember? You wouldn't believe how many violent crimes occur with a document in place at the time of the offense. Besides, I'm not trying to harm his reputation . . . I only want him to leave me alone."

"You have to do something. If you don't, he'll keep harassing you."

"I can handle him, but I do worry about what he might do to you, Mitzi."

"The only place I ever go is to the care center and back home, now that I can't do my Pink Lady routine with a broken arm. I could call and have my security system turned back on. It's been disconnected since Gabe took to wandering the neighborhood at all hours, forgetting to turn it off when he went out. The police weren't amused by all the false alarms."

Brooke nodded. "I'd feel better if you had a working security system here."

"No problem. I'll call them today. And to be on the safe side, what say we take the bus for a few days? There's a stop around the corner to the east. Besides, depending on other people to cart me around is the pits."

It was settled, and Brooke seemed relieved. We both rode the bus the rest of the week—Brooke to her office and me to the Guardian Light. And on the day of my orthopedic appointment to get my cast, I called a cab.

When I arrived on Friday, Maple, who'd been off for a few days, was fussing over Gabe.

"Mercy, Miz Steiner, what'd you do, break your arm?" She eyed my cast.

"A simple fracture, that's all." I was already sick of telling the story. "Don't you think the bright red cast is just the ticket for Christmas?"

"You got the groove on, no doubt. You going to sing for Mr. Gabe today?"

"Who knows? You never know when I might burst out in a song. Maybe a little soft shoe. You and I could dance together, Maple. It might shock Gabe back to his normal self."

Her ample padding jiggled as she moved with efficiency to fill Gabe's water glass. "The two of us dancing might scare the whiskers off Santy Claus himself."

She tenderly coaxed Gabe's medications into his mouth. "Say, Mr. Gabe. Looks like that bleeding in your gums has cleared up. It sure can cause a fella misery, can't it?"

To me, "You reckon you can manage his breakfast one-handed?"

"It hasn't given me any problems so far."

"If you need help, give me a holler." She sashayed toward the door, then stopped and turned around. "Don't know if you've heard or not, but there's been some flu going around. In morning report, the night nurse said five of the residents have symptoms already. I know I don't need to tell you what that means."

A bitter taste formed in my mouth. I knew the turnover rate was high at the Guardian Light. After all, it was the last stop before glory. We didn't need a flu outbreak to speed the process.

"I'll mind my hand washing. Any restrictions on visitors?"

"Not yet, but if it gets as bad as when that swine flu went through here, we'll get put on quarantine."

"Oh, I hope not. A friend of ours will be here in a few days. A young man who's interviewing for a hospital internship."

"A doctor, eh? We'll call his visit a consultation."

"That would be some consultation... Drew's going to be a pediatrician."

Maple's face broke out in a smile. "He'll fit right in. Half the folks here have the minds of little children."

Sadly, she spoke the truth. Gabe lived most of his waking hours in his childhood. More than ever, he rambled about his days in Brooklyn, working at his family's dry cleaning shop, singing in talent shows with his brothers on the weekends. When his eyes rested on me, he would blink, a vacuous expression in his coal dark eyes. I counted each yarn he told a blessing as I memorized the sound of his voice, the lines in his face growing deeper each day.

There was no doubt about it: our time was short. The flu could snatch Gabe from me in an instant. Fear that its long talons would whisk Gabe into eternity clawed at me. Not that I didn't have peace concerning the ever after. It was my being on this planet alone that harangued me.

I leaned over and kissed him full on the lips, hoping for once he would return the kiss.

You've always been a dreamer.

Tears welled up and fell on Gabe's cheek. Through the moist blur, all I saw was the man I'd chosen to walk this earth with; after a handshake from Jesus, Gabe was the next person I wanted to see when I stepped into glory.

I brushed the wet spots from the crevices of Gabe's cheek and whispered, "Don't you even think about leaving me, Gabe Steiner."

His eyes widened for an instant, then closed as he turned his head away.

[CHAPTER 21]

Brooke

By the end of the week, I'd quit looking over my shoulder at every turn, expecting Lance to pounce on me. I'd heard nothing since his drunken phone call. Either he'd come to grips with reality or he was regrouping. Either way, I refused to live my life in fear.

Yeah, right.

With the weekend coming, I'd decided for the millionth time life would go on as usual. A visit with CiCi. Maybe another trip with Mitzi to see Gabe. When I returned from lunch—an apple and a carton of yogurt I snagged at the nearest coffee shop—Jenna gave me a finger wave and a coy look. "You have a visitor in your office."

Her phone buzzed before I could ask her who. Jenna raised one eyebrow at me and picked up the receiver.

Mitzi? Not likely. Mom? Perish the thought.

My heels clicked on the marble floor, a staccato sound in my head. When I got to the carpeted hallway of our wing, I slowed down, took a deep breath, and breezed into my office.

Lance's head shot up, a look of surprise that morphed instantly into a huge grin. He rose from my swivel desk chair and hurried around my desk, his arms open.

A momentary head rush left me dizzy. "Wh... what are you doing here? And why were you sitting in my chair?"

I set my purse on my desk along with the double-shot latte I'd brought to get me through the afternoon.

"No need to cross-examine me. I've come because I miss you. And I thought I could feel your presence better if I sat in your chair." His arms slid around me, and he buried his face in my hair, working his way down to my forehead, my cheek.

My body went rigid, my arms dangling at my side. Turning my head away, I deflected his intended kiss. "Lance. Please."

Standing back, he had a hurt look on his face, a cloudiness in his eyes, which had been sparkling moments before. "I'm sorry. I know you need time." He held up his hands in surrender.

I eased away from him, taking my time hanging my coat on the wall hook. Calmly, I took my purse and stashed it in the console behind my desk and sat casually in my chair. "You didn't answer my question. Why are you here?"

"I do miss you. That part was absolutely true." He reached into the inner pocket of his perfectly cut suit and pulled out an envelope. "I brought you something." He handed it to me. "Go ahead. Open it."

I settled back into the chair's leather, still warm from Lance having been there, ran my finger under the flap, and pulled out two tickets. Concert tickets for Norah Jones. *Oh my.*

"They're for a week from Saturday. Sold out weeks ago, but I was able to get us center seats in the tenth row. I know she's your favorite."

His eyes pleaded, and my heart twisted. How did he always know how to get to me? I loved concerts. Adored Norah. My fingers caressed the tickets. *Are you stupid?* No way was I falling for this.

I stuffed the tickets back in the envelope and pushed it across my desk toward him. "It's a generous offer. Very tempting, but I thought

I made it clear I don't want to see you. Not now. Not a week from Saturday. Please don't make this harder than it is."

He swallowed, seemingly trying to control his temper. "Brooke, baby, you're all I think about. The political campaign seems off without you beside me. This weekend I'm going to the Diabetes Foundation ball by myself. I need you. Can't you see that?"

"I'm sure the Parsleys will be glad to accompany you."

"They have plans—their grandson's band concert."

With my hands around the cardboard cup, I wrestled with what to say. Lance had no family—no fallback plan. Sure it was tough, but it was hard for me, too, although not for the same reasons. Having him appear like an Internet pop-up ad was unnerving. And I was sick of worrying about what I might say or do to incite the next episode of rage.

I met his eyes. "Lance, it's not going to work out between us. You need to get help. Anger management sessions or counseling to learn why you have these... outbursts. Until you do that and make some changes, I can't see you."

He kept his eyes wide, his face relaxed, but the air felt thicker, congested, as he snatched up the tickets. "I don't have an anger problem. You frustrate me, that's all. You give off those come-hither looks that turn to ice the minute I get too close. What do you want? Whatever it is, I'll do it."

"Get help. Not for me, but for yourself."

His eyes narrowed. "You've found someone else, haven't you? You never come home to your apartment anymore. Who is it?"

Before I could deny his wild accusation, he said, "You'd better hope to God I don't catch you. Rest assured, I'll be watching." He spun on his heels and stomped out of the office.

My knuckles whitened from gripping the cup as an ache rippled between my shoulder blades. I sipped the latte, the liquid warm and welcome in my chilled body.

He might have gone, but something I'd noticed while he was there seared my memory. On his right hand, Lance still wore my gift to him—the tigereye ring.

By Saturday morning, I decided Lance was bluffing, that his talk was only to scare me. Besides, I had things I wanted to do, so I ventured out in the Mustang. After dropping Mitzi off at the Guardian Light, I headed to CiCi's. I didn't want to upset her by telling her I'd broken up with Lance, but Mom had done so without my permission. Go figure. I was glad it was out in the open, though, and CiCi had actually taken the news better than Mom had.

"Things happen for a reason," CiCi said as she flipped through a pregnancy and parenting magazine.

"I'm glad I came to my senses before I married him." Knocked to my senses was closer to the truth. "Now I can concentrate on something other than whether I want marzipan or traditional icing on my wedding cake." I gave a hollow laugh. "Did I tell you I've taken up drawing again?"

"That's great, but it doesn't do anything to fix your relationship with Lance."

"It's not fixable, CiCi. That's what I'm telling you." I wasn't sure what she meant, but then Mom might not have told her my decision was final. In many ways, CiCi was like Mom. Bossy. Pouting. Skipping off to her own conclusions.

She peered over the magazine. "People can change, you know."

"Only if they want to, and I don't think Lance wants to. It's not a lover's spat. Lance's temper gets out of hand, and I'm constantly on guard for what he might do next. I wish I'd taken action sooner, if you must know."

She tossed the magazine aside, her eyes shifting as if she had something on her mind. "Listen, Brooke. I'm not saying this to make you feel bad. I know men can change. Todd did."

"What are you talking about? I'm sure Todd never laid a hand on you."

"Not physically. Mental anguish can be just as painful."

Gears started spinning in my head. Lance's warning about men and their wandering eyes popped up. Not possible. Lance was wrong about Todd, I was sure of it.

"Todd falls all over himself catering to you."

She got her signature pouty look. "I've never told you about the nightmare I went through."

"What on earth are you talking about?" I tried to remember if I'd heard this before. Nothing came.

CiCi crossed her arms, her turned-up nose flaring ever so slightly. "We'd only been married a couple of years. Still newlyweds almost." Her bottom lip trembled. "Todd had an affair with one of his patients. A college girl. I walked in on them in one of the exam rooms."

The air escaped my chest as if it had been caught in a vise. *No!* "I'm so sorry. I never knew. How awful."

"Worse than awful. I wanted to puke on the spot. I ran out, packed some of my things, and went to Mom's for a week."

"Mom never breathed a word."

"Exactly. I threatened to murder her if she did. It was the most humiliating thing I'd ever experienced. She told me she regretted how things worked out with Dad and asked me if I loved Todd. I knew I did—with every inch of my being."

"So you confronted him?"

"I didn't have to. He came to me, apologized, and begged me to forgive him." Resting her hand on her protruding belly, she turned her head into the pillow. "It was hard. Horrible." She lifted her chin and squinted her eyes. "But I loved him. And I forgave him."

Been there. Done that.

CiCi leaned over the edge of the bed, dug in a pile of magazines, and came up with a copy of *Tulsa About Town*. She flipped the pages, then held it up for me, her French-manicured finger jabbing at the heading on the page.

Tulsa's Next DA?

It was an article about Lance, accompanied by the picture taken of us with the Parsleys the night we went to see *The Nutcracker.* The light emphasized the unevenness of his nose, the only flaw on his smiling face. A familiar tug pulled at my heart, and I could almost smell his lime aftershave, feel the softness of his fingers across my cheek. When I took a closer look at the picture, I could remember the exact moment it was snapped—with Lance's lips brushing my ears, our fingers interlocked. Me hissing at him about making wedding plans without consulting me.

"Do you see the way he's looking at you, Brooke?" CiCi's eyes misted over. "Lance can't keep his eyes off you, and I'm sure he's sorry for anything he's done to hurt you."

My breath caught. "CiCi, trust me, your situation was different than mine—"

"I'm only saying, if you try and work it out together, something magical could happen. Todd and I found a counselor who recommended we start attending church together. RCC—Riverside Community Church—has a class for engaged couples. Some friends of ours went and thought it was wonderful."

Counseling was the bone I'd tossed to Lance. Get help or forget it. Did I need counseling, too? No doubt. Not premarital counseling, though. Victim sessions for me. Psycho rage classes for Lance.

CiCi leaned back into her cloud of pillows. "Why don't you go to our church tomorrow? Todd can show you around since I'll be laid up here. The secretary could tell you when the next class starts."

"Thanks, but no. I have things to do this weekend." I still hadn't told Mom or CiCi about staying with Mitzi. I knew I should, but

I kept having visions of Lance sweet-talking them into disclosing where I was. I needed more time to stay tucked away. To heal.

We spent another hour discussing baby names and a lot of nothing before I begged off and said I needed to go Christmas shopping.

Under a cloudless blue sky, the Utica Square shopping center pulsed with the outdoor feel of Christmas. I felt lighter and more carefree in the crisp air as I sprinted between the shops. I picked out a chenille bear with a candy-striped bow for Todd and CiCi's baby, a Crabtree & Evelyn gift set for Mitzi, and a periwinkle spa robe for Mom. I got a bowl of baked potato soup from Queenie's in the middle of the square and relaxed while watching the shoppers through the plate glass window.

Feeling generous, I bought pecan millionaires for Ben Harrington, who always kept a secret stash in his walnut desk. Silver hoop earrings for Jenna. I wandered through Saks Fifth Avenue, mostly to kill time until Mitzi needed to be picked up at the Guardian Light. When I drifted into the men's department, a turtleneck the same shade of blue as Lance's eyes hung on a poised mannequin.

"Looking for something for your boyfriend?" A clerk in a pinstriped shirt stood inches away from me. He wore the same lime aftershave as Lance, his nearness suffocating.

I faltered and stepped back, trying not to breathe. Would it always be like this? Reminders of Lance at every turn? The color of his eyes. His scent.

I swallowed, then had an idea. "I'm actually looking for some warm socks for an elderly friend of mine. Something comfortable that won't bind around the ankles."

"Right this way."

I bought four pairs and nearly fainted at the total. But as I walked out into the cold sunshine, my steps were light. A student choir had gathered in the square, their voices clear and beautiful. Strains of *fa-la-la-la-la* followed me all the way to my car.

[CHAPTER 22]

Mitzi

When Brooke picked me up at five thirty, daylight had departed and a sharp breeze bit the air. I welcomed the warmth of her car. Sure beat waiting on the Mercedes to warm up, if and when it decided to.

She helped me snap the seatbelt. "I've always wanted a smaller car. How do you think I'd look zipping up and down Utica in a Mustang?"

"I hope you're kidding. You won't be driving anytime soon. You're lucky your car was built like a tank. Otherwise, I still might be visiting you in the hospital."

"Good point. I'm thinking about buying a new one, though. Maybe Drew—"

"I'm not sure you need a car. What you could use is an eye exam and some new glasses."

"How do you know what I need? Realistically, you can't be driving me forever."

"Maybe not, but I want you to be safe, too."

"As long as I stick with familiar streets, I'll be fine."

"I don't know. Why don't you wait until spring to decide?"

"I hate depending on someone else." My stubborn streak was

showing, pushing against my insides. "And talking about needing your eyes examined. In case you didn't notice, you missed the turn to our street."

"Nope. Purely intentional. I'm taking you out to eat tonight. I've made reservations at Fu Li's Mandarin Restaurant."

My stomach did a samba. How had Brooke known this was one of our favorite places? Mine and Gabe's... a lifetime ago it seemed. "Oh, I look a mess. Maybe I should go home and change."

"You look fine. Great, in fact." Brooke pulled to a stop at the light, her fingers drumming on the steering wheel in time to the soft music on the radio. It was the first time I'd seen her so relaxed. Feisty even.

Moments later, we pulled into the restaurant parking lot. Brooke linked her hand in my right elbow. Then, arm in arm, we marched in, the smell of stir-fry and ginger pungent, enticing. Tears sprang unbidden from my eyes.

Brooke settled me in a chair. "You okay?"

"Never better. This place brings back such memories. Gabe and I loved coming here on Saturday nights. We'd see friends, knew all the waiters..."

"I'm sorry. I didn't mean to make it difficult for you."

I waved away her comment. "They were the best of times. Gabe never met a stranger, and he absolutely loved the Kung Pao chicken. Sure beat the pants off the ground-up stuff he lives on now." Scanning the menu, I saw things hadn't changed that much. Not as much as I had.

We had cream cheese wontons for appetizers; then while we both ate orange chicken, the manager came to our table. "Mitzi Steiner. My goodness, sweetie, it *is* you. I thought you'd fallen off the planet." I laughed it off, but the truth was, it sure can feel like it in the tsunami of Alzheimer's.

We chatted a minute, and he told me how sorry he was to hear about Gabe. "Don't be a stranger now, you hear?" Then, in a flash, he picked up the tab for our meal.

The moon winked through the trees when Brooke and I left, both of us giggling like schoolgirls. Back at the house, we curled up on the sofa with Cosmo between us, my new friend and me. And I couldn't help myself—I went into another nostalgic yarn about another friend from long ago. Namely, Penny Vaughn.

[CHAPTER 23]

Under her innocent veneer and childlike face, Penny Vaughn turned out to be complicated. Smoking was only the half of it. She kept her feelings bottled up and had brushed me off when I'd tried to draw her into talking about her family, her past. I had the feeling she'd had some hard knocks.

One afternoon, the twins pulled me aside while Penny was getting ready for work.

"You seem like a nice girl, Mitzi . . . ," Ann started.

". . . So we've been praying on how to tell you this," Nan finished.

They exchanged identical raised eyebrow looks, their faces grave. "Penny's not the sweet girl you might think she is."

Curious about their melodrama, I thought it would be polite to hear them out, especially since they seemed so earnest. "Why would you say that?"

"She does things single girls shouldn't," said Ann.

"And married girls, neither," Nan added. "Not only smoking her Kool menthols . . . but drinking, too." She whispered the last part, as if mentioning it might make her guilty by association.

I thought of the flask Penny carried in her purse and nipped from on breaks at Red's place or on the bus rides home when she thought I wasn't looking. Penny did seem troubled. Nervous. And waffling about, like me.

I shrugged. "I just think she needs a friend, someone she can talk to."

The twins exchanged wary looks, but Nan answered. "We hear she's got plenty of friends. The male kind. One of the clerks at the store saw her marching in the front door of the Broadway Hotel with a man twice her age."

"And she wears nice clothes, has money for makeup and jewelry. You know what that means," Ann said.

"It could mean any number of things, but it's awfully nice of you to be concerned. Have you talked to Penny about this?"

"Oh no." In tandem, their eyes grew as round as the chipped saucer on Idella's supper table.

"Maybe you should. I think you'll find Penny's just like us, trying to make a go here in the city. Thanks for the chat. Sorry to run, but it's time for work." The truth was, I suspected Ann and Nan were right. Penny hadn't come home the previous night, and she'd shown up just long enough to change clothes and catch the bus with me.

And surprisingly, she was giddy with excitement, gushing about meeting someone important at the Carlisle. "Can you believe it? I could become a starlet."

I gave her a sidelong glance. "That sounds a little far-fetched . . . More like Hollywood than Tulsa, don't you think?"

"Hogwash. It just so happens tonight I'm meetin' with a guy who's doing a low-budget film and looking for extras."

"One of our customers?"

"No, someone who knows someone."

"Promise me you'll be careful, Penny. A lot of these people take advantage of naive girls. It could be a con." I was one to talk—getting my handbag stolen in the bus station—but something about Penny seemed so vulnerable.

"Nope, this is the real deal. And he's got references."

"What kind of references?"

"You know, the names of other girls he's put in films. Some might even be famous movie stars by now." Her eyes had the dreamy look of seeing her name scroll across the big screen at the Royal Theater.

"Just promise me this: don't go off with someone you don't know."

She crossed her arms and looked out the bus window, then hopped off at the Carlisle without another word.

Red met me in the kitchen when I arrived. "Mitzi. I'm in a pickle. Ruby's come down with a case of the mumps and can't sing tonight . . . maybe not for two weeks even. I've been listening to you sing along while you zip in and out of the kitchen. You've got the pipes, girl. Think you could fill in?"

My skin tingled like I'd stuck my finger in the light socket. "Now? Tonight? I've never sung in front of an audience in my life, Red! Or practiced with the band." Take Ruby's place? Oh, my stars.

"Mouth the words, hum along. Git yourself in the stage dressing room. Stella and Claudette brought Ruby's dress, said they thought you'd do a bang-up job. Now, scat."

I floated off, certain my feet never touched the floor, humming the middle harmony part Ruby sang. I knew it by heart, but what if I tripped over the mic cords or got the Follett jazz band booed off the stage?

Next thing I knew, Waggs Follett and his band were warming up the audience and, on cue, Claudette and Stella herded me out, a pale moonstone between a pair of onyx gems. The rhythm of the drums vibrated the elevated stage, sending its beat from the soles of my feet to my vocal chords, which mercifully found the right notes. Spotlights blinded me, the audience a blur of faces in the smoke-filled haze.

The Folletts kept the tunes simple, only doing the most familiar ones, and when our set was over, a sheen of perspiration and delight caressed me.

Offstage, Red waited for me. "You sure you never sang before? Mercy sakes alive, girl, you were a sensation."

Stella and Claudette hugged me and gave me a slip of paper with an address. "Rehearsal tomorrow at four o'clock. Ruby don't know it yet, but she's in peril of becoming obsolete."

Flattery's one thing. Letting it go to my head was another. Two weeks of singing Mama's music thrilled me, but it also reminded me of my original *intent—find Mama's kin and piece together where I came from. After paying rent and bus fares, I'd saved a little. A couple more months and I'd be on my way to Missouri.*

A week after Ruby returned from her bout with mumps, Claudette came down with them, and once again I took the stage. Only this time, I sang her lead parts, quivering like a cottonwood leaf. Our audience—black and tan, Red called them, proud of the fact we were an integrated club—didn't seem to mind a white girl sharing the stage with a group of colored artists.

For me, all that mattered was the music welling up from the deep and the sheer joy of performing. I felt as if I had one foot in heaven and the other on earth.

Being in the limelight and rehearsing with the Folletts left me little time to keep an eye on Penny. Whenever I did see her, she danced around, starry-eyed, talking nonstop about the talent scout who was setting her up for a screen test.

"Finn knows all the right people. Dresses real snazzy. A man with clout, ya know?"

Finn this. Finn that. When I asked what his last name was, Penny shrugged. "Scouts don't give out their last names or else they'd have half the women in Tulsa ringing them up day and night, trying for an audition."

I'd yet to lay eyes on this Finn, since she only met with him after the club closed. Her wide-eyed, reckless spirit worried me even more than her brooding had. In the pit of my abdomen, I felt trouble brewing.

Red was having his own troubles. The Folletts got a good showing of their record on KVOO and decided to go on the circuit, play some clubs in Muskogee and Oklahoma City. Red would be stuck without a house band.

He fumed. Pulled at the three or four strands of hair left on his speckled head. "We need to lean with the times. We're only a middle-of-the-road joint, but the Folletts keep the regulars coming back. Ain't no way I can compete with the big shots over to the Big Ten Ballroom." He ranted some more, then told me to scoot and take the order from table six.

Every night Red let off more steam, and each time he did, my insides twisted with what I had to tell him. One night when I was wiping down the last of the tables, I got up my nerve. "Red, you've been a saint giving me work and all, but Tulsa wasn't my destination when I set out last summer. I'm thinking of going to St. Louis."

His face turned forty shades of purple. "St. Louis? You got any idea how big a place that is? You'd be as lost as a bumblebee in a tornado."

"My mind's made up. I've saved enough money to get there and live for a few weeks until I find another job." And Mama's kin.

Red stepped between me and the table I was running a rag over. "I hadn't meant to let this news out, but things are fixin' to change around here. Jazz is going off in new directions, starting to flow twixt the traditional and the mainstream. Thing is, we ain't gonna see the likes of Charlie Parker and Jelly Roll Morton no more."

Red talked with his hands, and now they flew around like kite tails as he talked. "New sounds are popping up. Bebop. Hardhop. It ain't even restricted to the colored musicians no more. More and more white folks are breaking on the scene. Here's the deal. I've been talking to a promoter who's full of new ideas. Fella by the name of Lou Caprice. He thinks we can take the Carlisle in a new direction. He's got a few guys lined up for a house band, and here's where you come in, Mitzi."

So there was a point to Red's rambling. Since I knew he was going to have his say, my eyes met his. "I'm listening. It doesn't mean I've changed my mind—"

"No. No. Of course not, but I think you'll be interested in what I'm thinking. Lou's group wants a singer—a soloist—and they're thinking a gal's what they want. You, Mitzi. They want to give you an audition."

Soloist? A steady job at singing? I couldn't connect the dots in my head. One part of me was jumping up and down, ready to sign on immediately. The other part, where my love for Mama held a special place, said wait.

Which is what I told Red. "I'll do the audition, but if it doesn't feel right, I'm still going to St. Louis."

"Fair enough. One thing, though. I'd want you to stay until we have

the farewell for Waggs and his group. The girls have asked if you'd share the stage with them that night."

Tears welled up. And in the tomblike stillness of the Carlisle at closing time, I agreed.

The Carlisle was packed to capacity the night of the Folletts' final show. I greeted a few regulars before the show, mingling to get a feel for the crowd.

When I went through the kitchen, Penny grabbed me and pulled me aside.

"He's coming tonight. Finn's coming. Wants to see me in action. Oh, tell me, how do I look?" She twirled around.

Her pinafore gapped, and I could tell she'd put on an underwire to push up her walnut-sized breasts. Henna highlights in her hair glistened in the glare of the kitchen lights, but it was Penny's radiant face, full of energy and expectation, that pricked the hair on my neck.

"You look wonderful, Penny. I'll say a prayer for you. And, if you think of it, you might whisper one for me, too. Sharing the stage with the girls is a mighty big honor, one that's got me quivering in my all-together."

A quick hug, then Penny went off to wait tables while I went to the dressing room to get ready.

The Follett girls wore shimmery red dresses for their closing night, part of the new wardrobe they'd be sporting on their circuit tour. They'd brought me one of Ruby's white gowns with the same sleek cut and sheen. Secretly, I was glad my dress wasn't red, as red dresses made me think of Mama's left-behind dress, and tonight was no time to think about Mama.

Before I knew it, we slipped onto the stage, humming along with Waggs and the band. Spots came up, and for the first time, I looked into the audience, making out smiling faces, singing my low alto part like I'd been doing it from the womb.

Applause. What a sweet, sweet sound. Song after song, until our final number, when Stella sang the solo for "Sentimental Journey." It was a fitting farewell for the band and Red, and my throat got a sticky feeling.

As we turned to the left and swayed in unison, my eye caught Penny making her way to the entrance. Like a hummingbird flitting from honeysuckle to hollyhock, she bobbled along. Then she linked arms with a man in a double-breasted suit who sported a gentleman's hat, her face uplifted to his. Finn. He'd come. I tried to feel happiness for her, but nothing came.

Ruby sang the second verse while I hummed and echoed my part, the lump in my throat thickening. Together we sang the last chorus, then we ended with a flourish and sweeping bows. When I came up for a final wave, the only faces I saw were Penny's and the man's who had promised her stardom.

Recognition barreled its way through my body. I knew that face. And what penetrated my belly was revulsion. Finn, who had not told Penny his last name, was Finster Poole. My papa.

[CHAPTER 24]

Brooke

Mitzi's voice had grown thin and faint, her pale, mottled hands folded in her lap. I wanted to know so much more, what happened to Penny, and whether Finster Poole had become a new man after his family's disappearance. Mitzi, though, had lapsed into silence, her eyes far away.

"Come on, Mitzi, let's call it a night. Then tomorrow you can tell me the rest of the story."

She took my hand and let me help her stand up. She rose to her full height, and for a moment, I saw Mitzi as a young woman onstage at the Carlisle, her mellow voice blending with the other girls', and I wished I'd been there. Mitzi Steiner was no fragile woman who let the world define her. My heart swelled at merely being in her presence.

And, as I should have expected, the next morning she was going full throttle again, asking me to pick her up at two o'clock so she could start organizing the house for Drew Caprice's arrival on Tuesday. *Caprice.* Of course, she'd mentioned someone named Lou Caprice. Some of what she'd told me came back. Drew was the grandson of a dear friend. I knew there was much more to Mitzi's story than she'd told me, and for the first time I wondered what Drew Caprice would be like.

The weather channel forecasted a warm-up for Sunday, but it turned out to be damp and blustery instead. When I took my pastels and sketch pad to Swan Lake, the swans were nowhere to be seen, perhaps nestled in the plumed grasses out of the wind. Settling onto a bench with a good view of the Victorian home I wanted to sketch, I made the preliminary outline—the intersecting roof lines where Christmas lights were strung, the turret anchoring one corner of the grand house, a twenty-foot fir twinkling multicolored behind the leaded glass. After choosing a pencil in the vibrant aqua of the double doors, I feathered them in. The angle seemed off, so I sat absentminded, a bit chilled. And restless. Maybe a walk would bring inspiration.

After stowing my supplies between a light pole and a winter brown azalea, I shoved my hands in my pockets and circled the miniature lake. Ahead of me, a girl of five or six wobbled on a pink bicycle, trying to keep her balance. A man in a Nike jogging suit kept a steady hand on the back of the bike seat. "You're doing great! Keep pedaling. Thatta girl!" The bicycle shot off ahead of him, the little girl pedaling like mad, blond hair flying behind her.

A memory so sharp it almost buckled my knees assaulted me. My dad had taught me to ride a bike. I lifted my face to the wind, remembering how he'd come for my birthday and surprised me with the bike—pink, with streamers hanging from the hand grips. He'd spent the afternoon running beside me up and down our street, holding the seat steady, shouting encouragement. My breath came in gasps as it had that day. I'd totally forgotten—not only the best birthday I ever had, but also the sound of my dad's voice.

I quickened my steps on the path, hoping to recall more about that day, but by the time I reached the spot where I'd stashed my art kit, nothing else had come. I snagged my sketch pad and pencils and headed back to Mitzi's. Maybe Mom was wrong and Dad wasn't such a rat after all.

A white PT Cruiser stood in Mitzi's driveway. The Dust Bunnies? No, the cleaning crew Mitzi had hired to give the house a thorough cleaning wasn't due until Monday. Who then? No clue.

I slowed, unsure if I should approach the house or continue my walk. Perhaps Lance had hired a private investigator and hunted me down. The warmth I'd felt after the hike around the lake evaporated, caution taking its place.

A figure stepped from the porch. Tall. Long, gangly arms. Stylish rectangular eyeglasses. He lifted his arm in a friendly wave. "Oh, miss, could I ask you something?"

My muscles tensed, and I wished I had a free hand to retrieve my cell phone from my pocket. "Yes, what is it?"

"I'm looking for Mitzi Steiner. No one seems to be at home. Do you happen to know her? Or where she might be?"

"Yes, I know her. She must be out... since she didn't answer the door."

"Shucks, I was hoping to surprise her. I bet she's with her husband. I'll drive over there and check. Sorry to bother you."

In three long strides he was at his car door.

An attorney? No, too casual. Insurance salesman? Not on Sunday.

Drew? Had he come early? He lived in Boston, but that was no East Coast accent. More like California or Arizona. Curious, I half sprinted to the stranger's car and pulled to a stop as he tucked his legs under the steering wheel.

"It's no bother. I didn't catch your name."

"Forgive me. I forgot my manners. I'm Drew Caprice. Mitzi's been a friend of the family forever."

"Oh, Dr. Caprice! Mitzi wasn't expecting you until Tuesday. I'm afraid your room is still cobwebby."

Ducking his head to look through the open door, he said, "I don't mind a few cobwebs, but I'm confused. Do you live here with Mitzi?"

"For the time being, yes."

"She never let on she'd had to hire a live-in. Tell me, is she okay? What I mean is . . . she's not ill or slipping . . . like Gabe?" He chewed his lower lip, his expression one of concern.

"No, not at all. Matter of fact, I should be paying her to stay here." An awkwardness fell in the space of the open car door separating us. Drew didn't need to know the details.

He eased out of the car, unfolding his legs, and rose to his full height. Now instead of looking level with him in the car, I had to peer upward to see his face.

Extending his hand, he said, "Guess it's my turn to say I didn't catch your name."

"Brooke Woodson." Bobbling my art kit, I tried to shake his hand, but my sketch pad slipped from under my arm, the half-finished drawing fluttering up in a wind current. As I reached for it, my cedar art case clattered to the ground, my Caran d'Ache pencils scattering like Pick-Up Sticks.

Heat rose in my face, the old shame of being a klutz bubbling up, too, as Drew loped off to catch my errant sketch. I swallowed hard, scooping up my pigmented pencils and telling myself to get my act together.

Returning triumphant, Drew handed over the drawing. Silly. Only a few off-kilter lines similar to my thoughts. The main thought being I'd not put on any makeup this morning, meaning only to putz around Mitzi's all day. My pulse throbbed in the scar on my cheek, and I imagined it flashing neon at Drew Caprice, who hovered over me eyeing my feeble attempt at capturing the Victorian on paper.

I slid it into the pad. "Thanks. And sorry to be so clumsy."

"My fault entirely. I should apologize to you for interrupting your day, scaring you like this." He bent down to retrieve a pencil I'd missed, his hands smooth, strong, as big as catchers' mitts. "So, you're an artist?"

"No, just a dabbler. A hobbyist."

With everything back in order, we stood a few feet apart, not knowing what to say. He had an easy manner, and he was clean shaven but with a hint of five o'clock shadow on his angular face. Not handsome, but studious. Sincere. I nodded toward the house. "I was going to get Mitzi at the Guardian Light in a few minutes. Maybe you should surprise her instead."

"Better yet, why don't you ride along with me?"

"Thanks, but I'll straighten up the house while you're gone. Don't want to scare you too much with our clutter."

"Trust me. If you saw my place, you'd know I don't scare easily." He opened the car door, looked over the top at me. "Last chance?"

I shook my head.

"Okay, then, see you later."

Inside the house, I leaned against the door. Drew Caprice. Not what I expected. I laughed at my own naïveté. I'd pictured someone with a receding hairline, a white coat, and a stethoscope slung around his neck. Not a towering giant with a voice of velvet and manners that made me blush.

[CHAPTER 25]

Mitzi

The door to the chapel at the Guardian Light eased open behind the padded pew where I sat soaking up God's presence. Having just poured my heart out on behalf of Gabe and Brooke and Lily Davis, Hadley's wife, I needed the calm, the reassurance I always got in this quiet place. With only six small pews and a kneeling altar, the chapel had become my refuge more and more. Not unlike Mt. Olivet, the small church I'd found after Finster Poole had shown up.

The answer I received at Mt. Olivet years ago was a gentle nudge to seek God. Wholly and completely. As I wept in God's tender presence back then, he'd reminded me he cared for Penny the same as he did me. That I must let him water and feed my spirit as he carried hers. As I pressed into him, warmth enveloped me.

Penny weighed heavily on my spirit then, as Gabe, Brooke, and Lily did the Sunday Drew showed up. Poor, fragile Lily, who fought not only Alzheimer's, but now the flu sweeping through the care center. On Friday she'd been fine. By dawn on Saturday, a hollow cough racked her skeletal chest. She'd grown feverish, her agonizing screams wafting through the halls of the Guardian Light.

Hadley stayed by her side from Saturday on, coming out for air only when the battle became too fierce. We'd talked over a cup of coffee at noon on Sunday, his eyes bloodshot and sagging at the corners.

When I told him I was praying, his chin jutted out. "I'm prayed out, Miz Steiner. I've done beseeched the Almighty to put an end to her suffering. It's just the hole she's leaving behind. I don't know how I'll manage." He looked away, his face hollow. Helpless.

I ached for him. The terror of being alone hovered endlessly beneath the surface of my thoughts; yet when I looked into Hadley's grief-stricken face, a twinge pinched me, provoking guilt that Gabe had escaped the respiratory demon holding Lily in its clutches.

A hand rested on my shoulder in the chapel. Expecting Hadley, I turned and looked up into the face of Drew Caprice.

My heart leapt like a deer over a pasture fence, suspended in midair, then crashing to the ground. Dear, sweet Drew.

Fanning my face with my hand, I said, "You right near gave me heart failure. You're early, aren't you? And how did you know where to find me?" I slid over on the pew, giving him room to sit.

"One of the gals at the nurse's desk told me. And yes, my interview was changed. In the rush of switching my flights, I didn't get a chance to call you." With a sheepish grin, he draped his arm around my shoulders, asking first about me, wanting to know about my broken arm. I glossed it over, telling him I'd had a fender bender.

His look over the top of his glasses told me he didn't believe me, but he let it pass and changed the subject. "How's Gabe?"

"Hanging in there. Seeing him every day I don't notice the changes. Maybe you can tell more since it's been a while since you've seen him."

"Too long, and I'm not proud of that fact. Would you like me to sit here with you for a while?"

"No, I'm finished. I've laid the burden at Jesus's feet. Something I'm having to do more and more."

"That's all you can do. Can I peek in and see Gabe then?"

"Nothing I'd like more."

The smell of fresh-brewed coffee met us when Drew and I got home. Brooke turned from wiping down the kitchen counters. In the air, the scent of lemon Pledge lingered.

"Goodness, Brooke. I didn't mean for you to spiff up the house. Drew here told me you'd met. What he neglected to tell you is he's family. He knows I'm a wreck at keeping house."

Brooke smiled. "It's my mess, too. Besides, Drew's not my family."

Drew held up his hands. "I come in peace. Mitzi's right—no need to clean up for me, but I sure would appreciate a cup of coffee."

Brooke pulled out three mugs and brought them steaming to the breakfast table. Small talk. The weather. How much warmer it was in Tulsa than Boston.

Resting my broken arm on the oak surface felt divine. "Your folks, Drew. How are they?"

Turning sideways to stretch legs that went on forever, he said, "You know Dad. Work and golf. Still miffed I went into medicine."

"My lands, you'd think he'd be over that by now."

"Yeah. Whatever." He turned to Brooke. "The coffee's great. So tell me, has Mitzi told you about her illustrious life?"

"Some, but I have a feeling there's a lot I haven't heard. Like where you and your family fit in."

"Why, that's the best part. What do you say I cook dinner for the two of you, then afterward Mitzi can tell us both."

Brooke's eyes widened. "You're a doctor *and* you cook? That's some combination."

I knew I was a doddering old woman with no business entertaining fanciful thoughts, but from the first minute we sat down at the table, I had a feeling something good would happen between Brooke and Drew. Not that I would prod it along, you see. In my eyes, Drew was still a wide-eyed second grader, but I did notice a touch of curiosity when he looked at Brooke.

He smiled and teased her. "I'm a doctor in name only until I finish residency and boards, but years of bachelorhood and a steady diet of fast food can turn a guy to strange behavior." To me, he raised his eyebrows. "So, whaddaya think? Salmon? Rosemary chicken?"

"You know I don't keep a well-stocked kitchen, Drew. We'll have to go to the store."

"Not you, Mitz. I've been looking at your fingers sticking out from that cast. They're swollen. You need to keep your arm elevated. Maybe Brooke will prop some pillows under it while you sit on the sofa. It wouldn't hurt to put your feet up for a while, too."

"Me, oh my, but you're bossy. I'm not a child."

"No, but I'm a pediatrician, so I get to treat you like one. Now, scoot. Where's the nearest market?"

"Reasor's, over on Fifteenth. Maybe Brooke can go with you."

Brooke shook her head. "I'm going to finish the laundry we started." She gave me a knowing look.

Ah—the linens we'd washed for Drew's bed. I didn't argue. How could I with a fussy ten-foot-tall doctor ordering me around? Instead, I handed Drew a wad of bills from my purse and told him, "I don't like salmon."

Brooke insisted on cleaning the kitchen after the melt-in-your-mouth chicken linguini Drew whipped up, so while she loaded the dishwasher, Drew made a fire in the den. He made me sit on the sofa and fussed over getting the pillows situated under my arm. Only then did he sit in Gabe's chair, his legs unfurled before him.

"Tell me, Drew, what did you think about Gabe?" I'd been curious for his opinion all afternoon, but admittedly I didn't want to hear anything grim.

"He seems much the same since I saw him last. Almost a year ago, now that I've had time to think about it. The arthritis symptoms have progressed. I couldn't help but notice the enlarged joints on his fingers and wrists. Probably quite a bit in the other joints, too. Does he complain?"

"No, more like resistance to the range-of-motion exercises, and six or eight months ago he started screaming every time they got him up in the wheelchair. It got so I couldn't stand the tortured look on his face. They put him on an anti-inflammatory, and now they only get him up once in a while."

"The activity is good for circulation, but unfortunately there's an increased risk of fracture if he's resisting." He stopped, tenting his fingers before him, his forehead creased in deep doctorly thought.

I followed the fracture trail. "Every month, one or two get whisked from the Guardian Light to the hospital with broken hips. Something I'd rather prevent." No need to add that half of them never returned.

"There's another thing."

A tumbling-rocks feeling coursed through me. I waited for him to continue.

"Gabe's lost a lot of weight since I saw him. He always had a large frame, strong muscles, but now . . . he looks shriveled, weaker somehow. Is he eating well?"

"Not really. I keep the Ensure handy, since they've told me it's loaded with protein, but it's like wrestling a grizzly to get him to drink it. The doctors mentioned putting in a feeding tube when the time came. Do you think it's time?"

"It's up to you, but most of the recent studies have proven feeding tubes don't prolong life and may instead increase the risk of infection. My gut tells me that families do it to alleviate their own guilt... their sense of helplessness."

"I know that all too well. What bothers me most is losing our connection, reading each other's thoughts, sharing our lives. Now I could be a Martian for all the recognition he shows." Saying it aloud stung. And Drew, bless him, didn't press me any further.

Brooke had slipped into the living room and tucked her feet under her on the opposite end of the sofa. A long, uncomfortable silence filled the room, each of us with our unspoken thoughts. The fire crackled, and for a fleeting moment, I imagined it was Gabe who had his legs stretched out across the room from me. Foolish woman.

Drew cleared his throat. "You know, Mitzi, Gabe trusts you, and the truth is, no one knows what synapses are still firing in his brain. At some level, he may know who you are and what's happening. I do believe it's God's grace that protects Alzheimer's victims in the late stages from knowing how much their loved ones are hurting. It would be unbearable."

A chill penetrated me in spite of the heat from the fire. Shifting my position—and my attitude—I forced a smile. "Is it just me or are you two as thirsty as I am? I think I'll make some iced tea."

Drew piped up. "Better yet. I raided your pantry and found a bottle of Chablis. I took the liberty of splashing some in the linguini, but there's enough left for the three of us. How about it, ladies? Care for a glass of wine?"

With our glasses in hand, Drew proposed a toast. "To the love of old friends and treasured memories."

I added, "To new friends and new beginnings."

After we sipped, Drew leaned over, elbows on knees. "If I recall, Mitzi, you promised Brooke you'd tell her how you first met my granddad."

"You sure y'all want to hear this? I mean, it's ancient history."

Brooke nodded. "You promised."

It didn't take an arm twist for me to slip back to those days.

[CHAPTER 26]

The week after Waggs Follett left the Carlisle, Red introduced me to Lou Caprice. He fixed T-bone steaks for us, and I have to say, I took an instant liking to Mr. Caprice. It was all ma'am *this and* pardon-me-for-asking *that as he inquired about my singing experience and what training I'd had. With slim expectations of being considered, I told him honestly about my lack of everything in the way of voice lessons and public singing. My subbing with the Follett girls aside, of course.*

"I'm looking for raw talent, someone who lets the music come from within." He sliced his steak, and when he did, I noticed the thin gold band on his left ring finger.

My face flamed when he caught me staring. Not that I'd been attracted to him as a suitor, but he was so polite, so charming, I guess I wouldn't be human if I hadn't been at least curious.

His eyes lit up as he told me about Mary Ruth, his wife. "Been married just shy of three years. She just got her first job as a nurse. I reckon you and Mary Ruth are going to get along fine."

"I'm sure we will." Toying with my food, I had the feeling that with Mr. Caprice being so open, I should level with him.

"I'm not sure if Red has told you, but I'm only staying in Tulsa a while longer. I'm planning on moving to St. Louis in the near future."

Red cleared his throat, but shoveled a forkful of fried potatoes in his mouth without protesting. Lou, in turn, raised an eyebrow and asked, "A career move or some fella?"

"Neither. More to find out about me, I guess. I don't want to give the wrong impression on how long I'll be available . . . if you even want me, that is."

"St. Louis is still a hopping place on the jazz scene. Not quite as big as Kansas City, but Tulsa's in a fine position, too. We've got the mecca for western swing right here at Cain's Ballroom, and there's an explosion of other sounds emerging, too. Ballads, singing trios, and quartets. I'm bringing some of those newer groups to the Carlisle, but Red still needs a house band to cover the weekdays and warm up the crowd on weekends. Red tells me you're quite the torch singer."

That made me laugh, and I sputtered the Coca-Cola I'd just sipped, barely catching myself before it spewed onto Lou. "Oh, mercy, I'm sorry. Red's only heard me a few times. He's prejudiced, I'm sure."

This time Red didn't stay silent. "Why don't you let Lou and the boys he's got lined up decide? Tell her what you have in mind, Lou."

"Gladly. We're targeting the service boys and their sweethearts. I'm a veteran myself, so I know how these guys think. They're settling in with steady jobs and starting families, but they're still young. A lot of 'em are hankering for a night out once in a while, maybe taking their wives dancing in a respectable joint." When Red stiffened beside him, he chuckled. "Not saying you haven't always been respectable, Red, but we'll be catering to a specific segment of the market."

Lou sounded like he knew the business and how to promote. When he asked if he and Mary Ruth could take me to lunch the next day, I accepted at once. The idea of having a new friend was nice. My shock and fear at seeing Penny with Finster had paralyzed me, and I was happy to have someone else to visit with. Although I wanted to say something to Penny, the time never seemed right. Then she started missing work and even stopped coming home to Idella's. For weeks, my insides gnawed, worrying if she was with Finster Poole, and knowing she probably was.

The new group—the Fireflies—helped take the edge off my concern. They had a more modern sound than the Folletts, but they were easygoing and got generous applause from the crowd. We hit it off from the start, and it gave me a kick singing with them. I began to think I was as infatuated with the spotlight as Penny was with being a movie star.

One evening, weary after an especially busy evening at work, I plodded up the bus steps to go home, eager to flop into my bed. Halfway down the aisle, a hand tugged my skirt.

A sharp intake of air pierced my lungs as I snapped instantly on alert.

"It's only me, you goose." Penny slumped in the seat and yanked me down beside her.

"Penny! Where have you been?"

"Never mind. I need to talk to you."

"I should hope. You've had me worried, disappearing the way you did. Are you okay?"

She smacked a wad of chewing gum. "Of course. I'm busting to tell you the good news, and I only have a minute."

"We've got all night. The twins and I have been frantic, wondering where you went."

"I'm not coming back to Idella's. As a matter of fact, I'm getting off at the next stop. Listen. Are you interested in my news or not?"

"You know I am."

"I did the screen test. I was a nervous wreck, let me tell you, but it was swell. Finn says I'm a natural, and we find out tomorrow what part I'll get."

"In a film?"

"A short this time. Finn says I have to start small, but he thinks I have star potential. Can you believe it? Anyway, I was hoping you'd tell Red I had to leave town so he won't be mad at me for not giving notice."

Red wasn't my concern. I swallowed the bile worming its way into my throat. Penny was in danger. Of what I wasn't certain, but her precious Finn was not to be trusted.

"Penny, listen to me. Finster is only going to get you into trouble."

"Finster? Oooh, I love it. What a perfect pet name for him. I can't wait to try it out."

Inside, I groaned. A slip of the tongue? A sign I should tell her about Finster Poole, what a low-down snake he was? I couldn't risk it. Then we'd both be vulnerable. I had kept my identity secret for this very reason. If Finster knew I was his daughter Maggie, he'd drag me by the hair and . . . I shuddered to think what might happen.

"Don't try it. I doubt he would be amused. I just don't think Finn is your ticket to fame. I'm not sure you should trust him."

She drew up in a huff. "How can you know that? You don't even know him."

"I . . . I've seen his type before. He's using you."

"Some friend you turned out to be. I think you're jealous because you're stuck at the Carlisle, and I'm having this once-in-a-lifetime opportunity."

"I'm not jealous. I care what happens to you. If I didn't, I wouldn't have been praying my socks off for you."

"Don't pull the church girl routine with me. I know what I'm doing. You oughtta get a grip and learn that in the real world, you have to take chances."

"Come home tonight, please. I want you to think about it."

"Nope. My mind is made up. Sorry I bothered you."

The brakes of the bus hissed. Penny looked out the window, then shoved her way past me and stormed out the door. Craning my neck, I watched her swinging her purse as she scampered down the street and turned into a small hotel with a neon vacancy sign. Red lights glowed in the second-story windows.

Icy blood coursed through my body.

Mary Ruth grew up on a farm, like I did. Nursing baby chicks and delivering litters of puppies gave her the idea of becoming a nurse. She was tiny, not the way I pictured a nurse. We took lunch at the Woolworth's counter several times a week. She talked ninety miles an hour, and whenever Lou's name came up, her eyes were like sparklers on the Fourth of July. Then off she'd go to her evening shift at the Sisters of Mercy hospital while I graced the stage at the Carlisle.

Every night was a thrill singing with the Fireflies—"Straighten Up and Fly Right," "Chattanooga Choo Choo," and "Dream a Little Dream of Me."

Red strutted around like a kid in a new pair of britches when business picked up, and he gave Lou full rein with the weekend gigs. By late October, with the leaves in a blaze of color and a crispness in the air, I'd decided to stay until I found out what had happened to Penny. Every night, I scanned the crowd, hoping she and Finn would pop in. They never did.

Sometimes I'd get off the bus at the hotel she'd gone into that night, hoping to find her. Once I'd even gone in myself and asked the clerk for her room. He eyed me in my gathered skirt and crisp white blouse and told me the guests were entitled to their privacy and to hightail it on out.

I'd been rehearsing a new number with the Fireflies. New to them, anyway, but not to me. We decided to end our set on Friday night with the new number, right before the Coney Island Boys took the stage. As usual with anything new, Red was jittery.

"Don't know what the town of Tulsey's gonna think o' them Jew boys from Brooklyn. I'm afraid Lou's gone off the deep end with this one."

"They have a hit record, Red." I was nibbling a soda cracker in the kitchen to settle my nerves before going onstage. "That ought to tell you something."

"Yeah. But New York ain't exactly the middle of America, you know."

"Quit your fretting. And by the way, Red, did I ever thank you for giving me the opportunity to sing?"

"Only sixty times a week. Now, scoot." He slapped me on the bottom and went back to pacing.

The Carlisle was packed that night as the Fireflies and I breezed through our numbers, feeding off the vibes of the crowd. As our final song approached, my palms sweated, and my underarm deodorant shut down. Still, I swayed and smiled, and with an outstretched arm, invited the crowd's enthusiasm.

The lights dimmed, and when I nodded to Denny, our sax player, he started in soft and smooth, setting the mood. On cue, I stepped into the spotlight.

Why should I feel discouraged, why should the shadows come,
Why should my heart be lonely, and long for heaven and home.

It was Mama's song—"His Eye Is on the Sparrow."

With each line, my confidence grew, the sound coming from below my diaphragm. No clinking glasses in the audience. No murmured chatter. As I sang the chorus, smiling faces nodded their approval, and although tears filled my eyes, my voice carried on.

As I sang the second verse, a tall figure with dark hair appeared at the back of the room, his eyes meeting mine. The distance between us kept me from reading his expression, but I no longer looked at the crowd—only him. His dark eyebrows lifted when I went into the chorus, sending tiny spiders of excitement shimmying down my spine.

At the last note, the stage lights went black. Thundering applause pulsed the air as shouts of "Encore!" echoed. Denny counted, "One, two, and three," and we gave the audience their request.

I sing because I'm happy,
I sing because I'm free,
For his eye is on the sparrow,
And I know he watches me.

When the house lights came up, I did my usual bow and scanned the crowd for the tall stranger. In the swarm of guests, he'd vanished.

[CHAPTER 27]

Brooke

Mitzi's eyes glassed over as she spoke, mesmerizing Drew and me as she must've done with the crowd at the Carlisle.

Drew leaned back, his long fingers stroking Cosmo, who'd been curled on his lap the entire time Mitzi was talking. "I bet you were something, Mitzi. Don't keep us in suspense. Who was the tall, dark stranger?"

Mitzi threw up her hands. "As if you didn't know! How many times have you heard the story, Drew Caprice?"

"Not enough, that's a fact. So ol' Gabe's always been a charmer."

"Right from the start. Not that he was perfect, mind you..." A faraway look came into her eyes, and I thought she might continue.

When she didn't, I glanced at Drew, his eyes shining, intent on me. The sensation that we'd vicariously stepped into the smoke-filled haze of Mitzi's world at the Carlisle Club hovered between us. The air felt charged with mystery, a tune with no name, but pulsing, calling out to me. A tingle started at the base of my spine, sparking its way through me. I looked away, crossing my arms, my hands on my shoulders as if I could hold the feeling in... or shut the world out.

"Are you cold?" Mitzi's soft voice penetrated the silence. "The fire has gone plumb to ashes while I carried on. Maybe Drew would throw another log on."

I shook my head, willing the tension in my limbs to relax. "I'm all right... ready to call it a night. Do I need to drop you off to see Gabe in the morning?"

We discussed Drew's schedule. No appointment until ten, so he volunteered to chauffeur Mitzi and visit Gabe again.

As I climbed the stairs, Drew's voice called out, "Nice to meet you, Brooke."

I turned. "You, too."

On jellied legs I fled into my room, shoving away the thoughts gathering in my head.

[CHAPTER 28]

Mitzi

When Drew and I arrived at the Guardian Light the next morning, a sleek white hearse filled the portico in front of the building. My heart two-stepped in my chest. "Mercy, I hope it's not Lily they've come to fetch."

"Lily?"

"Hadley's wife. Sweetest couple. She's suffering with the flu everyone's worried about."

"I'll go in with you, say hey to Gabe."

"I'll be okay. You run on...Don't want to be late for your appointment." Brave words coming from someone who felt the foundation rumbling underfoot. The hearse stood like a great white whale between me and the entry. When had they started making them white? Less ominous than black? Not hardly, to my way of thinking.

My steps were leaden as I walked into the care center. Two men in somber black suits wheeled a gurney from the room at the far end of the hall. Not Lily's room. Heaving a sigh of relief, I pushed open Gabe's door, suddenly frantic to see him.

His breaths came without effort as he lay on his side, still bathed in sleep. A silver Kewpie curl rested on his forehead. I brushed the strand away and stood beside the bed watching him sleep, wondering what dreams he had. An ache crept into my throat.

My legs throbbed from standing so long, drinking in the rhythm of Gabe's slumber, being thankful no fever racked his body or flushed his cheeks. When the aide brought in his tray, I coaxed Gabe to eat, then we did his morning exercises. Only then did I venture out for a cup of coffee. Hadley nursed a cup of his own at a small table in the nutrition center, where family members often sat to gather their wits. He looked half-expired himself.

"How's Lily?" I shook two sugar packets into my cup and sat opposite him.

"Better this morning. Fever is down, but 'twas a rough night. Her lungs are still full of crud. She plumb near beat herself to death coughing and carrying on. Our kids are coming in from Oklahoma City later on."

"Maybe they can help out and let you get some rest."

"You know how that goes. They got their own problems. Good boys, both of 'em, but they have families and jobs to tend to."

No, I didn't know, since the closest thing to kids for Gabe and me was Henry, our godson, and Drew. But I understood what he meant.

Hadley pushed himself up from the table and raised his eyebrows. "Gabe doing okay?"

I nodded. No need to mention he seemed his normal healthy self. Whatever that was.

Hadley refilled his cup and lifted it to me. "Think I'll mosey on back and see what Lily's doing. Take care."

"You, too."

Another resident left this earth later in the afternoon. A gentleman who'd been there longer than Gabe. I popped the top on a can of Ensure and wheedled Gabe into taking four swallows. Maybe the protein would give him strength if the flu came his way. I shuddered at the thought.

Drew came breezing in at five o'clock, all smiles and kidding with Gabe. "There's a distinct possibility I'll be moving this way. You know, I'll be pestering the daylights out of you two. And don't you worry, I'll be keeping an eye on Mitzi. Can't have her misbehaving."

Gabe turned his head and looked out the window.

Drew pulled up a chair and asked about my day, whether Gabe had eaten well—small talk. It crossed my mind that Drew rarely talked about himself. Here I'd been entertaining thoughts of him and Brooke together without considering whether he was attached to someone in Boston. He squirmed when I brought it up.

"You might as well know. I was engaged to a girl whose dad is a top heart surgeon in Boston. Melody and her family have been pressuring me to switch to cardiology so I can join her dad's practice."

"Back up. You said you *were* engaged, past tense. Don't tell me you got cold feet."

"I wish that was it, but no. My heart's been set on peds the whole time I've been in med school. I guess it started when I spent those two years traveling the country and saw the kids in Appalachia. The poverty and sickness those people suffer did something to me."

"And your dream of practicing pediatrics doesn't sit well with your fiancée?"

"Not by a mile. After two years of trying to convince her, I had to make a decision. I've never been very good at doing what others expected of me. I knew I'd be miserable, since I'd been called to do something else."

"So you broke off your engagement?"

"More or less. Melody's dream is of a house on Cape Cod and playing the socialite wife of a heart surgeon. I thought if I left Boston, she might reconsider, so I decided to come to Tulsa and see what happens."

"Well, shoot, I thought it was because you wanted to spend time with us old fogies."

He eased back into the chair and chuckled. "That's just one of the perks. I'm going to look at apartments while I'm here, and don't forget, we've got a date to go to the Jazz Depot."

"I didn't forget. Matter of fact, tomorrow works for me, if you don't have interviews."

"I'm meeting with a faculty panel in the morning. Should be free by two o'clock. Want me to pick you up?"

"Best offer I've had all week."

[CHAPTER 29]

Brooke

The next morning I was still rattled. I couldn't get Drew out of my head, and then the minute I stepped through the double doors of CH&B, Jenna glared at me. "I thought we were friends." She cocked her head, her mouth turned up in a smug grin.

Unsure what she meant, I shrugged. "Well, yes. I think we are." Not bosom buddies, but we got along.

"Friends usually confide in each other about certain things." Her eyes narrowed. "Like broken engagements."

I shifted from one foot to the other. "I'm sorry, Jenna, I should've told you. I've been a little stressed."

"Well, I'd be freaked out too if my fiancé dumped me. Not that I have one, but still..."

He dumped *me*?

Jenna's words buzzed in my head as I headed to my office. She'd heard from a girl in accounting whose sister had run into Lance at the diabetes gala on Saturday night. He'd gone stag and had quite a time it seemed. Long story short—the accountant's sister ended up going out with him after the event, and he told her he was trying to recover from a broken heart. One thing led to another and he told her his fiancée was cheating on him, so he'd had no choice but to call off the engagement.

Bile rose in my throat that he was so brazen, but then I laughed. Why was I surprised? He told me I'd be sorry. How apropos. And maddening, because it bothered me. I swung my leg back and kicked my desk just as Mr. Harrington spoke from my doorway.

"Having a bad day I see." It was an observation, not a question.

"It's nothing. Fixing to start to work. Did you have something for me?"

He handed me a stack of files. "I have to say, Brooke, you've taken a cavalier attitude with your work of late. You'll see that some of these files are repeats from last week." He jammed his finger against the folders I hugged to my chest. "You know we can't afford to be less than 100 percent accurate. Your neck is on the line if I lose a court case or upset a client due to your mistakes."

"Yes, sir. I'll try to be more careful."

"Not careful. Meticulous. You got that?"

He swiveled on his custom-made wingtips and disappeared.

My face flared, and rather than kick the desk again, I dug into my work, trying not to think of the crummy job I'd done and what other surprises Lance might throw at me. When another interoffice memo popped up on my computer screen about the Attorneys Association Christmas party the next day, I groaned. I'd forgotten to get my black silk dress when I'd gone to my apartment to collect the mail. I'd have to pop over there and pick it up. But at least it would be an excuse not to have another cozy evening with Drew scrambling my thoughts.

When I arrived at Mitzi's house, I was feeling an odd mixture of anticipation and dread. The attraction to Drew had been imagined on my part, I was sure, since I'd been such a wreck lately. So needy. Trusting my emotions was like trusting a train to stop on the tracks when you jumped in front of it.

The house was empty except for Cosmo, who gave me one whiff, then went off to stand by his food dish. An idea formed. Impulsive. Risky. I sprinkled the kibble into Cosmo's bowl.

"What do you think about going back to our apartment for a few days?"

Cosmo arched his back, which could've meant anything.

I packed a few things and put them and Cosmo into the Mustang. Wrote a quick note to Mitzi and propped it against the sugar bowl. She and Drew could spend time together without me interfering. And I could use the solitude to sort out my own life.

An uneasy thought crept in. What if Lance showed up? I wished I'd taken Mitzi's advice and gotten some pepper spray, but I hadn't. One thought consoled me: once I was inside the apartment, I didn't have to answer the door. Feeling braver, I backed out of the drive and refused to think of the what-ifs.

When I set Cosmo's carrier in the entry hall and opened the hatch, he hissed and snarled, arching his back when I tried to coax him out. Great. Not a happy cat.

The apartment had a stale, neglected feel. Chilly. The fridge reeked when I opened it—sour milk, a plastic container full of green mold, a deflated orange with a dry, shriveled rind. I went to work cleaning it, moving next to the cobwebs and dust in the dining room. My glass-top tables, which I had thought were so chic and defined me as an up-and-coming future wife of a prominent attorney, had a dull coating that begged for Windex.

When every surface shone and berry-scented cleaner filled the air, I flopped on the smooth leather sofa and called for Cosmo. Either he wasn't a fan of Windex or he was hiding. After catching my breath, I got up to look for him. He wasn't under the sofa or in the closet. Not under the bed. While on all fours looking under the bed, I saw the sequined teal dress I'd kicked in the corner. Still crumpled in the box as I'd left it. Strangely enough, I felt no remorse for not returning it to Lance or the shop where he'd bought it.

Another realization crept over me. The apartment felt foreign, like a pair of high heels that hit my arch wrong and threw me off balance. The rent did, in fact, throw my checkbook off balance every month. I remembered the brick house I'd been in before Lance convinced me to move downtown. The house, built nearly a century ago, had been split into four apartments, two up and two down. The faucets leaked and the windows rattled, but it had oak floors that shone with a patina of having survived many dwellers before me. Its wide door moldings and plaster crown along the ceilings suited the place with their dents and scars. While living there, I'd felt settled and content. Not in an ever-present state of confusion.

Cosmo had still not appeared, so I went back into the living room and checked his carrier. He lay curled on his pillow, holding something between his paws. Kneeling down, I reached in and stroked his fur, carefully extricating the object he held. I leaned back on my haunches and caught myself from falling as laughter bubbled up inside me.

The treasure Cosmo hoarded was one of Gabe Steiner's pipes, no doubt stolen during some late-night prowl through Mitzi's house. I reached farther in, patting around the edges, and came up with one of Mitzi's satin bedroom slippers.

Cosmo was a thief! When had he done this? Weirder still, why had he done it? It was ridiculous to think he felt some kinship to the house by Swan Lake, but then, I loved it there, too, with Mitzi and her memories.

A picture of Cosmo curled on Drew's lap while the soft, gargantuan hands of the doctor stroked him flashed before me. Cosmo—the connoisseur of the good life.

Scooting on my bottom across the terrazzo floor, I leaned against the kitchen wall and held out my arms. Cosmo leapt into my lap, batted at the pipe, then stretched his paws in the air. I ran my fingers along the fine silver fur of his tummy until he purred like a truck engine.

The irony washed over me. Cosmo purring. Me cross-legged on the cold floor a half a dozen feet from an expensive leather sofa. I'm not sure when they started, but I noticed the burning in my eyes first, then a single tear rolled down my check. And another. Wet pearls falling on Cosmo, running in tiny rivers off his midsection. He righted himself and took off, leaving me empty-armed and aching.

More tears came, cries from corners of my heart that I'd long ago walled off. I didn't bother trying to hold them back. Guttural sounds filled my ears, my eyes a virtual spring of pent-up emotion. A minute, an hour, an eternity passed, as my chest heaved for air. And as time stood still, newness took hold. Ideas poured in and raced through me, giving me a sense of lightness. Of freedom. I wiped the wet from my face with the sleeve of my sweatshirt and rose to take charge. Right or wrong, it was time to move on.

After a restless night, I rose early, showered, and snapped digital pictures of everything in my apartment. Then, with great care, I donned my little black dress for the party. I piled my hair on top of my head, letting a few strands escape in a provocative way, took extra care with my makeup, and at the last minute snagged the baguette diamond bracelet Lance had given me for my birthday. Why not? It suited the dress, and I had nothing to be ashamed of.

The party wasn't until eleven, but I arrived at Cooke, Harrington, and Baumgartner at seven fifteen, brewed a double espresso in the machine, then slipped into my office.

Ignoring Mr. Harrington's folders perched on my credenza, I composed a letter on the computer to my apartment management company. Thirty days' notice. That should be enough time to find another place.

Next, I loaded the digital pictures of my chic modern furniture and lamps, along with the artwork Lance had helped me choose at the art fair on Cherry Street. I set up an account on Craigslist and posted them all at ridiculously low prices, leaving my cell phone as the contact number. I considered putting my various *I'm-so-sorry-I-hurt-you* jewelry gifts on the list, but then I decided I might do better by taking them to one of the upscale shops in Brookside. My skin danced with anticipation at how much the baguette bracelet was worth. Wicked.

By the time Mr. Harrington stuck his head in my office, I was happily working on the breach of contract suit our client Mr. Neville was bringing against one of his electronic supply vendors.

"Well, Brooke, I guess you're taking our chat from yesterday seriously."

"Yes, sir." I reached into my desk drawer and pulled out the gift I'd bought for my boss. "Merry Christmas."

"You didn't have to do that, but thank you." He removed the bow and the wrapping and held up the pecan millionaires, an appreciative look on his face.

"You're welcome. I hope you don't mind, but I'd better get busy if I'm going to finish this brief before the party."

"Right. See you there."

I'd made appointments with three people interested in my Craigslist ads by the time the party was due to start. Although Cosmo had voiced his sly opinion on where we should be living, I decided to wait a couple of days before going back to Mitzi's. It would save on going back and forth showing potential buyers my stuff. Hopefully, at the prices I'd put on everything, it would be gone soon. Two of the callers had expressed interest in taking a look at everything I had to offer. *Yes!*

The champagne was flowing freely when Jenna and I arrived with two other girls from the office. I made a point of going with the group to try and squash my reputation for being standoffish, thanks to Lance. We filled our plates with hors d'oeuvres and were seated at one of the scattered tables, chatting about the holidays, when Lisa from accounting joined us.

"Sorry to hear about your breakup with Lance, Brooke." She wedged a chair in next to Jenna and leaned over, her breasts all but spilling out of the glittery spandex dress she wore.

Shrugging, I said, "Life happens."

She seemed intent on zeroing in on me. "Nice bracelet. Was it a gift from your new boyfriend? Come on, tell us who it is." Her full red lips drew into a pouty Cupid pose.

Lifting my arm so the light caught on the diamonds, I sucked in air and returned her pouty look. "Actually, it was a birthday gift. From Lance. It's nice, huh? I will hand him that; he has great taste in jewelry."

"You didn't answer the question. Who's the new guy? C'mon, you can tell us." Lisa tapped her rhinestone-studded acrylic nails on the table, seemingly impatient with me.

"No boyfriends. No fiancé."

"Not according to Lance." Lisa elongated his name so that it ended with a hiss.

"That's interesting. The Lance I know has a wee problem separating truth from fiction. This, apparently, is one of his fantasies." I drained my ginger ale and pushed away from the table. "Refills, anyone?"

Jenna shook her head. "Not for me. I'm going to drift over to those guys who just came in. New recruits from Buchwald and Sons. I hear a couple of them are unattached." She teetered away in her four-inch heels, her ample hips swaying.

Poor Jenna. She really wanted a boyfriend, but her approach was all wrong. I wished I could tell her to tone it down a bit, be herself. Like I was such an expert. On the way to the buffet, I nodded at Mr. Harrington, who stood laughing with a couple of well-heeled clients. I hated these gatherings. Fake smiles. Pretentious showing off.

Standing in line at the drink bar, I calculated how long I would have to stay at the party to be polite. An hour or so, I guessed, until the champagne and eggnog had stupefied the guests. I was anxious to pick up some boxes and start packing the things from my apartment I wanted to keep.

A voice near my ear whispered, "Hello, gorgeous."

Inside, I went rigid, but I turned around with a smile on my face. "Hello, Lance. We were just talking about you."

"Really? I hope it was good." He moved into my personal space, voice low. "Let's sneak away from the crowd and you can tell me all about it and what you've been doing lately." He sounded odd, sort of breathy, but then alcohol did have a certain effect on him. Charming. Teasing. Unpredictable.

"I'd rather not, and anyway there's not much to tell. Just work and staying busy." A cluster of people behind me kept me from backing up any further.

"I hear you're quite the vixen." A waxy smile hardened his face as he gripped my elbow and led me to a less-congested area.

My skin felt dirty from his touch, and as I shrank away from him, he whispered, "Smile, Brooke. We wouldn't want anyone to get the wrong idea."

Whirling around, I opened my eyes wide. "About what? That you—"

His fingers touched my lips, stopping the barrage I was ready to unleash on him. "Maybe you should hear what I have to say before you get too indignant."

"Whatever."

"I ran into someone you know. An intimate someone."

Wheels spun in my head as I tried to figure out what he meant. I waited.

"Your old boyfriend congratulated me on our engagement at the diabetes gala last weekend. Seems he's a brittle diabetic and loaded to boot. He's a heavy supporter of the charity, and he was interested in contributing to my campaign. Said you were one sweet romp in the sack. Ring any bells?" His head tilted, mocking.

"You are completely delusional. I think you've had a few too many drinks. As usual. Excuse me." I turned on my heels and took two steps before he clamped my elbow in an iron grip.

"Maybe there've been so many, you're having trouble remembering. Try this on for size: Chad Lamb."

The air swooshed from my lungs in one colossal gust as my hand flew to my mouth. My boyfriend from college.

"So it comes back, huh? All your puritan ways. Ha! Come to find out you're nothing but a liar." His blue eyes had turned to ice. "I hate being made a fool. You will pay, sweetheart. Trust me."

He spun around and stalked off.

Glasses clinked. Sparkles of laughter popped throughout the room like miniature Roman candles going off. And from invisible surround sound speakers, holiday voices crooned merrily, "Have a holly, jolly Christmas."

[CHAPTER 30]

Mitzi

Waiting for Drew to pick me up at the Guardian Light on Christmas Eve, I chatted aimlessly to Gabe. "Brooke finally called and she's coming back to the house. I can't help but think she was avoiding Drew, and of course, he feels responsible for scaring her off. Could be she's afraid to have feelings for someone so soon after that mess with her fiancé."

Pacing the room, I picked lint from my sweater sleeve, straightened the aftershave and Fixodent on the shelf over the vanity sink, and smoothed the covers on Gabe's bed.

"Can't get my hopes up too much, I guess, but I have a feeling in my bones. Brooke and Drew are meant for each other."

Gabe stirred, his eyes roaming the room. I moved to the head of his bed. "I know, you think I'm meddling."

Leaning over, I kissed the hollow of his cheek. He closed his eyes and, within minutes, relaxed into a deep sleep. An ache in the back of my neck had been pestering me all afternoon, so I slipped out and went to the family break room for a glass of juice to take a couple of Tylenol.

I found Hadley Davis nursing a cup of coffee. "Looks like you could use some Christmas cheer. What say you go with Brooke and Drew and me to Mt. Olivet tonight?"

"Mighty kind of you to ask, but Lily's fever's gone back up, and I aim to stay here with her. Say a prayer for us if you would." He turned his head and coughed into a wizened black fist.

"Have you had that rattle checked by a doctor?"

"Yes'm. Touch of bronchitis is all it is. Doc Sample put me on some pills big enough to choke a horse. Says it'll ward off the flu should I be gettin' what's ailing Lily. No never mind to me since she ain't long for this earth, and I'd be happy to be trailing after her into them pearly gates."

"Hadley Davis, I won't tolerate your talking like that. I'm sorry about Lily, though. Anything I can do?"

He shook his head. "She probably won't make the night. Can't hardly stand the thought of her going on Christmas."

I patted his hand. "There's never a good time, is there?"

We sat in silence, reality pressing in on us. Hadley looked up, his eyes crinkled. "I had this vision last night. I was standing on the shore watching Lily sail off. On the horizon, all I could see was a boiling tempest. I reached out to her, wanting her to turn and take my hand, but she had her face full into the wind. As she got farther away, the tempest broke up, split smack down the center, and there on the other side, arms reached out, welcoming her home." He wiped a tear from his cheek. "That's when I knew my Lily was packed and ready to go. All I got to do is turn her loose—something the Almighty and I are still wrestling on."

"I'll be praying."

Drew stuck his head in the doorway with a "Hey, here you are."

"Hey yourself. You remember me talking about Hadley Davis—well, here he is."

"Nice to meet you." Drew offered his hand.

"Same to you. Y'all have a good time at the service. And when you see Brooke, tell her merry Christmas."

~

Brooke's Mustang was in the drive when we got home. A sporty black car angled in behind it, blocking Drew from turning into the drive. As we got closer, I could see a nice-looking young man bent over, talking to Brooke in her car. A premonition skated along my bones. Something wasn't right, and from the way Drew gripped the steering wheel, I knew he felt it, too.

He asked, "Do you know who's talking to Brooke?"

"I have an idea. Could be trouble, if it's who I think it is. Guess we won't know if we don't get out."

Together, Drew and I approached the man who was talking to Brooke through her half-rolled-down window. Drew spoke first. "Hi there. Something I can help you with, sir?"

A tousled blond head jerked up, a smirk on the face of the young man. "Who the devil are you?"

Before Drew answered, Brooke stepped out of the Mustang. "Mitzi, Drew, this is Lance Evans, an acquaintance of mine."

Lance's sneer dissolved into a casual grin. "Pleased to meet you. I came to ask Brooke some questions. Personal, if you don't mind."

Brooke looked from me to Drew, then spoke to Lance. "This isn't a good time. I'm leaving soon with my friends." She reached into the backseat, took out the cat carrier, and started up the steps to the back door, but Lance grabbed her by the elbow and spun her around. I'm ashamed to say I held my breath so I could hear what he said.

"Hey, sweetheart. I was hoping we could, you know, talk about some things." He looked at Cosmo's carrier. "What's with bringing the cat over here? Did he get in the way of your emptying your apartment? What's going on, Brooke?"

"I'm making some changes, Lance. And I don't owe you any explanation."

Lance rocked back on his heels, then tensed—a tiger ready to spring. Drew stepped into the space between them, but Lance was quicker and leaned out, his face splotched crimson. "Your friends must be quite the influence. Any chance they're responsible for these so-called changes?"

The way he said *friends* made me indignant, but Brooke didn't budge. "Lance, please. There's no point in making a scene."

"You." Lance sneered and pointed a finger at Drew. "I bet you're the reason behind this. Looks like my suspicions about Brooke finding someone else were right."

Drew stood rock solid. "Mr. Evans, I'm not sure what's going on here, but it does appear Brooke doesn't wish to talk right now. Maybe you should leave before someone says something they regret."

Lance relaxed, changing gears it seemed. "Let's let Brooke decide. What do you say, sweetheart?" When she didn't answer, he nodded at me. "Is this your home? I don't believe I've had the pleasure of meeting you."

The ache in my neck burned into my shoulders. "I suppose not. Brooke is right, though. We're fixin' to go to the Christmas Eve service at my church. Would you like to come along?"

I stole a look at Brooke, her face a mass of horror. Drew now stood beside her, relaxed but ready to intervene again, if necessary.

Lance gave me a dismissive sniff. "Better take a rain check on that." He pivoted, and in one smooth motion went to Brooke, cupped her chin in his hand, and gave her a brief kiss. "Don't worry, sugar; I can see you're not thinking clearly right now. We'll talk later. I promise."

He quickstepped over to the sports car, revved the engine, and roared off, coming within inches of skimming Drew's rental.

In the dusk around us, Christmas lights twinkled, a hush settling on the neighborhood. I couldn't shake the feeling that Lance was a man who kept his promises.

~

Drew joined me in communion at the Christmas Eve service, but Brooke seemed deep in thought and didn't go with us to the altar. When I returned to my seat, she was blotting the corner of her eye with a tissue. Her encounter with Lance had obviously opened the wounds I'd hoped were healing. His constraint with us present had been obvious, but the underlying tension had come through in spades. In the quiet of the old church with its glowing stained glass, I bowed my head and prayed for Brooke, for Hadley, and for Lily. Then I tacked on a prayer of thanksgiving for my blessed friend, Drew Caprice. And as ever, of course . . . for Gabe.

The vision of the Lord's table in heaven opened to me. How long, Lord? For Gabe? For Lily? A tiny cherub choir sang *pa-rum-pum-pum-pum*, and in the stillness around me, peace descended.

We rode home in silence to a meal Drew had whipped up earlier in the day and required only a few moments to get onto the table. We dined on chicken salad croissants, homemade tomato soup, and wide slices of French silk pie.

"Your chocolate pie was divine." Brooke sipped the coffee she'd made and brought to us in the living room, trying hard, it seemed, not to let the afternoon's incident spoil our evening. "You'll have to give us your recipe."

Drew's ears reddened. "Okay, I'm so busted. I found a bakery over on Cherry Street. Merritt's, I think it's called. I went in for the croissants and couldn't resist buying the last pie in the showcase. I'm glad you ladies approved, though." He added another log to the fire and stoked the ashes. As new flames leapt from the grate, my face flushed with its warmth.

Shifting my position to ease the ache across my shoulders, I didn't hear what Brooke said. "Sorry. You were saying?"

"You promised Drew and me you'd tell us about your romance with Gabe—a tall, dark stranger I think you called him."

"You sure you wouldn't rather watch something on TV?"

"Absolutely not." Drew winked at Brooke. Or maybe it was me he winked at, and my brain mixed the signals. Perhaps talking would help me relax and fight off the weariness descending on my body.

[CHAPTER 31]

While the Fireflies cleared the stage to make room for the Coney Island Boys, I dashed into the dressing room and changed into my pinafore and straight skirt, hoping to catch a glimpse of the man whose look had intrigued me. Being part of the house band didn't change the fact that Red still needed me to wait tables. Besides, the tips I squirreled away might come in handy when I left to find Mama's kinfolk.

I herded the two new girls Red Carlisle had hired and began showing them the ropes. Swerving between tables, I took a few orders myself for the overflow crowd. Lou Caprice's strategy was paying off, and every night we had more new customers at the club. The place buzzed with talk about the new group—those damn Yankees, according to Red—but I scarcely had time to pay attention to the stage.

When the lights dimmed and the band came on, a catch came in my throat. The tallest of the three brothers was the man whose eyes I'd met. He had a rich baritone voice that carried the melody of their hit song, "Milk Glass Moon." It had a swinging upbeat sound and harmony so sweet you could taste it. The crowd went wild, whistling and tapping along with the music. The next song, a ballad, had a haunting melody, with echoes that had shivers dancing on my arms. All I wanted to do was stand back and watch, but I heard a bit of a ruckus coming from table six.

One of the new girls had gotten an order wrong. After smoothing things over, I went to the kitchen to clear up the misunderstanding. Lou stood, arms crossed, a smile lighting up his face. "So whaddaya think of the new group?"

"Nice. You sure know how to pick 'em, Lou."

He winked and gave a thumbs-up as I scurried back out with the correct order.

By the fifth or sixth song, the crowd was fully engaged in the show, so I stood at the back to catch my breath and drink in the music. This wasn't the sound of my mama's jazz, but crooning, full of fun and life. A beckoning hand came from two tables over. I sighed and went over to them.

"Whatcha say, darlin', think you could get me and my friends another round?" He reached out and circled his arm around my waist, eyeing me up and down. A frown creased his brow when he tilted his head and looked me in the eye.

With a wink, he said, "And if you're not busy later, maybe you can come and put on another one of them shows for me and my friends at my gentlemen's club."

The hairs on the back of my neck bristled. This was no gentleman. It was my papa, Finster Poole.

Panic rose in my chest, cutting off the air I struggled to inhale. Had he recognized me, as I had him? His putrid cigar fumes wafted toward me. Swallowing my fear, I regained my composure and gave a tinkling laugh. "My boss frowns on fraternizing with the customers, but I'd be glad to refresh your drinks." Sidestepping his embrace, I asked for their orders and fled to the kitchen.

Applause rippled through the room as the group onstage finished another number, but all I could think of was getting away. Red met me in the kitchen doorway, a scowl on his face.

"Those guys back in the corner bothering you?"

"Yes . . . no . . . you know how it is. They're adding their own booze to our sodas, forgetting all the manners their mamas taught them. Nothing I

can't handle." Cool on the outside, but inside I shook like I'd come down with the St. Vitus dance.

Finster smirked when I brought the tray of glasses. I intentionally passed them out from the side of the table opposite him. The men all eyed me, guffawing like they'd heard a funny joke, and I cringed to think it was something Finster had said about me.

Get hold of yourself, girl. There's no way Finster Poole knows who you are.

But what if he did? I slid away as quickly as I could, my heart wrenched, wondering if somehow he did know.

Collecting my wits, I assigned one of the new girls to the table, then told Red I had a headache and wanted to go home. It wasn't a lie. My head throbbed, the pulse in my ears pounding so hard I thought I might explode.

He gave me a questioning look, then said, "Go on. Get some rest. Can't have my star performer feeling punk tomorrow night."

"I'll be fine by then." I slipped out the back, letting the cold air fill my lungs as I stumbled into the night toward the bus stop.

In my dreams, faceless men lured me into a sleazy hotel room, where Finster Poole met me in a satin smoking jacket. A scantily clad Penny Vaughn dangled from his arm like a charm on a bracelet. Her eyes, dull and vacant, looked through me as if I weren't there, her right cheekbone bearing the remnants of a bruise. Watching her, I shrank back, trying not to think about how she'd gotten the bruise. Finster held out his free hand, the snarl on his face changing to a smile that could coax the scales off a rattlesnake. The more I backed up, the closer his fingers came, clawlike as they grazed my neck, catching on the fabric of the chiffon dress I'd worn onstage. The dress was out of place. It wasn't the one I'd been wearing when the dream began. Then in a flash, the filmy fabric slid down my shoulder, leaving me exposed. He didn't speak, but his look said enough. And in my dream, my cries caught in my throat.

When I sat up in the bed at Idella's boarding house, my flannel gown drenched in sweat, I could still smell the alcohol and tobacco on Finster's breath as if he were in the room. My pulse accelerated until I thought my heart would crash into my ribcage. Through the threadbare curtain at my window, the first pink light of dawn crept into the room.

Penny. What has he done to you?

The scowl he'd given me the night before brought fresh fear. Did he know who I was? Leaving on the next bus to St. Louis would be the smart thing to do. I was fairly certain I could look for Mama's kin and not cross paths with Papa. But if I left, I might never learn what happened to Penny. What if she'd fallen into something horrendous and needed me? No, leaving was not an option. I would simply have to stay alert and out of Finster Poole's path. How had Mama ever loved him?

An ache rose into my throat. Mama had left her parents—sweet, caring folks, if I was to believe the letter they'd sent her—to marry Finster Poole. Had she been head over heels in love and defied them? Or had he promised her the moon before he'd turned into a weasel? He'd wooed Penny with a slick come-on. Had he done the same with Mama?

Come home, *my grandmother had written. Maybe I should do the same. Go back to Jess Barlow's farm.* Don't come crying to me when you find out the world ain't the rosy place you thought it would be. *No, I couldn't go home. Jess would be the last person to roll out the welcome mat.*

Which left me with Finster and Penny. If Finster came back to the Carlisle, I could follow him and maybe find Penny. Or a pack of trouble. As a last resort, I could tell Red who I was and ask him to protect me if things went sour. No. I couldn't tell anyone. Not if I was ever going to find out about Mama and her family. My *family.*

Lou met me outside my dressing room, a mischievous grin on his face. "Say, Mitzi, one of the boys asked me to give you this." He passed me a folded note.

Curious which boys he might be referring to and praying it wasn't some-

one from Finster's table the previous night, I waited until I changed clothes before I read the message.

> You have the voice of an angel. Can you meet me after the show tonight? I promise I don't bite. Sincerely, Gabe.

My first thought was that it was another ploy by Finster or one of his sleazy friends wanting me to give them a private show. Disgust roiled in my stomach. No thanks. Lou wouldn't do that, though. And he did have a rakish look when he'd handed off the note. Maybe one of the Coney Island Boys sent it through him. If so, why not just ask for an introduction?

I didn't have time to think about it. I ran my tongue over my teeth to get any lipstick smudges off and waited for my cue to go onstage.

Our set went even better than the night before, and at Lou and Red's insistence, we kept Mama's song as the finale. All during our performance, I kept my eyes on the crowd, searching, dreading the reappearance of Finster Poole. Later, while I waited tables, I watched. Once in the shadows across the room, I thought I saw him, but when the customer turned, it wasn't Finster at all.

The Coney Island Boys kept the audience in the palms of their hands for the second night in a row, and in between keeping my vigil for Finster, I watched the trio before me. Could the baritone with the chocolate eyes be the mysterious Gabe? The name fit, but who was I kidding? What would he want with a farm girl like me?

Then, as I was finishing the last of my shift duties, there he was, the one with the voice like warm molasses, leaning against the kitchen door, his hair ruffled, a boyish grin on his face. "Mitzi?"

I nodded, thinking he'd at least gone to the trouble to find out my name. "And you are?"

"Gabe Steiner. Happy to make your acquaintance." He stuck out a warm, soft hand, his long fingers enveloping my entire hand. His voice, thick with an accent that sounded foreign and inviting at the same time, sent a

warmth through me. After a few awkward attempts on both our parts to get past a shaky beginning, my tongue lost its tied-in-a-knot feeling, and we talked about the show, and wasn't it funny how stage nerves paralyzed you until the spotlight came up and the music took over.

Gabe had an easygoing way about him and reminded me of a farm pup wanting its ears scratched when he said, "Any chance you'd go out for a cup of coffee? I know it's late . . ."

Lou appeared and rescued me from having to give an answer. "See you two have met. Have you made plans? If not, I'm on my way to pick up Mary Ruth from work. Y'all wanna come along?"

I fell in love that night. Laughing, talking, enjoying Mary Ruth's cookies and cocoa. For a small-town girl who'd only had a handful of dates, I thought I'd shot the moon. Gabe was tender, yet witty, a towering, angular figure who seemed more like a boy on a first date than a singing sensation from Brooklyn. We had the love of music in common, and yet a vast chasm loomed between us filled with our differences.

Had I known what lay ahead, I might never have allowed myself to be carried away like I was.

[CHAPTER 32]

Brooke

Mitzi rested her head against the sofa, eyes closed, her cheeks flushed. Her voice, barely a whisper at times, came with sighs of remembrance, then with hardened passion, sometimes in the same breath. What had Mitzi endured? What had happened with Finster Poole? To Penny Vaughn?

A tear trickled down her soft cheeks that drooped with weariness, but what I saw there was the woman who took in strays. Like Penny. Like me. I had so many questions, but Mitzi's heart was wrung dry, her body spent from effort.

Drew was the first to speak. "What I'd give to have known you and Gabe in those days. My granddaddy, Lou, once described you as vim and vinegar, laced with a shot of peppermint schnapps."

Mitzi laughed, but when she did, a rattly cough came with it. She reached lethargically for a tissue and coughed again.

In a flash, Drew was at her side, the back of his hand against her forehead. "Mitzi, you're burning up. Why didn't you tell us you weren't feeling well?"

"I'm fine. Just getting a cold, I think. I'll take a couple of Tylenol and be good as new in the morning."

"Wait. I'm going to listen to your lungs."

Drew vaulted up the stairs, taking them two at a time, and returned with a stethoscope and a few other gadgets. He had Mitzi say *ahhh* and peered into her throat with a penlight. Took her temperature. Listened to her chest. He became the ultimate professional, with an unreadable face, while he conducted his examination.

When he'd finished, he turned to me. "Her fever is 102.4. Can you get a cool cloth and help her get ready for bed? Her chest is congested. It's not pneumonia, but it's definitely more than a cold. Probably the flu everyone's talking about. Mitzi, where do you keep the Tylenol?"

As I dashed off to get the washcloth, the Tylenol, and a glass of water, I remembered her worry over Lily Davis, who along with several others at the Guardian Light battled for their lives with a horrible, death-gripping flu. My throat was thick as I placed the cool rag on her neck and held out the pills.

After I'd helped her upstairs and into her nightgown, she turned to me. "Love is strange sometimes. Like me, I guess. Thank the Lord, he knows what he's doing even if we don't."

Another round of coughing racked her chest. I tucked her in and watched as she instantly relaxed into the pillow. She clasped my hand, weak as a baby kitten.

The sun slashed through my window the next morning. Christmas. I'd lain awake half the night listening for Mitzi, but except for an occasional cough and the two times I heard Drew pad into her room and check on her, she'd slept. Now, I rolled her haunting words over in my head. *Love is strange . . . The Lord . . . knows what he's doing . . .*

In the cushioned softness of the bed, I closed my eyes and said a silent prayer.

God, Mitzi seems to be on good terms with you. I'm not sure I even know what that means. Still, I'd consider it a personal favor if you'd protect her, make her well. Let me be the friend she needs.

An odd feeling came over me. Soothing, but elusive. While trying to pinpoint the feeling, I remembered Mom and CiCi. I was supposed to have Christmas with them. I hoped they understood my place was with Mitzi, but how could they? I'd yet to tell them about her.

The house was quiet, and after checking on Mitzi, who was still nestled in a deep sleep, I went downstairs to make coffee. The pot was half full and still warm. Drew had beat me to it, but there was no sign of him. Cosmo wove in and out of my ankles, making a throaty cluck that meant *feed me*. He followed me into the mudroom off the kitchen, where I gave him a packet of tuna kibble and checked outside for Drew's car. Gone.

Moments later, armed with bags from QuikTrip, he came breezing in. "Breakfast!"

"How did you know I was starving?" I peeked into the bags. Muffins. Cinnamon rolls. Rich, yummy smells.

"Sorry it's only pastries. I didn't know what you liked, so I got a variety. Also some orange juice. We both need the vitamin C with this flu going around."

"Do you think that's what Mitzi has?"

"No doubt. I also called one of the docs I met at the interview and told him about Mitzi." He held up a cardboard packet. "Antiviral samples. We'll get her a prescription tomorrow."

"Do the pills work?" I was touched Drew had gone out and taken control of the situation. He was much better at this than I was.

"Theoretically, yes, but the earlier they're started, the better. Which is why I want her to take one this morning. If she does have a respiratory flu, the pills should help her recover more quickly. Still, she'll need to stay in bed for a few days."

"Are we talking about the same Mitzi? She has more willpower than anyone I've ever known." I took two clean glasses from the dishwasher and poured the juice for Drew and me. I held up my glass. "Merry Christmas."

As we drank our Christmas toast, the phone rang. Drew stepped over and answered. "Yes, this is Mitzi Steiner's." He identified himself and nodded at something said on the other end.

I rinsed out our glasses and tried not to listen.

When Drew hung up, he came beside me, a grave look on his face. "That was Hadley Davis. Lily didn't make it through the night."

Pain shot through me as tears flooded my eyes. No! Not on Christmas. My heart ached for Hadley. For Mitzi.

Drew gave me space and let me cry, but an agonizing thought came. "Mitzi. We'll have to tell her."

"It's time we checked on her anyway."

She was stirring when we went upstairs to her room and didn't fuss when Drew took her temperature. Still 102. Propped up on one elbow, the other arm helpless in the cast, she let Drew give her the Tylenol and a dark blue pill from the packet.

After an extra sip of water through the straw, she flopped back on the pillow. "When this fever goes down, I have to visit Gabe."

Drew rubbed her hand gently. "Not today, I'm afraid. It'll be several days before you're well enough to go. Not only for your sake, but also so you don't give him the flu."

Tears welled in her eyes. "It's Christmas."

"Shhh. I know. I'll stay with Gabe today. Brooke can keep an eye on you." He cleared his throat. "We have something else to tell you, too."

Her eyes grew wide. "Lily."

"Yes. Hadley called. He wanted you to know she'd passed away."

Lying so still, her face void of makeup, age lines etched deep around her eyes. The pink in her cheeks was from the fever, no doubt, but the strength I'd admired so often had dissolved into a frail shadow.

She looked up and smiled. "Poor Hadley. He was afraid to let her go. Afraid not to. It must've ripped his heart out to open his hand and let her glide off into eternity."

She closed her eyes and, within minutes, had drifted back asleep.

Eternity. The mention of it had calmed Mitzi, brought a smile to her chapped lips. The feeling I'd been unable to identify earlier stirred, butterfly breezes beneath my ribcage, then almost as quickly, an icy fear gripped me. Mitzi had the same flu as Lily. *God knows what he's doing even when we don't.*

Drew interrupted my thoughts. "Sleep will be good for her. That and our prayers." He raised an eyebrow, his hands clasped before him. I bowed my head as he prayed for Mitzi and Gabe to be held in the cleft of the most high, for the loving arms of Jesus to comfort Hadley, and that our walk each day would be pleasing to God. In the stillness, a breath as soft as the down of a tiny sparrow filled the room. And before I opened my eyes, I thought I caught a glimpse of Hadley, his hand outstretched as Lily slipped through the clouds.

Drew and I tiptoed from Mitzi's room, and a few moments later, Drew appeared in the kitchen, briefcase in hand, and left for the care center.

Alone with my thoughts, I poured another cup of coffee and called Mom.

"Merry Christmas, Brooke. I'm on my way over to CiCi's. Guess you'll be along later."

"No, that's why I'm calling. I'm staying with a sick friend, a dear lady who's very ill."

"Would this be that elderly woman Lance told me about?"

I rubbed my temple with my free hand. "I don't know what Lance told you." *Why was he even talking to Mom?*

"He's concerned you've fallen for a sob story and thinks a man may be living there, too. You need to think of your reputation dear... and your future."

Irritation pricked my skin, so unlike the calm I'd felt only minutes before. Mom believed everything Lance told her, and I was relieved to have an excuse for not going. "I have gifts for y'all, but I'll get them to you later."

"Surely you could come for an hour or two. I've invited Lance to dinner."

"I'm sorry. To tell you the truth, Mom, I'm not anxious to see Lance. He's pretty volatile right now... having some issues with our broken engagement."

"I'd say you're the one with issues."

"Only because I'm afraid, Mom. Lance is unpredictable. Violent. Not just the time when you thought I antagonized him, but other times, too. Why won't you try to understand?"

My hands shook so much I could barely hold the phone. On the other end, Mom was so quiet I thought the line had gone dead.

Finally, she spoke, "So this person—"

"Mitzi. Her name is Mitzi. I should have told you about her sooner. That's my fault. And yes, she has a houseguest, someone who's been a family friend for years. There's nothing weird going on."

"How do you get yourself into these difficult situations? You should've come to me for advice about Lance—"

"Mom, I tried. You told me to work it out. I'm trying to do that now—work out my life."

"It's not just about you, Brooke. I'm sure Lance is frustrated, too. He's told me your melancholy moods worry him. I would think seeing him on neutral ground might be a good thing."

It was hopeless to argue with her. I'd been as truthful as I could without drawing pictures for her and spelling out every blow he'd inflicted, and still Lance had convinced her to believe him. The same way he'd convinced me so many times he was sorry. I changed the subject.

"How's CiCi doing?"

"Fair. Still on bed rest, which is why I'm taking the dinner to her house."

"Give her and Todd my love, okay?"

"And what do you propose I tell Lance?"

"How about the truth? I'm staying with a sick friend."

The second day of Mitzi's bout with the flu was the hardest. She coughed until her face splotched purple. Drew brought her codeine cough syrup and made chicken broth with egg noodles and a delectable mixture of herbs.

We got in touch with Hadley and found out they'd had a small family service at the funeral home. Mitzi, of course, was disappointed she couldn't go, but she had us send a bouquet to his home and a memorial check to the Guardian Light in remembrance of Lily.

I also gave CiCi a call and apologized for not coming on Christmas.

She sighed. "Mom was really upset, you know. Lance came for dinner, and he went on and on about how much you'd changed since you'd met that woman. Mom feels like she's been replaced."

"That's not it at all. Mitzi's been really sick; she's still feverish and coughing. I couldn't leave her, and besides..."

"Yeah, yeah. You don't want to be around Lance, I know. But you could have come later."

"Look, CiCi, Mom and I don't see things quite the same way right now. It would've been awkward." The truth was I hated not being with them, but until Mom quit trying to patch things up with Lance and me, I just couldn't see her.

CiCi said, "Whatever."

We left it at that, but she seemed happy when I promised to come by Saturday morning. Drew spent that day with Mitzi, and when I got back from CiCi's, he told me he'd canceled his flight to Malibu. That his folks had encouraged him to stay and see to Mitzi's well-being.

"It's a relief of sorts. My folks entertain nonstop during the holidays, and I never know exactly where I fit in."

"Your parents. What do they do?"

"Dad's an entertainment attorney. Took up where my granddad, Lou, left off. Only he has a string of Hollywood stars as clients, not like Granddad Lou, who was Gabe and Mitzi's exclusive manager."

"You must've had an interesting life."

"I suppose, but I'm afraid I'm a big disappointment to my parents, going into medicine instead of following in my dad's footsteps."

"Didn't Mitzi say Mary Ruth was a nurse? Your grandmother?"

His face brightened at the mention. "Yes. Sweet and caring right up until she died of leukemia. I guess I take more after her."

"I know you're a godsend for Mitzi."

"She's the best. And Gabe, too."

The week after Christmas, I had a short workweek. I had just started my year-end reports when my phone signaled a text message.

How about New Year's? We could make a fresh start.

I didn't have to look at the number to know who sent it. I deleted the message and three others that followed, but it left me on edge. The texting was unnerving, but not nearly as jarring as the two occasions I'd caught sight of his Lexus in my rearview mirror.

If he was trying to rattle me, it was working. I feared it was only a matter of time until I became unhinged.

We closed the office at noon on New Year's Eve. *Yes.* Three and a half days out of the office. Maybe I could relax.

Drew had gone to see Gabe when I got home, and Mitzi, still feeling weary, went upstairs to take a nap. An idea for a surprise for Mitzi had been flitting about in my head, so with her tucked away, I propped a canvas on the portable easel I'd picked up after Thanksgiving. Working from the preliminary sketch I'd done, I wished for the hundredth time I'd pursued art in college so the project I had in mind would be more professional. I didn't tell Drew what I was working on. No sense embarrassing myself if it turned out a disaster. By the time he returned, I had my art things tucked safely back in my room.

Drew put a sack of groceries on the counter. "How's Mitzi?"

"Better, I think. Still napping."

"Good. I have something I want to show you. Grab a jacket, okay?"

I followed him out and he motioned toward the back of the house. The afternoon light had faded, wrapping the neighborhood in sepia tones. When Drew took my elbow to guide me up the winding path, I tensed, engulfed by familiar prickles of warning. Shuddering, I flicked my elbow, and Drew released his gentle hold, falling a step behind me. I plunged ahead on the cut-through to Swan Lake, my face flaming at how rude my reflex must have seemed. Drew was nothing like Lance, but I still felt rattled and annoyed that Lance could control my reactions even when he wasn't present. When we emerged from between two sky-high magnolias, the lake lay before us, shadowed in a jigsaw pattern by the near leafless maple and oak trees on the other side.

As we leaned on the wrought iron fence that circled the lake, Drew spoke. "I used to come here when I was a kid. Gabe would bring a bag of Wonder bread for the ducks and swans. It's one of my best childhood memories. Sometimes, when the hectic pace of being a sleepless intern overwhelms me, I think of this place." He turned to me, his eyes as soft as the air around us.

"Me, too."

"What? You mean you knew about Swan Lake?"

"Doesn't everyone? It's my favorite place to sketch or walk off my frustration." Already the placid water, the moist evening smells enveloped me, and the tension that had crept into my neck melted.

"Shucks, I thought it was just me. I'm glad to know we share it, though."

The swans floated by as if carried by an underwater current. Ripples fanned out and faded into the glassy stillness as they waltzed a perfect duet.

Drew, thoughtful and quiet, rested his elbows between the spikes on the fence. When the swans disappeared into the feather grass at the water's edge, he turned to me.

"I've been wondering."

"About?" I lifted my eyebrows.

"You. Why you came to Mitzi's. About your fiancé."

"Former fiancé."

"Are they connected? Your staying with Mitzi and your broken engagement?"

"Have you asked Mitzi?"

He swallowed hard, a sheepish grin on his face. "Yes, I did. She told me I should talk to you."

"Not much to tell. Lance is running for political office. He's a high-energy mover and shaker. I'm not. We had some misunderstandings, and it turned out he wasn't the same guy I thought I'd fallen in love with."

Lowering his eyes away from me, he said in a low tone, "Any of this related to the scar on your cheekbone?"

My breath left me. It wasn't an accusation, only curiosity. But not something I wanted to discuss, which I quickly pointed out.

This time he did look at me. Intently. "I didn't mean to pry, but as a physician, I notice such things. Are you all right?"

I stuffed my hands in the pockets of my windbreaker. "Sometimes more than others. This week has been one of the better ones. Turnabout is fair play, though. Do you have any girlfriends or former wives you want to tell me about?"

His eyebrows shot up. "Hmmm. I see what you mean. Being in the hot seat's not near as comfortable as being the inquisitor."

"Sounds like a cop-out to me."

"You struck a nerve, that's all. Not with your question, but what you said about your former fiancé. The misunderstanding part." He shifted positions, now leaning casually against the rails, facing me. "I have... had a fiancée, too. We don't share the same vision for what we want out of life."

"Which is..."

"For now, finish a residency in peds. Then work in a region where there's a shortage of medical care—Appalachia or maybe the Navajo reservation in Arizona."

"Hmmm. I pictured you on staff at a successful practice in a big city."

"You and a lot of other people. I guess I don't fit the mold other people want to put me in. It's not that I like swimming upstream... or maybe I do, and I haven't figured out how to conform to the world's standards. Somehow I think God shows us his desires and then equips us to carry them out."

"It must be nice to have it all figured out." A damp breeze blew from the water, bringing a chill that made me wish I'd worn a heavier jacket.

Drew felt it, too, rubbing his hands to warm them. "Let's walk around the lake before it gets too dark."

I turned one direction at the same time he turned the other, so we almost collided. We were so close I got a whiff of his pine-scented aftershave. We did a little dance to get out of each other's way, but when we headed west together, Drew's arm was firmly around my shoulders, drawing me into his warmth.

Flutters came in my stomach. How had that happened? His closeness felt natural and pleasant, but at the same time, terrifying.

Drew carried on as if nothing had happened. "So, back to you. You work as a paralegal, right? Any plans for law school?"

"No, although I started out in pre-law. I was antsy to get on with life, so after college, I took the one-year completion course at Tulsa University and worked for a few years with Legal Aid. Not the way to get rich quick."

"Being rich is overrated. I bet you met lots of interesting people, though, huh?"

Images came to mind. Young couples who were trying to adopt. An elderly woman whose children had hijacked her estate. Real people with real problems. Not angry social snobs arguing over who got the Jag and who got the condo in Maui.

I nodded. "Some sad situations, but I did feel good about helping people."

"Tell me about your drawing. Is it a hobby or have you had classes?"

"What is this? Twenty questions?"

"Sorry. It's the practitioner in me. Gather information. Study the results. Make a diagnosis."

"I don't recall asking for a consultation." I stepped away from him, but he took my hand in his, and in the glow of the streetlamp, I saw laughter in his eyes.

"My apologies. I get carried away sometimes."

"Yeah, well, you'd better perfect your technique, Dr. Caprice."

"How about I kiss you instead?"

My mind went blank, as if the sidewalk in my brain had shifted when I wasn't looking and I couldn't get my footing. "You're kidding, right?"

He cupped my chin in his fingers. "No, I'm not. It's been on my mind ever since the first time I met you and your colored pencils went flying to kingdom come and your sketches blew all over the neighborhood."

My face felt hot, and I was thankful for the encroaching dark so Drew wouldn't see my cheeks turning red. "I thought you were a con artist, coming to make trouble for Mitzi. I was ready to read you the riot act."

He didn't move, but kept his eyes steady on mine. His hand curled warm around my trembling fingers.

I shook my head. "No kiss. Not today. I don't want to complicate things for Mitzi." *Or me.*

"I suppose you're right." He kissed my forehead instead, then led me onto the stone path toward Mitzi's.

Turning back for one last look at Swan Lake, I saw a black Lexus parked along the side street, with a straight view of Drew and me. The streetlight had come on and cast a blue light on the driver. Lance's face was as dark as his car.

My stomach turned sour.

[CHAPTER 33]

Mitzi

Something had changed between Brooke and Drew. Nothing I could put my finger on, but while I watched Drew glide from fridge to stove, chopping, measuring, pouring a fine stream of olive oil into a smoking skillet, I sensed he was preoccupied. Brooke fussed over me, avoiding Drew, it seemed.

She brought me a cup of tea and the mail. My heart fluttered as I noticed I'd received a thank-you note from Hadley. I eagerly ripped into it, then rested the note in my lap, a twinge of disappointment that it was a preprinted card. Hadley hadn't even scrawled a *missed you at the service* line at the bottom. I was sorely tempted to pick up the phone and give him a call, but what would I say? *I'm sorry about Lily. What will you do now? Wanna play some gin rummy?* I'd lost a friend; he'd lost his wife.

The smell of caramelized onions and sizzling beef brought me back from my muddled thoughts. "Drew, that's the first time I've been able to smell since this nasty flu bit me. You know you're spoiling us."

Brooke stepped in from the dining room. "Spoiled is right. Before long you're going to be stuck with me and Lean Cuisine again."

Drew laughed it off and put the dish he was preparing into the oven.

Half an hour later, we sat at the dining room table, eating off china that hadn't been used in twenty-five years. Drew had even scrounged up a couple of candles and set them in crystal holders I'd forgotten I had.

As delicious as the sautéed tournedos of beef and the pan-seared asparagus were, I couldn't help thinking this was a finale of sorts. Drew would be leaving soon. He and Brooke spoke politely, but without their usual banter. When Drew asked what our New Year's resolutions were, Brooke surprised me.

"I've been doing some thinking, and I had an epiphany of sorts. Something Drew said got me thinking about taking art classes, trying something different. Next week I'm going to check into taking a couple of night courses at Tulsa University."

Drew reached for Brooke's hand. "Good for you. You have some real talent, you know."

Waving him away, she said, "That remains to be seen. I'm certainly not good enough to be a professional, but I want to expand my horizons. I don't have it all worked out yet..."

"What's to work out?" I felt the excitement in Brooke's voice, the way she glowed when she talked. "We'll set up Gabe's old office as a studio for you. I've been needing to clean it out for ages. Might be good therapy for me, too."

Alarm crossed Brooke's face. "Mitzi, I can't ask you to do that. You have your own life, and as much as I've enjoyed staying here with you, we both knew it was only temporary."

"You can't leave. Not now." I didn't mean to say it so harshly, but for a minute I had my own brush with panic, and peering into Brooke's eyes, I could tell I'd hit a nerve.

"I can't accept your hospitality forever."

"It's not hospitality. I've gotten used to you being here. You're like the granddaughter I never had."

"Which is why I can't stay. It's not safe. For you." Her voice faded into a whisper, her face clouded.

Lance. Something had happened.

Drew listened, not interrupting, but I saw his tensed jaw. Maybe he had a beef with me asking Brooke to stay, but when he didn't jump into the middle of our conversation, I flared my nostrils and charged ahead.

"Has Lance threatened you?"

Brooke stiffened the way she did whenever the subject of Lance came up. How he could have this effect on her sent my conniption meter into the danger zone.

Her voice was soft, more of a breath than an utterance. "Sort of."

"Well?"

She blew out a breath, her gaze wandering to the crown molding. "He follows me. Sends me text messages wanting to talk or get together. Not threats exactly . . . "

"Which explains why you check the alarm three or four times every evening."

Drew looked from me to Brooke, his eyes flashing. "I know it's none of my business, and I don't know all the details, but I noticed the same thing you did when we left Swan Lake." Drew turned to me, probably seeing the confused look on my face.

"Yeah. We went for a walk while you napped. I've always loved Swan Lake, and come to find out, Brooke does, too."

"I've always thought Gabe was a genius for insisting we buy in this neighborhood. So what did you two notice?"

Brooke swallowed. "A Lexus was parked by the grassy spot on the north end. It looked like Lance, but with the streetlight, I'm not totally certain, and it's possible there are other cars like his around—"

Drew cut her off. "Not likely. It's apparent he's trying to intimidate you. I'm even of the notion you should take action to stop him. A restraining order or something."

Brooke shrugged. "I could ask for a protective order, but Lance is an attorney—a smart one. He'll have someone else follow me, report where I am, what I'm doing."

"Do you think he would intentionally hurt you? Or Mitzi?"

Brooke slumped in her chair. "I don't know. It's a tape I play every minute of every hour in my head. The thing is, I don't want Mitzi to get caught in the middle. I would never forgive myself if she were harmed."

Drew fiddled with his fork, pushing the remaining mushrooms from his half-eaten beef dish around on his plate. "You can't let him get away with it. You'll be looking over your shoulder the rest of your life."

Snorting through her nose, Brooke said, "It's not like I haven't tried to stop him. I thought being firm and keeping my distance would be enough to discourage him, but it's only made him more determined."

Drew frowned, his eyebrows drawn together, but he didn't speak.

The wine sauce on my plate congealed, the aroma no longer tempting. "Brooke, I've made my opinions quite clear, but that's immaterial. I don't want you to leave on my account. The fact is, Lance already knows where I live. He could show up at any minute. Moving away won't solve anything. I've been on the receiving end of some pretty nasty stuff, and though we think we can change people, there are those who don't want to change."

Drew whisked the plates off the table, rattling the silverware, stomping back and forth from the kitchen to the dining room. When the table was cleared, he switched on the overhead lights, snuffed out the candles, and sat down. "What can we do to help?"

Brooke shook her head. "Nothing. I need to work it out myself." She folded her napkin and rose from the table, leaving Drew and me staring helplessly at each other.

"As much as I hate to say it, Brooke was right about one thing." Nestled on the sofa, I watched Drew start the fire. "Some things have to work themselves out. They can't be rushed, even if there is danger involved."

Drew looked over his shoulder at me. "And you know this from experience?"

"Unfortunately. It can drive you to the edge of insanity. I thought I could keep Finster from sucking Penny Vaughn into prostitution or those awful movies I knew they were making. I couldn't. All the while, I felt guilty for not having some affection for the man who'd provided half of my genetic makeup. What if I turned out to be like him and not Mama?"

"Sounds like another fireside chat to me." Drew looked over the top of his glasses, his eyebrows raised.

Brooke. She'd slipped down the stairs and now rested her hand on my shoulder. "What do you say, Mitzi? Want to tell us about your courtship with Gabe? And what happened with Finster and Penny?"

She took her place on the other end of the sofa, her hair pulled back into a ponytail, her face freshly washed and made-up. No traces of the earlier worried Brooke. And I saw in her the spirit of a younger me. The one who kept on believing that somehow things would get better.

[CHAPTER 34]

After the Coney Island Boys played their last night at the Carlisle, Gabe pulled me in close, smelling of stage sweat and Old Spice aftershave. His kiss was sweet and lingering, splitting my heart like an ax that made its mark on a chunk of firewood.

"Hey, you two, enough of the kissing!" Eddie, Gabe's older brother, whisked by, a saxophone case in one hand, a trumpet in the other. "Time to make tracks if we're going to make Philly by tomorrow evening." He disappeared into the back of their travel van.

Another kiss, longer than the last. Gabe whispered, "I'd give the world to take you with me. Eddie and the guys won't have it, though." He cupped my chin with his fingers, smothering me with last-minute good-byes, then sailed off, his promises to write and come back at first chance wafting like music in the air.

I stood in the alley behind the Carlisle, watching until the twin red taillights faded into the inky horizon. When I shuffled into the kitchen, Lou met me, shaking his head. "Sorry, kid."

At least he hadn't told me to get my head out of the clouds the way Red had. But then, Red had his reasons—one being Penny Vaughn, who'd skipped town with Finster Poole. He didn't want to be left high and dry again when things were going so well.

I rode the high of being in love for the first week after Gabe left, trying to remember the sound of his voice as he whispered bubbala*—Yiddish for "darling," he'd explained—and nibbled my ear. When no letters came after two weeks, the first rumblings in my heart began. Red was right—I* did *have my head in the clouds. What an idiot I was to think someone as sophisticated as Gabe Steiner had fallen for a sorry farm girl who happened to know how to carry a tune. The pictures in my head of a smiling Gabe were replaced with the scowls his brothers had shot our way, the garbled phrases they tossed out—Yiddish endearments, Gabe had told me. I began to think they weren't endearments at all, but rather not-so-subtle reminders that we were of two different worlds.*

The Fireflies and I went to work on some new material. They wanted to go in the direction of swing; I wanted to sing jazz with a few gospel numbers thrown in.

"You aiming to make like the next Ella Fitzgerald or Billie Holiday?" Harvey, our self-appointed leader, asked. "You ain't got skin black enough to make a passable imitation."

"The color of my skin has nothing to do with it. It's the music my mama sang, the beat stirring in my soul."

We compromised, letting Lou settle arguments more than once. The one thing I insisted on was ending the show with "His Eye Is on the Sparrow." I was no Ethel Waters, but it never failed to bring a few sniffles and tears from the audience.

Secretly, I knew I was being difficult. And even though singing had become as much a part of me as breathing, I seriously considered throwing it all in and heading to St. Louis. When six weeks passed without any word from Gabe, I made my decision. I would stay through the holidays out of respect for Red and Lou, then give them my notice.

During Christmas week, we added a few holiday numbers in keeping with the spirit of the season. Red grumbled over the light crowd on Christmas Eve and having to close the club the next day. When I asked about his family, I got a quit your meddling *answer, and it dawned on me that the*

Carlisle Club was his family. When Lou and Mary Ruth invited us all over for Christmas dinner, Red said he had things to do. We knew better.

Since the twins had gone home to Webbers Falls for the holidays and Idella had gone to visit relatives, I accepted the invitation and told Mary Ruth I'd come early and help with the cooking. Nostalgia for the farm wormed its way into my thoughts on the bus ride home. Hattie, bless her soul, always cooked like there was no tomorrow, whipping up the best cornbread dressing you ever tasted, and I got teary-eyed thinking of the sand plum jelly I'd be missing on her light-as-a-feather yeast rolls. A doughy lump filled my throat. No one but Hattie had the touch for making those rolls, and she was gone.

As I slipped into Idella's boarding house and climbed the stairs to my room, my thoughts were still on Hattie and the farm.

The minute I switched on the light, I saw her. Penny Vaughn. Crumpled on my bed, her legs drawn up, lying in a pool of bright red.

"Penny! You're hurt! What happened? How did you get here?" No response. My mind raced, wondering if she was even alive. Two quick steps, and I saw she was at least breathing. Her eyelashes fluttered as she tried to open her eyes. Her dress, a flimsy summer weight fabric, was hitched up to her thighs, and the blood seemed to be coming from the lower half of her body.

She raised up on one elbow, groggy, blinking at the light.

"Mitzi . . . sorry . . . didn't know where else to go . . . what to do."

"You did the right thing coming here, but you need to see a doctor. What on earth happened to you?"

Slumping back onto the pillow, she waved her hand dismissively. "I'm fine . . . Need to rest. That's what they told me."

"Who? The person who did this to you? Do you know you're bleeding?" I tried averting my eyes from the bloody mess, but I couldn't.

"Only a little spotting. That's what's supposed to happen."

"This is not spotting, Penny. It's like a flood. You could bleed to death." Scenes flashed through my head. When Lucy Mae, a friend of Liberty's back home, was seven months along, she got a shooting pain in her back, and

before she could get to the doctor, blood gushed like a dam had broken. She and the baby had both died. I grabbed a towel from my closet and stuffed it between Penny's legs and looked at her abdomen. As flat as the day she took off with Finster Poole.

Anger built up like a pressure cooker, ready to blow. Finster had something to do with this. "Penny, are you pregnant?"

She moaned and shook her head. "No. They fixed it."

The room spun before my eyes. "Who fixed what? Who's they?"

"The ladies Finn knows. 'Safe as a walk in the park,' he said."

Adrenaline coursed through me as I tried to think of what to do. Take Penny to the doctor? She was in no condition to walk. I didn't think she could even sit up. An ambulance? The only phone was downstairs in the dining room. They fixed it. *The words thudded to a stop somewhere behind my eyes.* No, Penny, no!

Flying down the stairs, my body trembling, I found the phone and called the only person I knew, praying she would know what to do.

Mary Ruth's groggy voice came on the line.

The words tumbled out, my plea frantic, the explanation miraculously understood on the other end.

After the ambulance hustled Penny to the hospital, I sat with Lou and Mary Ruth waiting for the doctor. None of us talked, our thoughts shrouded with questions and uncertainty. In a drab anteroom in the emergency department, the doctor gave us the news. Terms like critical, removed the uterus, transfusions, *and* unsanitary abortion. *The last part he muttered under his breath. "She'll be on penicillin injections for now. There's sure to be infection. Are you her family?"*

When we shook our heads, he asked if we could try to locate them. "She's not out of the woods yet. May not know for several days."

Lou and Mary Ruth offered to help me search Penny's belongings for clues about her family, but I sent them home; they'd helped enough already. Most of Penny's things were in my room since I'd rescued them from Idella, who wanted paying boarders, not those who skipped out without notice. A new girl would be moving into Penny's room after the holidays.

When I got back to the boarding house, thinking about finding Penny's family, the first thing I saw was the bed where I'd found her. The blood on the sheets had turned a crusty brown, and the sight of them brought bile rushing to my throat. I rolled them up and deposited them in the trash barrel in the alley, mentally shopping at JCPenney, asking the twins to help me find the linen department. Realizing Penny had to have let herself in downstairs with a key, I searched first for her purse and found it tucked in a corner under the bed.

I dumped out everything on the bed and grabbed the wallet first, surprised at the feel of expensive calfskin. It wasn't a recent acquisition—the pebble grain was worn smooth, the silk lining frayed. Rummaging through it, I found a couple of grainy photos of a woman I didn't recognize. A sister, maybe? Her mother? Nothing was written on the back. The wallet's only other contents were four dollars and twenty-four cents in change and a yellowed in-case-of-emergency card, blessedly with a telephone number but no name or address.

Back in the dining room, I disobeyed one of Idella's cardinal rules—no long-distance phone calls. Although it was grounds for eviction, I dialed the operator and gave her the number, praying I didn't get Finster Poole on the other end.

A man answered, a refined but cautious quality to his voice. Yes, they had a daughter named Penny. No, they hadn't seen her in two years and didn't know she lived in Tulsa. A clatter in the background kept me from determining whether the man was happy to hear news of her or angry I'd called. I gave him the name of the hospital, told him there'd been an accident, and got his assurance that they would come. In clipped tones, he replied it would be a minimum of five hours. I hung up without asking where they lived.

Penny floated in and out of delirium, her temperature raging, but her bleeding was at least under control. Her parents arrived before dark. Her dad, stiff and unsmiling in his gray suit, introduced himself as Dr. Landon. Her mother had red-rimmed eyes and the same pixie face as Penny. Her eyes averted mine as she wrung her hands and sniffled. When she saw Penny, she wobbled, steadying herself on the rail of the hospital bed.

Dr. Landon turned to me, his face sour instead of worried, as I thought it would be. "What exactly is going on here? What happened?"

There were too many questions, and I didn't know where to begin, so I mumbled, "I'm Mitzi Barlow, Penny's friend."

Dr. Landon frowned at me, then drew his attention to the clear bottle of intravenous fluid dangling above her. "I'd like to speak to the doctor caring for my daughter."

His tone sent chills to the tips of my toes, and I wondered if I'd delivered her from Finster and handed her over to someone worse. Over the next two days, Penny hovered in a semiconscious state. The Landons had little to say to me, sending vibes that since I was Penny's friend, I was somehow to blame. I didn't dare tell them it was my own father who was responsible. I could scarce think it myself.

Lou had already filled Red in on what happened when I reported for work two days after Christmas, and Red lit into me. "Crying shame. That's what happens when you girls get them highfalutin ideas, letting men lure you into the devil knows what, leaving people behind who happen to care about you." Gruff, but in a lovable sort of way.

Giving him a playful punch in the arm, I said, "You're a soft touch." And as I took the stage, it dawned on me that Red had been more like a father to me than Finster Poole or Jess Barlow. That's why I dedicated a number in the middle of our program to him.

"Ladies and gentlemen. Thank you all for coming. This next song is for the man who gave me the first opportunity to stand on this stage, the one who took me in when I didn't have two nickels to rub together and treated me like a daughter. Thing is, folks, I'd have been lucky to have a daddy like him. So, here you go, Red Carlisle, the words you'd sing to me if you could carry a tune."

Straighten up and fly right, straighten up and do right.

Laughter and applause broke out, and when I looked out over the audience, Red's face was a reflection of his name, but he beamed as if I'd given him a fistful of silver dollars.

At the end of our set, a jazz trio from Oklahoma City took the stage, and I assumed my waitressing duties. It took more effort than usual to concentrate; thoughts of Penny drifted in and out, distracting me. I'd just taken an order from table nine when someone whispered in my ear, "Hey, doll, ya got a minute?"

I whirled around to face Finster Poole. My blood stopped cold, and my first thought was to run, replaced immediately with the urge to pound on his chest and hurt him the way he had hurt Penny.

Instead, I sucked in a bucket of air, braced my shoulders, and said, "Yes, sir, what can I get you?"

He steered me under the glow of the exit sign, my skin alive as if crawling with ants. His teeth, stained brown, hung in between gaps, where I imagined he'd lost them in some brawl or another. He wasted no time in stating his business.

"Fella over there pointed you out. Said you's the one named Mitzi. Come to find out, we're acquainted already, and Lord knows I got an earful about you from my little darlin' Penny. Seen her lately?"

Acquainted? *I shuddered and shook my head. "Can't say as I have. Sorry."*

"Sorry don't cut it. Ya see, I'm needing to get a hold o' Penny. Can't imagine where she slipped off to. I got a doozy of a picture show lined up for her. Guess she told you 'bout how I'm gonna make her a star?"

"I haven't seen her." And I'd heard way more than I wanted. Star? More like an object for his perverted pleasure.

"I figger she'll be in touch. Give her a message from her man, would you? Tell her Finn's got big plans." He cupped my chin in his square hand. "See you around, darlin'." A chaw of tobacco bulged in his left

cheek, producing spittle that oozed in the spaces between his teeth. His air of familiarity gave me a nagging feeling that he knew more about me than he let on.

I backed away, so sick to my stomach I thought I might heave.

Finster winked, then swiped the back of his hand across his mouth and left.

The rest of the evening went by in a blur, Finster disappearing the same way he'd appeared—like a nightmare that comes unbidden but leaves behind a cloud of doom. And I swear I saw his blocky, hunched body under a streetlight from my bus window when I went back to Idella's.

Luckily, I hadn't mentioned Penny to Idella or the twins, but the next morning I told them I'd had a run-in with an unsavory character at work and to be on the lookout. "Under no circumstances do I want you to let anyone in who asks for me."

Idella scoffed. "House rule: no men allowed. I don't care if they're unsavory or pure as the driven snow, you bring men in here, and you'll be out on your backside faster'n you can whistle Dixie."

Idella's staunch rules were a relief. But my run-in with Finster also meant I couldn't visit Penny. It wouldn't have surprised me if he'd followed me home and was watching my every move. When I got to the club, Lou assured me he'd have Mary Ruth tell Penny why I wasn't able to visit. He became the grapevine, bringing news of Penny and her reluctance to reconcile with her parents. Mary Ruth couldn't put her finger on it, but she could tell they had a rocky history. Whether it had to do with her leaving home to follow her marshmallow dream of stardom or something else, no one seemed to know.

A guilty film wrapped itself around me like a spider web. Penny must've had her reasons for leaving home, the same as I had when I left the Barlow farm. It's never quite that easy, though, is it? I'd abandoned my brother, Chet, and for that, Mama would've been sorely disappointed in me. Maybe I wasn't so different from Penny after all.

Two days after Finster's visit to the Carlisle, I shuffled out of Idella's and headed for the bus stop. Lifting my chin a smidgeon, I saw a figure step toward me with a familiar gait, his features shaded by a clump of crape myrtles. Emotion clogged my throat.

The last person on earth I expected to see picked up his pace, arms wide.

Gabe Steiner.

[CHAPTER 35]

Brooke

The clock on the mantel read 11:45. Mitzi looked up, her eyes bleary. "Well, look at the time. Guess we'll be ringing in the new year soon."

Drew rose from Gabe's chair. "You girls want to watch the ball drop in Times Square?" He rummaged for the remote on the end table and clicked the TV on.

Mitzi shook her head. "Not me. I'm turning in. You kids carry on without me."

My mind was still on Mitzi's story. "Wait. What happened with you and Gabe? You can't leave us hanging."

She winked. "I don't think you want to hear about the next sixty-one years tonight. Besides, it's not so hard to figure out, is it?" And off she went, climbing the stairs with more energy than she'd shown for more than a week.

"I'm going to call it a day, too," I said. After gathering our mugs, I went to the kitchen, aware that Drew's gaze followed me. When I turned, he stood inches away, giving me a start. A feeling of déjà vu from our earlier encounter at Swan Lake swept through me.

"Sorry, I didn't mean to scare you."

"It's okay. Guess my mind was wandering. Did you want something? A drink of water? Some juice?" It sounded stupid. Spastic.

"Nothing for me. So what were you thinking about?"

What I was thinking was that the ball would be dropping in Times Square in mere minutes and that even a cursory New Year's kiss from Drew terrified me. What I said to him was, "Just thinking about Gabe and Mitzi. Why she didn't hear from him, and then he shows up. He must've had quite a line explaining himself."

Drew smiled, an I-know-something-you-don't smile. "Maybe she'll indulge us before I go back to Boston."

"But you know what happened."

"More or less. It's quite a story."

"Rats. It's not fair that you know and I don't." Casually, I turned and began rinsing the cups. Over my shoulder I said, "Do you know Mitzi still has all the gowns she wore while they were performing? Dozens of them, in the cedar closet in my room."

"Doesn't surprise me. She does tend to hang onto things, memories and all."

"Which is why it startled me when she offered Gabe's office for a studio. I'd think she would want to preserve everything the way she has the dresses. You should see them... billowy chiffon, satin that swishes when I run my hands over them. Sometimes I think if they could, they'd waltz right off their padded hangers and onto the stage. Wouldn't that be fun to see?"

Drew leaned against the refrigerator, still sporting a silly grin. Whether at me for blurting out my fetish for hanging out in Mitzi's closet or at the image of a fleet of headless dresses bobbing around, I didn't know. Whatever the reason, I liked the way his eyes crinkled when he smiled. Glittery. Mischievous.

From the living room, the television murmured, the frenzied voices of the Times Square crowd beginning the countdown. *Sixty. Fifty-nine.*

Drew cleared his throat. "Funny you should bring it up. I think there are a number of people who would like nothing more than to hear Mitzi perform again."

"Like that would ever happen." I dried my hands and took a seat at the breakfast table.

Drew pulled out the chair opposite me and turned it so that when he straddled it, his elbows rested on the back. "Don't be so sure. You see, I took Mitzi over to the Jazz Depot before she got sick. The director there teased her about doing a show, singing a few songs for one of their Sunday evening performances. She laughed it off, but I could almost feel her itching to grab a mic and take the stage."

"Do you think she would?" Goose bumps cascaded down my arms.

"I'm counting on it."

Forty-two. Forty-one.

"I went by again yesterday to see if they were serious. Turns out they're thrilled and gave me a date. The last Sunday in February."

"But you'll be gone by then... You'll miss it."

"It shouldn't be too hard to arrange. Some things just can't be missed. Mitzi will be back to her feisty self by then. Now all I have to do is convince her." He wore confidence the same way he whipped out a gourmet dinner. Smooth. With a touch of class.

"Oh, she'd do anything for you, Dr. Caprice."

"I called my folks, and they've been wanting to see Gabe again, so everything's working out. I do have a favor to ask, though."

"Whatever you need."

"I'd like you to stay with Mitzi for now."

Biting my lower lip, I said, "It's not that I don't want to... and she has been so nice to let me store my things in her garage until I find another place... It's Lance—"

He held up his hand. "Moving somewhere else is no guarantee

he won't do something. Actually, I'm worried for both you and Mitzi."

"That's nice of you to say, but I'm quite capable of handling my own life."

The tiniest raise of his eyebrows told me he wasn't so sure. Thankfully, he didn't dispute it, arguing instead for what I could do to help Mitzi. Be her chauffeur. Make her take her medicine. Take her shopping for a new outfit to wear when she sang.

"You don't even know if she'll agree to it."

"She will."

Three. Two. One. Muted cheers from the television.

Drew rose and held out a hand to me. I took it and stood, afraid to breathe. He cupped my chin in his fingers, his kiss like a whisper on my cheek. But his voice was strong when he said, "It's a new year. Anything is possible."

And for a moment, I forgot he was talking about Mitzi and her engagement at the Jazz Depot.

On Saturday, Drew wanted to do some odd jobs around Mitzi's, and he offered to set up an Internet connection at Mitzi's, since I'd agreed to stay with her. I volunteered to spend the day with Gabe. It was the opportunity I'd been hoping for to carry out the rest of my surprise plan for Mitzi. I introduced myself at the nurse's desk and asked what I could do for Gabe in Mitzi's absence.

A jovial nurse showed me to his room. The head of the bed was cranked up, with Gabe in a semi-reclined position, and once again, his frailness pierced my heart. I didn't expect that he would remember me, but I didn't want to alarm him either.

The nurse spoke to him. "Gabe, you've got a visitor. You behave yourself, you hear?"

She could've been talking to a rock for all the response it brought, and my stomach went queasy.

The nurse turned to me. "Maybe you could massage his legs and feet the way Mitzi always does. Lawsy, she's a sweet one, clucking over him like a mama hen. With this flu floating around, we're run plumb ragged. No time for the extras." She fished in the bedside table and pulled out a bottle of lotion. "Wanna give it a try?"

I must have nodded, because she handed off the lotion to me and pointed to a CD player in the corner. "Mitzi puts on their old music sometimes, too."

Okay. First, some music. "Fly Me to the Moon" was the first song on the CD, and its sweet harmonies wafted through the room as I uncovered the lower part of Gabe's legs and removed his socks. The skin was as transparent as tracing paper over calves that seemed to be only bones draped with loose skin. His knee joints, like flesh-covered softballs, were pale and waxy looking. I worried that touching them would inflict pain.

Warming a bit of lotion in my hands to gather my courage, I watched Gabe's face to see if he was freaked out by my being there, but he didn't flinch. No eye contact, just a far-off look toward the window. Up and down, over legs with no muscle tone, I massaged gently, trying to decide if I should talk to him, although I couldn't think of anything to say.

Song after song filled the room. Some were sassy and full of fun; others rich and mellow. More than once, tears sprang to my eyes as I rubbed more lotion into Gabe's thirsty skin, then I took the new socks I'd bought at Saks and pulled them onto his feet. I tucked the covers back around his legs.

Gabe and Mitzi sang "Moonlight Serenade" as I settled into the armchair in the corner of the room, where I had a good view of Gabe. I pulled out my sketch pad and charcoal pencils and went to work, the excitement of the strokes on the page coursing through me.

When the CD changed to a new track, Gabe stirred, his eyes opening wide, and for a moment, I thought they focused.

Mitzi's solo voice came through, strong and sorrowful. Gabe moaned as Cosmo sometimes did, throaty and low, trying to communicate some feline message I never understood. Gabe's mouth, though, moved as though he was trying to speak. I tucked my art things in the tote I'd brought along and went to his bedside. Over the padded rails, I took his hand in mine. It was cold. Fragile.

A lump filled my throat as Mitzi's voice began the chorus.

I sing because I'm happy,
I sing because I'm free . . .

Tears obstructed my vision. Mitzi's song. The one she sang the night she first met Gabe. I blinked back my tears to look at Gabe. His lips no longer moved, and a look of peace now graced his face. My insides felt raw, but nourished somehow.

Their song.

A song that spanned a lifetime.

[CHAPTER 36]

Mitzi

A hollow feeling burrowed in the morning Drew left for Boston. There were so many things I wanted to tell him, medical questions I hadn't asked. Having him and Brooke around had filled the house with a zest that hadn't been there in a blue moon. Maybe it was the electric vibes they gave off—all their youth and promise of the future. Granted, Brooke's life was still as tangled as the wires in Gabe's head.

When Brooke dropped me off at the care center, a thread of apprehension knotted itself. *Gabe. Had he missed me?* I hurried down the hall, patting my hair to tame any flyaway strands the wind had whipped up.

Gabe lay curled on his side between his protective rails, his shoulder exposed above the coverlet. The hospital gown gaped as well, its ties undone, trailing across his back like apron strings. A pale scar floated along his protruding collarbone. Beneath that, the ribs of his upper chest poked out like those of a half-starved stray cat. My own chest caved in reflexively, caught unaware by how much thinner he seemed in only a week.

Before I kissed him good morning, I adjusted the gown and the blanket. In his sleep, Gabe twitched, barely visible jerks that left me more unsettled than his bare shoulder.

"Why look who just rolled in, would you?" Maple's voice behind me was like warm honey on a biscuit. "We been wondering how you were. 'Twas pure delight having that hunky Mel Gibson look-alike stepping in to stand your watch while you was down with the flu."

"Maple, you call all white men under the age of fifty Mel Gibson look-alikes."

She laughed and went about her business while I took off my coat and turned on the CD player. Might as well start tuning up my vocal chords for the silly notion Drew got about me singing at the Jazz Depot. *Mercy.* Who would give a flip for an old has-been like me?

Gabe looked a tad better after Maple fluffed him up and washed his face. He stirred, a moan pressing through cracked lips.

"How's Gabe been since I left?"

"'Bout the same. Figger he might perk up some now you're back. Got that oozing in his gums again."

I slipped into the routine of feeding Gabe his breakfast and smoothed a towel across his chest to catch the dribbles. I held my finger over the end of the straw and let a half teaspoon of Ensure run into his mouth. It was like feeding an orphaned baby bird.

When I went to get my morning coffee, my throat clogged. The table where I'd shared so many lingering cups with Hadley stood empty, the absence of my friend a hollow spot in my chest. What I would've given to see Hadley's wooly white head pop through the door, his toothy grin all set to bedevil me. He'd lost his dear Lily, and I'd lost the pleasure of Hadley's company. The room, though scarcely bigger than a closet, seemed cavernous. My hand shook as I carried my cup back to Gabe's room.

Standing at the window, I saw the mottled gray and white bark of a sycamore, the tree reaching bare armed toward a colorless sky.

Good grief! Why was I being such a whiner? The gist of a long-ago sermon popped into my head. *If you've never experienced the valleys of life, how could you possibly know the splendor of the mountaintops?* I thought of Jesus, prostrate in the garden on the eve of his betrayal, asking the Father to take this hour from him. Then he submitted to the Father's will and met his destiny. The one designed for him from the beginning of time.

Tears fought their way to the surface, the sting of my selfishness nipping at me like a pesky mosquito. *We're not promised tomorrow. Only today.* The words came as a gathering mist, the way the Holy Spirit so often did when I needed an attitude adjustment. I'd had more than my share of mountaintops. Vistas that took my breath away. Who on God's green earth hadn't seen heartache and sadness? Terror. Pain. And my lands, yes, victory. Letting a bad attitude rob me of whatever joy I had left was nothing but a waste.

"Straighten Up and Fly Right," from our *Tribute to Jazz* album, sizzled from the speakers. I burst out laughing. Gabe jerked, startled from whatever mental valley he'd been in. His eyes popped open, meeting mine, and for an instant we connected. Stark recognition. As real as the flesh on my bones.

Today. We only have today.

A grunting noise escaped Gabe's mouth, his chin jutting up, his eyes fluttering, then rolling up into his skull. All at once, his body tensed, twitching over every inch of it, gaining in intensity until I thought he would flail himself out of the bed.

No, God! No. Not now. Not yet.

"Help! Maple! Someone please help." My hands patted Gabe's rigid body while my eyes searched the bed for the call button. Beneath my touch, the jerking continued.

I ran to the door and yelled into the hall, "Help! I need someone fast!"

[CHAPTER 37]

Brooke

When I got back from a late lunch at Ping's, the takeaway down the street, a vase of red roses on Jenna's desk caught my eye. Maybe something had worked out with the new interns she'd been panting over at the Christmas party. I hoped so. Jenna, with her iPhone to her ear, looked up, startled, then gave a fake grin and looked away. She'd been weird all morning. Crisp. Not chatty. Whatever; I had plenty to do besides worry about Jenna.

A new stack of files had appeared on my desk while I was at lunch. A child custody hearing. A suit filed by a woman whose dog had died in the care of a veterinarian. The name on the file made me gulp. Judith Zabel. The woman Lance played Scrabble with every Sunday afternoon.

Why would she have picked our firm and not Lance's? Why would she even be bringing a suit? She was richer than the Rockefellers, according to Lance, so it wasn't the money. Strange. A note was paper-clipped to the manila folder.

Please see client at 2:00. Her home. She's a shut-in and won't take phone calls. Address inside. BH

Since it was already 1:45, I needed to leave. When I zipped past

Jenna's desk, she muttered, "See you later." Didn't even look up from her computer.

At 2:05 I pulled into a curved drive two blocks off Lewis. Shrouded by trees, a daunting stone house the color of winter stood on a spacious lot that made Mitzi's place look modest. Did Mrs. Zabel live here alone? I tried to remember how Lance knew her. Was she a friend of the family, or maybe the widow of one of his firm's partners? It wouldn't come to me.

A housekeeper answered, her diminutive figure immaculate in a crisp pinafore apron, her dark hair pulled taut into a bun. I handed her my card. "Missy Zabel back this way. Expect you five minutes ago."

She led the way to a sunporch off the kitchen, the air fresh with dozens of poinsettias, their pointed blooms tinged green, pink, red, and a luscious deep salmon I'd never seen before. Mrs. Zabel, also slight in stature with rounded shoulders, yet regal in her bearing, dismissed the housekeeper, then peered at me from her seat in a high-backed wicker chair—the kind I'd always thought of as a queen's throne. A walker with tennis balls on the back feet stood sentry beside the chair.

"You're late."

"My apologies. I only found out about our appointment a few minutes ago." I offered my hand, which she waved away with a single word.

"Arthritis."

"I'm sorry, I didn't tell you my name. I'm Brooke Woodson." She took the card I handed her and tucked it into a pocket of the carry-all attached to the walker. "May I sit down?"

When she nodded, I took the chair closest to her, another wicker one with a faded floral cushion.

"Not that one. It is Philippe's."

As I moved to another chair opposite her, I asked, "Who is Philippe?"

Through a sniffle, she spoke. "My baby. The reason you are here."

"Perhaps you can tell me about it."

Philippe was a seven-year-old schnauzer who'd been the last gift from her deceased husband. She poured her grief like cream from a pitcher, as if poor Philippe had died five minutes ago. He'd been gone a week already, but in her mourning, she hadn't had the stamina to notify an attorney about suing for damages for the "botched" treatment Philippe had endured.

"Tell me more about Philippe's illness."

She shuddered. "It was so horrible I can hardly bear to think about it. He was like my own flesh and blood. More precious to me than a child. If only our regular vet had come last month to give him his heartworm medication..."

Her voice trailed off as if she'd lost her train of thought. When she didn't continue, I prompted her. "The vet came here? Isn't that unusual?"

"Philippe was special. It's difficult for me to get out, but the vet also came for another reason. Philippe had a delicate issue requiring the kind of assistance only another man should attend to." She squirmed like she had a hitch in her panties, then gave me a stern don't-make-me-go-there look over the top of lavender-framed glasses a shade darker than her nearly transparent hair. "Discretion was of the utmost importance." A tear rolled gently down her cheek. "As you can well imagine."

No, not exactly. I'd never thought of a dog having privacy issues, but the way she shifted her bottom around made me think perhaps Philippe had a problem with his anal glands. Which, even with my meager knowledge of veterinary medicine, hardly seemed like a fatal diagnosis.

Shuffling my papers, I found what I needed. "I will need a signed consent from you to obtain Philippe's records, but first, tell me what your vet told you."

"I haven't talked to Philippe's personal physician. He's in Belize. He couldn't come in December because of the dreadful snow, so Philippe missed his monthly check-up. Three weeks later, my darling was deathly ill, so I called to arrange a home visit. A new person was in charge—a snippy little thing who told me they didn't make house calls and to find someone to bring him in if I couldn't. Lance, the poor dear, escorted him to the vet's office, but it was too late. Philippe was weak beyond imagination and died undergoing treatment. Lance feels simply dreadful."

I let the reference to Lance slide. It would have been completely within the scope of my paralegal profession to clarify her relationship to Lance, but I had the creeping feeling she knew who I was without veering into that catacomb.

"I'm truly sorry. Do you know the cause of death?"

She flinched. "Poor Philippe had a bowel constriction or some such. And they subjected him to such inhumane treatment." She lowered her voice. "I'm certain you'll find out all about it, honey, and make it right."

It seemed illogical, but her distress was real, her grief visible. There was little I could do without looking at the dog's medical records. I scribbled some notes and handed her the release form to sign. "I'm not the one in charge of the case, you do understand that, correct?"

She wobbled a scraggly signature onto the page. "Yes, but Lance assured me you would understand what it was like to love a pet more than any human being."

"I'm afraid I don't carry much influence—"

"Lance says you have a cat... Think how you would feel if you lost your dear Cosmo." The sniffles and tears were replaced with a steely look that sent chills up my spine. She knew Cosmo's name. Had Lance put her up to this?

Before I had time to come up with a question, she rose, her back so curved that her body was scarcely taller than a ten-year-old's. She grasped the rail of the walker and took a first precarious step toward me. "You know, it's quite remarkable."

"What? I'm afraid I don't follow."

"You. You're the spitting image of Betsy. I saw it the moment you walked in."

After such a bizarre afternoon, I was almost afraid to ask, but I decided to humor her. "Really? I don't think I know a Betsy. Who is she?"

Her gnarled hands gripped the walker, her head cocked to the side as if checking to see if I wasn't the real Betsy. "Of course you don't know her personally... She's deceased. But you know of her. Betsy Evans. Lance's mother. She loved cats, too."

Her smile curdled the egg drop soup I'd had for lunch.

Refusing to let my discomfort show, I stuffed papers into my valise. I'd think about this later. I stood, started to offer my hand, then remembered her arthritis and retracted it. "Thank you, Mrs. Zabel. We'll be in touch. And although I know it doesn't ease your pain, I'm truly sorry for your loss."

I let myself out the front door, my thoughts a jumble as I picked my way down the flagstone walk that led to the drive. Looking up, I nearly lost my footing. A black Lexus sat beside my Mustang, and leaning against the side of his car, arms folded, was Lance.

My heart turned as cold as the January air that bit my cheeks. He had arranged this. How convenient. And me... I'd been stupid enough to fall for it. I gritted my teeth and forced myself to take another step.

With a friendly grin, he sprinted the half-dozen steps between us. "Brooke."

"Lance. What a coincidence, meeting you here." Act cool. Calm.

"Sorry. Sometimes love calls for desperate measures."

Love? I wanted to puke. "Pathetic, you mean. How could you use a sweet old lady like this?"

"I'm not using Judith. She has a legitimate claim. It's just not something my firm handles. I knew you'd be perfect for her."

Ignoring my role in this, I said, "Not hardly. And I seriously doubt she needs the money, even if her claim is legit."

"There's no price on grief, Brooke. Think how you'd feel if you lost Cosmo."

Mrs. Zabel's words.

"So what's this about, Lance? A threat that something *might* happen to Cosmo?"

He held up his hands. "Hey, don't get defensive. I've missed him, as I have you. You can't fault me for that, can you?"

"You and Cosmo weren't exactly what I'd call good friends."

"I'd like to change that. What's important to you matters to me, too." He stepped closer and clamped his hand around my wrist below my sleeve. Not tight enough to hurt, but with enough squeeze to let me know he had control. I clung to my briefcase, ready to use it as a weapon if necessary.

He released my wrist and cupped my chin in his fingers. "Matter of fact, I'd let you have a dozen cats if that's what you want." He leaned in and brushed my lips with his.

I wanted to spit. To laugh in his face, but it was all too weird. What if he was using a new tactic to try and coax me into . . . what? Not a relationship. We were beyond that. My mind clicked at death-defying speeds, wondering if he was going to try to grab me and shove me into his car. *Make me pay*, as he'd so aptly put it.

Willing myself to keep my wits, I eased away and replied honestly. "I don't want a dozen cats, I want to get on with my life. As you should."

"I've had time to think. Christmas was the loneliest day of my life, and I realized you were right. I do have to change." He shrugged, a half-grin, half-pleading look on his face. "Would you come to my place for dinner tonight? You can even bring Cosmo. No kissing or advances from me. We'll make it a strategic discussion about our mutual acquaintance." He jerked his head toward the hulking gray house of Mrs. Zabel.

I gazed at the bare branches overhead and thought of the way Mrs. Zabel talked about Betsy. My remarkable look-alike. No, even if Lance's offer came with a hands-off promise, there were too many unknowns. Creepy unknowns.

"Not tonight, Lance." His posture stiffened, an old familiar reaction that usually preceded action. I curled my hand around the key chain in my pocket and clicked the remote unlock. I backed up, maintaining eye contact and control in my voice. "I have work to do, but Mrs. Zabel would probably love for you to spend the evening with her."

He shrugged and gave me room, but as I ducked into the Mustang, I noticed his blue eyes had taken on another familiar characteristic . . . that of a brewing storm.

Back at the office, after jumping through hoops to retrieve Philippe's records from the vet's office, I collapsed into my chair. *Think. What is going on here?*

The medical records indicated that surgery was done for a gangrenous bowel, which had apparently twisted in on itself. As I waded through the jargon, the phrase *inadvertent incision through the peritoneum* jumped out at me. A slip of the knife? Three pages later, I laid the papers aside. There was the distinct possibility that Philippe's treatment *had* been botched. The vet clearly wasn't responsible for Philippe's condition, but the dog might have survived without the error during surgery. Mr. Harrington would have to engage experts to check into it, but perhaps Mrs. Zabel wasn't just another bizarre pet owner looking for a lawsuit. My heart ached for her.

It didn't change the manipulation Lance had tried to pull. And as much as I wanted to dismiss it, I couldn't. My nerves felt like they'd been frazzled by a dull razor blade.

Think.

My boss's voice echoed in my memory, "Never overlook the minutest scrap of information." Maybe if I wrote it all down, it would make more sense.

I grabbed a yellow pad and my favorite Montblanc pen and let my thoughts flow freely.

Mrs. Zabel suffered a loss. Did Lance suggest a lawsuit? Tell her to ask for me? Apparently.

Betsy Evans and I looked alike, acc. to Judith Zabel. Has Lance ever mentioned this to me? Can't recall. He might have said I reminded him of his mother, but I don't recall him ever saying I was her spitting image.

Did Lance know Mrs. Z would notice the resemblance?

What was the relationship between Mrs. Z and Betsy Evans? How did they know each other?

Betsy Evans loved cats.

I studied the last four words, my fingers white-knuckled on the pen as I underlined them. There was something weird about Lance and his relationship with his mother. Did it have to do with her cats? Maybe I *should* be worried about Cosmo.

Lance wasn't stupid. Hurting Cosmo wasn't the way to win me back. Unless revenge was his goal now. His threat at the Christmas party came to mind. He was capable, no doubt, and under it all, I knew it was because I rejected him. And somehow I was starting to get the odd feeling that I wasn't the first person who'd dealt him rejection.

Find out more about Betsy Evans.

Check on Cosmo.

Buy pepper spray.

Okay, the last item was because I'd promised Drew and Mitzi I would get the spray in concession for not getting a protective order. Better safe than sorry.

I leaned back in my chair and let my thoughts wander. My head spun with possibilities, none of them pleasant. Lance was up to something, but I couldn't figure it out. He had everything he wanted: money, a great career, the admiration of his colleagues, a political future. Just not me. Perhaps I was being paranoid. Maybe Lance had loved his mother dearly and was attracted to me because he missed her. When I turned out to be a poor facsimile and didn't nurture his needs, he became frustrated and reacted with criticism . . . and violence.

Still, Lance was accountable for his own actions. Gifts, notes, pleading phone calls, and orchestrated meetings didn't change the truth. Not knowing when he would show up was making me crazy. Living my life in fear was weak. Why hadn't I pressed charges against him when he hit me the first time? So what if a protective order didn't always work? Didn't I have to make the effort?

Think how you would feel if something happened to Cosmo.

Bile pierced my tongue. Cosmo might be in danger. Or even worse . . . Mitzi.

Oh no you don't, Lance Evans. This time I'm fighting back.

[CHAPTER 38]

Mitzi

Dr. Hogan, a staff physician and one of three doctors who managed the care of the Guardian Light residents, leaned over, stethoscope to Gabe's chest. With eyebrows knit in deep concentration, he listened. When he'd finished, he looked up. "Lungs clear. Heart strong and regular. I'd say the worst is past."

"What happens now?" My senses had returned after a long day of waiting, watching Gabe for signs of another seizure.

"Hard to predict. It may have been a one-time occurrence or the beginning of another phase of Gabe's condition."

I appreciated the word *condition*. So much better than *disease*, which some of the other doctors let roll off their tongues as if they were talking about the weather. It was the words *another phase* that threw me. From the family counseling I'd had when Gabe first entered the care center and Drew's more recent observations, I understood that Gabe was in the late stages of Alzheimer's. Physical decline, groaning, unaware to a deeper extent of his surroundings. Was there a definitive final phase? Was this it?

Dr. Hogan placed a strong hand on my shoulder. "We'll start Gabe on an anti-convulsive, which may help, and I've left orders for the IM Valium in case he has another seizure before the blood levels of the medication are adequate. Does he have any difficulty swallowing?"

Shrugging, I said, "I've been gone a week with the flu, but before Christmas he was eating poorly, choking every once in a while. I'm pretty sure this morning Maple persuaded him to take his medications."

"We always have the option of inserting a nasogastric tube for feeding and oral meds. We usually leave that option up to the family."

I shook my head. "Gabe would be mortified with that. He's been through so much already."

With kind eyes, Dr. Hogan looked me in the face. "It's up to you. As a comfort to you, though, I must say Gabe doesn't seem to be suffering. For some reason, pain receptors and the normal body responses disconnect in ways no one fully understands. The feeding tubes are often for the family members."

"I'm okay with leaving it out." The words sounded so glib, like I made these decisions every day. My outward calm certainly didn't reflect the true depths of fear clattering like a Santa Fe railcar through my body.

When Dr. Hogan left, I pulled a straight chair closer to Gabe's bed, keeping vigil for the slightest tremor. He slept peacefully, his breaths inaudible. With my hand lightly on his shoulder, I prayed for strength and mercy.

The soothing whir of the overhead vent brought a gentle rush of heat into the room. I closed my eyes, listening for the still, small voice of the spirit to visit, to wash peace over me. I was still waiting when the door swung open and Brooke came in.

"Hey. How'd it go?" Her heels clicked on the tiled floor as she came to my side, putting a gentle hand on my shoulder.

The energy drained from me, and I realized that her presence was the balm I'd been waiting for. Tears welled up as I stood and wrapped her in my arms.

"Mitzi, what's wrong?" She looked over my shoulder at Gabe's withered form. "Has something happened?"

I brushed a tear away and gave her the basic gist of it, leaving out how terrified I was Gabe might slip off into eternity.

She led me gently away from the bed. "I'm so sorry. I would've been here sooner, but something came up."

"I hadn't noticed the time. Did you have an emergency at work?"

"Not exactly. More of a disturbing set of circumstances." Her voice wavered, and I noticed the haggard look on her face.

"Need I ask if it involved Lance?" When she nodded, my own dander riled, infusing me with fresh energy. "He's not hurt you or threatened you again..."

"No, he hasn't hurt me. I'm just tired of all the mind games. The manipulation. The fear of what he might do next."

She prattled on, words tumbling for attention as she told me about visiting Mrs. Zabel and finding Lance outside when she left. His pleas and the not-so-subtle hints about Cosmo. Cheeky fella, if you asked me.

Then she cocked her head and said, "I've made a decision. Tomorrow, I'm going to visit the DA and ask for a protective order. I have to at least try. Next time he might be drinking, and I won't be so lucky."

Gabe stirred, a low moan in his throat.

Brooke hop-skipped to his bedside, while I stood opposite. She ran her fingers over his forehead and spoke. "Gabe. Sorry you had to hear all that. I think we both know how special Mitzi is. Thanks for letting me dump all my worries on her."

His muscles relaxed, the deep sleep once again stealing him away. Brooke smiled at me and said, "You are the best, you know. Whenever you're ready, we can go home."

"I'm good here. Think I'll spend tonight in the recliner."

Brooke nodded and offered to get me a bite to eat. Bless her.

When she returned with burgers and fries from Goldie's Grill, she'd changed into jeans and a turtleneck, explaining she'd run by the house to check on Cosmo.

"And?"

"He was lounging in the middle of Drew's bed. I warned him about Lance, but you know, Cosmo's got this sixth sense. If Lance showed up, he'd dive into a closet or someplace where he couldn't be found. Besides, I made sure the alarm was set and turned on half the lights in the house."

While we ate, Brooke riddled me with questions. What did the doctor say about Gabe? What was the medicine? How was my cough? She ran out to the car and brought in an overnight bag, pulling out my slippers, my satin-covered bed pillow, and my cosmetic bag.

"If you're going to spend the night, you might as well be comfortable."

Since she didn't seem in a rush to leave and offered to fix us a cup of tea in the family break room, I decided it was time to tell her the rest of my story about Gabe.

And Finster Poole.

[CHAPTER 39]

When I got over the shock of Gabe materializing before my eyes by the crape myrtle tree, I got spitting mad. Gone all this time, then he stood there, arms open, expecting me to fall right into them.

When I didn't rush toward him, those long arms hung slack as a pair of Jess Barlow's coveralls on the clothesline. "It's not what you think, Mitz."

I walked past him and hollered over my shoulder, "Not interested."

He loped along beside me, babbling he had every intention of writing, of coming back sooner. He could've come with an armload of roses and a bushel basket of hundred-dollar bills, and I still wouldn't have listened to him. Gabe followed me up the steps of the bus, where I practically jumped over the lap of a man wearing a hard hat who smelled of sweat and road tar so I wouldn't have to sit by Gabe.

When we got to the Carlisle, Red slapped Gabe on the back and gave him a prodigal's welcome with a steak as big as a dinner plate. I disappeared into the dressing room, waiting for the band and our turn on the stage.

For four nights in a row, Gabe showed up—pleasant, helping out in the kitchen, cleaning up, whatever needed done. Me—I pouted, acting so childish I could hardly stand myself. Stubborn as a Missouri mule, I refused to listen to Gabe. Finally, on Friday night, Lou pulled me aside.

"You've got your reasons, I understand, but the least you can do is hear what Gabe's got to say."

"Why? So I can be duped again by a smile that promises everything and then takes off like a feather in the wind?" I stomped off, swinging my hips, going toward a customer with a beckoning hand. Tears stung my eyelids, blurring my vision so that all I saw was the form of the man I approached. I cocked my hip and asked if I could help him.

His voice boomed. "Whaddaya know? A gal with some spunk. You remember me, don'tcha, doll?"

Finster Poole. In the flesh. Peachy. In my dither to avoid Gabe, I'd plumb forgot to keep an eye out for Finster.

I swallowed the venom I wanted to unleash on him and said, "Sure. You're Penny Vaughn's friend."

"How is our sweet girl?"

"I wouldn't know." Lying was sinful, that I knew, but delivering a lamb to slaughter was worse. Penny, luckily, had recovered enough to go home with her parents, although when I took a chance and went to the hospital to tell her good-bye, I could tell she dreaded going with them. Still, Finster couldn't have pried the information out of me with a crowbar.

He gave me a skeptical look, then switched gears. "Thing is, doll, I got me a problem. Had this gig all lined up and now I'm left holdin' the bag. What I need is a pretty girl like yourself—" His thick fingers brushed the back of my arm, gentle, caressing. Disgust shot through me like I'd been goosed with a cattle prod. He smiled and said, "What say you meet me when you get off?"

"Sorry . . . I don't go out with customers." I tried to ease away, but he clamped his fingers around my wrist.

"Your friend Penny did."

To her peril.

The group onstage ended their set, telling folks to sit tight and they'd be back for some more bayou blues. The applause gave me the break I needed, so I broke free from his grasp and said, "I'm not Penny. Excuse me, I have work to do."

Hurrying to the kitchen, I nearly ran over Gabe, who leaned back in his chair near the stage.

Gabe. *He could protect me, and even though I knew it was weak, I came to a stop beside him and leaned over to say, "Lou tells me I should give you the courtesy of an explanation. How about when I get through here?"*

When the Carlisle closed for the night, Gabe and I took the bus back to Idella's and sat on the front porch steps. Our breath made marshmallow puffs in the cold night air. He told me that two days after their gig in Philly, his dad had suffered a heart attack and died a week later in the hospital.

My I'm so sorry *fell short of the shame I felt, but his excuse didn't make up for the time since then when he could have written. Even a postcard wasn't much to ask. "It would've been nice if you'd let me know—"*

"I know. I'm a yutz.*"*

I held up my hand. "A what?"

*"*Yutz. *You know? Clueless idiot. Teched in the noggin. A* schlemiel.*"*

"What kind of talk is that?"

"Hey, I grew up in Brooklyn. It's the way we talk."

"Yiddish. Gibberish. They sound the same to me."

His eyebrows shot up, his eyes crinkling into half moons. "Point taken, but I guess it will always be part of who I am . . . or was."

As foreign as it sounded, it fit him. Dark. Mysterious. With a bit of fun in those laughing eyes. But could I trust them? What if Gabe decided one day to pack up and leave again? Where would that leave me?

As if reading the doubts scribbled on my brain, he said, "Going home convinced me of one thing. I don't belong there. I haven't in a long time. I've got other dreams now." His dark eyes glittered, holding me captive for a moment.

"And those would be?"

"Us. We belong together, Mitz. You and me."

"You're right on one thing. You're definitely teched in the noggin." I felt bad about the death of his father, could even pardon him for not writing, but I did have principles. What about courtship? Getting to know each other?

And what on earth would I have in common with his Yiddish-speaking mother?

I scooted away from him on the porch. "Looks to me like you've gotten way ahead of yourself, Gabe Steiner. You've got it all figured out, don't you?"

"Not hardly. I know I have to establish myself with you, gain your trust. I'm willing to do that. However long it takes, I'll wait. I'll crawl on my hands and knees if I have to, Mitzi. I want to marry you."

"That might be difficult . . . I'm leaving Tulsa soon. Didn't even plan to stay this long."

He frowned. "Where are you going? And why?"

"If you must know, I'm going to St. Louis to get on with my life. You can go back to Brooklyn, play weekends there as the Coney Island Boys, find a nice Jewish girl . . ."

"I don't want a nice Jewish girl. I want you. And as for the trio, it's kaput. We've been on the outs for a long time. Eddie and Simon have their families to take care of, and neither of them is interested in the group anymore. We've had our run. One hit record."

"So what are you going to do? Surely there's something you've thought of."

My eyes wandered to the overhead stars, a sky lit with a thousand eyes, as I waited for Gabe's big plan.

"Actually, there is. Lou and I have talked of nothing else. We have a plan."

A star shot through the darkness, an instant slash in the sky, sprinkling stardust into my thoughts.

Gabe's arm slid around my shoulders, pulling me to him. "Did you make a wish?"

"What a childish notion. Wishes don't come true."

"Mine will. You'll see."

After three days, I gave in to Lou and Gabe's preposterous idea. A duo. Gabe and me. The first session was like sparks spitting out of a campfire. The sound was a cross between a pair of fighting tigers and an automobile misfiring every two blocks. The only reason I kept at it was because Finster Poole had become a regular at the club, trying different lines on me every night. If Gabe hadn't been there to escort me home, I shuddered to think what might happen. Once I went to the bus station to buy a ticket for St. Louis and saw Finster in the line next to me. I picked up a bus schedule and sauntered out, ducking into an alley until I saw him get in his car and drive away.

I told Mary Ruth I was leaving, but she begged me to stay. "Lou has good business sense, and he's been friends with Gabe a long time. Mercy sakes, Mitzi, give it a chance. What have you got to lose?"

The next rehearsal I tried harder and didn't argue about the key we sang in or which songs we'd sing. Lou had an arranger working on numbers he thought suited our voices. We worked long hours, the harmony of our voices surprising us both, and without intention, the chemistry between us flickered with magic. True to his word, Gabe made no more mention of marriage, but the attraction—an unexpected smile or an accidental brushing of our arms here and there—skimmed below the surface until sometimes I could barely keep my wits about me.

As much as I believed Gabe was the man of my dreams, another thought niggled at me constantly. Jess Barlow, pigheaded as he was, devoured the Bible at least once a year and never faltered in spewing its wisdom. "Unequally yoked" was one of his favorite subjects, ever since his cousin on his mother's side had married a Catholic. A Catholic? Who in the name of Saint Peter would call that unequally yoked? I shuddered to think what he would say to me for so much as speaking to someone of the Jewish faith. Yet the ripples in my heart gave me pause, a shadow of wariness. But it didn't keep me from going on with Lou's plan for our debut.

It was to be on a Friday night, and Mary Ruth made me a new gown as a surprise—red chiffon. It made me think of Mama and the red dress she left behind in St. Louis. I didn't have the heart to tell Mary Ruth about the gnawing feeling in my stomach that I took to be a sign of impending disaster.

Right up until five minutes before we went on the stage, Gabe and I continued to argue over who got top billing: Gabe and Mitzi or Mitzi and Gabe. The next thing I knew, Lou grabbed the microphone and announced, "Ladies and gentlemen, for the first time ever sharing the stage, may I present the latest sensation—Steiner and Barlow."

It rattled me so much I wobbled onto the stage, but the moment the spots came on us, enchantment took over.

The crowd cheered and clapped as we sailed through song after song, and when Gabe's eyes locked onto mine on "Paper Doll," I could scarcely breathe. Somehow, I made it through, and when the time for the last number arrived, I stood alone in the spotlight. The one thing I'd refused to budge on was singing "His Eye Is on the Sparrow" for the finish.

Lou and Mary Ruth—who'd gotten the night off from her nursing job to watch us—had tears in their eyes when we left the stage. Red's face was as flushed as a ripe tomato when he clapped me on the shoulder and told me I'd earned a night off from waitressing.

He chortled and said, "Just don't get used to it."

A rollicking group from Louisiana played "N'awlins" jazz to an enthusiastic crowd while Gabe and I found a table near the back. With shoulders touching, we enjoyed one of Red's special steaks, a bit of the stage intoxication still bubbling between us. Gabe lifted his glass, "L'chaim—*to life." Before I could return the toast, a customer slid into the seat directly across from me. And although I shouldn't have been surprised, I was. It was Finster Poole.*

The evening's euphoria drained through the bottoms of my feet, leaving me lightheaded. Gabe shifted beside me, a slight tension in his body, as he gave me a questioning look.

Finster leaned over, one arm resting on the table, the other in his lap. His eyes flashed with laughter, whiskey fumes unleashed when he opened his mouth. "That was some performance tonight."

Gabe, obviously unaware I'd had a conversation or two with Finster, said, "It was, wasn't it? I'm glad you liked it."

"I didn't say I liked it, only that it was some performance. Figures a Jew boy like you would take up with a trollop." He leaned back in his seat, an arrogant smirk on his face.

"To each his own." Gabe lifted his glass to Finster. "Although I do take issue with you referring to Mitzi as a trollop."

"She comes by it naturally. And that is precisely why I need to have a private conversation with the little lady. You mind?"

Gabe looked at me for direction. I rested my hand lightly on his arm, applying enough pressure for him to know I wanted him to remain beside me. Inside, my nerve endings pulsed with premonition.

Meeting Finster's steely gaze, I said, "Finn, may I introduce you to Gabe Steiner?" To Gabe I said, "Finn is acquainted with a friend of mine—Penny Vaughn." I prayed he'd get the connection, since he'd heard Penny's story from Lou and Mary Ruth.

Finster snorted. "Another trollop."

Gabe clasped his hands together on the edge of the table. "Perhaps you can state your business, so Mitzi and I can get on with our dinner before it turns cold."

My heart danced in my chest, a frenetic samba fighting its way to my throat. Finster wasn't to be trusted. He knew. *Exactly what, I couldn't say, but his cockiness assured me he was here to cause trouble, embarrassment for me and the club. Red didn't deserve to be drawn into this. He'd worked hard for a clean reputation—and being the envy of other club owners in Tulsa.*

Finster's lip curled back, the gaps in his teeth showing. "As you wish. It seems your Mitzi Barlow here is nothing but an impostor. Posing as someone she's not." His eyes narrowed, venomous and hard.

My throat had closed off. Breathing took every ounce of effort I could drum up.

Finster shifted in his seat, never taking his eyes from me. "What do you have to say for yourself, Maggie Poole? Think you could fool the likes of Tulsa? Of the whole freakin' world? You ain't fooled me, not for an instant." A serpent's tongue couldn't have cut deeper. "The minute I saw you singing that coon-ass song about the sparrows, I knew you were the she-devil come a courtin'. Spittin' image of your mama, taunting me."

His voice got louder with each jab. "I had suspicions all along, but tonight you gave me all the evidence I need. Tell him, Maggie. Tell him who your papa is. Who you really are. And while you're at it, you can tell me what the Sam Hill happened to your mama."

I opened my mouth but no words would form. The shame I felt was not in lying about who I was, but that this man had been the one responsible for Mama's black eyes and heartaches. Gabe's arm slipped around my shoulders, his muscles twitching.

When I didn't answer, Finster reached into his jacket, and against the satin lining I saw a glint of steel. "Your mama was nothing but a two-bit floozy, singing in them two-bit clubs, sneaking off when I was working my tail to the bone. Made a fool of me, she did. And no one makes a fool of Finster Poole. Not your mama. And certainly not you. You gonna tell me about your mama or will I have to resort to another means of persuasion?"

A flame leapt to life in the pit of my stomach. I glared at Finster. "Mama died. Not that it's any of your affair. Not after the way you treated her. I don't care who knows what my real name is. The reason I go by Mitzi is —"

The steel flashed and instantly a shot exploded. Gabe slammed into me, throwing me to the floor. Another shot came on the heels of the first one, and I knew Gabe had been hit. Probably killed. I think I screamed, but the noise in the room deafened me. From my spot on the floor, I turned to see faces above me. Animated. Shoving. Shouting.

"Police!" "Ambulance!" "Who's been shot?" "Where's Mitzi?"

I heard the words, but they came so fast I couldn't register them all.

Someone pulled me up, asking where the bullet had gone in. Someone else shook me. The smell of burnt gunpowder stung my nostrils, but no pain screamed from my body. Gabe, though, was slumped, slack jawed against the table. In the next instant, a tangle of strong arms lifted him. A fist-sized splatter of blood grew as big as a cantaloupe in a matter of seconds until his shirt was ripped from him and someone jammed a fist over the hole in his shoulder. I couldn't tell if he was breathing or not.

The room spun. I searched frantically to see where Finster had gone. The adrenaline leeched from me when I saw his sprawled body in the chair across from me—a gaping hole in Finster Poole's lifeless chest.

[CHAPTER 40]

Brooke

Mitzi squeezed out the final words, her forehead dotted with perspiration as if what she'd told me had happened yesterday, not more than half a century ago. The streetlight outside Gabe's window bathed the room in a phosphorous light.

"How awful you had to go through that. And Gabe—what a heroic man." I was having trouble imagining it. "Is that why you decided to spend your life with him?"

She cocked her head, a half-tilted smile with it. "Wouldn't you? He was willing to give his life for me. Both him and Red."

"What do you mean?"

"Red was hovering nearby; he'd been watching Finster from the minute he came into the Carlisle. After what happened with Penny, he was wary. Didn't want trouble to come to the club. He saw Finster pull the gun from his jacket and meant to shoot it out of his hand, but things happened so fast he shot him in the chest instead. And killed him."

A new wave of sympathy cradled me. "Surely no one believed it was murder."

"Red was arrested and got a plea bargain for a lesser charge—manslaughter, I think—on the grounds he was protecting his clientele. Still it was a media hoop-de-doo. Cameras flashing. Headlines in the papers like it was D-Day all over again. Outcries over the evil of clubs like the Carlisle. A religious coalition demanded all the clubs in Tulsa be shut down, calling jazz the work of the devil. Of course it never happened, but the Carlisle suffered a fatal blow."

Mitzi gripped my hand, her face gaunt, but it was as if a fury had been unleashed, and in a flurry, she continued, "The club closed, and Red, humiliated, sold the building and the fixtures to pay his legal fees and moved to Galveston. 'Gonna fish till Jesus comes,' he said. That threw me. I never thought of Red as a man of God, but one never knows."

Gabe stirred softly a few feet from where we sat. Peaceful. Unaffected by Mitzi's story. I stood and stretched. "I bet you could use a drink of water and some rest."

"I'm too keyed up to sleep, but some water would be nice."

I got her a glass from the nutrition room and snagged a cup of coffee for me. When I returned, Mitzi had changed into the nightclothes I'd brought her.

"Tell me, did you and Gabe have a wedding?"

"That's a story for another time."

"I've no place to go." I tucked a knitted throw around Mitzi and took a sip of my coffee. "So tell me about your wedding."

"Gabe spent a week in the hospital, and not a day went by he didn't hound me to get married. I knew I was deeply in love with him, but Jess Barlow's voice in my head wouldn't be quiet. *Unequally yoked*. I pushed it aside and prayed daily for a sign from God, hoping perhaps he'd sent me to be the rescuer of Gabe's soul."

"Was having the same beliefs that important?"

"I was no Bible scholar, but yes, I thought it was important. Not that God can't work any situation for good, but I'd seen the disaster of my parents' marriage, and I wanted more. I felt it in my bones and in my belly, where I'd burned an ulcer fretting over it. But every time I went to the hospital, I chickened out of discussing spiritual matters. Then Gabe was discharged and went home to Lou and Mary Ruth's. I stayed away for four days, afraid of what might become of me if I did the wrong thing. Scared witless to bring it up with Gabe.

"In the end, it was all for naught. One night I got up the nerve to bare my soul. Gabe and I sat as far apart as humanly possible on the scratchy sofa in Lou and Mary Ruth's living room. 'Gabe, about our getting married... We come from different worlds. I believe in Jesus and eternity, and as much as I respect the Jews being the chosen people, I can't see beating myself up the rest of my life because I married one. No doubt we'd have shouting matches and a brood of kids who won't know which one of us to side with. So unless we can come up with—'

"Gabe burst out laughing. Laughing, mind you. Then he knelt down beside me, taking my hands in his. 'Mitzi, I've tried to tell you. I don't belong in Brooklyn, in my family. Matter of fact, I'm the same as dead to them. If you'd been paying attention, you'd have noticed that Lou and I don't spend all our time planning what songs we're putting in the show. He's my spiritual mensch, the one I shared a foxhole with during the war. The one who asked if he'd see me in heaven while mortar fire sounded all around us. I didn't even believe in the hereafter—it's not part of the Jewish belief. But I'd sure enough seen hell in Germany, so I didn't know what to say.

" 'The next day we lost a third of our battalion, and that night, Lou told me about Jesus. I might be hardheaded, but when you look death in the eye, it doesn't take an Albert Einstein to figure out what to do.'

"Gabe and I got married the following Saturday in the Mt. Olivet church, with Lou and Mary Ruth as our witnesses. We left right after and went to St. Louis to look for my grandparents. All those years I'd thought it was Quincy, Missouri, but it turns out it was West Quincy. We found a couple of people who remembered my mother, and at the newspaper, we found my grandparents' obituaries."

Mitzi tossed the throw aside and reached for her glass of water. Sadness welled in her eyes.

I asked, "So they'd already passed away?"

"Murdered. And here's the eerie part. It was the month after Mama got lost in the dust storm. The newspaper claimed a vagrant robbed the house and shot them, but I've spent sixty years wondering if Finster Poole went there looking for Mama and us kids. That after shooting Mama's parents, he moved around to avoid suspicion. Who knows why or how he ended up in Tulsa, but I've always felt that God watched out for me when I didn't even know I needed watching."

A hollow spot in my chest seemed to swell. Not in sadness, but gratitude that Mitzi had been spared so many brushes with disaster. With death. My own pitiful circumstances felt small.

I asked, "So if you didn't sing at the Carlisle, how did your career start?"

"After West Quincy, we went on to New York. Gabe wanted to introduce me to his family, hoping his mama might have a change of heart and welcome me into the family."

Mitzi sipped her water.

"I guess she didn't."

"No, that took ten years. It wasn't until we sang on *Ed Sullivan* that she decided to welcome us. Funny what notoriety can get you. She was the sweetest lady you'd ever hope to know. She even taught me a bit of Yiddish over the years."

Mitzi fidgeted, pausing like she'd taken a side trip through time. "When we'd been in New York a couple of weeks, Lou tracked us down and said he had a gig for us in Philadelphia. Told us to get on over there; he and Mary Ruth had a surprise for us."

The door creaked open and a nursing assistant popped her head in. "You ladies all right? You need a pillow, Mrs. Steiner?"

"No, I've got my own, but thanks for asking. I don't think we've met. Are you new here?"

"Brand spanking. I'm Sue Horton. Night nurse."

Mitzi yawned. "That late already? Maybe I ought to call it a day."

I left soon after, promising Mitzi I would go to the DA's office the following morning. Walking to the car, I made a mental note to ask Mitzi what surprise Lou and Mary Ruth had in Philly. A falling star shot across the sky. More than sixty years ago, under this very sky, Gabe had made a wish. A wish that had come true.

I closed my eyes and wished for a miracle—one more magic moment for Gabe and Mitzi.

Mitzi's house shone with all the lights I'd left on, but after letting myself in and resetting the alarm, I called for Cosmo. Nothing. Thinking he'd given up on me coming home, I went into the den and found him crouched in Gabe's chair, his silver fur bristled like a porcupine. A shiver went through me as I did a quick look around. Gabe's pipe holder lay on the floor, the pipes scattered like toys on the carpet. My first thought, of course, was that something or someone had frightened Cosmo, but as I bent to scoop him up, he had one of the pipes tucked under his front paws.

I laughed, but it sounded hollow. My imagination was getting the best of me. After the day I'd had and hearing about Finster Poole, I knew I needed to get a grip. Cosmo had been bored. All day alone. My one quick zip in and out of the house hardly constituted quality time.

Still, the weariness I had moments earlier evaporated. I picked up the mess Cosmo had made and went to the kitchen to make a cup of tea. Chamomile to relax me. Cosmo followed, still acting skittish, and to satisfy myself, I rechecked all the doors and the alarm system and made a surreptitious peek around the drapes to see if anything looked unusual out front. Nothing.

Settling into the chintz chair in the kitchen, I pulled Cosmo up beside me and opened my laptop. I still couldn't wrap my brain around my unusual afternoon with Judith Zabel. I connected to the Internet and keyed in her name. Choosing the first article that popped up, I read about how she and her husband, Farris, had made contributions to the Tulsa Zoo, the ASPCA, recreational facilities, and political candidates, including L. Monroe Evans. Lance's father.

A few more clicks and I found a newspaper article about the Zabels celebrating with Betsy and Monroe Evans—his third victory as a state senator. Several society page quotes paired them again.

I switched to a search for Senator Evans, and on the first try I found the front-page article in the *Oklahoma Times Herald* reporting the airplane crash that claimed him and his wife of twenty-nine years, Elizabeth "Betsy" Evans. I enlarged the screen to see the photo, chilled at once by the striking similarity between Lance and his father. Betsy wore a plastic smile, her dark hair touching the shoulders of a prim, tailored suit. My throat clogged. It could have been my photo taken from my college yearbook. I swallowed hard, unable to keep from staring at her image on the screen.

Was it an act of fate that Lance picked me from the sea of paralegals at the seminar where we first met? I wondered.

I noted the date of the paper and searched the obituaries for the following day. The senator's was long and glowing, citing his many achievements. A shorter piece about Elizabeth followed.

> An avid animal lover, Betsy gave tirelessly of her time to the greater Oklahoma City Center for Animal Rights. Her constant companion and dearest friend, her Russian

> blue cat, Adonis, perished in the plane crash along with her.
>
> Survivors include a son, Lance M. Evans Jr. of the home and an aunt, Judith Gladys Zabel from Tulsa, OK.

The words stared back at me from the screen. Mrs. Zabel was Betsy's aunt. Why had Lance never mentioned she was a relative? And more disturbing, why had he not told me Cosmo was the same breed as his mother's beloved Adonis?

I remembered Lance's reaction when I'd brought Cosmo home from the shelter. He sneered and told me I should have consulted with him first, and for the first week or two, he shooed Cosmo away anytime he came near. I'd teased Lance about being jealous and he'd muttered, "I have no use for moronic creatures." I'd brushed it off, but I now wondered if Lance's disdain for cats, Cosmo in particular, stemmed from his relationship with his mother. A gut feeling gnawed at me.

I closed the laptop and carried Cosmo upstairs. As he purred beneath the covers, I knew what I had to do: visit once again with Judith Zabel.

[CHAPTER 41]

Mitzi

After Gabe's morning routine, I took advantage of the shower in his bathroom. I hummed a few bars of "New York, New York" while applying the fresh makeup Brooke had thankfully brought me. Things had worked out for Gabe and me. Not quickly and not without trauma, but I was blessed.

I was still humming and thinking of the first time Gabe and I went on the road when I stepped from the bathroom. I stopped cold when I saw Lance Evans sitting by Gabe's bed. Maybe Brooke's worry over Lance's vindictiveness was justified. She'd been afraid for me. And Cosmo. Neither of us had thought of Gabe.

Lance rose and rushed around the end of Gabe's bed. "Mrs. Steiner, how good to see you again."

"The only Mrs. Steiner I know is my mother-in-law, God rest her soul, and she's been gone for thirty years." I ignored the manicured hand he extended.

"Oh, I beg your pardon." His smile was dazzling, his composure graceful. Enchanting, if I didn't know better. "I remember my own mother, God rest her soul, saying the very same thing when people called her Mrs. Evans. My sincerest apologies. What would you have me call you?"

"Mitzi is fine. What can I do for you, Mr. Evans?"

"Please call me Lance." He reached behind him to the bedside table. "Here, I've brought you something." He extended a box of Godiva chocolates decorated with a gold bow.

"What's the occasion?" I ignored the box.

"No occasion. Just an offer of friendship. You've been on my mind so much lately. You and Brooke. Two very special ladies, I might add."

His teeth gleamed, two perfectly straight rows, set in a mouth more handsome than Cary Grant's. The smile never faltered as he continued. "I had hoped to see Brooke last night and apologize for something I said. I came by your house—waited outside until nearly midnight—but when you didn't come home, I feared something was wrong. Please pardon my intrusion. I had no idea your husband was in a vegetative state."

Anger seared my bones. Vegetative state indeed.

Gabe's eyes blinked open. "New York, New York. My kind of town."

I gasped. He'd heard me humming. Some thread had registered. I took Gabe's hand, noticing Lance's jaw had dropped. I hoped he'd swallowed his tongue. Gabe's eyes roamed the room, settling on a far corner. He mumbled, his words now unintelligible.

I turned to Lance. "My husband, as you can see, is not vegetative. You've intruded on a very personal part of my life, and I would prefer it if you would leave. As for Brooke, I'll let her know you stopped by. Whether she calls you or not is entirely up to her."

"A thousand pardons. And don't worry, I'll get in touch with Brooke myself." He laid the chocolates on a nearby chair and scooted out the door.

Gabe closed his eyes, an ethereal smile on his parched lips.

[CHAPTER 42]

Brooke

Jenna's roses were still on her desk when I arrived at seven fifteen the next morning, the first one in the office. The message envelope, still on the plastic pick, was from Andrés, Lance's florist of choice. Whether just curious or feeling a bit reckless, I slipped the card out and read, *Thanks for everything. Lance.* A shudder went through me. Lance and Jenna? Creepy.

I slipped the card back into place and went to my office. I pulled up Judith Zabel's file on my computer screen and wrote the report on my visit to her, trying not to color it with my own ideas of why she'd chosen our firm and had requested me in particular. Satisfied the report was complete, I emailed it to Ben Harrington and turned to my year-end comprehensive review, which was due on January 15.

The spreadsheets blurred before my eyes as I copied and pasted information back and forth. After finishing the first quarter, I noted the time. Jenna would be on break, and I wanted to slip out unnoticed for the two items on my agenda. Because the district attorney's office was closer than Judith Zabel's house, I went there first.

The receptionist clicked her maroon fingernails on the desk and asked my name and what time my appointment was.

I handed her my card. "I don't have an appointment, but was

hoping to speak to someone about a personal matter."

She studied the card with a furrowed brow and told me to take a seat. Moments later, she led me to the office of an assistant, a wiry man with John Lennon glasses who told me his name was Rory.

"How may I help you, Ms. Woodson?"

"I've come about obtaining a protective order."

"For a client?" He glanced at my card.

"No, for myself."

A cautious look crossed Rory's face. "I see."

He drew out a form as I told him briefly about my abuse. He probed me with questions. How many times had it occurred? How long had it been going on? Why had I decided to wait until now to file the order?

"I should have reported it the first time I ended up in the hospital, but I had hoped things would get better." I explained about the second hospital visit and breaking the engagement.

"My former fiancé has persisted in calling me, showing up at unexpected times, and threatening me in obscure ways. I'm weary of wondering what he might do next. I'd like a protective order."

"Are there any witnesses who've heard him make threats?"

I shook my head and remembered Lance's visit to Mitzi's on Christmas Eve. The exchange had been heated, but the only threat was that we'd talk later, which is what I explained to Rory.

"Do you have a therapist who can verify that you've been a victim?"

"No."

He scribbled a few notes, then leaned back, flipping a pencil back and forth between his fingers. "The abuse seems to be in the recent past. It can be unnerving, I know, but is it possible that you're imagining the current threats?"

"I am on edge, but no, they're not imagined."

"You seem like a reliable individual. We'll look into it. Check your records. In the meantime, are you in a safe place?" Rory made more scribbles on his pad, seeming almost bored.

"I work in the same building as Lance. It's hard to avoid contact."

"Lance? Last name? We'll need it for our investigation."

"Lance Evans."

The air thickened. "*The* Lance Evans? I knew you looked familiar." Rory's jaw went slack, his eyes round, and I detected a tremor of excitement in his voice.

The hair on the nape of my neck dampened as the realization hit me as well. Not only was I seeking insurance for my safety, I'd also put Lance's political dream in jeopardy. In an absurd moment, I wondered if that would work for or against me.

When I left, Rory effused charm with the assurance that my request would receive top priority. Shudders went through me as I imagined Rory and the DA holding a press conference, calling into question Lance's character. Or would they simply give an anonymous tip to a hungry reporter?

Although I knew what I'd done could come back to haunt me, I had no regrets. A light mist mixed with ice crystals had started when I emerged onto the street, but a flame licked its lips within me, fueling me onto the next item on my agenda. I stopped by a florist on Twenty-first Street and picked out a flowering kalonchoe, its tiny blooms reminiscent of the tint of Mrs. Zabel's hair.

She received it with grace when I presented it to her. "What a lovely plant." From her wicker queen's chair she directed me to place it on a low table by the sunroom window, then asked me to sit down.

"I hope you've not run into a snag in Philippe's lawsuit."

I wiggled into a more comfortable position. "No. Everything's in order."

"Then why have you come?"

"Merely a social call. I thought we might continue our conversation from yesterday. I left rather abruptly and beg your forgiveness."

"No offense taken. Would you care for some tea?"

"That would be perfect."

I asked about her poinsettia collection and inquired about her health and whether she liked to read books. She chatted and seemed much more animated than the day before, and I began to feel a little guilty that I was there under false pretenses. After the housekeeper brought our tea and we'd settled into drinking it, I said, "Yesterday you mentioned I looked like Betsy, Lance's mother. Could you tell me more about her?"

"She was lovely, as are you. Very shy most of her life. Contemplative."

"You were related, I believe."

"Oh my, yes. She was my niece, my sister's girl, but more like my own daughter, especially after her parents died." Tears filled her eyes.

"That must have been difficult."

"More than you know. Monroe—he was her husband—didn't understand her grief and thought she should be at his side for every rally and social gathering that he, as a state senator, attended. Having a child—that would be Lance—made her nervous as well, and I'm afraid she couldn't handle the pressure."

"I can only imagine."

She paused, seemingly slipping into another place as she continued. "She became withdrawn, taking comfort in her kitties. I didn't know the true depths of her despair, though, until the senator won his second term. Betsy had an engagement to cut the ribbon on a new animal shelter, but it coincided with a dinner the senator was to attend at the governor's mansion. Betsy called me from Baptist Hospital in Oklahoma City. Her face was a bloody mess and her arm broken. Compliments of the senator." Mrs. Zabel plunked her teacup on the table beside her, her lips drawn tight.

"I tried to get her to divorce him, but she wouldn't. And of course, the press covered up the incident. Betsy said she had to consider Lance, who was by now in junior high or so—an impressionable age. She was afraid Monroe would seek custody if the marriage ended, so she stayed. Truthfully, I think he would have killed her had she tried to leave. I know it was God's mercy that he took them both in a plane crash. And I'm grateful every day Lance has turned out so well-adjusted."

A sheen of disgust covered my body, but with it came a realization that Lance must've had his own childhood trials, maybe even a nightmare.

"I'm so sorry to hear of Betsy's sorrow. I know how hard it is to talk of abuse when it's someone you love. Tell me, was Lance ever a victim of his father's rage?"

She studied her gnarled fingers, her chin quivering ever so slightly. "I've often wondered. I noticed bruises on occasion, and when Lance was about ten, his nose was broken. Betsy assured me it was from playing peewee football, but . . . I don't know. Betsy was so fragile herself, I'm afraid she couldn't protect him."

My mind spun, trying to remember if Lance had ever mentioned a football injury or a broken nose. Nothing came. There were so many things about Lance I didn't know. Might things have been different if he'd confided in me?

Mrs. Zabel's wobbly voice pulled me back to the present. "Lance was a good boy. Such a blessing to me now." Her eyes twinkled full of pride. And love.

I'd seen that look in my dad's eyes when I'd learned to ride a bicycle. My eyes smarted with tears. What an odd thing to think of. It was as if it just popped loose, a stray memory. Had Dad loved CiCi and me and left to keep peace in the family? Of course not. He cheated on Mom and was the root of her bitterness.

Strange. I'd never heard my dad's version of the story, and for a moment, I was lost in my own rambling thoughts.

I blinked back to the present and saw that Mrs. Zabel's shoulders slumped even more than usual. I apologized for having made her tired, promising I would come back soon for a visit. But I knew I wouldn't. And the gravity of it sank like a stone as I turned the key in the ignition and pulled out of the drive.

Since it was time for lunch, I swung by the house and checked on Cosmo. No scattered tobacco pipes. Everything in order. I ate a sandwich, checked the alarm system, and went back to work. Fifteen minutes after my return to the office, Ben Harrington rapped on my door, then burst through it, red-faced and scowling. "We need to talk."

"Yes? Did you get my report on Mrs. Zabel?"

"Yes. That's not why I'm here, though. I had a call from the DA's office." He stood, looking over the top of his glasses like this information was going to make me start blubbering out an apology.

I widened my eyes and tilted my chin up a fraction. "And?"

"That's all you have to say? What in the name of thunder do you think you're doing? Lance warned me you might have gone over the edge. A protective order? What grounds do you have for such action? And trust me, you'd better have some. There are repercussions for making a false charge, and I'll not have you dragging this firm and my name through the mud."

His eyes looked like they might pop out, and I felt my own face flush, not in embarrassment, but disbelief. *What nerve.*

"False charge? Not hardly. Although I am guilty of not being more open in the beginning about Lance's abuse."

"A broken engagement is not abuse. What are you implying?" He had the stance of a bull. Immovable. The only thing missing was smoke pouring from his nostrils.

"Mr. Harrington. We handle cases regularly where you recommend protective orders if there is some danger. My absences over the last two months were the result of Lance's physical abuse."

"And you have proof of this?"

"I have emergency room records. Unfortunately, I told the hospital my injuries were from accidents. They weren't. Now I'm being harangued with visits and phone calls from Lance. Frankly, I'm afraid of what he might do. Believe what you will, but I think Lance will do something. I'd like to know I can count on you if that happens."

"Evans was right then. You are delusional. Your memory is also flawed. I hired you because of his recommendation. He is a friend of this firm. I cannot let your tantrums affect our reputation. I assured the DA that this was utter nonsense. He's agreed to keep it quiet for the time being and speak to Evans." He folded his arms, scowling, then jerked to attention. "Until this is straightened out, I have no alternative but to put you on an administrative leave of absence. Consider yourself fortunate. You could be fired."

"What about Mrs. Zabel? My year-end reports?"

"You're not irreplaceable. Good-bye, Miss Woodson."

He spun on the heels of his shoes, leaving me blinking, unable to speak. And as delusional as it might sound... relieved.

I collapsed into my chair and spun around like a three-year-old. Did a mental cha-cha-cha. Then it hit me. Lance had set me up by telling my boss I was unbalanced. Not only that, he had access to my office via Jenna, who he plied with roses so she would inform him of my comings and goings. I could see it all now—Lance and Jenna weren't a couple. He was using her. She no doubt called him the minute I left for lunch or an appointment so he could follow me or sneak into my office and sit in my chair so he could feel close to me.

The hair on my arms rippled. Lance could easily be checking

my computer, messing with my files, even reading my email. I did a quick check and found nothing personal except for posting my furniture on Craigslist. Was that how he just happened to be watching my apartment when the buyers had come to look over my things?

I hit delete on all my personal mail and cleared my Internet browsing history. My paralegal training kicked in. *Save your files.* I inserted a DVD and transferred all my work to date to be safe.

Lance would not get the best of me. I pulled out a box of printer paper, emptied the contents, and filled it with what few possessions I kept in my office. A coffee cup. The grooming items I kept for emergencies. My Day Planner. The DVD of my files. Pretty pathetic when I surveyed the items barely covering the cardboard bottom.

From my coat tree, I took a wool scarf and remembered I had gloves and an umbrella in my credenza. With my purse now nestled on top, I hefted the box up and sauntered out, not even locking the door behind me.

Jenna wore a silly fake grin when I approached her desk. "Going home early, Brooke? Jeez, it seems like you're never in the office anymore."

"Deal with it, cupcake. And while you're at it, you might speed-dial Lance and tell him Brooke has left the building." I breezed out the door.

[CHAPTER 43]

Mitzi

When Brooke arrived at the Guardian Light to pick me up, she brought with her a sight for sore eyes. Hadley Davis. He'd lost a good deal of weight, which I wouldn't have thought possible, since he was as skinny as a willow branch in the dead of winter to start with. He still had his spunk, though.

After a round of greetings, I asked what in mercy sakes he was doing with Brooke.

"Now, Miz Steiner. You know I'd a come sooner, but there's more to tending to the business of the deceased than you can imagine. Brooke, though, convinced me that staying holed up forever ain't no good for a body."

"I've missed seeing you, I'll admit."

Brooke, who'd been hanging back, also had a twinkle in her eye. "Mitzi, I've engaged Mr. Davis to attend you for the next couple of days. I've had a slight change in my schedule and have to go out of town."

"Something for your job?"

"Not exactly. I am apparently not needed at Cooke, Harrington, and Baumgartner any longer and am on an administrative leave of absence."

"Oh my stars. Does this have anything to do with your errand this morning?"

Brooke nodded. "Unfortunately. And don't worry, you don't have to be secretive with Mr. Davis."

Hadley interrupted, "*Miss Woodson*, how many times do I have to remind you to call me Hadley?" Then to me. "Brooke told me about her restraining deal. She's got another mission now."

"What Hadley is trying to say is I may have started an avalanche with my visit to the DA, so I'm going to disappear for a day or two. I'm taking an honest-to-goodness trip to Texas to see my dad, to hear his version of our family story."

The room vibrated with chatter, Brooke and Hadley interrupting each other like a set of twins, but I finally pieced it all together. Since Brooke didn't know how long her leave would last or even if she would have a job afterward, she wanted to do some things to get her life back on track. I gave her my own bit of news.

"See that box of chocolates?" I pointed to the table. "Lance brought those by. Said he'd been meaning to get to know me better. I know a polecat when I smell one. I sent him on his way, but you know, I think your leaving town might be a good thing. Lance made it clear he was looking for you."

Brooke's eyes narrowed. "He'll be livid when he finds out what I've done, if he hasn't already. It's not me I'm worried about. He could still try to coerce you into giving him information."

Hadley again. "That's where I come in. I always wanted to be a bodyguard. So now let's figger this out. What time do I need to pick you up in the morning and come fetch you in the afternoon?"

Shaking my head, still feeling like a chicken leg two dogs were fighting over, I told him, "You ought to remember I get here early, before the breakfast comes around. And you can suit yourself in the evenings. Six, seven, it doesn't matter. So tell me again, Brooke, when are you leaving?"

"As soon as I can pack a few things. I'll spend the night in Dallas and drive down to Georgetown in the morning."

"Does your dad know you're coming?"

"Not yet. And I'm not telling Mom or CiCi either. Truth is, I can't wait to get on the road. I've never done a spontaneous thing in my life. Oh, y'all will have to take care of Cosmo while I'm gone. Can you handle that?"

Hadley. "Sure can, missy. I've been hankering for some company. I'll take him on home with me when I drop Miz Steiner off." He stepped over to Gabe's bedside. "Sleeping like a lamb." Hadley's Adam's apple wobbled. "Sure am grateful now my Lily's at peace." He reached over the bed and pulled the covers over Gabe's shoulder. The one where Finster's bullet went in.

Brooke brushed a kiss on Gabe's forehead, gave me a hug, and thanked Hadley for helping out. "See y'all in a few days."

Hadley stood on one foot, then another. "Sure could use me a cup o' coffee. You don't happen to have a gin rummy deck around here, do you?"

[CHAPTER 44]

Brooke

I was on the Indian Nation Turnpike when my cell phone rang. Drew. So much had happened since he'd called to say he made it back to Boston. I smiled as I answered.

"Hey, Brooke."

"Hey yourself."

It seemed as if he'd been gone a year, not five days. First, I had to tell him about Gabe's seizure. How Mitzi pretended I didn't know she thought Gabe was dying. That I finally knew what happened to Finster Poole. My unexpected job situation, and what I'd learned from Lance's aunt, Judith Zabel.

"Do you think Lance will find out you filed for a protective order?"

"More than likely he already knows. Ben Harrington said the DA would be talking to him."

"Lance won't let it slide. He'll retaliate in some way."

"Hey, are you trying to scare me? I've been doing a good job of that all by myself. But I can't let that concern me anymore."

"Listen, just because you've changed doesn't mean he has."

"True, but I'm tired of avoiding him, and trying to second-guess what happens next. I'm ready to get on with life. I didn't tell you, but I'm thinking of enrolling as a full-time student at TU and getting my art degree. I'll have to apply for financial aid and take out a loan, but it excites me to think about it."

"And your current job?"

"I imagine Mr. Harrington will find a way to fire me. Even if he doesn't, I'm not going back. I can do part-time legal aid to pay for gas and groceries."

A casino near the Texas border lit up the night sky with flashing neon lights and a marquee with the name of a country star who was performing. It made me think of Mitzi's upcoming gig at the Jazz Depot. A few minutes later, the WELCOME TO TEXAS sign appeared, so I told Drew I'd better watch my driving.

"I've missed you, Brooke." The words were like stardust in the encroaching dark.

"I've missed you, too."

~

It rained all the way from Dallas to Georgetown the next day, a miserable continuous rain that kept my attention on the road and off the insanity of what I was doing. Dad had sounded surprised, but pleased, when I'd called him. He told me to meet him at Woodson Electric on Austin Street. "It's on the main drag. Can't miss it. There's a blinking neon blue sign that says 'Let Us Fix Your Shorts.' A little Texas humor there."

Eew. What have I gotten myself into?

I couldn't recall the last time I'd seen Dad, and I honestly didn't think I would recognize him. But I did. He was fit, tanned, had more gray hair than blond, and he had the same blue eyes as CiCi. He welcomed me with a hug and told a guy at the counter he was taking the rest of the day off.

I followed his truck to a tidy house half a dozen blocks from downtown. The rain had stopped, giving a fresh-washed look to the white clapboard bungalow. Sage green trim. A rock garden in front and a swing hanging from a high branch in an oak tree. A swing my stepbrother and sister, whom I'd never met, had undoubtedly swung on through childhood bliss. The taste of longing was bitter in my mouth.

"Eva's gone to help Marcy move into an apartment. It's her senior year over at Stephen F. Austin." Eva. My stepmother, who'd stolen my dad away from Mom. I vaguely recalled Marcy was his daughter.

"And your son?" It sounded so odd, talking with my dad about this whole life he had separate from mine.

"That would be Will. He's a freshman at Texas Tech. Wants to be a pharmacist."

We bantered around, both of us polite but guarded. And as much as I hesitated to admit it, I found myself drawn to him. The dad I barely knew. Down-home. Pleasant. And a hard worker from the looks of the leather recliners and cheerfully decorated home. A tad too much Texas paraphernalia, but nice.

He went through a door to the kitchen, hollering over his shoulder, "Can I get you a beer? A Coke?"

"Diet Coke if you have it."

He brought back a Bud Light and my soda and offered me a seat.

He kicked up the footrest on his recliner and said, "So now, what brings you to Texas?"

No more time to dance around pleasantries. It was showtime. "You. Mom. I want to hear your version of what happened. Why you left." *And why you never came back.*

His fingers tightened on the beer can, pale eyebrows drawn together as though trying to come up with the answer. "You deserve some answers, can't argue there, and I can only imagine what your mother's told you. Sure you want to know?"

"Would I drive nearly four hundred miles in a blinding rain if I didn't?"

He looked at the ceiling for a moment, then directly at me. "Your mom and I married young, but I was a fool in love with her. Didn't take long 'fore I realized we had different ideas. I was working on my journeyman's license to be an electrician. She wanted me to be the CEO of the power company. I knew where she was coming from. She grew up without much and was determined to do better."

I motioned for him to go on.

"You girls came along early in the marriage, so we didn't have much in the way of extras, but she wouldn't let up. Wanted me to apply for office jobs. Go into insurance. She got more antsy, more demanding, more everything. The pressure built until I thought I would blow a gasket." He took a long, slow swig of his beer.

He'd described life with Mom to a tee. "So I guess you felt justified in having an affair."

Dad coughed, sputtered, a spray of beer ejecting from his mouth. "That's what you think?"

"Well, it's true, isn't it?"

He wiped the beer with a handkerchief from his Levi's pocket. "Guess your mother and I also have different memories. She went out sometimes at night when I got home and could watch you girls. She told me she was going to Tupperware and jewelry parties. I found out from a neighbor she was meeting a married man old enough to be her father at a club on Sheridan."

My heart fluttered like a canary trapped in a shoe box. "I've never heard this before. How do I know you're not lying to me?"

"You don't. You asked what happened. I'm telling you. She denied everything and called me a liar, the way you're thinking now. Threw me out and served divorce papers within a month."

My head couldn't connect the dots with what I was hearing. Mom threw him out?

"Surely you had visitation rights, some way to stay involved in our lives."

"Having rights and getting past your mother were two different things. I saw you girls once, maybe twice a month the first year. She used you as leverage to punish me for not measuring up. And quite possibly for revenge, because I heard later her affair didn't work out."

"So you left without looking back?"

He shrugged. "You and CiCi were the only things for me in Tulsa. A buddy o' mine heard about some jobs in Dallas, so we went there. I came to Tulsa several times over the next year. Same song and dance from your mother. Although I did get a judge to let me see you once. I'd bought you a pink bicycle for your birthday and wanted to give it to you in person." A hitch came in his voice.

The memory of his face when he taught me to ride the bike came to me. I knew he was telling the truth. He brushed his bronzed forearm across his eyes. "You learned to ride that weekend. Best memory I ever had of you."

Me too. My only memory, to be exact.

"Thank you for telling me. I admit it's not what I expected to hear. I know you sent money, and of course you know Mom never married." It seemed ironic in a way. Dad had a good life. She was still beating against the current.

We went out to eat Mexican food, and he told me about meeting Eva, coming to Georgetown, and, after a few years, buying his own electrical business. I hadn't intended to stay any longer than it took to get the facts and satisfy my curiosity, then head back to Tulsa. I hadn't counted on feeling such a connection to Dad and was surprised at the fierce craving I had to reclaim the last twenty-five years of my life. So when he offered, I accepted his invitation to sleep in Marcy's room.

After a breakfast of Cheerios and milk, he took me out to Lake Georgetown, showed me his favorite fishing spot, and asked a million questions about me and CiCi. What were our favorite foods? Movies? What did we dream about? I told him CiCi was pregnant and thought I noticed his chest puffing out a little at the idea of being a grandpa.

We walked on wide boards to the end of a boat dock. Below us, the lake breathed murky green sighs. Dad jammed his hands in his Levi's and turned to me. "What about you? Anyone you're seeing?"

"Not now." Wet lake smells enveloped me as I decided what, if anything, I should say about Lance. A chill breeze rose from the water. "It's a long story."

"They usually are. I'm a good listener."

It was easier than I imagined to tell him how I'd fallen in love with Lance. How handsome he was and the way he'd spoiled me. And how quickly the relationship had soured. I left nothing out.

His nostrils flared against a red face. "Thank God you didn't marry him. Hope there's no trouble in your future."

"Lance hasn't disappeared gracefully. I'm taking one day at a time."

"I've got your back if you need me."

Having my dad believe me and come instantly to my defense made me regret I'd missed knowing him. I dangled my keychain in front of him with the pepper spray I'd attached to it. "Girl's secret weapon. I'll be fine. I'm staying with a dear friend."

"Lord have mercy. What kind of twisted world do we live in that my own daughter has to carry pepper spray?" Dad shook his head, and before long we left the dock and talked of other things. Endless conversations, skipping from subject to subject like the rocks he taught me to skip earlier that day. When the hour grew too late for me to make it back to Tulsa, I agreed to spend another night. As we ate the burgers he cooked on his backyard grill, I told him about

Mitzi and Gabe and tried to pass off Drew Caprice popping into my life lightly. Dad saw beneath the veneer and wiggled his eyebrows with a knowing look.

After he put my suitcase in the Mustang the following morning, he hugged me long and hard. Then he held me at arm's length. "Don't be mad at your mother. I gave up that hunt long ago. Thing is, we all make mistakes. And I have a feeling she needs you more than you think."

He opened the car door for me and winked. "I'm betting on the doctor. You're welcome to bring him down anytime."

As I pulled away, I glanced in my rearview mirror. Dad had one arm raised, the hand of the other swiping across his eyes. I turned the corner, found my way back to Austin Street, and headed north.

[CHAPTER 45]

Mitzi

Hadley took me to the doctor to get the cast off my arm and had the decency not to wince when he saw it shriveled and peeling from being in the dark so long. It itched like fire, so I had him drive me home to take a long soak in the tub. "Thanks. See you in the morning."

"Anything you say, Miz Steiner." He nodded in that elegant, gentlemanly way he had and watched from the car window until I unlocked the door and waved him on.

Stillness bore down in the house. I'd missed Brooke something fierce since she'd been gone, and I couldn't wait to see her. She'd called to tell me she'd be in late and sounded relieved when I told her I hadn't had any more run-ins with Lance.

After my bath and scrubbing my arm until it was pink as a baby's bottom, I turned on the CD player and warmed up my voice by singing along. Foolish to think anyone would want to hear me sing. And all that nonsense about picking out the right outfit for my stint at the Jazz Depot. I had a closet overflowing with gowns. One of them would surely suffice.

I cranked the volume on the music and went upstairs to the cedar closet in Brooke's room. The smell was intoxicating—wine for the senses. I pulled the string on the light and wandered into the closet. Memories washed over me like water through my fingers. "What on earth were you thinking? An encore performance by an old has-been like me?" The words muffled in the tiny space, absorbed by the fox and mink coats standing like watchmen in a forest of chiffon and brocade. I plucked a half dozen of the newer dresses, the ones from when rhinestones and shoulder pads were in style, and draped them over my arm.

In the distance, Gabe sang a solo part on the CD, his voice so real I could almost imagine him appearing in the doorway to sweep me off my feet once again.

When you smile at me, I see heaven in your face.
When you take my hand, I feel the Master's touch.

Tears sprang unbidden to my eyes. The garments standing at attention on their hangers blurred into a collage of the finest years of my life, and the more I blinked the tears away, the more they came. I gasped for air while groping for the door to get out. The music came louder now, the chorus where our voices joined.

You're the one. The one who fills my senses.
And I thank Him for the dream of you.

My shoulders shook, violent jerks as I dropped on the edge of Brooke's bed. Our song. The one and only one Gabe wrote for me. My mind drifted back to the hospital room where I lay in shambles, my womb emptied prematurely for the third time.

Gabe held me then, stroked my hair, kissed my tears. The next day he took me home, and presented me with his special gift—"I See Heaven in Your Face." It sold a million copies.

Oh, the sweetness...the ecstasy of walking this road with Gabe at my side.

I gathered up the gowns, now stained with tears. Who needed these old rags from the past? Drew and Brooke had given me another chance to share Mama's music—and Gabe's—with the world. And dadgumit, I wanted a new dress. I deserved it. Flutters came in my chest.

Yes, I knew exactly the dress I wanted.

[CHAPTER 46]

Brooke

The drive home took nine hours, with two stretches of construction slowing me down. I didn't mind. A part of me wanted to stay away, forget the past, forget the present. Like that would ever work. What the drive did give me was time to process. Dad hadn't intentionally abandoned us. Nor did he have an affair. Of that I was certain . . . and glad.

Why hadn't Mom told CiCi and me the truth? At the very least, she owed us the courtesy of an explanation. Not only for the lies, but also for denying me the right to have a dad. My fingers grew numb from gripping the steering wheel.

It also annoyed me that she never believed me about Lance. I did feel bad that I hadn't gone to see her over the holidays. Maybe I'd been punishing her for not believing me. Or *in* me.

Dad said to let it go. Not directly, but from his open approach, his acceptance of what was.

By the time I got to the I-44 turnoff in Tulsa, I'd made a decision. Talk to Mom. Ask her for the truth and see what happened. Accept the consequences if things got messy. Personally, I was ready to carve out the new Brooke. More than ready to call Rory at the DA's office and proceed with a protective order. Ready to explore the longings that pierced my heart when Drew had prayed over Mitzi on Christmas morning. Maybe CiCi's church would be a good place to find the answers, to get in touch with God.

Night had crept in by the time I turned onto Mom's street. Once a modest subdivision, it now had cars in various stages of disrepair lining the streets. I swung into the last parking spot in front of her mailbox. The gas lamp in the yard had quit working years ago, but lights glowed in her living room window. I took a deep breath and grabbed my purse, then hurried up the sidewalk.

The TV blared behind the front door, actors shouting, canned music muffling the words. I rang the doorbell, clicked the key ring lock button for the Mustang before slipping my keys into my pocket, and waited. No answer. Another shout, this one not from the TV. A sense of foreboding started in my toes, snaking its way upward all the way to my throat.

I tried the doorknob, surprised when it opened freely, and promptly stumbled over a magazine basket. Catching my balance, I jerked my head toward the sofa on the far wall.

Mom sprawled in an awkward, half-sitting, half-reclining position, a figure hovering over her.

Lance.

With one knee on the sofa, he leaned in, sinewy hands clamped on her shoulders. "For the last time, tell me where Brooke is. And don't give me that bunk about not talking to her for two weeks."

Mom's eyes were wide; her face twisted, as whimpers pulsed through her lips. Our eyes met, and a million words traveled unspoken between us.

Dawning.

Understanding.

And terror.

Adrenaline barreled through me as I groped for the key ring in my pocket, getting a grip on the canister of pepper spray. I rushed toward them. "Stop! Get away from my mother. Now."

Lance whirled around and jumped to his feet, his dark look penetrating. "You! How dare you? Where have you been?" His voice bounced from the walls, his body taut, fists knotted.

"How dare I? What right do you have to intrude on my mother's privacy, demanding information? What were you going to do? Beat it out of her the way you did me?"

In my peripheral vision, I could see Mom inching toward the end of the sofa, away from Lance, but I dared not take my eyes from him as he sneered, trying to collect himself.

He hissed through clenched teeth. "You had no right to accuse me, to go to the DA."

"I should have done it months ago. It wasn't until I realized how desperate you were that I knew I had to stand up for myself. You're always wanting to talk. Let's talk."

"There's nothing to talk about—"

"I think there is. Let's start with Judith Zabel. Why didn't you tell me she was your aunt?"

He backed up a fraction, the pulse in his neck throbbing. "It's immaterial. She's just an old woman."

"She thinks you hung the moon. Couldn't quit talking about you. And she was kind enough to tell me about your mom, the way she stood by your dad, even when he sent her to the emergency room."

"My mother deserved it. All of it. She never once protected me or kept my old man from knocking me around." Lance's eyes flashed, his muscles so tight I thought he might explode.

Inside, I felt my own buildup of steam, and like a neon flash, I remembered the night in my bedroom. *You're no different from her.* I stumbled back at the impact of the memory and whacked my thigh on the end table. Wincing, I clutched the pepper spray tighter in my coat pocket.

"Your mother didn't deserve to be abused, Lance. And neither do I."

"You've ruined me. My career. How could you?" He snarled—almost feral—but it was too late for me to back down now.

"I tried to convince you to get help. I thought—"

"No one cares what you thought. You could've had everything with me. Now you've wrecked it all." He lunged forward, his hands reaching but not quite grasping my arms. I pushed him away with my free arm, holding it as a shield in front of me. I pulled my keychain from my pocket, ready to blast him with pepper, but he was quicker. He flew at me, whacking my arm. The keychain skittered across the floor. With his forearms, he backed me against the front door, his fingers encircling my throat.

I spit in his face, swinging my arms, stomping my feet.

His bourbon breath assailed me as his grip tightened. "No one makes a fool of me."

In my mind, I heard Mitzi's words. It was the same expression Finster Poole had screamed at her before he pulled out his gun.

I gasped, squeaking out my retort. "You made yourself into a fool."

The pressure of his hands cut off my windpipe. Still I squirmed and tried to shout, my voice hoarse. "Get away from me. Go. Leave us alone."

The air grew thinner. Spots before my eyes. No air. No breath. Nothing but a loud crack and the sound of tinkling glass as all resistance left my body.

I floated, my body free, no chains around my neck. Rest. Sweet, beautiful rest.

The air around me moved. A gentle breeze. Cool on my face. My eyelids fluttered, and I wondered if I was in heaven. The light was blinding, but a hand held mine and hovered above me. Perhaps it was an angel.

I forced my eyes open, expecting to see a winged cherub. Instead a figure knelt beside me, a flashlight panning inches above my face. Someone spoke. "She's coming around. You got the guy cuffed?"

Then on the other side, Mom—on her knees—cradled my cheeks with bleeding hands. Tears trickled from her eyes, making pale streams through her desert beige makeup. She smiled and whispered, "I'm so sorry. So sorry. How can you ever forgive me?"

"What happened? Where's Lance? Why are you bleeding?"

She looked surprised at her blood-stained fingers. "Oh my. Must've cut my hand when I whacked Lance with my genuine reproduction Waterford vase. Smashed it to smithereens." She picked a shard of glass from the sleeve of my coat. "And I'd do it again in a heartbeat."

I reached for her face and smoothed away a tear. "Thanks, Mom. For everything."

[CHAPTER 47]

Mitzi

The window of La Belle Formal Wear sported the latest looks for Valentine's Day. Bubble dresses with pink polka dots. Skimpy after-five numbers in Barbie doll sizes. But one bald, faceless mannequin wore a red evening gown that pert near gave me heart palpitations. This was the one. Brooke steadied me and held the door for me as her mother, Beverly, trailed behind.

The clerk, a busty girl in sling-back pumps, hurried over to us. "What may I do for you ladies?"

Brooke nodded toward the window. "The red dress, please. For her." She pointed to me.

"Really? We have a number of dresses suited for older women over here. I'm sure we could find something in lavender or one a bit more understated."

"No. Her mind's made up."

The salesgirl smiled politely, asked for my size, and scurried off.

Beverly ogled the dresses on the racks, peeking at the price tags. "Sheesh! You could get these at half the price on the Glamour Network."

"Mom. You promised. No more home shopping."

To which Beverly waved her away. "Okay. So I have a vice. You must admit, I got a great deal on the outfit I'm wearing to Mitzi's concert."

"Whatever."

When the salesgirl returned and showed me into a changing suite, I had second thoughts. Why had I told Brooke I wanted to wear red? Had I lost my ever-lovin' mind? Shimmying the sequined creation over my head, I told myself for the umpteenth time it didn't matter what I wore; no one was coming to hear me sing anyway.

Brooke knocked on the door. "Need any help?"

"Matter of fact. Be a doll and zip this up for me."

She tugged on the zipper while I held my breath and held the fabric in at the waist. I turned this way and that, looking at my image in the mirror. "What do you think?"

Brooke peeked around my shoulder, her face glowing, the bruises around her neck now faded to pale yellow. "It's fabulous. Just like you're going to be."

"You're a dreamer, Brooke Woodson."

Outside the dressing room, a cell phone rang, and we heard Beverly's voice. Then her knock on the door.

"Brooke, Mitzi. Sorry to interrupt, but it's CiCi. She's in labor. We have to go."

Brooke's eyes widened. "Today? Now? She's not due for another three weeks. Yes, we'll hurry and go, but don't you think CiCi and Todd can manage until we get done here?"

Beverly huffed off and hollered over her shoulder. "It's my first grandchild."

A few minutes later, with the red dress in a box as big as a trombone case, we piled into Brooke's Mustang. She tuned the radio to a soft jazz station and asked if I wanted to go home or to the care center.

"The Guardian Light. Hadley's coming over to show me something."

"And what would that be?"

"Just something."

"Mitzi. You can't fool me. What are you hiding?"

"I know you won't approve, but a man in Hadley's neighborhood went into the nursing home over on Peoria last week. He has a perfectly good, twelve-year-old Cadillac he needs to sell. He doesn't have many assets, so I'd be doing the poor man a favor by taking it off his hands."

Brooke threw up her hands. "Have you discussed this with Drew? With Henry?"

"No need. I'm a big girl. Ever since I got these new glasses, I've been itching to get behind the wheel. And it's a nice, heavy car. Lots of muscle."

"You're impossible. And nuts!"

Beverly chimed in from the backseat. "Good grief, Brooke. Give Mitzi the benefit of the doubt. When did you get to be so bossy?"

"I guess I learned from an expert." She looked in the rearview mirror at Beverly in the back. "Kidding, Mom. You know I love you."

Brooke wheeled into the Guardian Light parking lot. "Here you go. Give Gabe a hug, okay?"

I took the dress box from Beverly. "Call me about the baby. And be careful."

A breeze whipped a plastic bag across the parking lot as Brooke rounded the circle drive. I gave the two of them a wave. A heaping lot of good getting new glasses did. I could barely make out the Mustang for the tears in my eyes.

[CHAPTER 48]

Brooke

The last Sunday in February

A white limousine waited in front of Mitzi's house when Mom and I arrived to go with Mitzi and the Caprice clan to the Jazz Depot. A lot had happened in six weeks, but things seemed headed in the right direction. After Lance's attack, the media coverage had been extensive, but Mom had been my champion in keeping reporters away from me.

Drew called from Boston as often as his intern schedule would allow, and I'd told him everything about Lance: the attack, his arrest, my good fortune that my larynx was only bruised, not crushed. When he'd arrived in Tulsa two days before Mitzi's big day, our time alone was brief. A visit to Gabe. Dinner with Mom. One quick walk around Swan Lake where we'd held hands and I'd given him the latest update.

"Lance is no longer a candidate for DA. His hearing is still three months away. No clue what will happen. First-time offense for assault will probably get him probation and a review from the bar association."

Drew had stopped and looked deep into my eyes. "I'm sorry. You deserve more justice than that. And I worry about your safety, whether he might retaliate now that his reputation is ruined."

Before me, Swan Lake lay in glassy stillness. "It would consume me if I let it, and I still catch myself looking over my shoulder at times. I know now Lance was a victim himself. The therapist CiCi's pastor recommended has helped me a lot." I gazed into Drew's kind and gentle face. "I'm going to be all right. Mitzi told me not to borrow trouble—'we're only promised today.'"

He chuckled. "She ought to know."

"By the way, Jenna from the office actually called and apologized to me for ratting me out all the time to Lance. According to her, Lance told a friend who told someone in accounting that he was considering moving to Dallas when this is settled. With Jenna, who knows? The funny thing is, she asked me to go to lunch next week. She wants to talk about going back to school next fall. I'd like that—someone to hang out with in the Student Center."

Drew told me about his rotation in pediatrics and smiled when I showed him a picture of CiCi and Todd's bundle of pink. Mom and I had both fallen in love with Hannah Beth, who'd arrived the day after our shopping trip. Valentine's Day. Tiny but healthy, and already taking after Mom and CiCi with her bossiness.

Mom and I seemed headed in the right direction, too. We had more than a few emotional discussions about my dad. Nothing was settled, but we were both trying. That was something at least. I'd even gone to stay with Mom to make room for Mitzi's guests.

When I pulled into Mitzi's drive, Drew came to greet us. Three long strides.

Mom whispered, "Having a doctor in the family could have its perks, you know."

"Don't go there, Mom. Today is Mitzi's day, so behave yourself, okay?" I gave her a bug-eyed, teasing look that made her laugh.

Drew took the package I handed him from the backseat. "So what's this?"

"A surprise. Something for later." Mom and I followed him into the living room. Drew introduced us to his parents, Jill and Henry

Caprice, who'd arrived late the night before and I was meeting for the first time. Handshakes and I'm-so-happy-to-meet-yous all around. I took an instant liking to both of them. Warm. Friendly.

To me, Henry said, "Mitzi can hardly wait for the surprise she has for you."

"Really? Drew mentioned the same thing. Where is Mitzi, anyway?"

Drew took my hand. "You'll see."

My insides fluttered. Just being in the same room with him made me woozy with longing. Then Drew cleared his throat, and Mitzi—shimmering in her red sequined gown—stood at the top of the staircase. Beside her a petite older woman smiled, linking arms with Mitzi. Slowly they descended.

I'd never seen the woman before, although she looked familiar. She was pixielike, with sparkling eyes and a flowing leopard print pantsuit.

Mitzi's eyes gleamed, too, as she walked toward me. "Brooke. There's someone I want you to meet." She presented her friend's hand. "This is Penny Vaughn, my friend I told you about. Penny, please meet Brooke."

My heart leapt. "Penny? Your friend from the Carlisle? I had no idea. You never told me what happened."

Mitzi chuckled. "There's a lot I haven't told you, but Penny and I have remained friends all these years. I told you Lou and Mary Ruth had a surprise for us in Philadelphia. It was Penny. She traveled the world with us as my personal assistant. Mercy, I can't tell you how many colors of the rainbow she's dyed my hair."

Mitzi winked at Henry. "It was Henry's idea to bring Penny. She likes sunny California more than Oklahoma these days, but she jumped at the chance to fly out with Henry and Jill."

Penny came quickly to me. She looked exactly as Mitzi had described her. Only soft with age. She took both my hands in hers.

"I'm so glad to meet you. I think you and I have a lot in common." I thought she meant our brushes with disaster, but she said, "We've both been best friends with Mitzi."

Mitzi interrupted. "Hurry up. We don't have all day."

The limo's first stop: the Guardian Light. Maple whispered to Mitzi in the hall, "I got your man spruced up for you. My, but that aftershave of his made me wish I was married to him myself."

Although he smelled nice, Gabe looked as gaunt as usual, his skin draped carelessly over his frame, like a throw slung over the back of a chair. Our tidy group burst with small talk all at once, then lapsed into stillness. It was Penny who stepped in and got the ball rolling.

"My lands, Gabe, do you know what a coon's age it's been since I heard y'all sing? Mitzi here promised us a little concert. You listen up now." She nodded at Drew to start the CD player as Gabe's eyes blinked twice, then closed.

Sweet orchestra music with a muted trumpet filled the room. Mitzi stood at the foot of the bed, back erect, eyes shining. Sweet and low, her voice rose from her chest as she sang "I See Heaven in Your Face." The wrinkles in Gabe's face seemed to melt for an instant, but his eyes remained closed. Mitzi sang on till the end, then bowed at the boisterous applause from the six of us. Her hand trembled ever so slightly as she smoothed a wrinkle in Gabe's bedspread.

Drew had stopped the music, waiting for a signal from Mitzi. She bit her lip and nodded.

Why should I feel discouraged, why should the shadows come,
Why should my heart be lonely, and long for heaven and home.

Mitzi closed her eyes, the melody vibrating within her as if in anticipation for something to break free. The coverlet over Gabe's body shifted like the ocean waking up. From his head-elevated position, his lips parted, the wobbly motion of words trying to form. Mitzi inhaled deeply, her voice filling every corner and crevice in the room.

I sing because I'm happy.

Gabe's eyes fluttered open, his gaze stopping momentarily on each of us circling his bed until they rested squarely on Mitzi. He blinked, his reedy neck taut as he righted his head. Mitzi sang on, her eyes locked on Gabe's, until the final violin strains waned into silence. Drew, standing beside me, took my hand and squeezed it softly. No one dared breathe, our gazes set on Gabe, whose lips curved into the lopsided smile of his youth.

Finally, he spoke. "My wife used to sing that song. She was pretty as a songbird." It sounded like gravel was clogging his vocal chords.

Mitzi hurried around the bed and leaned over him. "Gabe. You remembered."

"She was something, you know." His eyes glittered as his gnarled fingers touched Mitzi's face. "Say, if you see her around, would you tell her I said hello?"

Tears tracked a crooked path down Mitzi's cheeks as she caressed Gabe's hand. With a sigh, he relaxed back into the pillow, eyes closed, his smile sagging like the evening sun over the horizon.

Mitzi

I couldn't get over all the fuss. The Jazz Depot exhibit hall was popping at the seams with all the people streaming in, shaking my hand, wrapping me in their arms.

Then, before I knew it, Drew guided me into the high-ceilinged auditorium, and a flood of memories took over. The old Union Depot, one of the magnificent art deco buildings of Tulsa, had been restored to its reminiscent look of days gone by, and a sense of pride coursed through me in that moment. A little spiffing up gives all of us antiques new life.

I stood to the side of the stage while the manager of the Jazz Depot introduced me. Applause burst out, and the audience rose in a giant wave of black and tan.

Mercy sakes.

When the band started, I closed my eyes and let the spirit move me. Gabe's music. Mama's music. And mine. I took a dozen bows, and before my finale, the manager sprinted onstage and to the mic. "Isn't she fabulous?"

Hoots and hollers from the audience.

"Mitzi, it's our great honor to have you, one of the jewels of Tulsa, here with us. We wish Gabe could be here with us, but we know that even though he's resting at the Guardian Light, he's with us here in spirit."

The applause and standing ovation lasted a good five minutes. When I reclaimed my bearings, I stepped to the microphone. "I came to Tulsa quite by accident, you know. But in case you haven't noticed, there are no accidents with God. He directed me here, brought a wonderful man into my life, and gave us an astonishing career. If not for him and all of you, I wouldn't be here today. I'm honored and blessed."

While I spoke, Brooke joined me on the stage. Confused at her presence, I said, "Did they send you up here to make me behave?"

Brooke made a terrible effort at suppressing a giggle. "Mitzi, you've become more than a good friend. And I'm glad I'm one of the coincidences in your life. I hardly know how to say thanks, but I have something for you. I hope you approve." She presented me with a gift-wrapped box.

My fingers trembled as Brooke helped me with the ribbon and lifted the lid. I gasped. "Oh, my stars!"

A framed drawing of Gabe and me was nestled in the folds of the tissue paper. The two of us as a couple of young, stars-in-our-eyes dreamers. When I lifted it out, I saw shadowed above our youthful images pastel likenesses of the way we now looked. Soft. A little worn. But still with a twinkle in our eyes.

Brooke had captured a lifetime on canvas, and I could scarcely breathe. I drew her into my arms, thanked her, then shooed her off the stage as the soft beats of the last song started. Before me, Brooke snuggled into the crook of Drew's arm at the VIP table. With them, Henry and Jill, Penny, and Beverly completed the circle. As I drew a deep breath, I saw another familiar face. In the front row, an erect figure with hair of pale wool gave me a nod of appreciation. Hadley Davis. His smile could've lit up a city the size of Tulsa.

I closed my eyes, wanting to hold onto this moment for all time. I gripped the mic and began singing. Floating. Remembering.

For his eye is on the sparrow,
And I know he watches me.

[A NOTE FROM THE AUTHOR]

Alzheimer's is an epidemic today: 5.3 million Americans have the disease. With the advancing age of our population, this number is predicted to soar in the next decade or two. Early diagnosis and treatment may slow the progression of the disease. You can find out more about the symptoms, current treatments, and ways to cope if a loved one is diagnosed with Alzheimer's at *http://www.helpguide.org/elder/alzheimers_disease_symptoms_stages.htm*.

Each day thousands of women and children (and some men) are abused in the home, workplace, and in dating relationships. If you are a victim of abuse or know someone who is, I want you to do two things. First, pray. God loves you and wants the best for you. Second, please know that you are not alone and help is available. Talk to a friend, family member, pastor, or counselor. Here are a couple of resources that may help you. My prayer is that you would be safe and find healing.

- Helpguide: *http://www.helpguide.org/mental/domestic_violence_abuse_types_signs_causes_effects.htm*
- National Domestic Violence Hotline: *http://www.thehotline.org* or call 1.800.799.SAFE (7233)

[READING GROUP GUIDE]

Discussion Questions

1. The young Maggie had rocky beginnings, losing her mother and then being brought up by strangers. When she leaves as a young woman to search for her past, what was the significance of changing her name? Have you ever wanted to change your name and start a new life?
2. Did fame change who Mitzi was at the core? What effect did her early years have on the woman she became? How did her faith act as a compass and give her strength during tough times?
3. The first meeting between Mitzi and Brooke appears to be coincidental. When they meet a second time, Mitzi declares it providential. Do you believe in providence? Have you had incidents in your own life that went beyond coincidence?
4. Mitzi wants to help Brooke and offers her refuge. Later, Brooke helps Mitzi. Have you ever had a friend who was much older or younger than you? What did each of you gain from that friendship?
5. Brooke's sketch of the sparrow with a broken wing represented her own brokenness with her family and her fiancé. Why was she willing to stay in the relationship with Lance? How might

her life have turned out if she had not called off her engagement? What advice would you have given her?

6. How did it make you feel when Brooke's mother refused to accept the truth about Brooke's abuse from Lance? How did her mother's ambition and denial of the truth in the past play into this?
7. Lance was a victim of abuse, too. What was your view of him by the end of the story? How might his relationship with Brooke have been different if he'd gone for counseling as she suggested?
8. Gabe and Mitzi were victims of another sort—that of Alzheimer's disease. When we first see her, Mitzi has accepted the future, but dreads the day when she loses Gabe. What does Mitzi fear most about her future? What sustains her? Have you ever lost a loved one who you knew had a short time left? How did you prepare for the eventual loss?
9. Mitzi discovered she was meant to be a singer. Drew Caprice chose medicine in spite of his dad's wishes. They both followed their hearts, but Brooke gave up her drawing to pursue what others thought she should do. Have you ever felt drawn to do something but didn't? What kept you from it? Would you do things differently if you had the chance?
10. Red Carlisle gave Mitzi a job and the opportunity to sing. Have you had someone recognize your talents and encourage you? Do you encourage others when you see they have a special gift?
11. Music can stir strong emotions and link us to others the way that "His Eye Is on the Sparrow" did for Mitzi. What songs do you remember from your own past? Are the memories joyful, sad, or poignant? What is your favorite pop tune past or present? Your favorite hymn?
12. Brooke has begun to fall in love with Drew by the end of the story. Do you think she is wise to proceed with caution? What do you predict happens with Drew and Brooke in the future?

13. The swans at Swan Lake represent the lifetime love of Mitzi and Gabe. Do you think it was always easy for them to remain devoted? Does faith help in building strong marriages? Have you known people who modeled love that lasts a lifetime? What was their secret for success?

[ABOUT THE AUTHOR]

Carla Stewart's writing reflects her passion for times gone by, as depicted in her first highly acclaimed novel, *Chasing Lilacs*. Carla launched her writing career in 2002 when she earned the coveted honor of being invited to attend Guideposts' Writers Workshop in Rye, New York. Since then, her articles have appeared in *Guideposts*, *Angels on Earth*, *Saddle Baron*, and *Blood and Thunder: Musings on the Art of Medicine*.

In her life before writing, Carla enjoyed a career in nursing and raising her family. Now that their four sons are married and they've become empty-nesters, she and her husband relish the occasional weekend getaway and delight in the adventures of their six grandchildren.

Carla enjoys a good cup of coffee, great books, and hearing from you, her readers. You're invited to contact her and learn more about her writing at www.carlastewart.com.